STEVE EXTEN

Club 5eightZero6

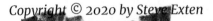

Contents

Acknowledgement

For everyone who has followed my progress, I hope it lives up to your expectations. And that you enjoy reading and getting to know the characters, as much as I enjoyed writing about them.

1

Seven weeks... should be ample

"Oh no! Look at my hai...!"

"Lucy?"

"Oh, ah, sorry Prof, I just caught sight of my...," and Lucy's outburst stumbled to an embarrassing halt when she realised the eyes of the tutor group were on her. "Ah..., sorry Prof." Lucy had just caught her reflection in one of the Prof's cupboards.

"Can I continue now?" the professor asked.

Lucy nodded vigourously. "Yes, sorry."

"Thanks Luce," the Prof said, his lips curled in a smile. "I'll try again, shall I. And so, ladies and gentlemen, as I was just about to say, it's time to put everything you've learned to the test." The professor paused and looked about the room, making eye contact with each of his students. "We have come at last to the final assignment: The Random Target Subject." The students scribbled feverishly as he set out the guidelines. "This person should be known to someone within your circle, but not necessarily known to you, and they should only be approached if someone within your sphere can vouch them safe. This is very important. You must never put yourself into an unsafe situation."

After spelling out his Rules of Engagement, Professor Beske'haht, affectionately known as the Prof to students and faculty alike, looked up and smiled.

"Tut, tut. Rabbits in the headlights," he said, and chuckled as he shook his head. "Don't look so worried, you can do it. Come on, cheer up, you've already done it in controlled environments. Now all you have to do is pull together everything you've learned. After all," he said, spreading his palms, "it's not as if I'm asking you to do something that's genetically impossible. You all possess the Homid Gene; telepathy is one of *your* natural assets. You guys can do it."

Then he smiled and continued, this time speaking directly into their thoughts. [>*"I'm giving you seven weeks for this assignment. That should be ample."*<] Again the students scribbled. [>*"By the end of four weeks, you ought to have established a definite contact. By five, you and your target should be chatting across the mindPlain and building a rapport. At six I would expect you to be making arrangements for some sort of meeting; a coffee perhaps, or something in that vein. And by seven? By seven I would hope that you can introduce your target subject to me."*<]

The Prof waited a few moments whilst his students finished their notes. Lucy Hettler was first to put her pen down and sit back; she was smiling, and she had a plan.

Beske'haht returned her smile and topped it with a wink. She winked back. Then, as the rest of the group rested their pens and looked up, the Prof said, [>*"Now don't forget I want to see you all back here in four weeks with your interim report, and in seven I want to be introduced to your new friend."*<]

Before he sent them on their way, he reiterated the guidelines verbally and emphasized the safety warning. "Never put yourself into an unsafe situation; I am deadly serious about that, as there are some nasty people out there. Okay?" He waited, looking them one by one in the eye, and only when *he* was satisfied that *they* understood, he spoke again directly into their thoughts. [>*"Good. Now off you go, no time to lose. Get to it."*<]

Lucy gathered up her notes, arranged them into some sort of order and slipped them into her bag. For a couple of minutes, she chatted with the other course members whilst she put on her coat, then took out her comb and glanced again at her reflection. The students were milling about, reluctant to make a move, all thinking out loud about how they might approach the task. She was excited.

"This is the one I've been looking forward to," she said. "I have two people in mind to make contact with, I've just got —" But she stopped short and gasped. "Oh no, it's worse than I thought it was. It's such a mess." Lucy twiddled when she concentrated, and her hair was in knots. "This needs more than a comb," she muttered, taking her beret from her bag and pulling it down to her ears. "That'll have to do for now. See you all in four weeks," she added, and after a few hugs and kisses, they went their separate ways. But as she picked up her bag the Prof called to her.

[>"Can you spare a couple of minutes Luce?"<]

Lucy had always had goals. Number one, she wanted to go to Mecklenburg Uni; she's there. The second, she wanted to be a lawyer; she's studying for that. And the third, well maybe that should have been the first. Lucy wanted to have a good time, and in the first six months, she certainly did that. Lucy, and her room-mate Cristi, fully immersed themselves into the Meck-U scene: they joined everything. They were living the dream and they partied hard. And of course, it took its toll. Lucy failed her first unit, bringing her down with a bump. She found out the hard way that if you wanted to do both, you can't do them both to an extreme.

That F was her wake-up call, and she flipped her priorities and spent the next six months doing extreme studying instead, and re-sitting the first unit whilst doing the next in parallel. Lucy threw herself into her studies and settled down. And she met Billy.

Billy helped her get back on track, and they were good together for nearly a year until they went their separate ways. It was a mutual split; it had run its course, and it wasn't a messy parting, they just had different paths to tread.

However, the hard work coupled with Billy's calming influence had paid off, and at the end of her first year Lucy was awarded a training contract with Beadles Legal, one of the top five law firms in Meckloe. During her second study year, Beadles invited her to join a team that was leading a government initiative to Mii'een, the green planet in the Belt of Homid, the homeland of the nomad sheep drovers.

The Mecklenburg government was keen to set up a supply-chain part-nership with the livestock markets on Mii'een, to victual their mining enterprises, and Lucy was present at all of the major negotiations. She had been asked primarily because she possessed the Homid Gene and could do a bit of telepathy, although at that time she wasn't particularly proficient. The little she did know proved useful. That was one of the reasons she was included in the party. The other? Well to put it simply, Lucy was stunningly attractive. She was tall and lithe, with long and shiny dark hair. She had a slender neck, was neatly proportioned, gently curved, and had legs that went on forever. At Meck-U, Lucy had been voted *'Horny and Gorgeous'* and *'Miss Body Perfect'* by both the boys and girls student unions. And, of course, Beadles weren't about to let that go without putting it to some use. But it works both ways, and one evening whilst the team was relaxing after a day of intense meetings, and Lucy was eavesdropping with the little bit of telepathy she knew, she was able to listen in on a hushed conversation between two senior lawyers.

"I always say," said one to the other, "a little bit of eye candy never goes amiss when the negotiations flag."

Lucy thought and smiled, [-"*If showing a bit of leg helps me get on, then maybe I'll show a little bit of leg.*"-]

There are two planets in the Belt of Homid; Mii'een and Sckeria: Sckeria is the closer of the two to Mejjas Major. Lucy was Sckerian, born and bred, but she had spent most of her life on Mejjas Major because of *'a father's love for his family'*. Her father, Colonel Kurt Hettler, the Fleet Supply Director, had for many years commanded a Fleet Supply Vessel but had taken a surface-based post in Meckloe because he loved his family more than he loved cruising the void: Each supply trip would take him away from home for three months at a time, which meant Kurt was missing seeing his family grow. It was the little things he missed the most; helping his girls with their homework; shining their shoes for school and brushing their hair. His wife Annie did it all, and he just wanted to share those everyday things with her.

So Kurt took a desk job at the Central Command Centre, a few miles from the seaport city of Meckloe, the capital city of the Mecklenburg State on Mejjas Major. It meant relocation, and the family moved, hopefully for the last time, from their lovely home on Sckeria to a nothing-special company house on Mejjas. It was a small sacrifice that was far and away outweighed by its benefits. At long last Daddy was able to go home every evening to be with his family and to be with his wife to watch their twin girls blossom through their teenage years and mature into young women.

2

Is this really your very last assignment...?

Lucy and Cristi jostled for position in front of the mirror in their tiny wet room as they put the final touches to their Friday night make-up. There was just enough space for a loo, a basin, the all-important mirror and a shower, but not much else.

"What time did we say we'd see them?" Cristi asked.

"Eight-thirty, under the *Hoof*, but I bet they'll be late," Lucy replied as she tightened her lips before colouring them.

"What, later than us," Cristi said, chuckling, "it's eight-fifteen now! And that bus is always late. It's going to take twenty minutes at least. I reckon it'll be more like 9:00 before *we* get there."

That evening their bus was on time. They had to run for it, and as they squeezed into the last two seats, Lucy turned to her friend and asked, "How long before Sam and the others get back from their Fleet duties?"

"Two more weeks, why? Have you got your eye on one of the others? You've kept that quiet."

"No," she yelped, surprised her friend would suggest such a thing, "nothing like that, and anyway you've got the only one worth a second look. No, it's to do with my final assignment for this course unit," Lucy replied. Cristi gave her a sideways glance as Lucy continued. "We have to make contact with a Random Target, and I want to try that boy that Sam's group always shun and pick on."

"Really? You want to hook up with JD, honest?" Cristi was surprised by her friend's choice. "Each to their own I suppose. You don't believe in *easy*, do you? As it happens, I had a text from Sam this morning. Says they've been given a real pitz of a job and that he misses me loads, and they will be two more weeks."

"Great, that means I've got two weeks to do some catching up with my studies, and a chance to take things a bit easy too." Lucy laughed.

"How long have you got for this assignment?"

"Seven weeks."

"But they're not back for two weeks, will you have enough time?"

"Yeah, of course, I've had some really good results so far and he looks like he needs a friend. I'm going to nail this. You just watch me."

"Well, if you're sure. You don't want another fail. Billy isn't around anymore to sort you out, is he?"

"Don't worry, it's in the bag. I'll be okay."

As they'd thought, the other girls were later than them; and they were fifteen minutes later than they had predicted too.

"We needn't have rushed."

"We didn't," Lucy replied.

"But *they* don't have to know that do they," Cristi whispered as the two girls hoisted themselves onto the statue's plinth and made themselves comfortable under the horse's *Hoof*, their usual meeting place. Cristi and Lucy shared a small attic apartment in a quiet street that was twenty minutes that way, give or take, whilst the others had a part-share in a house twenty minutes in the other direction; the *Hoof* was a good central place to meet.

It was Friday night, the end of a hectic study week, and the girls were going clubbing. Tonight, they had tickets for a new club, the '*Club*5eightZero6', the 'hottest' venue in town, and with two weeks free, Lucy was looking forward to her fourteen late nights clubbing and fourteen even later rises. She could push back her mindPlain studies and catch up on other parts of the degree course, and have a bit of fun too.

7

"The night has promise," Lucy said, laughing out loud, "oh yeah!" She *was* determined to have a very good time.

Lucy shuffled up close to her room-mate but was puzzled. Instead of being excited and cheerful, Cristi was quiet and thoughtful and staring into the distance.

After a few minutes, Cristi whispered, "Is this your very last assignment, Lucy? Will you be leaving after you hand this one in?" She looked worried, and Lucy, picking up on her friend's nervous thoughts, wondered what was wrong. "What's up Cris?" she asked, but before Cristi replied Lucy realised.

"No silly, we've got another year," she said. "I'm going to stay as long as you do. And anyway, you and Sam are bound to be hitched and gone long before I am."

"No! No," Cristi exclaimed, "he's just a good screw, that's what I miss about him. He's not going to come between us. I'll stay as long as you do." Cristi had already stayed a year longer than she'd originally intended. She had finished her degree last year with a 2:1 and had taken a job as a research assistant with the Meckloe City Museum's archiving department, just so they could stay together. It didn't pay much, but it was enough to cover her part of the rent and food, and a bit of clubbing too. "It's been three good years, hasn't it Luce. It's been great, and I've never had such a good friend. I'll miss you y' know, when all this is over."

They had been friends since their very first day at Meck-U, when the halls were being allocated. Their eyes had met, there was an instant connection, and they believed they'd remain close for the rest of their lives.

"Oh come on Cris, we're supposed to be out for a good time. We'll always be friends, always," Lucy said and put her arms around Cristi, and pulled her close just as the others arrived.

"Put that girl down Miss Hettler, we're going to miss the opening," Judi shouted as they crossed the square.

3

He looks so pathetic ...

"Why the lonely boy?" Cristi called through the open door across the hallway, their conversation on the bus coming to mind. The girls were in their own beds after an exhilarating night of dancing. The '^{Club}5eightZer06' had been all that it had promised to be, and they were both overflowing with adrenalin and neither could sleep. Their attic apartment was always cold and often they would share a bed for warmth. But after a night of dancing, and the thrill of the new club, plus the bubbling goodwill of everyone present, as well as the freebies, and of course the ever-flowing alcohol, the coolness of their rooms was a welcome respite.

[-"*Somewhere up there,*"-] Cristi thought, as she stared at the stars through the un-curtained skylight, [-"*doing his pitz of a job*"-], "But *another* two more weeks? Ohh," she groaned as she slid her left hand between her thighs and clutched her swimming head with the other.

In the other room Lucy took her time in replying. To be honest, she wasn't sure herself; she just had a feeling and wasn't certain how to explain it. [>"*I suppose it's because he looks so pathetic.*"<] she said using mindSpeak and planting her words directly into Cristi's thoughts. [>"*I'm hoping that because he's a lonely outcast that he'll want someone to talk to. That's why Cris. I hope I'm right, and that I've read the situation correctly. Although I won't know that until I give it a try.*"<] She paused, then added, [>"*I suppose it's because I'd just like to get to know him.*"<]

But the swimming head had got the better of Cristi and she'd let the sleep take her as the alcohol displaced the adrenalin and Lucy, still in tune with her friend's thoughts, smiled as she read her slowly dissipating threads.

[>*"Thinking of Sam, Cris? Bless you."*<] She smiled, and slipped off her bed, tiptoed across the hallway into the other room and, staring down at her friend's naked body, thought, [-*"He's a lucky lad, is our Sam. Very lucky."*-] Then she gently pulled the duvet over her friend and went back to her own cosy bed.

4

I feel like shit ...

Cristi stumbled into the kitchen/lounge to find Lucy already sitting at the breakfast bar, dressed in her baggy joggers and her new, vivid pink *'Club'*5eightZero6' freebie t-shirt, and studiously writing something for her degree.

"I thought you said last night that you were pushing your studies off the table until the boys came back?" Cristi mumbled, wrapping her arms around her roommate's shoulders, as much for support as for friendship. "I need water and a couple of bombs," she moaned before giving Lucy a gentle peck on the cheek then lurching to the sink. "I've got a banging head and I feel like shit," she mumbled. "How about you?"

"No, I'm good. Feel great."

"Really? Ughhh. You put away as much as I did. You sure?"

"No, I really do feel great. Homid genes, see," she said through a smile. "I've had a couple of coffees, been up about an hour. No," she said and she crossed her fingers behind her back, "I said that I would push the mindPlain studies to the back and do some catching up on the other stuff, so that's what I'm doing." [-"Well perhaps a little mindPlain studying."-] she thought to herself.

"But up an hour, Luce?" Cristi refilled her glass, then asked, "Really?" as she twisted her arm to read her watch. The timepiece had rolled around her wrist and she hadn't got as far as taking it off last night, or, to be more accurate, earlier this morning. She'd just peeled away her sweaty clothes and fallen onto the bed. "It's not even eight yet Luce, what's got into you?" she exclaimed. "No, forget it, tell me later. I'm going back to bed." But her feet weren't her own, and she stumbled, slopping the contents of her glass and catching Lucy on the shoulder, splashing the front of her t-shirt. Lucy shrieked!

"Ahh!" Cristi gasped, partly in apology, partly in admiration, as the water turned the cotton translucent. "Oh, I'm so sorry Luce."

"Go to bed Cris," Lucy sighed after the initial shock. Thankfully the water had only caught her top and not her notes. "Go on," she added, and to make sure, she stood and led her friend back to her bed and covered her up. Then she nipped into her own room to change. "I don't know what it is," she said to herself as she held up the damp t-shirt and stared at the design on the back, "there's just something about this picture and that boy. Was it something someone said? Can't place it, just something," and she put it over the radiator, put on another and went back to her notes.

True, last night she had been adamant about no mindPlain studies for a fortnight. But now, sitting at the breakfast bar and thinking of her new 'Club 5eightZero6' t-shirt with its quirky 'Boy on the Rope' logo emblazoned on the back, she felt revitalized and ready to take on anything. Everyone at the club last night got a t-shirt, and despite everyone being rewarded, Lucy still felt special — only the girls had been given the pink t-shirts. There was something about getting a gift and being an 'opening-night customer'. And for some strange reason, wearing the t-shirt she already felt a connection to the boy. [-"Why, it's so weird?"-]. But it was a good feeling none the less, and she smiled.

5

The boys are back ...

"The boys are back Luce, they're back." Cristi was beside herself with joy, although there was a little bit of tempering to go with her news. "But they will be catching up with their studies this week — day and evening classes. So, they won't be able to go out to play until Friday. But I might see him at lunchtime." Cristi was so excited that Lucy couldn't get a sensible word out of her room-mate all evening.

"It's going to be a chilly one tonight Cris, so are you going to your own bed, to imagine and probably not get any sleep? Or do you want to snuggle in with me and my hot water bottle?"

"I'd better join you and the hot water bottle. I don't think I'll get any sleep if I'm left to my own imaginings. Lead on my lovely."

6

The eyes said something else ...

"Are you sure you won't join us, Luce?" asked Cristi, her hand firmly gripping Sam's. She wasn't letting him go after not seeing him for six weeks.

"Yes, come with us, Luce," Sam implored, "I really want to catch up with the both of you, y' know."

But Lucy knew that face. Cristi might have been smiling because she had her man, but her eyes were saying something completely different and her thoughts betrayed her too. Lucy knew when to back off. "No, it's okay Sam. You two go off and enjoy yourselves, and you'd better hurry, that bus is unpredictable. Now get out there and have fun. I've got an essay to write. See you tomorrow Cris," she added and ushered them out of the door. "Go on, the bus won't wait."

7

I kicked out ...

Lucy heard the front door shut and Cristi's footsteps coming up the stair. She was just pouring herself a breakfast coffee and waiting for the toast to pop. "Morning Sweetheart," she said as Cristi came into the kitchen/lounge, "how was last night? Did Sam like the club?"

"We never got to the club... well, err that's not quite true. We did get to the club, but for some reason, Sam, Robbie and the other guys wouldn't go in. Point blank refused. Said it was distasteful and sick!"

"Oh?" Lucy was puzzled. "None of them? Wouldn't go in? Did they say why?"

"No, no explanation at all. They were fuming," Cristi replied. "Just wouldn't go in, and when he saw my new t-shirt he almost threw a fit. He didn't say so in so many words, he's too much of a gentleman for that, but he wasn't happy about me wearing it. We came back here."

"You don't say... I heard. You've certainly missed each other, and *you* certainly made up for it last night."

"Sorry Luce, I tried to keep the noise down, but..." — Cristi smirked — "you know."

"Oh, I know. Oh yes, I know. I even listened to your thoughts for a few moments, until I couldn't hear the sweet nothings because of the slurping sloppy kisses, so I used one of those inhibiting strategies the Prof taught us and turned in for the night. I was having a wonderful dream, then one of you must have knocked something over..."

"That would have been the bedside cupboard," Cristi confessed, "when I kicked out. Sorry Luce."

"I don't think it woke me completely, but suddenly you were both in my dream. It seems only the cleverest can block in their sleep. Next thing I know I'm seeing Sam through your eyes. I've seen everything that you saw from that kick onwards! And I mean everything. I don't know how I'm going to face Sam again. Although I could certainly see why you've missed him."

Cristi gulped. "Oh Luce, I'm so sorry."

"I'm not," replied Lucy, "I liked what I saw. Loved the feeling too, but it was weird. It was like I was in bed with you both, but only seeing Sam."

"Hey, that sounds fun. Sam said he'd be up for it. He thinks you're gorgeous." [-"So do I."-]

"Shush, no." Lucy put her finger to Cristi's lips and shook her head. "Sam is yours, Cristi, let's keep it that way."

"Okay, but you only have to ask," Cristi winked. And Lucy nodded, smiled and gave her friend a hug. "Oh shit. Oh, I'm aching all over," Cristi groaned as Lucy wrapped her arms around her. "Oh but it was fun and I'm going to do it all again tonight," said Cristi through a smirk. "I'm afraid it'll have to be here though Luce."

"What's wrong with Sam's room?" Lucy pleaded.

"He hasn't got a room to himself this time, he's sharing with *your boy*. Robbie has the single room this term, so it's Sam's turn to share with the loner."

8

What do you want from me?

Lunchtime, three days later, Lucy was sat at her usual table with her notes spread before her. On the other side of the refectory the cadets were sharing a joke and tucking into their lunch. As usual, the 'boy' was sitting apart and as usual, they paid him little attention, though he didn't seem at all bothered. He was staring intently at something spread on the table, his food untouched.

She quickly bobbed out of her seat to see if she could see what held his attention. [-"Is that a photo?"-] In fact, the more she looked at the cadets, the more she thought there was something about all of them that was different from last term. Cristi *had* mentioned something at breakfast, but she'd had her head in her notes and Cristi wasn't really making much sense. She was jumping from one topic to another, which she did when she was geed up, and after another of their steamy nights Lucy had given up trying to make any sense of anything she said. Although she wished she had tried, because something was definitely different this term. For a start off—"Huh!" She gasped. Robbie had just bought everyone a coffee. [-"Wow, that's a new one! He's even bought one of those disgusting ziirt-coffee drinks for the boy. Gosh, they have changed."-] Lucy looked on in awe as Robbie passed the drink to Sam, who carefully set the ziirt down as the boy nodded in appreciation. "What the ffff's going on?"

That was certainly noteworthy, and she quickly jotted it down. [-"Well,"-] she thought, [-"while he's distracted this might be the time to try... here goes."-]

But as she prepared, she hesitated. Their new attitude was puzzling. [-"*Last term they would have poured it over his food and most likely over him too, so what's changed?*"-] But, not wanting to miss this chance, she closed her eyes, imagined where she wanted to be and let her thoughts roam. As she did so she failed to see Sam lean over and ask him if he was okay. She also missed the boy gently nod, then counter it with the faintest of sideways shakes.

Lucy was still very new at this and it took all of her concentration to keep herself focused. Slowly she felt her way towards their table, feeling between the other occupants of the room. As she passed, she picked up snippets of their drifting thoughts, but the boy was giving nothing away. After Sam's show of concern, he had shut down and once again his thoughts were hidden behind a locked door that Lucy rammed up against. But she wasn't going to be deterred that easily. She was almost there, so she tried again. [>"*Hello, my name's Lucy Hettler. What's your name?*"<] she whispered, and almost as soon as she had delivered her very short speech, her energy failed, and her thoughts retreated across the room.

"Damn. Never mind, let's give it another go."

"Hello, my name is Lucy Hettler, can I communicate with you?" she whispered aloud.

[-"*No, that's a bit stiff.*"-] Nonetheless, she noted it all down and was about to try again with something else when the cadets stood, but they didn't move from the table though until the boy stood too. He gestured for them to go first as he put on an old battered baseball cap, peak to the back, and slipped the paper that had been spread on the table into his coat.

"He still keeps to himself though." [-"*And still hangs back.*"-] She jotted down a note *whilst* she watched them through the side windows and followed their progress across the lawn. But unlike their usual practice of rushing off to make the most of their lunchtime, and the boy going off on his own, they stood around for a few minutes. None of them batted an eyelid when he stepped on to his hover-board and floated off across the lawns. Last term they would have tripped him or grabbed his bag and hurled it into the lake. There was none of that. Instead, they just left him to do his own thing and watched him skate away.

Lucy watched him float away too. It always made her smile, the thought of a Fleet Officer Cadet on a skateboard. [-"*It's so funny and so sweet,*"-] she thought. Then she gathered up her notes and followed, and as she walked towards the lawn, following the same track the boy had taken, she realised the other cadets were still hanging back and watching him. Lucy thought she heard them mention his name, and were quietly discussing him: [-"*That's odd. I must ask Cris,*"-] she thought as she continued in pursuit of her Random Target Subject. He was going to his favourite perch, the fallen log at the top of the rise, where he would sit for hours and stare into the afternoon and evening skies.

Cautiously Lucy followed and settled herself on a bench that was about fifty meters directly behind him. She waited for ten or so minutes to make sure they were both settled and comfy before she attempted to make contact. Then she closed her eyes and pushed out her thoughts.

And this is how her days evolved as she tried again and again and again for the rest of the week, the weekend, and into the next week too. Her days became a monotonous cycle of early morning gym, morning lectures, afternoon and evening attempts, followed by nights of groaning and humping from across the hallway, and very little sleep. On Tuesday (week seven) she was sitting once again on the bench and staring at the boy's back. [-"*Boy? He's hardly a boy, he's twenty-two, behaves like one though — on his board, so as far as I'm concerned he's a boy,*"-] she thought, churning it over and over in her head as she noted down her last effort.

She was exhausted and now, every time she closed her eyes to focus her thoughts, she felt herself nod off then wake with a start. Lucy was tired and tearful. She only had three days left before the Prof wanted to be introduced to the *boy*, and she still didn't even know his name. She'd had to fudge her way to this point with made-up reports. She had nothing. [-"*I don't know what to do. What have...? Oh, I don't know, why won't he talk to me? Why did I wait those two weeks? You're an idiot Lucy Hettler. You were just showing off. Why didn't I stick with Ped...?*"-]

And whilst she was in the middle of scolding herself, the Prof sat down beside her.

[>*"How's it going, Lucy?"*<] he asked, putting the words directly between her ears, but her thoughts were a jumble. He didn't want to get tangled, and as he withdrew he picked up on some of those ragged threads. Beske'haht knew immediately that things weren't going to plan, and a quick sideways glance confirmed it: There were tears, wet cheeks and sobs.

"I've been thinking," he said, keeping his eyes forward to save her embarrassment, "I reckon I was a bit over-ambitious in only giving you all just seven weeks. I was judging the time needed to complete on my ability and not my students'. It was a crass assumption." He knew she was struggling, a couple of the others were too, but he was concerned about her. So he had decided the best way forward was to give everyone in the tutor group some extra time. "I'm giving you all an extra three weeks, but only three weeks mind, as there has to be an end sometime. Can you do it in three, Lucy?"

"I don't know Prof," she said and sniffed.

"You'll do it, I know you will. You have always had great results. Just keep doing what you do best," he said. Then as he started to leave, added, "There are other ways you might want to try, but of course, I didn't say that."

She sniffed again, not paying much attention to what he was implying.

"Perhaps you should give your target a gentle prod. It's a little bit unorthodox I know, perhaps a little underhand. A gentle prod, a metaphoric tap on the shoulder... or even the real thing. Perhaps even a whisper within earshot. I'm not saying you should, but at this late hour, it's something you might consider. But you didn't hear that from me, okay?"

Lucy just didn't hear it at all, because whilst the Prof was giving his little bit of advice Lucy was rummaging in her handbag for another tissue.

"Well, I'll leave you to get on with your evening and I'll see you in a couple of weeks. Good evening Lucy." As he put his hand on the armrest and started to rise, he hesitated and asked, "Whilst I'm here, who is your subject? Perhaps I can help. Can you point him/her out, or do you have a name?"

"His name is eh... he's over there, on that fallen log. At the top of the rise. He's got his back to us. There," she said, pointing. "Just there, look. Oh, he's just getting up to go."

"Oh him," the Prof said as the boy slid past on his hover-board. "That's interesting, and puzzling?"

"Do you know him, Prof?"

"Only by hearsay," he hurriedly replied, then turned and watched as the boy skated across the lawn. [-"Well now, that's a bit of a coincidence, but I'm surprised Lucy's not making contact."-] he thought to himself. Then after bidding her good evening again, he left without saying what the hearsay was.

"Three more weeks....of, this," Lucy said and threw out her arms at the vacant log. "It might be easier to get an answer from that lump of wood. Oh, what's the point? I'm going to fail, and I'll have to do the whole course again. Why was I so blasé? Oh, you idiot! Oh, I've only gone and wasted six months," and she sniffed again as the tears rolled.

She was worn out and everything was just too much. She loved Cristi to bits. They were more than just friends; they were sisters; lovers even, sharing more than just warmth on cold nights. But when Cristi was with Sam... well, Lucy wished she hadn't latched into her room-mates' thoughts, because now she was an unwitting participant in their steamy evenings, and they went on for so long. "I just need some sleep. Can't I have a night off? Please Cristi, please."

At first, Lucy had employed her inhibiting protocols, and that had worked for a couple of days. But after a particularly arduous series of lectures, and an afternoon and evening of failed contact attempts, she had been too tired to adopt a protocol and had ended up an unwilling spectator in a particularly frenzied romp, and now she seemed to be out of kilter, a beat behind. She was exhausted! Her features were drawn and her complexion pale. There were dark rings around her eyes, and tears came easily. The poor down-beaten girl sobbed her heart out in great racking sobs, and passers-by looked on curiously or stepped away from the bench as they passed.

"Oh, come on Lucy," she said, scolding herself while dabbing her eyes with the sodden tissue.

Then... [>"What do you want from me?"<]. The voice was between her ears, taking her completely by surprise, a harsh whisper, crisp and clear. JD, the boy, was there in front of her, floating on his board just a few feet from her.

21

There was no voice, he hadn't vocalised the question, but he was there inside her head, and staring, eyes narrowed, deep pools of black. He enforced his question with a slight upward nod. *[>"Huh?"<]*.

"Er?" She had seen him leave, and now he was back, and after ignoring her for all these weeks *he* was asking *her*. Lucy was stunned. "Er." But another slight movement of his head tipped her over the edge, and she was furious, the cheek of him after all this time asking her. "You've got a cheek," she shouted as she stood up, "you really have. What do I want from you? I want a response. A simple answer, yes or no. Is that too much to ask?" she yelled, matching his height and shouting into his face. "And I just want to sleep. To get into my bed, turn out the light and get an undisturbed night of sleep. That's what I want. This mindPlain stuff is doing my head in. I'm not used to using it, but I need it to complete my degree, and you," she said, leaning closer, finger punching his shoulder and pushing him backwards.

He stood there, still staring.

"You just spoke into my thoughts. You... You've literally admitted you heard me, and you've ignored me all this time." She was livid! "If you didn't want to talk you only had to say something, drop me a note, anything. You could even have shouted across the lawn, *'Sod off you silly bitch'*. At least I would've known and gone back to the one who did answer. But I wanted to talk to *you,* so I kept trying, and it's not as if I don't know how to thought swap across the mindPlain. I've done it in class, I know I can do it. I even mindSpeak to my non-Homid best friend. Then she thinks of her answer and I read it back, so I know I can do it. I can even see through her eyes. But I can't switch her off because I'm so effing tired. I've had to endure every single night of sex she and her boyfriend have had for the last four weeks. Thank God for periods, it's the only time I get to sleep. Every groan, every grunt and every squeal, is in my thoughts, night after night, and it's all your fault. Your fault," she screamed, "'coz no one wants to share rooms with you. Now its Sam's turn. I'm not surprised they all pick on you, and you deserve to be lonely you little shit, ignoring people, ignoring me."

She screamed again, but he didn't flinch, and Lucy was too fired up to let up. "I hated the way the others treated you. I just thought you might want to talk to someone. Anyone else would have given up weeks ago, but you looked so lonely, so sad, and I thought you might talk to me. I've asked, and I've asked, and I've been polite. I've tried not to pester. Look, it's all noted down," she said and held up her notes and thrust them in his face. "It's all here, and you can look if you like."

Her voice was breaking, she was speaking in sobs, tears were glistening her cheeks, and this boy was getting the full force of her vented frustration and her lack of sleep. It was all coming out.

"What do I want from you?" Lucy paused, thinking deeply and doing her very best to keep those thoughts to herself. She was the prettiest girl on campus by far. She was regularly asked out and of late had regularly declined. Men were queuing up for her attention. "I've turned down dates to sit here and try to get your attention, and you just ignore me. What do I want?" Again she paused, and was calmer now. "What do I want? I thought we could be friends, that's all, nothing sinister. I just thought you and I could be friends..." Her shoulders dropped and she felt drained. There was nothing left to say.

The boy showed no emotion, he just hovered in front of her, balance perfect as ever. Then with the faintest of nods, he turned his board and skated away, leaving Lucy staring into the evening sky.

"Oh," she groaned and slumped down on the bench. "Is that it? Ohh..." She had emptied her heart, brought all her emotions to the fore, and he'd just skated away. For a while, she stared as the light blue-grey of twilight gave way to the deep blue of night and the evening stars began to twinkle, until she could hold back no longer. "I gave it my all and he simply floated away." Her bottom lip quivered, tears welled in the corners of her eyes, and she sobbed the sobs of the broken-hearted. It had all been for nothing.

Lucy woke refreshed and all cried out. She had tumbled into bed almost as soon as she had got home yesterday evening. She had slept right through and had only woken because of the rain lashing against the skylight. It had stopped now, and a feeble sun was glinting on the wet glass. She threw back the covers and quickly rolled out of bed.

"Brrrr," It was early autumn, and she slipped on her bathrobe, partly for warmth but mostly to save blushes should she meet Sam in the hallway. Carefully she opened the door. It was still before six, and although they disturbed her nearly every night, the last thing she wanted to do was to wake Cristi and Sam. This was her time and Lucy wanted to keep a few precious quiet moments for herself. As she crossed the hallway, she glanced in at the sleeping beauties and was surprised to see the bed hadn't been slept in. They hadn't come home last night. "No wonder I slept through. Oh, thanks Cristi, you're are a dear," she said to no one. "Wow. You know what, you know what," she repeated, "you know what. I'm going to go to the gym right now, that's what. Yeah, I'll shower there. I feel great and I feel like doing a good workout before breakfast. I'll get something in the refectory. Where's my bag?"

She was in the gym by six-thirty and went through her usual routine, giving it one-hundred and fifty per cent and at the end, instead of feeling wasted she felt she glowed. "That was fantastic," she said to the attendant, "absolutely fantastic. I reckon I can take on anything the day throws at me now. Fantastic."

In the refectory, Lucy settled at her usual table, and was spreading butter on her toast when a movement on the other side of the hall made her look up. Someone was sitting where the cadets always sat, and she had been too wrapped up in her refreshed state of mind to notice when she came in. It was the boy.

He was dressed exactly as he was when she had last seen him. His glasses were pushed back on his head, he looked dishevelled and sad, and his hair was wet. On the table to his right was a bulky roll which looked like a sleeping bag. The picture he was looking at yesterday was there too, and he was despondently picking at a bowl of porridge. [-"He's wearing the same clothes as he was wearing yesterday!"-] she thought, and wondered, [-"Has he been out all night? Is that the reason I had a peaceful night? Did Cristi stay at Sam's? Shall I ask him?"-].

But she didn't get a chance because at that very moment, as if on cue, he folded the paper and tucked it inside his coat, then he picked up his gear and his board, took his bowl back to the counter, and left without giving her a second glance. His glasses were still pushed back and she could have sworn that his eyes were tightly closed as he walked out. *[-"Surely not?"-]*

9

Well, that explains the wet hair ...

"You were sitting just like that when I went out on Monday. Have you even moved from there at all? I bet you haven't. I bet you're dying for a pee."

Lucy was sitting cross-legged on the sofa. She was wearing her baggy 'Club 5 Eight Zero 6' t-shirt, shorts and fluffy slippers. She had moved. Of course she had. But yes, she *was* dying for a pee. But as long as she didn't move, she was fine. "You need to get yourself out a bit Luce. You can't stay in every night hoping tomorrow will be the day that you're going to latch onto that boy's thoughts, it's just not going to happen. The guys all ask after you. You only have to snap your fingers, you know."

"Well I have made contact. Not sure it was a good thing though, or that I want to do it again. Apparently I latched on the very first time I tried. He just didn't respond. Oh, and when he said that, I was so angry that I let him have it. But he just stood there, said nothing and when I was finished, he simply pushed off with his foot and skated away."

"When was that exactly?" Cristi asked.

"The beginning of the week; four days ago. Tuesday. About seven."

"Oh, now that's interesting, because on Tuesday evening a whole bunch of us were drinking at the Union Bar when Jez walks in and taps..."

"Who's Jez?" Lucy asked.

"Your boy. His name is Jez, but the guys call him JD. Not sure of his surname. Anyway, he walked straight up to Sam, tapped him on the shoulder and whispered a few words in his ear, and since then we've had the room to ourselves every night this week. JD only comes in to collect fresh clothes. Neither of us have a clue where he's sleeping, but I believe he showers in the gym every morning."

"That explains the wet hair," Lucy nodded, then, "Ah ooh, whoops, no, no, no, it's no good, I've got to go," she muttered as she unfurled her legs, and wincing from the pins and needles, she rushed as best she could from the room. "Are you in tonight?" she called through the open door of the wet-room.

"Yeah, they're away for the weekend. It's a stag, not sure whose but they're all going, even your boy."

"He's not my boy, but at least I now know his first name," Lucy said as she sat down beside her. Then because of Cristi's expression, she gave her the full version of her heated tirade. "He's been ignoring me all this time. I actually made contact with my first attempt, and he's been ignoring me. Can you believe that? I've a good mind to give this assignment up and redo the course."

"No, Luce. You can't give up, and certainly not because of a boy. You'll have to sit the whole course unit again if you do, and that's another six months. Don't give up Luce," her friend implored her. "He's difficult, Sam says so. Says JD was difficult to fathom, and he got off to a very bad start back when they were on their Basic training. He wasn't very popular, and that's all down to him. Your first impression of him being sad and lonely is mostly true. But there's something about him that none of the others will talk about. To be honest, I think they fear him now. I know Sam's changed his opinion."

"Really!" Lucy was shocked. "All of them." She found that hard to believe, but Cristi was adamant.

"Yes, all of them. Something happened in those six weeks they were back at their base on the Star-Link Hub, something none of them want to talk about. And it's something to do with that boy," Cristi continued, "so if for no other reason than curiosity, you should keep on now that you know you've made contact. You would be silly to throw your course away now, having worked so hard."

"But how can I trust him?"

"Do you need to?" Cristi asked. "What's the worst he can do? It's a two-way thing you know, and he might feel the same way about you. Have you considered that?"

"Yeah, no, I suppose. You're right, it would be silly to drop out now and have to do it all again. [-"*Have I left myself enough time though?*"-] she thought, then to Cris she said, "I'll give it some good thought."

"Now that's more like it. So then, shall we make some supper and see what's on the box?" Cristi asked through a smile.

"Okay, you get the crisps and cake, I'll get the wine."

10

What a beautiful smile ...

As she always did before going to the gym, Lucy checked her post-cubby. There was the usual student stuff, mostly flyers for concerts and comedy nights, as well as a letter from her twin sister, a note from the Prof asking if she could pop in and see him today after lunch, and torn slip of paper that must have been posted sometime during the night as it was under all the other papers. The note said, 'Hi Lucy, do you fancy meeting for a drink? Yours, Pedrasz'. [-"*Huh, Pedrasz. I did wonder if he noticed, hmmm, might be nice.*"-]

That *was* a surprise, Pedrasz the footballer, she was flattered. She had toyed with the idea of making him her Target. She had even made a few mindPlain forays whilst she was waiting for the boys to come back. [-"*He's always got an attractive woman on his arm. Don't know what he sees in me though?*"-] She was flattered but her inability to get something going with the boy was sowing self-doubt and knocking her confidence. [-"*I reckon I must've made contact, and planted a thought... that would be why.*"-] She tucked the note into her bag for later.

Lucy hurried across the cobbled courtyard. She had a study-group session in an hour and was hoping that whatever the Prof wanted to see her about could be wrapped up quickly so that she wasn't late, she always seemed to be late these days, it was getting to be a habit and she didn't like it.

The Prof was standing in the doorway to his rooms. [-"That might save a bit of time,"-] she thought. He was talking to a well-dressed couple. [-"They're not from Mejjas."-] She guessed, by the way they held themselves, tall and erect, they were in their early to mid-forties. On closer inspection though, their faces suggested they were much older, careworn and strained. Beske'haht smiled when he saw her, but didn't introduce her, so she waited a little off to one side. There was another man with them too. He looked familiar, another lecturer she thought, and they looked and sounded as if they were having a very pleasant conversation. Chatting, like old friends.

The lady turned towards Lucy, and as she did, Beske'haht said, "No, I think it best not to," and the lady nodded, then she smiled and her whole face changed, as if all her cares melted away.

[-"What a beautiful smile,"-] thought Lucy. [-"Weird though, there's something familiar about her?"-] But Lucy couldn't place her, and thought no more of it, and waited patiently for them to conclude their business.

They chatted for a few more minutes and Lucy was conscious of them all turning her way at different times during their discourse. Then, as they said their goodbyes, Lucy heard the lady, who was holding both the Prof's hands in hers, say, "It's been lovely catching up with you dear Tomasz, and your parents. Now be sure to pass on our good wishes to them," she added, to which Prof Beske'haht said he would.

Then the gentleman at her side asked, "Will we see you next year, Tomasz? It's so lovely being able to catch up." Lucy saw the Prof nod.

"I'll be there," he said.

The other man nodded too, and said, "I'll be there. It'll be nine years," he added, then paused. "Seems like yesterday." To that, they all nodded and their faces became sombre.

"Let's not dwell on it Andy dear," the lady said, touching his arm, and they all nodded again as their smiles returned. "I think we should be on our way now Andy, we have a long flight ahead of us and we like to get settled into our cabin before we fly."

Andy smiled and offered her his arm. Then he took the gentleman's bag, said something to the Prof, who nodded in return, then he walked with the couple across the courtyard towards the waiting car. As the lady settled herself into her seat, and before the door was closed, Lucy was certain that she turned towards her and smiled that beautiful smile.

"Thank you for coming at such short notice, Lucy. Don't worry, it's nothing sinister, I just want to catch up with you properly as to where you think you are with the Random Target Subject," the Prof said and he gave her what he hoped was a reassuring smile. "Come on up," he added, and Lucy followed.

"So, how's it going?" he asked, and when he heard that she was having second thoughts about her choice he looked perplexed. He knew that she was taking a week off from trying to make contact, and he was prepared for that. But to give up now and to opt for doing the whole unit again? He couldn't believe what he was hearing. [-"This won't do,"-] he thought, [-"won't do at all."-] "Oh Lucy, no, think again. Think again. This won't do. Pushing this unit back and doing it the next time it pops up means you'll have to put your whole degree on hold for at least a year, and that's a dangerous thing to do. In my experience students who do that seldom pick it up again, and often never finish their degree. You've come too far and done so well to let it all go now. Think again Lucy, please think again."

She hadn't considered that consequence. She thought she could redo this unit and continue with her degree and hadn't considered that she would have to wait a whole year and that it would jeopardize the whole thing.

"Lucy," the Prof implored, "you've excelled in all the other units and even with all your student hi-jinks and drunken nights, and everything else," he added with a wink — which she acknowledged with an embarrassed nod — "I know you'll get that double-first you've always strived for. So please, please don't throw it away now," he begged. "You'll regret it for the rest of your life."

Lucy nodded, her eyes glistened, and a tear trickled down her cheek. "Yes, it would be a waste," she said, sniffing. "But I just can't get through to him. I know he's listened, he told me as much." Then she told the Prof about her heated outburst the other week. "It was just after you left me that evening, on the bench. The time I pointed him out and he skated past on his ridiculous board."

The Prof listened, nodding where appropriate, then said firmly, "Right then, you're not going to give up are you?" It was more of a telling than an asking and before she had time to reply, he said, "You have two more weeks to complete this unit and you've just told me that a connection has been made. So, build on that, and to help you I'm going to give you this, and he held up a sheet of paper. "Read it, understand it and incorporate it into your report. I have given similar studies to all the other students, so you're not alone in wondering what it's all about, and what it has to do with your current studies."

The sheet of paper contained a bullet list. Lucy quickly scanned them then said, "Sorry Prof, but I don't understand. There's nothing in this list that relates to the course, let alone this unit. And nothing I can see that would help me build up a genial rapport." She was dumbfounded and just stared at the paper.

"Isn't there? Are you sure?"

"No." She ran her finger down the list, then said, "'^{Club}5 Eight Zero 6', it's a club, was a club and, for reasons that no one's prepared to talk about, has been closed down. It was a great club, really quirky and it's been closed down."

"And why is that?"

"Beat's me," Lucy replied, adding a frown for good measure. "And this other stuff too, what's that all about? How is any of this supposed to help me get that little shit talking to me? For example, 'Praes~Eedan', what's that when it's at home?"

"Well that's for you to find out, and you only have two weeks in which to do it. If you want that double-first, then you had better get reading," said the Prof. Then he held up a finger, and added, "Or you could give up now. It's your choice, Lucy. Hmm?"

11

Oh, that's not good ...

"Hey Luce, are you about?" Cristi called, but she got no reply. "Sounds like she's out, come on, I'll get the wine out of the fridge, you get the glasses." But as she stepped into the kitchen/lounge, said, "Blimey, it looks like we've been ransacked!" There were papers strewn everywhere. "Watch where you step, Sam, looks like, yeah it looks like we're not alone." Lucy was lying on the sofa, a sheaf of papers in a cascade from her chest to the floor. She was fast asleep.

Sam tapped Cristi on the shoulder. She turned, and he held his finger to his lips and led her back out the way they had come. "Let's go out for a drink instead," he whispered, then winked. "Don't disturb her."

"Okay, just give me a mo," she whispered, nipping into her room, "I just want to change out of this work stuff."

He smiled and nodded, and whilst he waited for a 'mo' to turn first into five and then ten minutes, he gazed at the mess at his feet and shook his head. He was a soldier, disciplined and tidy. [-"How can anybody live like this?"-] "I certainly couldn't now," he said, and he stooped down to part the scattered sheaves to make a safe path to the hob and the sink. As he did so, curiosity got the better of him and he read some of Lucy's notes. "Oh. That's not good, or is it? I don't know. I suppose it could be. Hmmm..." But Cristi interrupted his deliberations and he put the paper down, and together they slipped silently out of the front door and left Lucy to her slumbers.

12

One more try...

On Monday afternoon Lucy took up position once more on the bench. Jez, the boy, was on the fallen log staring into the afternoon sky. Something in the heavens twinkled and she was sure he flinched, and he was also hunched. He looked sagged!

This afternoon she was going to give it one more try; she owed that much to herself. He had been in the refectory earlier, in his usual place, slightly apart from the other cadets, and she was amazed at how wretched he looked. If he didn't respond this time, then she was going to go right up to him and tap him on the shoulder. But seeing how fragile he had become, she was afraid that a physical intrusion would be too much for him. With so little time left for her to complete this part of her course, however, she was left with no other choice. Today he was going to have to talk to her. Because today 'No' was not an option. But before Lucy had a chance to prepare, she heard familiar voices and turned to see what it was all about.

Andy, the professor that had carried the bag of the lady with the beautiful smile, was walking towards her. He was followed by Sam, Robbie, Conner and a couple of other cadets. But they sped past her, although each acknowledged her with a nod or a wink. But it was the boy they had come to see.

"Come on my old mate," said Andy as he put his hand under Jez's arm and helped him stand. Then Robbie and Sam each took an arm, and with the others carrying his baggage and Conner carrying his board, they gently supported him back to college. Lucy found out later that evening that they took him to Andy's rooms, where they stripped him, showered him and put him to bed.

Back in the apartment, Lucy was chatting to Sam whilst he waited for Cristi to get ready. They were going to see a movie that Cristi particularly wanted to see, though chick-flix weren't Sam's thing, but if it made her happy then he was happy too. As usual her *'get ready in a few minutes'* was already close to half an hour, but Sam was used to this, so he always allowed plenty of time and it meant he could catch up with Lucy.

"This afternoon was my make or break moment, Sam. I was going to give it one more try and if necessary, tap him on the shoulder and make him reply. I was just readying myself, had just gathered my stuff and... and you lot turned up," she said.

"He's just not up to it Luce," Sam replied.

"Who's not up to what?" Cristi asked as she rushed into the room. "Have you seen my gold necklace, Luce?"

"JD," said Sam.

"Have you looked in the jar on the window ledge, Cris?"

"Oh yeah," she said and turned back the way she had come, calling over her shoulder. "What's he not up to?"

"No, not the one in the wet-room, the jar in the kitchen," Lucy cried, and she jumped up to look. "Here it is, Cris."

"There's even talk of sending him home for a few weeks," said Sam. "I hope they don't, but they might, and he might even get shunted back to another training group. I think the next one is Tech10. I hope they don't, he's a good mate, and I wouldn't want to lose that friendship now. He certainly needs some space though. Those weeks we spent at the Star-Link Hub were just too much for him. Poor sod. And because of Cris and I, he's been living rough. We never gave it a thought."

"Have you seen my red bag?" Cristi called from her room.

"Under your bed," Lucy called back.

"Got it, thanks."

"What exactly went on up there'?" Lucy asked.

"Well, nothing really. It's just the Memorial Stone, it took him back."

"Back where?"

"There were names on the stone that we think were relatives of his, and seeing those names certainly seemed to shake him. Then there was that trouble between the... eh, those other guys. A few fists were thrown."

"Fists?" Lucy was puzzled; Sam seemed to be talking in riddles. "Who was fighting Sam?"

It was Sam who was puzzled now though. "I thought you knew. Haven't you told her Cris?"

"Told her what?" Cristi asked as she arrived beside Sam. "Will I do? Was it worth the wait?"

"Wow Cris, you look great. You know it's always worth the wait."

"What am I supposed to have told Luce?" Cristi asked.

"You know, when those guys started wrecking all of our hard work."

"Yeah, I told you, Luce, at breakfast, weeks ago, when the boys came back. But you must have been rummaging in your bag or something. Sam didn't exactly say what went on, but whatever it was he said JD was in the thick of it."

13

For one scary moment ...

Lucy stood slumped against the railings across from the Claude Atkins Institute, thumbing through her notes and checking her watch, and twiddling her hair. Checking her watch and then thumbing some more. Her hair was in knots! It was ten weeks to the day since they had received their last assignment and she hadn't completed it; she still hadn't made proper contact with her subject, and all she had to show for her ten weeks research were her notes. She had watched all the others taking someone into the building and then each couple coming out, their faces cut with beaming smiles. Now there were just five minutes left before she knew, most assuredly, that she would fail.

"Five minutes, so at least I won't have to endure the humiliation in front of anyone else. Oh well, let's get it over with then," she muttered, pulling down her beret. Then she picked up her bag and strode boldly up the steps to the front door.

Lucy had realised that being of a Homid origin could be very useful when she qualified if she could learn and develop the mindSpeak skill. She had enjoyed her brief spell on the green planet, and had made a good impression with her seniors at Beadles because she was prepared to try. In trying, Lucy had laid the foundations of a very useful network. The Beadles' seniors had seen her potential and had enrolled her on the mindPlain course as part of her degree.

It had been strongly intimated, that when the supply-chain partnership was fully up and running, there would be a position for someone like her who possessed mindSpeak skills.

Mecklenburg University had the most renowned mindPlain Laboratory outside of The Belt of Homid, and Prof Tomasz Beske'haht was the acknowledged leading man in the field. He was probably only bettered by the nomad shepherd drovers of the Mii'een steppe who, for thousands of years, had worked symbiotically with their dogs, and communicated over the vast steppe, using the mindPlain as they drove their flocks.

"Ah-ha, Lucy, for a scary moment I thought you weren't going to come in." The Prof had been looking at her through the window, watching as she feverishly thumbed through her notes and constantly checked her watch. "What have you got for me? Do we have double-first material? I'm sure we do."

Lucy didn't say anything. Instead she just thrust her notes towards the Prof, and waited a few moments whilst he flicked through the sheaves. He was impressed, and she was puzzled.

"This looks good Lucy, meticulous as ever. I'm going to enjoy reading this. It looks really good." But Lucy turned to go. "Hold on Luce, where are you going?" he asked, surprised.

"That's all there is Prof," she said. "All I have is notes. I've written them up, and it's all there. There's nothing else."

"Oh?" the Prof replied, clearly puzzled by what she'd just said. "Are you sure?"

"Yes, of course I am. I should know," she said, her voice starting to break. She was about to run out when a chair grated and she turned to the noise. She hadn't taken in the room when she entered, as she was too intent on delivering her pathetic report and getting out as quickly as possible. It was the boy, who had been sitting at the back, waiting through the whole session whilst she was leaning against the railing agonizing over whether she should come in or not.

"This young man has been waiting patiently, I assume for you, because all the others brought their own conquests."

[>"*Have you been waiting for Lucy?*"<] the Prof asked.

[>"*Yes.*"<] the boy replied with an upward nod.

"Well, I just asked him if he was waiting for you, and he said he was. Perhaps you might ask him or tell him something that he could then tell to me," the Prof said to Lucy, "and then I can sign off your assignment." He gestured and smiled, then added, "Go on, I don't think he'll bite."

Lucy was flummoxed. She hadn't expected this at all, and she certainly hadn't asked him to come and didn't know what to say.

So Jez, who was reading her thoughts, hesitantly said something to her instead. [>"*Eh, I'm sorry I ignored you,*"<] he said. [>"*I didn't realize how much I was hurting you, sorry. Please don't tell him that, please. No, don't tell him that. Tell him, tell him...*"<] He hesitated again. [>"*Tell him, that I've only ever wanted to be a shepherd, a drover; yes tell him that.*"<] Then he gave her the faintest of smiles.

Lucy took out a slip of paper and scribbled a note, then said to Prof Beske'haht, "Ask him what he would like to be."

So the Prof did. It was a brief exchange. Lucy watched and noticed that the Prof put his head to one side and pulled back, the way folk do when they don't quite believe what they have just heard. When he did Jez gently nodded. The Prof then shrugged and turned to Lucy.

"Oh right, are you sure?" Jez nodded and smiled again. "Right then Lucy," the Prof continued, "your young friend says that all he's ever wanted to do was stay on the steppe and follow the flocks. He says that he only ever wanted to be a shepherd or a drover. Is that what you have written on that slip of paper?"

"Yes, it is," she replied, opening the folded slip so he could see.

Prof Beske'haht, nodded, smiled and shook his head. "Well it's not quite the rapport I was expecting, a little bit unorthodox, but you've obviously been chatting enough for Master Devii'rahl to be here when you delivered your report. Well done. I will now sign all the necessary paperwork, and you can move onto the next unit of your course. Well done Lucy, first class."

Lucy was cock-a-hoop, her day had started so full of dread. She hadn't managed to keep her breakfast down and had gone the whole morning with a foul taste in her mouth. "Thanks, Prof, thanks." Then turning, she said, "Jez do you want a coffee, let me buy... Huh? Where's he gone?"

Whilst the Prof was signing the necessary paperwork Jez had jumped onto his board and floated silently out of the room.

"Oh."

14

Prof Beske'haht writes ...

'My dear friends,' Prof Beske'haht began his letter. He felt that words written on paper were more personal than that of an E. True, an E would reach the reader within seconds and a letter might take a day or two, or as in this case, with the readers somewhere out on the steppe and unlikely to be near to a postal service, maybe a couple of weeks. But for the Prof and his longstanding, and fond friends, a paper letter was much the preferred choice of both parties.

'*A breakthrough has been achieved, though alas I fear it is too late for our purposes. Contact was made, but a rapport was never established and now our dear boy has been posted to the Jaeger Corps to start his eighteen-month soldiering training. But there is hope. You will recall me telling you of the altercation during the construction of the Memorial Stone. It appears that it's the same unit to which the injured Jaegers belong. So, I would hope that they, knowing this, would wrap a protective arm about him. I will write again when I know more.*'

Yours fondly
  Tomasz Beske'haht

15

Jaeger Basic - JB316 ...

"STAND STILL," the escort screamed, and Jez did his best to do just that as he struggled to keep his balance and to keep his kit bags from tumbling onto the polished floor of the Senior Ranks Mess. To do so he shuffled.

"Who said you could shuffle? Stand still!" the escort screamed, then turned to the seated Warrant Officers (WOs), and announced, "Devii'rahl.J OiT as requested, sir." Then she smartly left the room.

"We get all the shit," Regimental Sergeant Major (RSM) Tomsen announced without looking up from the paper in his hand. "So why then do we have you? Hmm?"

Jez didn't reply, he just stood to attention and waited under the gaze of the WOs that ruled the base. He'd been on the base for less than twenty minutes and had been summoned the moment he'd arrived. He had been run here at the double; he was panting, and he was finding it difficult to breathe in the room's stuffy air that was heavy with cigar smoke and brandy fumes.

"Very wise," the RSM continued, this time looking up and breathing out, adding to the smoky atmosphere. "That wasn't a question that required an answer. So why then do we have you, when your service record puts you at the top of every class? That doesn't make sense to me, does it you?" he asked the three other lounging WOs, who all shook their heads. "All I can say then," the RSM continued, "is you must have done something really bad to make all the other wasters shine brighter than you. *They* were all given the plum

43

postings: It just doesn't make sense, does it. As I said before 'we get all the shit'! So, it must then be something to do with the margin notes, and there are quite a few. *'Can't make up his mind who he wants to be'*, and over the page I saw," — he turned to the next page, studied it for a few seconds, then read — "*'little shit didn't even try'*. It seems you made yourself rather unpopular with someone on Tech-Basic. Someone has even been in touch, told us to give you a bloody good kicking he did. Told us to shake you up because you've been languishing at college this past year, and we might have followed that advice had you not defended three of our own when they were at their most vulnerable. But to look at you... " he paused and turned to the others. "Look at him, the skinny runt. I've seen more muscles in a bag of whelks!"

Jez *was* wiry yes, skinny no. His bulky uniform covered a muscled body, but the oversized jacket made his head look small and his hands hardly extended beyond the cuffs. Never-the-less, the RSM's remark raised a chortle from the others. Sensibly Jez just stood to attention, stared over their heads and said nothing.

"So in my mind, and knowing what was done and how quickly and efficiently it was executed, and seeing you now for myself, I have to say you're either one very brave son of a bitch, a very brave one indeed, or just very, very stupid," to which the others nodded and grunted in agreement. "Which is it I wonder?"

The RSM then turned to the third page of Jez's service record, frowned and shook his head. "Homid, hmm?" he said and nodded, "That might expl... " The RSM hesitated, then asked, "Reading my thoughts are you, boy?" and he canted his head to one side and asked again, [-*"Reading my thoughts?"*-]

But Jez was smart enough not to reply, even though he was.

[-*"Smart lad,"*-] the RSM smiled. "You've certainly upset someone." [-*"Well you're not going to upset me."*-] Did you get that? [-*"That does require an answer."*-]

But Jez still played dumb, and the RSM waited a moment before continuing. "So, do you intend to upset me?" he asked again.

"No, sir."

"And who do you intend to be, boy?" the RSM asked, referring to the margin note.

"Me, sir. Jez'ziah Devii'rahl sir. No one else, sir."

One of the others, who also had a copy of Devii'rahl's service record and was scanning the third page, noticed another comment. "'*Side-Stepper?*' What's one of them when it's at home, huh?" One of the other three leant across and explained.

The RSM tossed his head. "Homid mumbo jumbo," he muttered. "Or is it mumbo jumbo, Devii'rahl?" Jez said nothing and the RSM stared thoughtfully, looking him up and down. "You really are a wiry little sod... there's nothing to you is there. I can't see how a runt like you could inflict enough damage to take out nine newly-badged Jaeger officers unless our training regime isn't tough enough, or maybe it's not mumbo jumbo after all. Maybe it is possible. Just maybe. What do *you* think fellas?" he asked, turning to the other WOs. "Is it possible?"

"A side-stepper, aren't they supposed to be able to know where a punch is going to land and move — side-step — before it lands? If that's the case, boss, then that might explain a few things." The others, including the RSM, all nodded in agreement. "Those people can move quickly too, boss."

"I've heard it said, read about them too," said the RSM. "Never actually come across a live one though."

"That would tally with those that were there, saying they never saw anyone move or anyone else throwing a punch or taking part," one of the others added. "They all said it was just one; that one. Although no one saw him move, they just saw a blur, like smoke, and those nine laid out and groaning. They say he took out nine and the other cadets mopped up the other six."

"Aye that's what I heard," Tomsen agreed. "So, until I'm proved wrong Devii'rahl, I'm going to believe what I heard and what's written here. And because you saved the life of one of us, and saved two more of ours from serious injury as well, we," he said, encompassing the others, "are going to give you a second chance. As long as you play the game by our rules and put in the hard work then we will do our best to make you into a fine officer, you got that?

"The regiment is grateful, but our gratitude comes at a price. You're going to have to work for it, because it's not going to come on a plate, make no mistake. Oh no, make no mistake, because I've read about you, I know your background; a shepherd, a fell runner who has won prizes, and now we know you're a fighter. Yet for reasons known only to you, you kept all that a secret whilst you were at Basic. Well, it's not a secret now, and I expect you to be the best runner we've ever had. So I'm giving you a second chance."

He turned and swept his arm around the room, and the others nodded. "We are giving you a second chance. But mark my words, Devii'rahl, and get this into your thick Homid skull. If it wasn't for the Memorial Stone incident then you wouldn't even have got this interview. You would be shovelling shit for the whole of your time with us because we don't like Officers in Training. OiTs, we've shit'em. But the regiment is grateful, so *you* are getting that second chance. You will start by redoing your Basic, but none of that namby-pamby officer stuff that you did before. We're giving you the chance to prove that a boy from the steppe is as tough as they come. You join JB316 this afternoon. You got that?"

"Yes, sir."

"Good. I'll see you in six months. Now piss off."

The RSM watched as Jez shuffled out of the mess, doing his best not to drop any of his kit on the polished wooden floor. The boy from the steppe puzzled him.

"I reckon he can handle himself you know."

"Really?"

"Yeah, he looks like a runt but that's just the QM's joke, OiT, O for oversize. The QMs do it to all the OiTs, don't they? But I reckon he's going to grow into his. Yeah, he can handle himself alright. Got his head screwed on too I'd say, as it takes balls to want to leave the steppe and join up. And to know how to cover your tracks with a proper address and not use the standard PO Box. He obviously put a bit of thought into all of this. He's smart, maybe too smart. We'll keep a close eye on him, I think."

One of the others then spoke up. "This article might interest you, boss," he said, then passed him an old magazine, "bottom of the page."

"Okay, what have we got here? *'The Homid Smoke Dance'*, hmm?" The RSM frowned. "Right then, here we have it, a reference to *'side-stepping'*, so where does smoke come into it?"

"Didn't one of the stewards on the Star-Link say something about smoke, and you mentioned smoke too, and that they thought there was a fire and rushed up with extinguishers?"

"Yes, you're right. I think that was in the report," one of the others added.

The RSM read on. "*'Extrasensory ability', 'penetrate the thoughts of others'*, and you can bet your sweet arse that he knew what all of us were thinking whilst he stood there. But that's just an everyday Homid thing, and all those weirdos can do that. No, there's got to be something else."

Tomsen spent a couple of minutes scanning the paragraphs whilst the others chatted.

"Right then, here it is. *'The Smoke Dancer ability is only likely to surface in one in ten million'*. Wow! *'And could miss several generations too.'* That's a shame, imagine a regiment of them. Oh well, never mind. Now then, what else does it say? Erm, okay *'the average person of Sckerian or Mii'een decent has the extrasensory gene, but once in a while — one true Homid person, one in ten million — has a concentrated ability that can be as much as tenfold, and the gene bearer can not only penetrate the thoughts of others but can manipulate them too; seeing in the dark or with their eyes closed is another manifestation, or even seeing through the eyes of others. But the real phenomenon is their ability to speed up their movements, or as the legends say, appear as smoke. These traits are only ever found in the Mii'een nomad gene pool'*. Wow indeed," he finished, and the room hushed as they all considered the possibilities of what they had just heard.

"Jeepers."

"Can I read it, boss?" asked another.

"After you, Jim," said a third.

Then the RSM said, "We most definitely must keep an eye on Devii'rahl J. I get a feeling that, with the proper mentoring, he will one day be an asset to the Corps. Keep an eye on him, boys and girls. Watch over him. Keep him safe, as we might just have been in the presence of something great."

16

Some night off... !

Devii'rahl.J OiT fell in with the new Jaeger recruits as they paraded for the roll. This was their first roll call, so at least today he wouldn't be singled out as the *'late'* Devii'rahl.J OiT. He knew though, that before very long the NCOs, would make some sort of snide comment and turn the focus on the OiT. Officers in Training bore the brunt of an NCO's displeasure and were always assigned the worst jobs. The thinking behind the OiT programme was 'how can you expect to lead someone if you don't understand them and their lot?' It was the painful shortcut to earning mutual respect, yet it seemed to work. But for this OiT things would be different. Once through basic, Jez would learn what it was like to be an ordinary Jaeger-soldier and do all the necessary soldier things, although there was nothing ordinary about the Jaegers. Jaegers were the elite.

Jag Basic was more than tough, that was a given, but after that, there would be real learning, the OiT shit-shovelling and coal painting. But before Jez got 'all' the OiT good jobs, first of all though he had to get through this Basic.

Jaeger recruit intake JB316 shuffled into a sort of line and Jez quickly glanced down the line at the fresh-faced hopefuls. They looked keen and happy and he smugly thought, [-"*Smile while you can boys because the next few weeks are going to knock the shit out of you!*"-] Unfortunately for Jez he was in for a shock too. He should have heeded the RSM's parting remark regarding the namby-pamby officers' basic. That basic was a stroll in the park.

The next month would be a walk through hell.

The first four weeks of any basic was a relentless procession of mind-numbing, body-sapping and pointless tasks. The whole object was to break the spirit, and the recruits would be on the go for every hour in every twenty-four. They would even wear the same clothes as there'd be no time to change. No time to wash either, just enough time to relieve themselves, and about the same amount of time to eat. They would only get catnaps, and this would go on and on until they would obey without questioning anything thrown at them.

Jez would fare better than the rest, but even he was close to breaking point by the end of the month. He had endured this barbaric practice once already and, fortified by his own history and knowing what was going to happen a few seconds in advance, he managed to stay half a pace ahead.

At the end of the four weeks, they were all at least a stone lighter, and filthy. They were ordered to strip, and they rejoiced as they peeled away the fatigues that had become a second skin. They then filed into the showers and enjoyed their first wash since that very first roll-call.

"You get your uniforms now, because from today you learn what it's like to be real Jaegers. In five months you will be able to refer to yourself, if you make it, as a Jag. Now get in there and collect your kit. You will also be allocated a bed, and just this once you get the rest of the day off to arrange your kit. Tomorrow you start to learn. Lights Out at eleven."

Jez looked at his watch. [-"It's nine now, some night off,"-] he thought.

The lights went out at eleven sharp and the recruits continued by the glow of their cellfones, packing their new belongings as best they could into whatever space they had. Although, they would probably have to try again tomorrow morning before they were expected on parade. Jez and a couple of the others who had the Homid advantage of being able to see without seeing, once they had sorted their own stuff, they helped the others, and by twelve they were all able to hit the sack. They were just about to do so when the doors burst open and a new set of NCOs marched in. Not only did today mark the start of the real training, but it was also the day that this new group of NCOs took over that training. And this lot seemed to be playing by a different set of rules.

"Stand by your beds," they shouted. "It was Lights Out at eleven, and it's now twelve. Why are you not in bed? Outside now."

They all filed out dressed as they were. Jez had realised something was up only seconds before the door burst open, and fortunately he still had his trousers on. Others weren't so lucky.

"Okay you lot, get running. Once around the perimeter. Go," and off they went, regardless of whether they were shod or not. When they got back the new NCOs weren't happy, so they went again, and a third time, until their tormentors had had their fun. "When it's Lights Out, it's Lights Out. Got that?"

They stood beside their beds shivering, feet bleeding and tired. It was one o'clock and morning parade was at six. Then the sergeant asked again, "When is Lights Out?"

"Eleven!"

"Exactly. And not one second after," he confirmed, and he was just about to add another pearl of wisdom when a particular shiverer caught his eye. "Sheep Boy. It's you, isn't it? Step forward, now!"

Jez dutifully stepped forward and Sergeant Garrard was nose to nose with him in an instant. "Well, what have I done to deserve this?" he growled, then stepped back and eyed him up and down, then nodded. "I was told you had been posted to a Jaeger regiment, but I bet they didn't tell you I had too. Oh, we're going to have some fun, you and me. The rest of you, bed, now. You, Sheep Boy, around that perimeter one more time, and no holding back. Let's see what you can really do, shall we?"

A week or so later, when they had a bit of spare time and were all sitting around in the billet polishing boots and darning socks, and generally chatting and getting to know one another, a solid and intimidating tribesman from Mejjas Minor tapped Jez on the shoulder and grunted. "What's your story then?"

"Huh?" Jez had been in a world of his own shining his boots, the question had taken him by surprise.

"What is it 'tween Garrard and you?" the tribesman persisted: His name was Piko.

Jez turned. "I did Basic eighteen months ago. Garrard was the NCO and I was his fall-guy. The NCOs will single someone out, pour all their contempt on him, or her. In the end the whole squad is taking it out on the poor sap. The NCOs don't mind losing one along the way if it helps bond the squad. Garrard revels in the practice. I suppose somewhere in that first six months I didn't try hard enough for him. But at the same time I've proved him wrong because I'm still here. Simple as that."

"Is that all? Sheesh. He's riding you hard because in a past life he didn't think you tried hard enough. Really? Nothing more than that?"

"Well there's always more to it than that. I'm still here for one. But yes, that's the gist. Garrard's a bully and I didn't try hard enough."

"Sheesh." Piko thought for a moment, then added, "Are you still a slacker? I ain't carrying no slacker."

"I've never been a..."

"Hold on a minute," said another. "*Why are* you doing Basic again?"

"He's doing Basic again..." Sergeant Garrard bawled down the billet as they all scurried to stand beside their beds. "He's doing it again because Mr RSM Tomsen told him to do it again, and because the namby-pamby officer basic he did before isn't good enough for the Jaeger Corps. I now have the pleasure of knocking him once again into shape, and believe me, it's going to be a pleasure. Come with me, Sheep Boy, I've got something for you outside. Follow me," he demanded, beckoning with a finger.

Jez shrugged, put his boots on his bed and obediently followed him from the building. As he stepped through the doorway he heard one of the others say, "That didn't sound too good."

Less than half an hour later Jez stumbled back through the doorway. His face was bruised, and trickles of blood were running down over his ear and his forehead. His lips were split, a couple of were teeth missing, his nose was blooded and there was a vicious stud gouge the length of his shin. There was swelling around his left eye socket and his eye was so tightly screwed shut that it was almost lost from sight. As he limped to his bed, he clutched at his side. His fellow 316ers looked on aghast.

Garrard had led and Jez had obediently followed, concentrating on the NCO's every move. Watching and waiting for any sudden movement that might betray an attack of some kind, which was Garrard's style. Jez had been so intent on the man in front that he'd missed the three who came out of the shadows. They'd been on him before he'd had a chance to react. By the time he was able to read their movements a studded boot had been run down his shin, his legs had buckled, and he'd stumbled. Fists rained down, and another boot was planted into his ribs. The attack was relentless!

He heard someone shout, "Hold him, grab his ankles," and through the corner of his good eye he saw a foot raised to stamp on his knee as a vice-like grip pinned his legs to the ground. Jez braced for the pain, but the stamp never came. The stamper suddenly flew backwards, and firm hands reached down and lifted Jez to his feet.

"Up you come boy."

"Don't hit me again, please, not again."

"No one's going to hit you, son. Not while I'm here." The voice was vaguely familiar, and when he managed to look up at the speaker Jez was greeted by the concerned and battle-scarred face of the RSM. "Let's take a look at you. Has someone got a flashlight? Point it over here. Oooh! Dear me, sorry we didn't get here sooner, son. Sheesh, they certainly gave you a pasting, and if Terk hadn't pulled that guy up when he did, your running days would most certainly have been over. Why didn't you side-step?"

"Looking the other way sir, concentrating on the man in front. Peripherals. It's been a physical day, I'm tired and they took me by surprise, didn't see them coming. I need to work on my peripherals."

The RSM accepted the explanation and nodded, "Yes, good idea." Then he asked, "Can you walk?"

Jez had been clutching his scalp, and when he lifted his hand away and opened his palm it was red and sticky.

"Can you walk," RSM Tomsen persisted, "or shall I get the lads to carry you?"

"Er, no. I'll walk sir," he replied, shaking his head and raising his bloodied hand to gently touch his forehead. "I'll effing-well walk," he said defiantly, and slowly, dragging his right leg a little, he stumbled off towards the billet.

The RSM admired Jez's determination, but to be on the safe side he signalled for a couple of Jags to follow him. "Make sure he gets to where he was going," said Tomsen.

As Jez shuffled across the parade ground someone behind him screamed. The moaning was sickening. He tried to turn to see what was going on and stumbled and fell backwards. One of the Jags was there in an instant

"Steady lad, come on, you've proved you can do it. You're not going to make it on your own though. Come on, we'll get you to the door. And you can walk in unaided. Will that be okay with you?" he added and smiled.

"Give in to friendly help, mate," said the other, "there's no shame in it. Jags don't forget. Reeble is a friend. You *are* one of us. What you did on the Star-Link for Reebs and the others was good enough, but your determination, here and now, has settled it for me. We Jags are family, brothers. So let your brothers help you now. Come on," they said and they linked arms, made him a chair and carried him to the door. Behind him, Garrard had been felled by the RSM with a well-aimed kick followed by a stamp to the sides of both legs. The other three hooded attackers had been dragged into the shadows, after which there were more screams — a lot of screams — then the night was still once more.

"What the hell did you do to that guy to deserve this," Piko gasped as he pulled off Jez's trainers and ran a fighting knife up the front of his ragged t-shirt. "Man, this ain't real. Did you fight back?"

The beer fridge was raided, and a towel packed with ice was gingerly applied to his swollen cheek. The gouge on his shin was swabbed and dressed.

"Didn't get a chance. Jumped from behind. There were three in the shadows. Garrard just watched and laughed. He ain't laughing now though, the RSM fixed him," Jez lisped through his split lips and broken teeth. "Fists everywhere, and boots," he said, clutching his side.

"JD, I'm going to take a look at those ribs," said Jenka, the Sckerian survival nut, as he uncurled Jez's fingers and pulled his hand away. Jenka had lived a self-sufficient life in the wilds of his home planet before joining up, and was well used to treating his own injuries. "I'll try not to hurt you JD, but I've got to check there are no breaks." He carefully pressed on the blueish skin. He realised he was causing some pain, but as long as there were no yelps he continued to press. "You're a lucky bugger JD, just bruises, it's going to hurt though. Oh yeah, and how."

A few minutes later the RSM strode into the billet followed by a limping corporal and a couple of Medics. "As you were lads, as you were," he said. "These Medicos have come to check on your friend, but it looks like you've done a pretty good job already. Nevertheless, let them give him a once over," he added and he stepped aside to let them pass.

Whilst they were doing their checking RSM Tomsen turned and looked about the billet. It was a bit of a mess but he didn't seem to notice. However, he did see the beer cans that had been taken from the fridge. "Let's have a couple of those," he said, "its thirsty work mopping up the bad guys. Want one Reebs?" he asked the corporal, who nodded. "Be a good lad," Tomsen said to one of the squaddies, "and crack open one of those cans for my mate, would you? His hands are a bit out of action at the moment." The corporal's right hand was in a cast, and the fingers of his left hand were in some sort of sprung brace. "Thanks for the beer... who do we owe?" Tomsen asked.

"They're on me, sir," lisped Jez, and the RSM and Corporal Reeble turned, raised their cans in salute, then nodded and smiled.

"Will he mend?" the RSM asked the Medics.

"He'll mend, sir, but he's going to hurt for a few weeks. Shall we sign him off duties?"

Tomsen looked down on the injured OiT, his head on one side. "It's up to you lad," he said. "The Medicos can sign you off and I'll gladly counter-sign it. You can stay in your pit for a few days and rest up. It's your call."

Without any hesitation, Jez reached out and grabbed both the Medics' arms and pulled himself up onto his feet. Slowly, and painfully, he straightened up. "I'll be on parade tomorrow morning, sir."

The RSM nodded and smiled, then said, "Yes, I believe you will. You're a fighter, I can see that, but you have to admit that up to now you've been a prat. You rubbed Garrard up the wrong way and he's the sort that doesn't forget. In years to come he might just try again. Make sure you're ready." Jez nodded and winced.

Then the RSM gave the lads in the billet the official line. He told them that Garrard was a vindictive bully and that he had been on base as part of the training team now for nearly a year. In that year, he added, there had been a record number of recruits who were injured unnecessarily or had quit the service. The RSM said Garrard was too hard. "Don't get me wrong though, Jaeger Corps training is supposed to be hard, but there's hard and there's vicious hard, and vicious hard is something we don't do."

The squaddies learned that the Corps had been looking for a way to legally get rid of Garrard for some time, but they had to be careful; Garrard had friends.

"Enter your mate here," he said, gesturing in Jez's direction, "Devii'rahl.J OiT rubbed Garrard up the wrong way in his previous basic. Seems that he caused Garrard no end of financial grief. But I'll leave Devii'rahl.J OiT to fill you in on all of that." The RSM turned and looked at the injured man, and shook his head. "You've still got some growing up to do boy, and you can do that by coming clean to these good mates of yours. You can tell them everything that went on at the other basic," he said, then he wagged his finger, and leant forward so no one else could hear, and whispered, "but let's just keep it to basic, for now, no Star-Link stuff. Okay?"

Jez nodded. "Yes sir," he agreed.

The Medics packed their equipment and left, and before RSM Tomsen and Corporal Reeble did the same, Tomsen said, "Sergeant Garrard is a bully, and you all know what bullies are. Bullies are cowards, and there's no room in the Jaeger Corps for cowards."

Whilst the RSM spun out his bullying tale to the squaddies, Corporal Reeble was thinking of the real reason that Jez was attacked, which was totally at odds with what the RSM would have the squaddies believe.

The corporal turned to the injured man, smiled, and tapped his forehead. Jez responded by dipping into Corporal Reeble's thoughts. Jez returned the smile and they shared a nod. Reeble then took a step back and waited for the RSM to finish his yarn. Then the RSM and the corporal left.

Once they were alone, the other squaddies helped Jez into a more comfortable position. Then each cracked open another beer.

Cael asked, "So how the hell did you piss that arsehole off so much to get you this?" he gestured. "Come on, get it out into the open now, and then we can all move on and forget it."

So Jez explained. It was a simple tale that had gotten out of hand. He told them how his two brothers had both been killed in a tragic accident, and how it had been their dreams to join up into the service, but how he had never wanted that for himself. Jez Devii'rahl only ever wanted to be a shepherd and to roam the steppe of his home planet of Mii'een behind the vast flocks of the Rahl people. He wanted to keep his brothers' dreams alive though, so he joined up in their stead and sacrificed his own dream for theirs. He tried to live as they would, and it worked for a while. But then the grief of their loss resurfaced, and whilst he was trying to deal with that he stopped trying, and events that Miike or Peiite would have excelled at were lost, and Garrard lost money.

But at that time no one thought anything of it, and Garrard accepted that his Trainee Intake - Tech2, were simply not up to it. Someone then found an old Geographic magazine, probably in the barbers or at the dentist, which contained an article about the shepherds of Mii'een. Inside was a picture of a young shepherd from the Rahl tribe holding a clutch of medals earned for running: It was me of course. And that's when everything turned sour, and why Garrard had it in for him. "In short, I cocked up... big time."

"Wow, shit, that's one hell of a tale. Sorry about your brothers, mate," said Cael, and everyone else said much the same.

"Yeah, sorry."

Then Cael said, "That's the daftest scheme I have ever heard anyone admit to. How the mejj did you ever think you could pull it off? Surely you must've realised that someone like Garrard would see through such a hair-brained plan as that?"

Jez nodded, and agreed. "Yeah, I was a prat. I very nearly pulled it off though. I was within a month or six weeks of the Passing-Out Parade. I nearly got there. Then someone slipped Garrard that mag — don't know who — and my whole world turned to shit!"

"And is that everything out in the open now?" Jenka asked. "The RSM got quite close to you before he left, so is there more for you to tell?" [>"Are you holding anything back?"<]

[>"Yes. But it's got nothing to do with Garrard, maybe those other three. Maybe. It's not my tale to tell though, it's the Corps', and as much as we are Jag brothers that information is one step more that I'm not prepared to take."<]

[>"Tell the others that. No secrets."<]

[>"But I've told you, I can't tell you that or what went on."<]

[>"Yes I know you can't, it's a matter of honour, I get it. But you can tell the lads that you can't tell them, and you can tell them why you can't. If you want to be one of us and earn our respect, then you have to tell them that. Or do you want to be the NCOs fall guy again?"<]

Jez looked up from his thoughts just as Cael announced, "You're a daft bugger JD and you've had one hell of a beating. No one deserved that, but I for one am prepared to move on and leave tonight in the past."

The others nodded in agreement, all except for Jenka, who motioned for Jez to speak. "Go on JD, tell them."

All eyes turned his way and he mumbled, "There is something else though," Jez said, a slight tremor to his voice. "Something that happened, something that I was involved in that might have something to do with the three that jumped me from behind. It's something to do with the Honour of the Jaeger Corps and because it involves the Corps then I cannot tell you what it is. All I can say is that something happened some months ago and that everyone who witnessed it had to swear an oath of secrecy. I can't tell you any more than that."

"Did Tomsen say something about that when he bent forward, before he left?" Piko asked.

"Yes, Piko."

"And you can't tell us?" Cael asked. He looked annoyed.

"No."

"Look guys," Jenka piped up. "I asked him to tell us and to tell you why he couldn't tell us, and that's what he's done. It is Corps stuff, Jaeger stuff, it's honour stuff. What's he supposed to do? The RSM will have his balls if he tells us, and he'd have our balls as well if he knew that we knew. I want to keep mine, so I'm happy with what JD has told us. I certainly wouldn't want to be burdened with a secret like that. I should say we're lucky not to be keeping something of that magnitude. I'm prepared to put tonight behind me and move on."

The others agreed with Jenka, and to a man agreed to leave it and move on. Devii'rahl.J OiT was still one of them.

In the shadows, just beyond the open door, RSM Tomsen whispered, "Well done lad." Corporal Reeble nodded in agreement.

The following day Sergeant Garrard and his team were supplanted by the limping Corporal Reeble and four more lance-jacks (LJs), and if the squaddies thought that the limping corporal, with his injured hands, would be giving them a bit of leeway because of his own condition, they were sadly mistaken. He joined them on their daily fifteen-kilometre jog-march and managed to out-pace them at every turn. And each day, as his injuries healed, the marching pace quickened until they were all running, fully packed, for the whole distance.

Jon Reeble's training program was tougher than Garrard's, but it was fairly metered out and Reeble ran with them and did everything that he asked them to do. The other man never did.

As Reeble healed so too did Jez, and very soon they were trying to out-pace each other. The rest of the troop weren't enjoying the rivalry quite as much though, and one evening they took Jez to one side and asked him, in no uncertain terms, to ease it off a little.

"Look mate, we know you're getting better, and we're pleased for you, but our feet ain't. Slow it down will ya, JD."

Devii'rahl, when he was being himself, just wanted to show people that he was capable. But he listened to his mates, and he repaid their understanding a few weeks later when they were confronted with the blind exercise. Reeble must have been listening too, because the next jog-march was a much more sedate affair.

Reeble's regime revelled in wet and uncomfortable tasks, and most days the trainee Jaegers would either be up to their armpits in mud, or on their bellies crawling under barbed wire across waterlogged fields. It seemed to rain every day of that six months, and the trainees found out later that Jaeger training was only ever scheduled for the wet season. Their kit was always wet and stiff, and unforgiving, and the grit that gathered in the creases chafed their skin. Their bodies were riddled with abrasion sores, and stripped down they looked like tigers.

But that's what the training was all about. Jaegers had to be tough, they had to fight like tigers too, and be able to do that in all conditions. Everything that they did had to be automatic, and by the end of the six months, putting on wet combat fatigues had become second nature.

The rain was relentless, and it looked like it would continue raining right up to the last day. But when Corporal Reeble, flanked by his training team, announced that "It will be bright and sunny at the end of the week for the Regimental Games," eyes rolled in disbelief. "It never rains on Sports Day. But as you might be aware, today it is raining, just how we like it. Now, for today's march, I want you in full combat gear and outside in five minutes. Snap to it."

17

Blind faith ...

Today's route was completely different to any they had taken before. After eight kilometres as they followed a narrow track along a ridge, Reeble called them to a halt. Then he turned, smiled, and said, "It's a good day for it, don't you think?" JB316 were strung out in a single line on one side of a shallow valley. On the far side of the valley was a line of flagpoles, and between them and the flags there was a stretch of ancient oak woodland, maybe one hundred and fifty meters at its widest. Their full combat gear was sodden, they had already forded a swollen river and crawled across a peat bog, and the rain was still coming down in sheets.

[-"*What's the catch?*"-] Jez wondered as Reeble shouted, "Helmets off."

Obediently, and without a moment's hesitation, they each unclipped and removed their headgear. As they did so Jez pushed his thoughts out, down the slope and into the wood. [-"*A few fallen trunks.*"-]

"Today's objective," Reeble barked, "is to get to that line of flags on the other side of the wood. You have three hours to do it."

[-"*A ditch! That track might be worth following though.*"-]

"Huh?" They glanced at each other, shifting their eyes only.

Jenka, the only other Homid left in the squad, stared at the flags and thought, [-"*This'll be a piece of piss,*"-] whilst Jez continued to push his thoughts deeper into the wood.

Reeble smiled too. "It's not a very big wood, is it, and if it wasn't for this

60

light shower you might just be able to hear one of the obstacles gurgling."

The rest of the squad stiffened and turned, looking left and right, and up and down the valley, to see if they could catch a river's reflection.

Jez pushed on. [-*"There's a river! That might be awkward."*-] But try as they might, the trees obscured the view.

"Eyes front," Lance-Jack Brakken screamed.

Jez though *was* staring straight ahead at the wood. [-*"That low branch will be a good point to aim at, approximately two paces to the right of where the track leaves the wood. That should do it."*-] Whilst the others turned eyes-front, Jez withdrew his thoughts and retraced his route. [-*"I reckon I can remember that,"*-] he thought. [-*"Well, maybe."*-].

The helmets were collected and swapped for black-out hoods. Jenka smiled. [-*"Defo, a piece o'piss…"*-]

But his thoughts were cut short when Reeble said, "Ah Jenka, you're smiling, but just remember, the corporal always has the last laugh. Hoods on now! And lock."

LJ Brakken went back down the line to make sure each hood was securely locked in place. "You will be blind for the whole exercise. You can only unlock the neck halters with special keys, and there's one at the top of each of the flag poles. Come on Devii'rahl, you too."

Jez slipped his glasses inside his jacket, and as he slowly lifted the hood he focused and concentrated on a gap and the low branch. "Come on Devii'rahl, hood on now," LJ Brakken screamed," and as Jez did so everything went black.

Reeble called to Jenka. "Obviously I can't see your face now Jenka, but I'll hazard a guess that you can't see mine either and that smile has gone too. Am I right?"

"Yes Corp." [>*"I'm blind JD!"*<]

Jez didn't answer.

"Good, at last we have a level playing field. These are experimental hoods," he said as he moved slowly down the line, "the material is a prototype. We are testing the material to see if we can counter the Homid gene ability, and it would appear in Jenka's case that we have succeeded. As for Devii'rahl J

OiT, I don't think he would say even if we had, would you?" asked Reeble as he stopped beside him, then he whispered, "Well JD, have we blacked you out?"

Jez said nothing.

"I thought not." Then the corporal turned and addressed the line. "You have three hours. You *can* try on your own, or you can work as a team. The choice is yours. Now I'm going to stroll to the other side of the wood. I've a coffee on the brew. I will see you all there in three hours. Off you go."

Jez immediately shouted down the line. "I have a route, so I will lead. Trust me." [>"*I owe you.*"<] Jez was blacked out too, the fabric was good. Something in the weave was reflecting his seeing visual thoughts back at him. But it wouldn't stop his words, nor his memory. And before any of the others could baulk at his suggestion, he barked again into their thoughts. [>"*Follow my lead. Do as I say.*"<]. Then he shouted out loud. "Everyone hold the hand of the person next to you," he yelled, and as he reached out the squaddies on either side did the same and the line was linked.

Then, although the hood blocked his sight anyway, he closed his eyes. He found it easier to concentrate that way. "Okay guys, on my command. And only my command. The slope is slippy," he added. "We go slowly. We only take short steps. And we stamp them out. Got that?"

A muttered "Yes'" rippled down the line.

"Good. Right then, let's move. Stop when you reach the trees, and always wait for my command. As one. Go!"

Reeble, and his crew stopped halfway down the slope. He was impressed by the speed that they had mobilized, and Lance-Jack Maesie Thorpe asked, "Surely he can see through that hood Corp?"

"I don't know Maes, but at this very moment I don't think it matters, do you? Two things are happening here just now. We've got teamwork, which is great, and JD's leading them and they're following him, blind. There's some real trust in that line, and it's blind trust in Devii'rahl J."

Jez was a step or two ahead of the rest of the line. He was moving forward in short steps and they were nervously following his pull, going down the slope in an arrowhead. He reached the tree line first, and walked straight into a low branch. [-"*Spot on,*"-] he thought and took a deep breath [-"*Phew that was lucky*"-]. He was where he wanted to be, a couple of paces to the right of the gap in the trees. "Okay, hold it. Now everyone take two paces to your left, Okay, and now one pace forward... good."

They did as they were asked, and Jez, feeling his way with his foot, found the gap in the trees. "Right then, in turns, the one on my left, Jenka, take hold of the webbing on my back. Then the one on my right, Piko, take hold of Jenka's webbing, and so on."

One at a time they formed a snake, twenty long. "Right then, everybody pull back on the one in front, and when that tension on your back stops, you stop. We will move forward one pace at a time, and we will stamp each pace. There are obstacles, so we'll have to slalom through the wood. Now number off," he said, then shouted, "One!" and they counted down the line to twenty. "Who's twenty?"

"I'm twenty JD, its Cael."

"Cheers Cael. Okay then, let's move," and Jez boldly stamped into the wood.

It took them just over an hour to get to the riverbank, as they had to overcome several fallen trunks and at least one deep ditch along the way. After each forced turn or ditch, Jez paused the line and they numbered off. And all the while Reeble and his team, instead of waiting by the flags with their coffee, followed the snake's progress, fascinated and full of admiration for its head and the trust of its body.

"I'm still not convinced, Reebs," said Lex Brakken. "He's got to be seeing through it... he's almost too perfect."

Reeble, though, wanted to believe it was memory, although he too was in two minds. "You can test him when they get to the flags, Lex. But I still think it's memory. I'll put five on that."

"I'll take that bet Corp," said Brakken.

"Me too," said Bella Morton.

"And me," said Maesie Thorpe, and they all shook on it.

"Could be expensive for you Reebs," said Jim Donelson.

"Could be, but let's wait and see what happens shall we. I'm still plumping for memory."

"Was it memory Reebs?" RSM Tomsen asked later that week as they shared a beer, bought with Reeble's winnings.

"I don't know, boss, the guys seemed to think it was. They paid up after all," he said as he slurped his beer. "After they got across the river one of the squaddies shimmied up a pole to get a key, and we unlocked all the hoods except JD's. Then one of the LJs punched him hard in the stomach. JD didn't flinch or shy away like you would if you knew what was coming, he just doubled up and stepped back. The LJ said it was like hitting a cushion, as it was a soft and not tensed.

"Memory then?"

"Maybe. I honestly don't know. All I'll say is if he could see through the hood, then he has nerves of steel to let the LJ land that punch. I just don't know, and I suppose we never shall."

"He's certainly an enigma, is that young man," said Tomsen as he put the bottle to his lips.

Jez hadn't seen the punch coming. He was as blind as everyone else, but he knew that there would be one. He also knew it would be one of the LJs, either Maesie Thorpe or Lex Brakken, who wanted to test him out. So, when the murmuring suddenly hushed and he heard someone close by take a sharp intake of breath, Jez was ready. There was no magic, he simply relaxed and readied his feet. And when it did come, when he felt the LJ's fist ruffle the air, he was able to double up convincingly, and back away before the punch really landed.

18

You need a good woman ...

Under Corporal Reeble's guidance, Jez flourished, and JB316 bonded into a very tight-knit unit. Reeble treated everyone the same, OiTs and squaddies alike, and he was an inspiring yet very private leader. He gave very little away, and for the entire time they were under his tutorship they learned nothing about the man except for what they could see, a battle-hardened Corporal of Jaeger. Although, he did seem to have some sort of affinity with Jez, but no one ever found out why. They all had their theories, but they came to nothing and after a while they gave up trying to figure him out and got on with their training, taking the rough with the smooth.

When it came around to the Regimental Games, and the sun *was* shining just as he said it would be, JB316 won everything that they entered. In the individual races, they eventually got to see the running JD in action, and they weren't disappointed. That evening the RSM sent over several crates of beer to help them celebrate, but Jez didn't stay long. The occasion got the better of him and he excused himself and stepped out into the starry night.

"The lads said I would find you here," Reeble said as he settled himself down beside Jez. "You all did well today, and you surpassed all my expectations. So why are you out here, all alone and not celebrating with the others?"

"We're family, my family, brothers. Tomorrow we go our separate ways and I might never see them again. It's still too raw, Corp."

"Hmm, yeah. You know I know how you feel."

Jez nodded. [>"Yes, I do."<]

"Maybe my hurt isn't as immediate as yours JD, but I saw it go too, and I have hurt, like you, for years. Now I nurture boys like those in there. They're under my guidance for six months, and I grow to love them just like you have. And then they go. Then I get another squad and I go through it all again. It's the way of service life, mate. It happens all the time. You just have to grin and bear it, and move on."

"I know," Jez replied. "I know. I often think I'm over it, then in the quiet moments it resurfaces and I'm back there in that conduit, running for my life against that wind and getting nowhere. So I come out here and stare up at that evil twinkle and let the tears flow and wash it all away. That's what I do, Reebs," Jez confided. "It's the only way I know of handling it."

Reeble listened to Jez baring his soul, and whilst he listened to this young man's sorrow he thought of his own and a tear welled and trickled down his cheek. [-"So many poor souls; his brothers. My.... My... "-] but he cut his thoughts short, and in the earthy way of soldiers he turned to the young man beside him and said, "What you need matey is a good woman to give you a good seeing to. Someone to give your memories a spring clean."

"Huh?" Jez reacted with surprise, shaking himself back to reality. "Corp, you what?"

"What you need, my boy, is a good woman to hump your brains out."

Reeble had knocked Jez off balance and his thoughts were scattered. "Eh? Woman, right, yeah, okay. Yes. Yes, I do, and I thought I had one, but I blew it.

"And that's where you went wrong, it should have been the other way around," Reeble said and laughed.

"What?" Jez was lost. This line of conversation had completely thrown him. "Erm, eh, is that how you sorted yourself out Corp? Did you get a good woman?"

"Tried the theory with several. I still get those remorseful thoughts, so I just try again and not necessarily with good women. To be honest, I'll try it on with any woman, good or bad if it blocks out the sad times," he said and winked, then continued. "Write to her, she might just write back. Give it a try. What have you got to lose? Anyway, lad," he said, struggling to his feet, "lights out at eleven sharp. Don't get caught out and spoil your evening. You did well today, but it's a big day tomorrow. Good night."

The next day they passed out. There was no ceremony, they were just assigned to their new units. There were hugs and handshakes, and tears. And then they went their separate ways. As Jez shouldered his kitbag RSM Tomsen called him over.

"You've surprised me, Devii'rahl J, and I'm pleased, very pleased about that. You've proved to me that it wasn't a fluke or just Homid mumbo jumbo, and you *were* probing my thoughts, weren't you?"

Jez said nothing, just smiled.

"As I thought. You're a good lad, I like that," he said as he rested his huge hand — Tomsen was built like a bear — on Jez's shoulder and nodded. "In all my years I have never come across someone as determined as you, and it was plain to see when you staggered across the parade ground after that beating. JB316 saw that too. I've seen squads fail their Basic on the blind-test. But your lot literally put blind faith in your leadership. Just keep doing what you do best. Do that, and you will always have my support and the support of the Corps. Now off you go, Devii'rahl J OiT."

Jez was assigned to the engine room of a Jaeger Corps Assault Craft, the JCAS Laximus IV. His reputation had preceded him, and everyone aboard was well aware that he was *the one* in the Memorial Stone incident, and consequently, JD was instantly accepted as being one of the guys. There were other OiTs on the ship, OiTs who had been there longer, who were still treated as the lowest of the low. But not Devii'rahl.J, the champion runner and mysterious side-stepping smoke dancer.

This boy — this man — was a Jag.

19

Engine Mess – B ...

At the end of a twelve-hour watch about three months into his tour, and before the quiet time got the better of him, Jez opened his notepad and unscrewed his fountain pen. The pen had been a gift from his parents on his fifteenth birthday, and had become a personal treasure. The others in the mess knew this; it was JD's, and it was to be left alone.

Jez settled onto his bunk and stared at the blank pages. He knew what he wanted to say, he just didn't know how to write it. But he knew how to start. *'Dear Lucy...'*

And that's as far as he got, then he was back on another twelve-hour watch. A month later he tried again and got as far as *'Dear Lucy, how have you been, I have joined the Jaeger Corps...,'* and so it went on. Every couple of weeks he would open his notebook and try again, much to the amusement of his messmates, but none of them ever tried to see what he had written. To be honest they were all a little bit nervous of what a *side-stepper* could do. They simply smiled at a distance, offering their own rather fruity advice of course, because they knew he wasn't writing to his Mumma. It was similar to the advice that Jon Reeble had given him. Jez would smile and store their advice at the back of his thoughts. Then he would shut his notepad and join in with the banter to keep the demons from creeping in, or he'd take out his much loved and many times folded picture and stare at it until the sleep came.

His tour of duty on Laximus IV was twelve months, and in that year their craft would visit most of the outlying planets in the inner ring. Whilst they were exploring The Belt of Homid they touched down for a couple of weeks on Mii'een, Jez's home planet, and he was given leave by the skipper to visit his folks and stay with them for a few days.

Every one of the Rahl tribe came to see him, some even travelling for a week overland. Jez took a couple of his messmates, and the homecoming feast was spectacular. The visit though was all too short, and a few days later Jez and his mates were back on board, up amongst the stars and dodging the asteroids in the Homid debris field. But before he left the bosom of his family, Jez and his cousin Meeko shook hands on a partnership, 50-50, to raise their own flock; Jez would supply the funds and Meeko would do the droving. It was a partnership that would last a lifetime and would become very successful indeed.

Back onboard Jez took out his notepad and opened it. Now he felt he had something to write about. His messmates were a bit confused, and one of them whispered, "He's going to write to a girl... have you seen her picture? She's gorgeous, and he is writing to her about sheep? Each to their own, I suppose. But I ain't gonna say anything, although he's probably read my thoughts already. Have you, JD?" he asked out loud.

Jez smiled, but said nothing.

"But sheep, JD?" Jez just smiled some more. "Well, you know best. I have to say though," his mate said, then turned to all the others in the mess, "JD's family certainly know how to throw a spread... I don't think I've ever eaten so much."

They brought back several hampers too and each mess got a share.

"Cheers mate, thanks for taking us. You have a great family. And thanks for this."

Again Jez smiled as his messmates enjoyed their hamper, then he turned back to his letter and started to write.

20

Is that it? ...

"I've had a letter," Lucy said to Cristi. "It's from that Jez."

"Oooh!" Cristi exclaimed.

"Yeah, but... it's... very odd."

"Here, let me see," said Cristi. She looked at it, read it, and then looked again. "Huh, is that it?" she said, turning it over to see if there was anything on the back. "Just that?"

"Just that."

"I always thought he was a bit weird, and it's not what you'd call a love letter is it?" Cristi replied.

"I think it's so sweet. He's obviously very excited and he wanted to tell someone, and he told me. It's lovely." She took it back and read it out loud. *'Dear Lucy, do you remember me telling you that all I ever wanted to be was a shepherd? Well my cousin Meeko and I have just bought four hundred sheep, and we're going to be partners. We shook on it. How are you? Did you pass your course? Yours very affectionately, Jez Devii'rahl.'* "And he's signed it with three kisses."

"Wow. You know Sam tells me things he hears from around the Fleet, and Your Jez."

"He's not my Jez."

"Really?" Cristi gave her friend a very old-fashioned look. "Really Luce?"

"No, he's not, and anyway I'm going out with Jerry tomorrow."

"Oh yeah, of course, and who was it last week, Riki? And Phil a few weeks before, and before that, and don't forget that awful Pedrasz, who keeps leaving you notes. You're not going to date that creep, are you Luce?" but before Lucy could answer, Cristi continued. "It's such a shame you and Billy split, you were good together. You just can't settle, can you? Let's face it, you haven't been able to settle since JD turned up on the day you had to give in your assignment," Cristi said while shaking her head. "You even went out with the Prof."

"It was just one evening," Lucy replied quickly, "and he bought me dinner then drove me home. That was it, though I think he wanted more."

"I'm sure he did."

"But students and lecturers don't mix, and anyway he's married. So that was a non-starter."

"All these one-night stands, Luce. You don't want to get labelled."

"It's never anything physical, Cris." Lucy was shocked by the suggestion. "Just drinks or the cinema or a meal. It's nothing like that, and you know I don't sleep around! I pay my way when they let me. The last person I shared a bed with was you."

Cristi could see she'd rubbed a very raw nerve, so she steered the conversation back to JD. "Your boy is making quite a name for himself too. Apparently he plays hard and fights harder, though I'm sure Sam said something about him getting quite a beating when he first started in the Jaeger Corps. But he's better now," Cristi quickly added when she saw a look of real concern wash across her friend's face.

"He's not my boy, he just writes a lovely letter. You do think it's a lovely letter, don't you? It shows that even though he's a real ruffty-tufty soldier these days, that he's still an excited boy at heart. Does Sam know if he still has his hover-board?"

"Oh yes, he certainly does, and there are all sorts of stories doing the rounds about the 'floating Jaeger'. He's building up quite a reputation, and he writes a great letter too," she said and laughed, then added, "Sheep! I ask you Luce, sheep?"

Lucy had to admit it was funny, and the two of them fell together and

71

laughed some more. "He's got four hundred sheep Luce, how many of your other boyfriends can say that?"

"He's not my boyfriend Cris, and that letter is the most he's ever said to me. But... It is on paper, written with a pen, and it was sent to me. It's lovely isn't it, don't you think, Cris?" she said to her friend.

"Yes, it is. It really is," Cristi agreed.

And that was the start of it. Before Lucy had a chance to put pen to paper and reply, another one arrived. Then another. It seemed like the boy had found his voice, as he was telling her everything, where he'd been since he saw her last, where he was travelling to with the service, everything that happened daily. It was all there inked onto the page. At least once a week, sometimes two. And through those pages, Lucy was able to plot his course around the Endecca System. He visited all of the planets and moons of the Inner Ring. He told her how they spent a long time exploring the moons in The Belt of Homid, even visiting the namesake moon of their assault craft Laximus IV. Every one of his letters was brim-full of enthusiasm.

Lucy bought a map of the Endecca and pinned it to the wall, and with every letter that came she would plot the route that the JCAC Laximus IV had taken. Then she would smooth out the creases and carefully file the letters away. The very first one though, the one about the sheep, she had it framed, and it took pride of place on the cupboard below the map. She was still unable to settle though. "Oh, this won't do," she said to the map. "I want to be with *him*, not the others," and she found herself saying over and over, "He's the one, he is the one. He is the one for me, if only as a friend."

So, she made an instant decision, and with a quick cellfone call she cancelled her evening out, then made herself a cup of coffee and settled down in front of the TV. The programme was light and funny, and because she was laughing so much she didn't hear the door slam open as Pedrasz, the dropped boyfriend, stormed in.

"What do you mean, you don't want to go out with me anymore? As if it's your decision to make," he screamed, and having been taken unawares Lucy turned and fell from the sofa.

Getting to her feet as quickly as she could, she said, "Hey, how did you get in, the door was... "

"Locked? Yeah, I beat it down. You don't lock me out and you don't tell me it's over. I'll tell you when it's over. I'll be waiting for you downstairs," he yelled, and as he cast around the room looking for her coat to speed her up he noticed the envelope of the latest letter. "And I'm not sharing you with this, this... whoever this is, so you can get that out of your head as well. You're going out with me," he said, poking his finger into her shoulder. "Get your coat."

"I don't want to go out with you anymore."

"Get your coat."

"No. No! Now get out. Go on, get out. GET OUT. GET OUT!" Lucy screamed, her voice getting louder with every word, the force of her reply momentarily stunning him and putting him onto his back foot. "Go on, get out. I'm certainly not going to go out with you after this. Get out."

But he wasn't finished. He wasn't going to be talked to like that, not by a girl, even if she was the best looking girl on campus. The cheek of it. Who the hell did she think she was? He raised his hand to her, and as he brought it down and as she raised hers in defence, he suddenly swung away and vented his anger on her map instead, scooping his hand under an edge and ripping it from the wall. "I don't share," he shouted as he screwed her treasured map into a ball and threw it at her. As she ducked and turned away, he punched the framed letter, sending it flying across the room. "You can tell that soldier boy to stop writing those sickening letters and grow up. Next time I'll burn it."

"He's more grown-up than you'll ever be. Now get out."

"I expect to see you at the bar as arranged, and if you're not there in an hour I'm coming back for you. So be there," he spat, and with that, he left.

Lucy was all of a shake, angry and scared all at once. "How dare he? How dare he?" she muttered and whilst she was still *fired up*, she picked up her cellfone and called Cristi. Within twenty minutes Cristi, Sam, Robbie, Conner and a couple of the other OiT cadets were in the apartment, repairing the door and clearing up the mess.

Pedrasz didn't come back, so Robbie, Conner, Sam and the others went to look for him. They found him telling all who would listen about how he put her straight and how she would be back on his arm, and how he only had to snap his fingers. But when the cadets entered the bar, those around him melted into the far corners of the room, and whilst the guys had a quiet word with Pedrasz, Sam snapped his fingers. He seemed to get the message after that and never called again.

"He ripped up my map Cris," Lucy said, sniffing. "Look at it!" She slowly and carefully teased out the creases and spread it out on the wooden floor.

Together they laid a sheet over it and smoothed it with their very old smoothing iron. "I'm afraid we can't make it as good as new, Luce, but with a bit of sticky tape it'll be presentable. Will presentable be good enough?"

Lucy sniffed again and nodded. "Thanks Cris," she said and she leant across the map and hugged her friend. "But look at my lovely letter," she groaned. "There's glass everywhere... be careful when you step over there, there's glass all over the floor. The frame's smashed as well."

Cristi leant across and lifted the treasured letter and frame out of Lucy's hands and set about removing the sheep letter from the shards. "Why the mejj did you go out with that creep, Luce?" Cristi asked as she eased the letter out of the frame. "There, it's in one piece, just a tiny cut that a bit of sticky tape will fix. There you are sweetheart, good as new," she said through a smile, "although I don't think we can fix this," she added as the frame disintegrated. "Let me buy you a new frame," she said and offered a slight nod. "Can I? I'd like to."

"I just thought that if I went out with him the other night that I could tell him that was all it was ever going to be. But before I had a chance to say anything, he went off with his mates, and I had to get the bus home on my own!" Lucy brushed away a tear. "I was going to finish with him tonight anyway. We were going to meet at the Union Bar, but after plotting JD's latest letter I decided I wasn't going to meet him, so I called him instead, and this is what happened. Look at our lovely room," she muttered. "You and Sam, and

Robbie, Conner and the others, you've been so kind. I don't deserve friends like you. How do you put up with me? Over this last year I've been, been... so scatty, and... "

"And," Cristi said, holding up a hand, "that's ok Luce. Okay?"

The following evening Cristi and Sam arrived laden with goodies; they had a couple of bottles of wine, a ten serving cheesecake, a huge tub of crackers and several bags of sweets and chocolate bars and biscuits and mallows and... well, the bags seemed bottomless.

"Where did you get such a huge cheesecake? And how many more are joining us?" Lucy asked, and Sam just smiled and shook his head. "You mean it's just for us?" Sam nodded with vigour, smiling excitedly.

"Sure is," Sam said and laughed, "just us. We thought you might like company, you know, after last night. If you want it, that is?"

"Oh, yes please."

"And I wondered if this might be any good. I got it from the chart room... they were changing their stock. I think it's a bit bigger than your torn map, and it's laminated too so you can write on it." Sam rummaged in his pocket and pulled out some marker pens.

Then Cristi took a neatly wrapped package from her bag. "This is for you my lovely," she said and held it out. Lucy nervously accepted it and carefully unwrapped the package. It was a new frame for her letter. "Why don't you put the letter in now whilst Sam and I sort out plates and glasses?"

Lucy was putting the letter back where it belonged when they returned with the drinks. "Back where it belongs," said Sam, "and it's a cracking letter is that. Who'd have thought our lad could write such a thing. A really sweet thing, really sweet."

"Don't mock him Sam, it's a lovely letter."

"I'd never do that, Luce. He's turned himself around has that boy. No one makes fun of him these days, certainly not twice, that's for sure."

"Are you sure it's okay to have this star chart? It's in very good condition, so are you sure?"

"Absolutely. Apparently it's out of date, and it seems that since printing they have found a new planet and have established without a doubt the origin of The Belt of Homid. It's the remains of the broken Homid planet. Hence the new maps. So, yes, it's okay for you to have this one," he said.

Then Cristi asked, "Could we help you plot all the places that are on the old map onto this one?"

"That would be lovely. Yes, I *would* like that, thank you. I'll just get the letters."

"I'll pour the wine," said Cristi, "and Sam, you cut the cheesecake."

And that's what they did. They spent the evening re-plotting all the places that Jez's letters referred to. That, and drinking both bottles of wine and eating all of the cheesecake and most of the biscuits, as well as nearly all the sweets and the chocolate. Sam and Cristi stayed the night, Sam on the sofa. He said he couldn't stand, so Cristi covered him with a blanket then staggered to her bed alone. Before all of that, however, they rebuilt Lucy's wonderful map.

"He's been some places, hasn't he," said Cristi as she stuck a pin in the mining planet of Fhloria. "Where exactly is Fhloria, Sam? Have you been there?"

"Fhloria is in the Outer Rim. It would've taken about three weeks in their old assault ship. It's a spectacular journey, and the quickest way is through The Belt of Homid. Yes, I've been there. There are mining planets further out than Fhloria you know, and they all begin with the letter F. Ferios is the furthest out. It's been known about for ages, but for some reason it's only been on the charts for the last twenty years. It should be on this one." Sam studied the laminated chart, as best he could as his eyes were getting tired; the wine was definitely getting to him. "Ah, there it is," he said as he held his little finger over a bright orange dot diagonally opposite Fhloria. "That's Ferios. I met up with JD there."

"JD?" said Lucy

"On Ferios?" Cristi added.

Sam nodded. "Yeah Luce, your Jez is..."

"He's not my J...!" Lucy mumbled.

"Cris?" Sam was puzzled.

"Don't go there Sam, let it slide. What were you saying about JD?"

"Eh, oh. Yes JD. Yes, he's known as JD in the Corps too, although I'm not sure if Jez is his name. And no Cris, we met up on Fhloria. Ferios is patrolled by the Blue Fleet; we're the Red Fleet.

"Our craft had literally just docked on Fhloria as the Laximus IV came in. We got to spend twenty-four hours together before both crafts shipped out. JD and I see each other at least once a month, often when I'm here on Mejjas, and his craft is here for a bit of R and R. He'll crash-out on the sofa. He actually prefers to sleep on the floor; he's a Jaeger now as well as being a Nomad, and it seems he'll sleep anywhere."

"He stays with you and Robbie?" This was news to Cristi as well as Lucy. "I didn't think you liked him."

"That was then, Cris, this is now. Like I said, he's turned himself around, and he's a good mate now, the best."

"Golly!" Lucy exclaimed.

"I'll second that. Golly," Cristi agreed.

As the night wore on they read out snippets from his letters, and laughed and cried, because his letters rang with truth and a lot of it was painful. Jez had poured out his heart to Lucy and it was all there on every page. "He's told you everything," Cristi gasped as she blew her nose, "and I remember you saying some time ago *'can I trust him?'* Well he obviously trusts you."

Then Sam said, "JD has certainly told you a lot of things, but I know there's much, much more."

There followed a thoughtful silence as the three of them reached for their glasses. "Oh! Oh, we appear to have drunk both bottles. Oh!" Lucy gasped.

"Wait," said Cristi, "wait, I think I know where we might have another bottle, or two... hold that thought," she added as she clambered to her feet and swayed out of the room. Whilst she was gone Lucy slipped another letter out of the folder.

"How many have you got Luce?" Sam asked. "You just keep pulling more and more out."

"About a hundred I think, maybe a few more. I get a letter at least once a week, sometimes two, but a couple of weeks ago there was one every day. It's just great, just great. I especially like this one." The letter had a red tag and was well-thumbed. "It's all about his family, and his sheep. It's all about taking the flock to the market. He says he was there, on Mii'een, for a whole month."

"Yes, he takes four weeks off in a block to help the family. When he's onboard he works all his rest days and has the skipper's permission to take four consecutive weeks. I've heard it's a godsend for the crew. Don't get me wrong, he's definitely one of the guys make no mistake, but he can be intense, though they do say he's calming down. They love his stories of home. I spent a week with him last year, walking across the steppe."

"Was that when I went home to see my sister?" Cristi asked as she returned with two dusty bottles of red.

"Yeah, I think it must've been. Here look, I have pictures of the visit," he said and projected his cellfone onto the wall. "That's all the sheep the Rahl tribe was taking to market." The picture showed a flock covering at least a thousand square meters. "They said there were two thousand sheep in that picture, and at least another thousand behind me. Now then, this is a picture of his family; that's Meeko Beske'rahl, his cousin and business partner. And that's his Mumma and Pop, who really are lovely. And this is... "

"Can you go back to that last one, Sam," Lucy asked. Something in the picture had caught her eye. "I've seen that lady before, the gentleman too. I'm sure they were talking to Prof Beske'haht. They kept looking at me and nodding as if they were talking about me. I could be imagining it I suppose, but they did look at me more than a couple of times and nodded a lot."

Cristi, Lucy and Sam crowded round. Was this something else in JD's mysterious background?

"Beske'rahl, did you say, that's Jez's cousin? Are Beske'haht and Beske'rahl related?"

"Perhaps you could ask the Prof, Luce?" suggested Sam. "It does seem a bit of a coincidence, doesn't it?"

They pondered the names for a while, and the pictures. The girls had never seen so many sheep and were fascinated by Jez Devii'rahl's huge nomadic family.

Then Cristi groaned. The wine had caught her by surprise. "Ohh," she slurred, "all theesh names. I'm c-confushed," she stammered, then hiccupped. "There'sh Beske, Beske, Beske'haht and Beske'rahl... JD or Jez. And now Sam says Jesh might not even be his name."

"I'm confused too, and now the room's starting to spin," said Lucy.

"Eat more cheeshcake, that'll stop the spin," said Cristi. "And then there's Mii'een and Sckerian, and Homid. You're Sckerian, aren't you Luce?"

Lucy nodded. "Yup."

"So is Jesh Homid or, or, eh I thought he was from Mii'een. Is he from Mii'een? He is from Mii'een, isn't he? Isn't he Sam? And... ah, you're from Sckeria, Lucy, but you say you are Homid? I don't know what's what anymore," Cristi groaned.

"I have the Homid gene," said Lucy, who was staring into the distance, and squinting at her wine-glass, trying to look through the curve. The wine was getting to her too. "Erm, well," she began, but that's as far as she got.

So Sam tried to explain, although the wine was having its effect on him too. He'd had quite a bit of drinking endurance training at Basic and on the various tours about the Endecca, but that was beer. It hadn't quite taken full control, so he gave it a go. "The people from the planets of Mii'een and Sckeria are said to have, eh, no that's not it..." He paused and hiccupped. Sam wasn't used to wine. "The people who fled when the planet Homid broke up... " But he stopped again and shook his head. "Wine is stronger than beer," he mumbled and screwed up his eyes and shook some more. "Okay, the Belt of Homid, that's the asteroid or debris belt between Sckeria and Mii'een. It's made up of the remnants of the broken planet that's now the moon known as Homid, which was the planet known as Homid. It is said, *hic*," Sam screwed up his eyes and shook his head. Then tried again. "Those fleeing peoples, *hic*, integrated into the indigenous populations of Mii'een and Sckeria and the legacy of thish merging, *hic,* is the Homid gene, and Lucy has that gene. It endows the bearer with an extrasensory ability, and which is why she could listen in when we were eh... you know, at it."

Sam paused for a moment to see if either of the girls had reacted, but Lucy was still her wine glass and Cristi had turned to grab another bottle. "Oh." So he continued. "JD's people, the Rahls, the Nomad Drovers of the Mii'een Steppe, are said to be the true, *hic*, descendants of the people of Homid, and that they carry the full Homid genetic makeup, and they're still looking for a place to settle and they will keep roaming until they find it."

"Do you want some more wine?" Cristi asked. "What was all that about genes?"

"I washed your jeans yesterday," said Lucy, snapping out of her trance. "Mine fitted okay this morning, but they've shrunk," she said as she took another mouthful of cheesecake. "They're tight tonight."

"No, you silly bitch, not jeans, genes. Here, let me unbutton them for you. Hold this will you Sam?" she said and she gave him her glass, "and this one," she added, taking Lucy's and passing that too. "There," she said, then winked and smiled, "is that better?" As she popped the top two buttons, she kissed her tummy.

"When you two have quite finished," said Sam. "What was it you were asking about genes?"

"What about jeans?" Lucy asked.

"Cristi just said, '*and what's all that about genes*'. What about them?" said Sam.

"I said I washed them. Do you need yours? Borrow mine?" Lucy started to kneel and pull her jeans down.

Sam froze aghast and wide-eyed. "Ehh... eh, no, Luce."

"No no no, Luce, genetic genes not blue jeans. Pull them back on."

"Oh, those genes," she said and the girls roared with laughter as Sam heaved a huge sigh of relief.

"Those genes, not these jeans. Anyway, I thought we were talking about family names," said Cristi.

"Were we? Well I think we should... I think, er, perhaps we should... should... er, eh," Lucy slurred, and tried to hold up a finger and the words stalled. Then she tried again but it was just too much effort, "Er... ugh," and her head sagged into her chest.

Cristi nodded and shuddered. "Ugh, my head. I'm going to bed my lovelies," she said and held out her hand for Sam. But he just waved and fell back into the sofa. "I'm staying here," he grunted.

"Okay, I'll get you a... a blanket," Cristi replied in a fit of giggles as she managed to pull everything out of the linen cupboard, and in fending off the deluge she somehow flicked a blanket onto the comatose Sam.

The giggles were infectious and soon all three were laughing maniacally. "No no, stop," cried Lucy through her fits and giggles. "Stop," she gasped, "stop, I'm going to we... too late!" she groaned, looking down. "Too late." Then she burst out laughing all the more.

Cristi roared, "Lucy you silly bitch, you always leave it too late," then as she turned to go to her room, she crossed her legs but didn't move her feet and fell amongst the sheets and blankets. "Oh, this is nice, I think I'll stay here. Do you want to join me, Sam?" Cristi mumbled.

"Sam's asleep. Come on Sweetheart," Lucy said as she stooped down and pulled her room-mate unsteadily to her feet. "Let's go to bed and leave Sammy Sam on the sofa. Neither of us is any good for him tonight."

"Oooh Lucy, you said you wouldn't." But Lucy, who was rocking back and forth, totally missed Cristi's innuendo, or indeed what she had said anyway, "but *we* could," Cristi added.

Lucy shook her head. "Can't, not tonight. Love to but can't. Got to go to bed... my bed."

And they hugged and went to their separate ways.

21

No Cris, I wouldn't ...

All three of them slept till late and the sun was already high over the skylights by the time Lucy clambered out of her tangled bed. She slipped on her favourite t-shirt and bathrobe, although she didn't tie it, and her t-shirt hardly covered anything. She staggered into the kitchen to make a brew, and as she passed, she innocently knocked against Sam's dangling arm. He woke with a start and looked up as she turned to the noise of him waking.

"Lucy!" he gasped, "have you any idea...?" he started, then when Lucy realized that she was showing all she quickly wrapped and tied her robe. But Sam hadn't noticed, as all he'd seen was *Club*5eightZero6.

"Is that one of those t-shirts from that *effing* club?" he barked.

"Eh yes," she replied in a surprised squeak.

Cristi woke slowly and rolled out of bed onto all fours. It had been a heavy night, much too much wine, and *whose* idea was that cheesecake? Her head was pounding, and the wine, cheese and cream were still partying. She belched — "Urgh!" — flooding her mouth with unpleasantness, and her head. "Oh," she groaned and carefully lowered her forehead onto the cold wooden floor. "Burp!" She belched again and groaned. Then clutching the bedhead, Cristi slowly pulled herself upright and turned towards the open door, reaching out, and with her eyes screwed shut against the sunlight that poured through the skylight, she grabbed the doorpost and swung into the hallway. That's when she heard the crash of tumbling pottery, Sam's raised voice and Lucy's scream.

"NO!"

Cristi just managed to stagger out of the way as Lucy ran from the room, pushing past, hair awry, bathrobe off her shoulder and clutching the front of her t-shirt. Tears streaked her cheeks. Behind her, framed by the doorway, was Sam, his face dark and angry and his hands constantly on the move. This just didn't add up, the dark face, the disturbed clothes. Had Sam misheard last night?

"But?" No buts, you just don't do that. Her head still thumped, logical thought was beyond her, and she only knew what she had seen. Instead, she opted for instinct and launched at her man, her lover. Not even he does that to her friend.

"No Sam, no!" she screamed. "How could you? How... how, Sam? How?"

Sam's face was dark, his fists clenched, and he was shaking. Cristi confronted him again.

"How could you Sam?" she screamed, pounding her fists into his chest, but there was no recognition. Sam's stare was glazed, his thoughts somewhere else.

"Wait 'till Lucy comes back," he whispered and he lifted Cristi to one side and left the room. A few minutes later Lucy returned. She was wearing jogging pants now and had changed her club t-shirt for an old baggy one. Cristi suspected the worst and rushed to comfort her.

"There there my lovely, it's going to be okay. I'm sure Sam didn't mean it. [-"I hope he didn't?"-] she thought. "I really do," she added, and now it was her turn to shed a tear. He was the love of her life and now... what now?

"How could I have missed it?" Lucy groaned. "It was there on the page and I missed it. Oh, how could I... Oh!" she muttered, agonized.

"Shush my lovely, shush now. I'm sure we can sort this. Shush now. Shush," Cristi soothed. But what Lucy said when Sam returned took Cristi's breath away, and left her more confused than ever.

"Oh Sam," Lucy cried, "I'm so sorry. It was there on the paper that the Prof gave me and I just ignored it. Can you ever forgive me? I'm so, so sorry.

Can you?"

"No Luce, no, I'm the one who should apologize. I should never have barked at you like that, it's unforgivable. It's me that should be sorry."

Cristi looked from one to the other. What was going on? What had she missed?

Then Sam changed the subject. "Thank the heavens you two never tidy up," he exclaimed. "Oh Lucy, I could never hold a grudge against you, never," he said and bent forward and kissed her on the forehead, then said again, "Thank the heavens you guys never put anything away," he repeated, brandishing an old magazine.

"Err... I've definitely missed something?" Cristi gasped. "Erm, wha... what just happened?" She was totally confused. "I *have* missed something, haven't I? Sam, you didn't... did you? And...?" Cristi opened her arms, her shoulders tense and her palms up as she looked longingly at her man. "You didn't?"

"Of course he didn't," said Lucy. "What you saw was *me* trying to get the t-shirt off, not Sam. Sam barked that number at me, the night club name, and that's how many people vanished," — she snapped her fingers — "just like that. And some of Jez's rellies vanished too, didn't they. That hit home, I can tell you. I just had to get that shirt off. What you saw just isn't what you thought, it isn't. Sam's not like that, you know that," Lucy said, reaching out and grasping her friend's hand. Cristi nodded sheepishly and smiled.

"Who vanished?" she asked.

Sam just looked horrified and shook his head. "No, I didn't, and I never would Cris. How could I? How could you think such a thing?" he whispered, canting his head to one side. "Yes, I did hear you two drunken tarts slobbering over each other as you said good night. I did hear what Lucy said and I know she didn't mean it." He smiled, then said, "Lucy caught my dangling arm as she passed the sofa, and I woke with a start. She turned to the noise and that's when I saw her *Club*5eightZero6 t-shirt, and nothing else Luce. Nothing else," he added with a wink. "And I spoke without thinking. So I think now's a good time to tell you why that club was closed down."

"Who vanished?" Cristi asked again.

"I'm just about to tell you, babe," he said. "Sit yourselves down," and before they could butt in again, Sam began explaining. "Eight years ago, do you remember that big galaxy shattering disaster, the AtomSpheres, which was in orbit around Mejjas? Do you remember?" he pressed.

"Eh," Cristi wasn't sure, but Lucy was.

"It was on the list that the Prof gave me, wasn't it. I tossed it away because it didn't seem to have any relevance to my course. A lot of people disappeared didn't they? And did you say some of Jez's relatives too?"

"I could have said anything I was so angry. But yes, there were some of Jez's. I'd seen that list, you see, amongst all the other scattered papers. It was when Cristi and I dropped in some months ago. We didn't stay; you were asleep and that's why I was so surprised. Spher'rios and the AtomSphere were on that list. So when I saw you in that t-shirt, Luce, I'm sorry, I just flipped. I woke with a start, you turned to say sorry and that's when I saw your t-shirt. Lucy's robe wasn't tied," he explained, "and the t-shirt was short, and in her frantic efforts to wrap it and tie the sash, Lucy had elbowed the crockery. But I hadn't noticed. Honest Luce, I only saw the number on the shirt and I just barked. I'm so sorry. I told her in no uncertain terms just what that logo meant, and that some of JD's family were part of that number."

He paused for a breath, eyes fixed on the girls.

"And yes you're right Lucy, lots did disappear, thousands. Five-thousand, eight-hundred and six, to be exact! Yeah, that's right," he said as realisation swept across Cristi's face. "That club, they named it after the number that went missing, '5eightZero6'. Catchy wasn't it," he huffed. "Tasteless is too weak a word for it. You guys said it was a *hot place*, you and the girls, Cristi, you all wanted to show it off to us. I can understand that. It was just the wrong moment. Any other moment, well, I don't think we would've been so annoyed, although we still wouldn't have gone in. We might just have been a bit more polite with our responses. You weren't to know that Robbie, me and the others, JD too, had just spent six weeks on a job detail on the Star-Link Hub, building a memorial to all those poor souls who had disappeared." He paused, glancing upward. "It's up there," he said, pointing through the skylight. "It's my base and I get to see that memorial every day we're docked. That memorial seeps into you," he said and tapped his forehead. "Damn near screwed JD's mind it did, as if he wasn't screwed enough already."

"There are the names of two Devii'rahls etched into that stone; brothers, father and son, who knows?" Sam shrugged. "JD didn't say much about them, and hopefully they're just namesakes, but it makes you think, doesn't it? There's a Sam Jonsen and there are other Jonsens on the stone too. No connection to me whatsoever, but seeing your name, it stops you in your tracks I can tell you. Sadly though, JD did point out the names of an aunt, uncle and cousin. Seems they had saved for a holiday of a lifetime," he added and shook his head. "So you see we couldn't understand, when *we* saw it, why you girls thought the place was cool? I know you weren't with us Lucy, but you clearly had a feeling for it too or you wouldn't have been wearing that t-shirt. But no one these days seems to be aware of what happened or cares. It's as if it has been erased from the public conscience. Easier I suppose to forget about it than to deal with its consequences."

Cristi nodded. "But you guys never said why."

"We should have Cris, but it was too fresh I suppose. After all, we had been living and breathing the disaster for six weeks. It was all too fresh. Too fresh," he replied.

"You know," said Lucy, "I think I've always known about that number. I'm sure some friends of mummy, and a distant cousin of daddy's, were lost in that disaster. Do you remember me saying, Cris, that there was something about that t-shirt that made me feel close to Jez? I know, it sounds silly. Perhaps the mindPlain studies shook a memory loose." She took a moment, then added, "I'm sure there were *'Boy on the Rope'* posters on placards a few years ago. I would've been... yeah that's it, my gap year; I was travelling. I was eighteen. The posters were old. There were posters on top, and they were stripping off one layer to stick on another. The *'Boy'* poster was beneath. Yes, that's where I've seen it before. They must've been covered for the same reason that the club was closed: Tasteless and too fresh."

Cristi nodded. "Yes," — she did recall something like that — "yes," she said, "I do remember."

"It makes me shiver now just thinking about it. To think I've been glorifying the loss that Jez, Mummy and Daddy and thousands of others must feel every day... Oh," she groaned, "I feel so ashamed."

"Never mind Luce, you know about it now. Let's move on shall we. Sit yourselves down and I'll make that brew. First, though, I'm going to clean up this mess," he added and both girls looked down. The floor was sticky and splashed with coffee and scattered sugar, and there were broken cups too. "And whilst you're waiting, you might like to take a look at this article." He opened the magazine. "Look at the pictures," he said, "and read the columns that go with it."

With nothing better to do, the girls started poring over the pictures and words.

Twenty minutes later, when Sam was satisfied that the room was tidy and the floor squeaky clean, he pulled a chair up between them and announced, "This is a picture of the AtomSpheres. At one time it was *the* go-to-holiday destination. This is an artist's impression. It's not what was built, and it's certainly not how it finished up. This is the picture that the Praes~Eedan Corporation used to sell their idea to their backers."

It was true that the AtomSpheres started life as an idea drawn on a napkin.

"Look, there, the very thing," he said, and inset in the corner of the photo-spread was a photo of the framed serviette. The legend below it read: *'The AtomSpheres, the brainchild of Robert Atkins, Co-founder of the Praes~Eedan Corporation'*.

"Is that the Atkins that the Institute is named after?" Lucy asked.

"This picture," Sam continued as he returned to the artistic work, "is an almost faithful representation of that little sketch. It was supposed to look like a laboratory atom, hence the name." Then as he turned the page, he said, "I think it might be, Luce. It could well be. A lot of institutions benefitted when it was broken up. Anyway, this is an actual photo of the original set-up that went into orbit above Mejjas Major about two-hundred and fifty years ago. Subtly different, not as many spheres as hoped, but it was definitely an engineering masterpiece.

"The 'Atom' started life as a nucleus (Nucleo), an encircling ring (Taurus)

87

and an orbiting electron (Dominion), that was attached to the Taurus ring and slowly rotated around the nucleus. Nucleo was two kilometres in diameter with a smaller sphere inside: The inner sphere was one kilometre in diameter. The Praes~Eedan Corp pioneered large-scale gravitational engineering. It's said that you could walk in a straight line, in the inner sphere, and just over three kilometres later you would return to where you started. Those I know who holidayed there said that Nucleo was amazing. The plaza floor could be programmed with all sorts of patterns. It still orbits you know. You can still go there on holiday, but since the disaster, it's just a sphere on its own." He turned to the next page. "And..."

Cristi thought for a while, then asked, "How far, from where to where, is three kilometres, Sam?"

"Hmm, let me think. Three-klix, well that would be from here to... eh no, better to say from the Hoof to Uni. Yeah, that would be about three."

"Shit! Really?"

"Yep, I reckon so. Hmm, that sort of distance."

"Bloody hell, honest?" asked Lucy. "Blimey."

"Easily that distance, maybe a little more."

"Jeepers!"

Sam smiled and nodded. "Big eh? Anyway," he said, going back to the magazine, "this is what it looked like a few seconds before Spher'rios disappeared."

"WTF! It's immense, so many spheres and... eh, other stuff," Lucy said, and gasped.

"Shit, it's huge," said Cristi, "and cluttered."

"And it was all because of that sketch drawn by that Atkins guy?" asked Lucy as she stared at the magazine.

"That's right," said Sam, "Robert Atkins, and the Atkins family as well I suppose, and the result of after-dinner brandies, good cigars and a handy napkin."

They turned the page to the next spread. In this photo were six electron spheres, two encircling rings and a whole host of independently floating hotels and conference centres, plus smaller spheres emblazoned with adverts.

From the angle this snap was taken, it was only just possible to see the arc of Neucleo's circumference. The AtomSpheres in this picture looked less like the classical laboratory atom, and more like a virus!

"What went wrong?"

"It got too big," said Sam, "and then," — he slapped his right hand down over a pale-yellow sphere, completely covering it up — "Spher'rios disintegrated and so did everybody in it."

Whilst the girls were absorbing that startling bit of info, Sam turned to the next page. "And then there's this picture."

"Hey, isn't that the...? It is, isn't it? It's the picture that was on the back of the t-shirts, the one over the door of the club. It's *The Boy on the Rope*! It really was a boy. I never realised. Oh, that's so sick! Sick," Cristi said and gasped. "Sick."

"That boy was the last person to have any physical contact with the lost sphere. Unfortunately, this is the only clear snapshot they have of him."

The boy was flailing, falling backwards away from the camera, his long hair swept forward, his stripy coat too. There was a cord looped around his ankle, the cord was taut and a man wearing coveralls was grasping it with both hands. The man was held back by his safety line and harness, and that line was taut too. Walkway furniture was flying past the pair, sucked out by escaping air. The boy was silhouetted against the starry, empty blackness of the void, and the photo was framed by the severed end of the Star-Link Walkway, where the entrance doorway of the vanished sphere should have been.

"Don't we see his face in the club picture?" Cristi seemed puzzled.

"That might be the case, though that was probably for artistic effect," said Sam. "Every other shot I've ever seen of him has his face obscured either by his hair or by the body of the guy that saved him. When the sphere vanished, the sudden rush of escaping air spun him around. If it hadn't been for that man grabbing his ankle rope, the boy would've been dragged into the void too."

"Sheesh. He was so lucky," Cristi whispered, and Lucy nodded in agreement.

Then she asked, "Is the boy named?"

"No. There aren't records, as there was a lot of confusion. He was probably taken to the hospital, but the hospital records were lost if his name was ever recorded at all. There's no record of the guy who saved him either. The hospital and the Star-Link were sold off and they now form the Star-Link Hub, my base. But the records were misplaced I'm afraid. Incidentally," Sam continued, "remember me talking about Ferios last night, the newly named planet and the reason I had that chart?"

The girls nodded.

"Well, apparently the sphere that disappeared was named Spher'rios in honour of the newly named planet. It's a sort of play on words."

Then Cristi interrupted. "Hey, sorry Sam. He's a boarder. Look, that's his board," she cried excitedly. Sure enough, just above the right shoulder of the rescuing man was a hover-board. "That cord around his ankle, it's just like the one that JD... eh, Jez has. Oh, why can't he just have one name? It's so effing confusing, all this Jez JD, JD Jez," she said.

"He's been called JD since the first week of Basic. First off he was Dev, but there was a Dave who was much more open and interesting, so Dev was dropped. Then he was Jez, but Jerry said that was his preferred name and we couldn't have two Jezzers. So it was either Devii'rahl, which is a mouthful, or something else. We settled on JD. But you know the stories, he didn't mix, he was a pain in the arse and we hardly spoke to him at all, so he was mostly known as Shit Head. Then we did the Mem job and everything changed... "

"Mem job?" asked Cristi.

"That detail upon the Star-Link Hub, you know... when we built the memorial for the missing five thousand," Sam answered. "To be honest, after that incident he could've called himself anything he liked and we'd have been more than happy to change our names to suit."

"Incident?" the girls replied in unison.

Then Lucy asked, "What the mejj could he have done for all you guys to make such a reversal in attitude, Sam?"

"We had underestimated him. We thought he was a prat, treated him like one too. But in that moment, by that stone, we suddenly realised we had been prodding a tiger, dancing in a minefield. He's unpredictable and, dare I say, scary! Someone poked too hard and the JD bomb exploded at the memorial."

"What did he do?" Cristi asked, gasping.

"He scares *you*?" Lucy joined in.

"Scares the shit out of me," Sam said in a whisper.

"But there's nothing to him, he's slight, a shadow in the line-up. What could he have possibly done to bring about such a change?" Cristi asked, agreeing with her roommate. "He's just a boy and there's nothing to him," she said.

"We *are* talking about the same JD, aren't we?" asked Lucy. "What did he do, Sam?"

"He... " But Sam stopped short. "Ah," he paused again, thoughtful, with conflict in his expression. "I can't tell you. It's a fleet secret. More than my career's worth. Sorry."

"But Sam," Cristi said, aghast, "this is me and Luce, surely?"

"Sorry Cris, I can't. Sorry. I've said too much already."

The next few minutes passed in an uncomfortable silence with everybody looking at each other, and Sam shaking his head until eventually, he said, "I'm sorry, no, I can't. Just can't. Anyway, I ought to be going, I've got to be on duty one pm." He gathered up the rumpled heap of clothes and went into the wet-room for a shower.

"What was that all about?" Cristi said to Lucy.

22

Too intense for such a small ship ...

Devii'rahl J OiT stood smartly to attention at his CO's desk.

"Your name," the CO announced, "has been suggested by a Captain Jimi Shallop, whoever he is, and a Professor Andrew Hobbins. Now, I know who he is — the belt man. There is a new project, Linear Spheric Propulsion, LSP. Apparently it is the way forward, though I can't see it myself. It's a new power source developed from something discovered or derived from, though I'm not sure which, the AtomSpheres disaster. Apparently, you know all about it and these two people want you to join their project. I'm inclined to agree with them; you are too intense for such a small ship. Don't get me wrong son, you are one of us, a Jag, and the guys all think you're great. But I just can't get my head around someone that never takes a day off, then takes off a month to go and follow some sheep. So do you want to go to this LSP Project?"

"This is the first I've heard of LSP, sir. Although I have known Andy Hobbins a long time, nearly eight years now, and if he thinks that I should be part of his team, well?" He took off his glasses and sucked on one of the arms. "I met Andy on the AtomSpheres, our last family holiday. I'm not certain about Jimi Shallop. I think I met her on that holiday too. She was fussing about some technical problem."

"Oh, so Shallop is a she, thanks for that, could have been awkward. I have a video call with them both tomorrow. So I will ask you again Devii'rahl, are you interested..." but he stopped short, and asked, "Why do you wear glasses,

Devii'rahl? I mean, it's not as if you can see through them. I don't think I've ever seen you clean them!" They were greyed over with thumbprints and looked as if they had been dragged on the floor. "May I?" asked the CO, who took them off him and held them up. "Really Devii'rahl? Really? I can just make you out and you're less than a metre away." The CO shook his head and gave the glasses back. "Are you interested in this LSP Project?"

Jez pulled himself back to attention and replied. "Yes sir, I think I am."

"Okay Devii'rahl I will sort out all the necessary paperwork, and next time the Laxi docks at the Hub your tour with us finishes and you can join the LSP Project. I will be sorry to see you go matey, you didn't quite make the twelve months, just short of ten, never mind. You might be an intense son of a bitch but you've done us some very good service, and you're well respected among the crew. You are the shortest Jaeger I've ever met, but you are one of us. You will always be a Jag. Stand tall, be proud."

23

Green, and blue? ...

Jez left the JCAS Laximus IV three weeks after his meeting with the CO, foolishly thinking that he might simply slip away quietly with a few handshakes and maybe a couple of hugs. The engine room boys had other ideas. The CO had dropped a few hints too to other parts of the ship. Jez was popular and every mess wanted to toast his farewell. So the leaving party went on and on for hours, and Jez didn't walk away from Laximus IV as he had planned.

Instead, Jez was carried to his shore side billet, and woke up three days later. It was a throbbing pain in his left upper arm that had eventually stirred him from his slumbers. It was red and hot, and painful to the touch, but just out of eyesight. His head was full of cottonwool, his thoughts wouldn't travel and his balance was all over the place. He needed a mirror, but [-*"That can wait,"-*] he thought and lay as still as he could, staring at the ceiling until he drifted back to sleep. When he was finally able to clamber out of bed and find a mirror he just shrugged and shook his head. In all his time on the Jaeger craft, Jez had refused the offered body art that all Jaegers seemed to adorn themselves with, citing cultural objections. But for those objections, he had been sober. Fortunately though for Jez, the Skipper had got a whiff of what the rest of the crew were planning and had stepped in.

The Skipper had been adamant. "Yes to the Jag tatt, he's one of us after all," he said, then firmly added, "Nothing else. I don't want the lad to be embarrassed. Got that? He could be your boss one day, could be mine too. I want him to be proud of his time with us. Okay?"

Jez now had a beautifully and professionally drawn Jaeger Corps tattoo on his left upper arm. Like it or not, Jez was now a Jag for life, and although it was a shock, he was actually quite pleased. It was only after he had showered and was standing in front of the full-length mirror that he noticed the rest! "Bastards," he said, and he shook his head in disbelief, "no wonder I was itching. Bastards." Then he shook his head again and smiled. "Well, the top will give people something to talk about, a real ice breaker. The other, I don't suppose that will have any viewers anytime soon."

He was due to start next Monday. He'd wanted to start straight away and had intended to walk off the Laxi and report for duty at the LSP Project that same day. But that didn't happen. Jez had never been so drunk in his life and had lost three days already. At least he no longer thought he was going to die, but he did know it would take the rest of the week at least to get his head in gear. He was picking up the weirdest of thoughts too.

As soon as he was able to walk and string a sentence together he moved out of his billet on the Star-Link Hub and down to his new accommodation at the LSP Project, which was adjacent to the Mecklenburg University. He decided to report immediately to Captain Jimi Shallop, and hoped she would let him start early.

The Orderly showed him into Shallop's office. "Devii'rahl J OiT, Skipper."

Shallop looked him up and down. "It's been a long time," she said, extending a hand, "you've shot up a bit since... well you know. You can take your cap off Devii'rahl. We're not that formal at LSP."

Before Jez could reveal his embarrassment, the Captain asked, "Your initial, J, what does the J stand for?"

"Jez, ma'am."

"Jez! Hmm?" Jimi frowned. "And what did they call you in the Corps?"

"JD, ma'am."

"JD?"

"Yes, ma'am."

"And are you okay with that?"

"Yes, ma'am."

"Right, then if it's okay with you we'll stick with JD, we already have a Jaz, and she's used to being called by that handle. I wouldn't want you two getting mixed up, it could be a bit awkward if you know what I mean. Okay then JD, stand easy, and as this isn't the Jaeger Corps we'll have none of this ma'am business. I'm the Skipper or Jimi the Skip, got that? We're a bit more relaxed at LSP, so take off your cap... it's not going to rain in here." Jez took off his cap, "Ah, I see," she said, shaking her head. "The Jaeger Corps certainly like to party. The trouble is you lot just don't know when to stop." Jez said nothing. "I suppose they used highlighter pens and printer ink, that's the usual trick, and ruffled your hair so it's down to the roots. You have light hair too. It doesn't wash out, does it?"

"No ma — I mean Skipper."

Shallop shook her head some more. "Well I think we can wait until Monday, don't you?" she said. "I want that hangover out of your system before you set foot in my workshops. As for the hair, bend your head forward and let's have a closer look." After a quick inspection, she said, "Yep, right down to the scalp. Ah yes, and that trickle by your ear. Close cropping isn't going to help, and it wouldn't be back to normal by Monday anyway," she said, shaking her head again and chuckling. "There's only one way you can play this JD, and in my experience, it's the only way. You've just got to front it out. The project team know you're from the Jaeger Corps, and they know Jags play hard. Is there any more damage?"

He showed her his tattoo, and as she turned his notes back a couple of pages, she nodded. "Ah, of course, you are that Devii'rahl J." [-"He has come a long way since I last saw him. Oh yes, he's going to do just fine. But why is he calling himself Jez, I could have sworn he had a different initial?"-] "Just front it out JD. Don't try to hide it, because if the dye is on your scalp then no matter how much you crop that hair of yours the colour will be on your skin for weeks. Go away now, go on, and I will see you on parade on Monday morning, at eight o'clock sharp. Don't be late." As he turned to leave her office, she asked, "Did they highlight anywhere else?"

"Yes ma'am, they did." And Jimi the Skip smiled.

[-*"Eight o'clock, they're relaxed! I thought shore bases started at seven or seven-thirty, but she said eight sharp, so who am I to argue."-*]

So with nothing to do for the next four days, Jez picked up his board and spent the rest of the day gliding over the campus lawns.

Cristi was away visiting her sister. Sam, Robbie and Conner, who were already assigned to the LSP Project, were away with other team members collecting parts for the project, and Lucy, because everyone was away, was at a loose end too. So she went to her usual bench to do some studying.

[>*"Hello, can I buy you a coffee?"*<] Jez was in her head. She looked around to see where he was, but he was nowhere to be seen. The lawns were empty, so where was he? She could push out her thoughts, say twenty feet, but Jez... where the hell was he? Whilst she scoured her surroundings he swooped in from over the hill.

[>*"Do you want a coffee? Can I buy you one?"*<] he eagerly asked again?

"Eh yes, eh no," she said, gasping. He *had* startled her. [-*"Where did he come from!?"-*] "Eh no, I owe you one from the other day, it's my shout," she said.

Jez didn't reply, and instead he just looked at her with his head on one side. He tapped his forehead. Lucy looked at him puzzled, then he tapped again, still with the same response from Lucy. So then he put his fore and index fingers and thumb together and worked them like a pecking bird, then tapped his forehead once more. Suddenly it dawned on her, and Lucy said, "Of course, yes. You want me to," and she pointed at her head. "Right." Then continuing on the mindPlain, she said [>*"Okay."*<] then added, [>*"I owe you a coffee from the other day."*<] She nodded and he nodded back, then he hopped off his board and bent down and picked up her bag.

[>*"Your shout then, I'll not argue with that. Lead on,"*<] he said.

In the coffee bar, Jez stopped using mindSpeak and Lucy heard his voice for the very first time. She thought he sounded very nervous. "I'm sorry," he said, his voice hushed. "I heard you the very first time you tried all those months ago. I have no excuse." He apologised and she detected a slight accent, just like those she'd heard on her trip to Mii'een. His voice was soft and quiet and she just couldn't understand where the fiery aggression that Sam had hinted at could come from? [-"Plays hard, fights harder?"-] She just couldn't see it.

"That's okay," she said, "its all water under the bridge now. You turned up at the Prof's, that's all that matters to me. Thank you."

Jez nodded and sipped at his coffee as they sat in silence, each hoping the other would say something. When they did speak, they both spoke together, stalled, then fell silent again. Over the next hour though, the tension eased and they let each other talk, although Lucy couldn't get Jez to open up. She felt as if she had done most of the talking.

"I like your letters," she said, then across the mindPlain she added [>"I have a map and I plot all the places you talk about in your letters, so I can see where you've been. Sometimes at night, when I'm in my bed, I look up at my map and all the places you have been to and I wonder where you are at that moment."<]

Jez reddened a little at the thought of someone in bed thinking of him. [>"I like writing them, I like writing to you,"<] he replied. Then he said, "Your mindSpeak is good."

"Thank you. But I don't think I will ever be as good as you."

Jez smiled; that compliment meant a lot to him. "You could be," he said, "in twenty years perhaps," and as he chuckled his whole face lit up. Lucy was reminded of the lady with the beautiful smile and the photo that Sam had shown her and Cristi.

They chatted some more, talking about this, that and nothing at all, filling the spaces, often with waffle, not wanting to get bogged down by pauses. Both were still nervous of the other's company, but equally wanting more.

It was a sunny day and the only free table had been in the window, in direct sunlight, and Jez's head was getting hot. [-"Front it out, that's what she said, front it out."-] So he took off his cap and straightaway was conscious of Lucy staring at him. He knew why of course. [-"Orange!"-] And he knew also she was doing her best to inhibit her thoughts. [-"Pink!"-] But the strategy she was using was awkward. [-"Red?"-] And difficult to control. She was trying hard to stifle a smirk too, and her thoughts [-"Is that purple?"-] slipped out

[-"Green and blue?"-] until it was all too much and they both laughed out loud.

"The Jag boys," he said, "at my leaving party. Highlighter pens and printer ink, and we're not allowed to close shave. I could close crop. I would be put on a charge if I shaved it right down. My new CO says keep cropping if you like, it might grow out by Monday, but it's on my scalp. I'm going to leave it and front it out. She says everyone knows I'm from the Corps, and says no-one is going to say anything to my face. I suppose after one of them does say something behind my back, thinking I can't hear them... well it would only happen once, wouldn't it," he added and gave his head an upward jerk and creased his lips with a faint smile, "however big they are."

Lucy had noticed the jerk of his head and the faint smile and thought again of what Sam had almost said.

They talked about his new posting. He was very excited and tripped over his words as he tried to explain. He told her of his surprise at being selected, especially as he hadn't actually applied, and that his name had been suggested by the two leading experts in the LSP field. "I didn't apply, didn't know that such a project existed. Sam's on it y'know, and Robbie. Conner too. It was advertised when the Laxi was on Fhloria. We were sorting out a problem at a mining camp, so I didn't see the ad."

"Laxi?"

"The ship I was on, Laximus IV. There was a dispute that got heated, and the boys had to sort it," he proudly explained. Then he asked, "Would you like another coffee? My shout this time."

With two fresh coffees on the table and the conversation resumed Jez was starting to feel relaxed. "They did this as well," he said and he pulled off his hoodie to reveal the bright red throbbing tattoo at the top of his left arm. "The bastards got me drunk, stings like f..." but he cut himself short. "Sorry, didn't mean to say that, that was erm... Anyway, I'm a Jag for life now," he continued, and the thought of being one of that Corps forever warmed his soul and a beaming smile lit up his face.

"You should smile more often, you've got a lovely smile." *[-"You look like your mum."-]* And then, without stopping to think if it was a good idea or not, she asked, "Why do you sit on that fallen log and stare at the stars?" Almost immediately she wished she hadn't asked, because she felt a vacuum suck across the mindPlain, and saw all the joy drain out of his face! "I'm so sorry, I shouldn't have said that," she said, "it was out of order. Please forgive me."

His response though surprised her. "That's okay. Anyway, it's getting late. Can I walk you home?"

"Eh, yes please, of course, yes. Yes, I'd like that," Lucy replied.

It was a mostly silent walk. They did speak a little whilst they waited for the bus, but in the streets and on the bus Jez was reluctant to engage and stayed quiet until they reached her door. "There's nothing to forgive," he said. "It's not a comfortable log. I sit there and I think and I remember."

She was about to ask what he was thinking about and remembering but thought better of it, as she'd realised it was a touchy subject. So she said nothing and they stood facing each other, neither knowing how to break away. It was Jez who broke the silence.

"Could we meet again tomorrow, in the afternoon perhaps? I can't start until Monday, so I've got nothing to do and I enjoyed our chat today."

So they met the next day in much the same way. Lucy was sitting on her favourite bench, scribbling notes, doing a bit of revising and thinking about her very brief encounter with Jez's parents, although she never actually engaged with them. *[-"Why did they keep looking at me? Were they talking about me?"-]* But her thoughts were cut short when Jez just appeared and asked how she was. They went for a coffee, sat at the same table, chatted until it was getting dark and then he walked her home. They met the next day too, but Lucy couldn't meet with him the day after that because it was Sunday and she was having dinner with her parents. They arranged instead to meet after Jez's first day at his new job.

24

I'm not so sure now ...

Jez arrived as commanded, at eight sharp, expecting, as it was so relaxed, to be the first there. Hesitantly he opened the workshop door and stepped into a frenzy of toing and froing, and drills and hammers, and before he could work out what was going on a rather irate sergeant was in his face.

"Where the hell do you think you've been? What time do you call this? Late starters are they in the Jaeger Corps? Stand to attention when you're addressing me. We know all about you," the sergeant screamed and the workshop fell silent. "Where's your safety hat? This is a hard hat area, so get that Jaeger scrap off your head right now."

Jez swallowed. He was convinced Captain Shallop had said eight, but now he wasn't certain at all, and everyone had stopped and were staring at him. It felt like daggers. *[-"She said front it out. I'm not so sure now."-]*

The sergeant's stare was burning right through him and now his upper lip was starting to curl in a silent growl. Jez reluctantly removed his hat and, immediately from each side of the workshop, familiar voices shouted, "Love the hair mate," and, "Is that the latest Jaeger style?" and "Sexy mate, really sexy, that's bound to pull the women."

Before he knew what was going on Robbie, Sam and Conner were at his side and patting him on the back. "Great to see you JD. It really is."

He was overwhelmed. He had been so excited about starting on the LSP Project that as usual he was only focused on the immediate and not on the peripherals. It was his one big failing and he'd been well and truly ambushed, again. [–"I must stop doing this… check your peripherals you idiot!"–] "I fell for that one," he groaned, "hook line and sinker. I thought it was a bit odd when the Captain said eight. Was she in on it too?"

"Her idea mate. The Skipper's okay, says she knows you from way back, and says you know Andy too. She was in hysterics when she told us about your hair." Robbie laughed and slapped him on his arm. "It's great to see you again," he said, but he recoiled when Jez yelped and Robbie said, "Sorry, mate."

"What's up JD, inoculations?" Sam asked, a little concerned by Jez's reaction.

"Na, this," Jez replied as he slipped off his jacket and showed them his Corps tattoo. "I got this as well as the hair. I rather like it too."

"They've done a good job on you there JD," the sergeant said, "that's a really good pro-job, that is. My name's Pete," he said as he thrust out his hand, "good to meet you JD."

Pete then turned to Sam, Robbie and Conner. "You wasters take JD and get him kitted out with all the gear he's going to need. Have you got any tools JD?" Jez shook his head. "Never mind," he said, "fix him up with a tool kit too, find him a locker and then put the kettle on… he looks like he's seen a ghost. I'm sure you could do with a coffee or something." Sergeant Pete then called out across the workshop. "Take five everyone and get to know the new boy." Then he turned back to Jez. "We'll go outside. I could do with a smoke and I need to calm my nerves a bit. Always been nervous of Jags. And I've heard about you, JD, your reputation precedes you." He leant closer and whispered in Jez's ear. "Me and Jon Reeble go way back, he's a very good friend of mine. Anyone who would do what you did for Jon is okay by me."

Jez nodded and tapped his forehead. [>"Thanks, Pete."<] Pete looked a bit startled at the delivery, then nodded and smiled. Then Jez asked, "Is there any ziirt?"

"Yeah, there's a big jar in the corner mate. At long last a fellow drinker. Help yourself matey."

The kettle boiled, then they made their drinks and they all filed outside. It was a bright morning, both moons were on the wane and the sun was midway to the noon high. Sam and Conner pulled up four chairs and the four of them sat, chinked their mugs together and smiled.

"What's your room number?" asked Sam.

"Forty-seven."

"Magic, I'm in forty-eight next door, Conn's in fifty-six and Robbie's in forty-three. We're all on the same floor. It'll be just like old times," said Sam.

"Hope not," Jez replied.

"No. No, you're right, perhaps not. We *were* bastards, but you *were* a prat, be honest," Robbie said. "Wasn't he lads? You were, weren't you?"

"Yeah JD, you didn't help yourself, did you," Sam agreed.

"I know, I know. But that was then and things changed, didn't they? I finally woke up to what a prat I was, before it was too late. It didn't help much though, Garrard was the NCO on Jaeger Basic too. I got a kicking, good and proper, probably because of the Mem Stone incident," and he showed them his gappy smile and scar on his shin. "It was Garrard's doing, along with three others. They all got busted too. I've heard Garrard can't walk, but that was for more than just setting on me. He's ruffled a few Jag feathers, and that's something you just don't do."

"We never heard about that."

"Another Corps secret. Jaegers don't wash their dirty linen in public, you know that."

Their drinks had cooled a little and they all drank and thought about what JD had just told them. A couple of others joined them too, eager to hear what the new team member had to say, and were startled when he announced, mostly for the benefit of Sam, Conner and Robbie, that "I'm not a prat any more boys, and that stupid nomad who thought he could live the lives of others has wandered back into the steppe. The Corps taught me to be a team player, and they also taught me how to colour hair, so watch your backs," he said and chuckled at his little joke. The others chuckled too, glad another joker had joined the team.

Jez's first day went well. Captain Shallop turned up around mid-morning, and brought doughnuts and a beaming grin. She laughed aloud when Sgt. Pete relayed Jez's first moments in the workshop. She stayed for most of the day, watching and listening, and even rolling up her sleeves and helping with spanner holding and such like. First and foremost Jimi Shallop was an engineer; she had been assistant to Ted Rawlins, the Chief Engineer on the AtomSpheres, and was actually talking on her cellfone with Rawlins when Spher'rios vanished. Rawlins vanished too. Jimi Shallop was now one of the two leading experts in the field of LSP. The other LSP expert, in fact, Mr LSP himself — Professor Andy Hobbins — dropped by in the middle of the afternoon, eager to see Jez, and the two of them chatted for some time before he made his apologies and went off to a meeting.

"Andy worked out what was wrong with the AtomSpheres and was seconds away from delivering his report to Ted." Jez didn't turn, and knew without looking or listening that Captain Shallop was behind him. "Luckily," she continued, "he was delayed,"

[-"Yeah, I'm glad he was."-] Jez thought.

"Only by a minute or so, but it was just enough of a delay."

[-"That was enough"-] Jez agreed.

"Andy's calculations about the alignment of the spheres is the science behind LSP. He's a very clever man. Very clever indeed."

The shift finished at four but there was no rushing off to wash up and clock out. They were all as easy-going at quitting time as they were for the rest of the day, and they all milled about and chatted for quite some time before eventually going their separate ways.

The four lads left together and were strolling across the campus towards the Union Bar when Sam asked, "Is that Lucy?"

"I think she's coming this way," Robbie replied. "Yes, I think it is, so perhaps she's coming to meet me? Well, I'll see you later lads."

"In your dreams," said Sam, "and anyway, Judi would be more than a little upset, don't you think." Lucy continued to walk towards them.

"Hi Sam, hi Robbie, Conn," she said then smiled and added, "Hello Jez, how was your first day?"

"You haven't wasted any time," Conner whispered over Jez's shoulder.

Sam smiled and glanced sideways at Robbie, then they both looked across at Jez who was blushing from head to foot. Sam nudged Robbie, and said, "We'll see you tomorrow JD, and don't forget we start at seven-thirty. See you mate, and have a good evening."

Their usual table, by the window, had just become vacant. "That was lucky," said Lucy as she pushed the dirty crocks to the waitress who had swooped in to clear and wipe the table. This was the Coffee Bean's busiest time, as it was popular with both students and workers alike, as well as families. The Bean was a good place to meet after lectures or at quitting time, before either hitting the town or tackling the commute. Lucy loved the hubbub of different conversations, and Jez just liked being with Lucy. At last, he had found a friend he was able to talk to. With Lucy and Sam, he now had two good friends.

Jez was eager to tell her all about his day. He told her of being set-up by the Captain, which Lucy thought was a little bit unfair, but Jez just laughed it off. He told her too of his conversation with Andy Hobbins, and of how *he* had been looking forward to catching up with Jez. "We've known each other for about eight years, perhaps a bit longer. He's the brains behind LSP."

Jez knew that Lucy was crossing the campus lawn on her way to meet him. He had felt it across the mindPlain whilst he was packing up and putting his gear into his locker. He had been so eager to meet her that he now needed to excuse himself. "I'm just erm... just, you know, I'll get some drinks on the way back. I've just got to, eh... "

Lucy smiled. He was still very nervous. "Just go," she said then opened her magazine and turned to an article she had been reading earlier in the afternoon. A few minutes later she looked up when he pulsed, [>*"There's a bit of a queue."*<] He was looking her way, so she nodded and smiled and went back to her article as Jez shuffled towards the counter. So she was a little bit surprised when a drink was set before her a few seconds later, and looking up she was confronted by Pedrasz, who said, "I hope you haven't been waiting too long. I've got tickets, so we should be going. Get your gear."

"What?"

"I've got the tickets, come on. You know that band you're always going on about, well it was tricky but I got them."

Lucy was speechless. "What are you talking about? What band? We're not going out Pedrasz. We've never been an item, we never were and we never will be. You just wanted a trophy on your arm. Please go away, you're in somebody's seat."

"I told you before, I decide if we're going out or not. Get your gear, because we are going," he confirmed and sat back, smiling at her as he sipped at his king-sized crushed ice drink.

Lucy glared back, but just then Jez appeared behind him carrying two large cups, one of coffee, the other of ziirt. He looked confused, and Lucy thought he looked hurt. [>"I'm sorry, he just sat down,"<] she pulsed.

[>"Should I go?"<] Jez asked.

[>"No! No, don't go. I promise I'll get rid of him."<]

Jez glanced to his left. He was standing between the tables and an older man, probably the father of the family on the table to Lucy's left, was gingerly navigating his way between the tables with a heavily laden tray. Jez was in the way. Lucy saw him look and assumed he would step back, but he didn't move. Instead, Jez pulsed [>"Go to your right. Go now. Now."<] She hesitated. [>"Who me?"<], so he pulsed again, [>"Go now, go right and duck down."<]

The man with the tray was by Pedrasz's shoulder. Jez hadn't moved and Lucy had done as he'd told her. She was at eye level to the table and this is what she saw.

Pedrasz's arms clenched into his body, and at the same time, his hand squeezed and crushed his drink, bursting the base of the cup, dumping half of his icy drink into his lap. Then his arms punched outwards and upwards, flicking the man's tray into the air and depositing the contents, hot drinks, cold drinks, cakes and shakes, onto everyone in the vicinity. The sudden travel of Pedrasz's right arm threw what was left of his icy drink over the lady to Lucy's left, and over the walls and the pot plants and anyone else unfortunate to be within range.

When Lucy felt it was safe to sit up the whole café was in an uproar, everyone was shouting at everyone else, and the woman to Lucy's left was screaming as the blue dye from the iced drink soaked into her white dress. It was a scene of utter devastation and there, standing in the middle of it all, was the boy with the multi-coloured hair. He looked tired, his face ashen and his cheeks hollowed, and there were shadows under his sad eyes, and she felt he was staring straight through her.

[>*"Are you okay?"*<] she asked, concerned, and worried.

He blinked twice, and he was back. [>*"Sorry, I was somewhere else?"*<] Then he bent forward and whispered something in Pedrasz's ear. Pedrasz nodded. Jez straightened up, then looked straight at her. [>*"Bench?"*<] he asked, and he was smiling now.

[>*"Bench,"*<] she replied, returning the smile. She quickly gathered her belongings and carefully picked a safe passage through the debris and mayhem.

As they stepped out into the late afternoon sun, and the furore suddenly hushed as the door closed behind them, Lucy asked, "Did you do that?"

"Might have."

"How?"

"I'm not sure, it's just something I've always been able to do," he said. "All three of us could do it, as natural as breathing. Used to play tricks on each other, we did. Did it as kids. The sensory equivalent of banging a paper bag next to someone's ear."

"Who's we?" she asked.

"Huh?"

"You said '*we*', '*all three of us, we used to do it as kids*', so who's '*we*'?"

"We? Oh, we... " He looked puzzled and surprised. "I meant, erm, me and, and... Meeko and eh... Jix. My cousins."

"Oh, I see," she said but Lucy wasn't convinced. Why had he hesitated? But she thought better of pushing it though, after all, he had just saved her from that creep Pedrasz. She would leave it for another time. Instead, she commented again on what she had just seen. "It was very effective, and what was it that you whispered?" she asked.

But Jez just smiled. He wasn't going to say, and instead, he said, "It's a Homid thing. Makes the muscles violently contract and then expand so the recipient lets go. I mean, lets everything go," he added, and Jez's smile widened when he said, "I wouldn't want to be downwind just now."

"Oh dear," Lucy replied through a grimace, then asked, "Could you teach me? Sounds like it could be useful?"

"Hmm?" He thought for a while then said, "Probably not, well certainly not at this stage in your understanding, but maybe in a year or so. I can teach you a failsafe inhibiting method though."

"I already know several protocols the Prof taught us on the course."

"I'm sure he did, and your thoughts leak like a sieve when you get excited, or work the other way when you're disturbed in your sleep. The Prof taught you those methods because he knows they can be breached; he had to be able to check up on how you were getting on. Those methods are for kids. I'm going to show you something that will really work, and it's so easy." He placed his hands on her shoulders. "Now all you have to do is this," he said and leant forward and whispered the secret. "And that's all you need to know. In time it will be second nature, as natural as breathing. Using that you can draw your thoughts in, and also push them out. Go on, do it now. Think of something, anything you like. I promise I won't know what it is."

So she did exactly as he had explained, and she let her most burning innermost thought rise to the surface. [-"I want you,"-] she thought. "Did you get that?" she asked.

"No," he said, shaking his head, "not a bit of it, and that's how it should be between friends. I don't want to know your secret thoughts until you want to tell me."

[-"Oh it's not a secret."-] Lucy flushed and tingled as she thought it. Jez though didn't notice her colour.

"My turn now," he said. "See if you can read it. [-"I think I love you."-] He studied her expression, looking for a reaction, but there was nothing so he asked, "Anything?"

Lucy shook her head. "No," she said and it took a few moments for her to realise just how liberating it would be. Then it slowly dawned. "Oh wow. Oh wow. Wow wow wow," she exclaimed and she felt as if a huge weight had been lifted from her shoulders. "Thank you so much." She leant forward and kissed him on the cheek. He hadn't expected that and reeled back. He hadn't expected that at all and touched his hand to the dampness.

"Thank you," she said again. "At long last I can have a decent night's sleep. Thank you so much, Jez."

It was Jez's turn now to tingle. She had kissed him. It was the stuff of dreams and he searched for something to say, but all he managed was, "Bench?"

"Bench, yes bench," she replied and they silently moved off, both elated, both thinking the same thing.

[-"I kissed him."-]

[-"She kissed me."-]

Lucy was thinking of everything and nothing, but a few paces further on she said, "But."

"But?" Jez replied, the spell broken.

"Yes, there's a but."

"Huh?" And for a few seconds, Jez regretted teaching her how to inhibit, because her thoughts weren't there to be read anymore. She was a quick learner, so he had no inkling about what she was uncertain of. "What but?"

They shuffled a few steps more.

"You've told me the secret."

"Uh-huh." He was more than a little puzzled now. "But, there's a but," Jez said and put his head on one side, waiting for her question.

"Can you still find your way into my thoughts?" she asked. "The same way you can read anyone else's. You can still do that, can't you?"

Jez nervously smiled. He didn't want her to think he could cheat, or that it was just another method that could be breached. His smile had faded, and he was nervous now. "If I really wanted to, I could, but it would be difficult though," he said, shrugging his shoulders. "It's just the same as listening to a whispered vocal conversation. If you listen hard enough you can hear all you want to hear. But as much as I would love to know your innermost secrets and what you're thinking, I don't want to know."

He paused, then thought, [-"Oh, how much I'd love to know your innermost *secrets, love to be part of those thoughts."-]* "I want to get to know you better, person to person, but I only want to know what you want to tell me." *[-"Did I just say that?"-]* "More than anything though, I just want to be your friend, and I want you to be my friend, my own friend. I've never had a friend of my own before," he added, and once more he hesitated. "We, eh no, no... I mean eh, what I meant was when I was at home, everything was shared." He looked down at his cup and said, "My ziirt's getting cold, your coffee too, so where's that bench?" and the subject was changed and the door that Lucy thought was opening had slammed shut again.

[>"I've always wanted to be your friend too."<] she pulsed, and he heard that. But the next thought stayed with Lucy. She wanted so much to tell him, but didn't want to scare him off. *[-"But what I really want is to be your lover."-]*

And he wanted to prove to her that he wasn't going to listen to her inner thoughts unless she specifically invited him in, so he pulled up the barrier.

The conversation had faltered and there they were in the middle of the campus lawn, staring at each other moon-eyed and with nothing to say.

"Eh..."

"Um..."

"Bench?"

"Yes bench," Lucy replied. But something he had said was still puzzling her, *[-"Who or what are the 'we' that he keeps letting slip?"-]*

25

Just good friends ...

"I didn't expect to see you tonight JD?" Sam called down the hallway. He had just done some laundry and was opening the door to his room. "Thought you'd be…"

"What's that Sam?" Jez replied.

"Y'know, with Cristi still away 'till the weekend, I thought you'd be, y' know…"

"Huh?" Jez hadn't caught what he'd inferred.

"I thought you'd be staying for breakfast. Just surprised you haven't that's all. Oh, and have you heard about Robbie?"

"What about Robbie?"

"His father has been taken seriously ill. The Skipper called him back into the office after you and Lucy left. Robbie has to go home to look after his mum and younger siblings. Jimi has managed to get him a temporary posting close to home for six months. He's already gone, but he said to say '*Hi and bye, and it was good to see you again*'. He said he'll see us in six months unless he can get back sooner. I mean, he's going to want to see Judi, isn't he. Wouldn't you? But it's not all doom and gloom, as he's left us his beer fridge. It's full. Do you want a drink?"

"That's a shame about Robbie's father. I hope he's going to be okay. But he does buy a first-class beer. So like you say, not all doom and gloom. Yeah, I'll have a beer… thought you'd never ask."

They took a bottle each and knocked off the caps. And as Jez swept Sam's old magazines off the easy chair and sat, he said, "Me and Lucy are just good friends, right?"

Sam stared at his face for a few moments, waiting for a smile, but none came. "Okay JD," he said, "if you say so mate."

26

We ...?

"Hello the house," Cristi called from the open doorway. "Make yourselves decent, I'm coming up."

Lucy met her at the top of the stairs. "I'm home alone sweetheart, it's just me, and Vi... " Lucy winked, Cristi smiled back, then Lucy said, "The wine's poured and I've turned down your bed."

As Cristi struggled up the stairs, Lucy leant forward to take one of her bags and asked, "How was your trip, and how was your sister? And how was the little one?"

"She's fine and the little one is just gorgeous. I've got loads of snaps. I could've sworn you would've had company though. I had a text from Sam, says you and JD are, how did he put it, *'Are walking out?'* Very old fashioned, but I got the gist."

Lucy shook her head. "Yes and no. Meeting for coffee, yes, and walking together... he always walks and sees me home. But that's about it."

"Oh Luce, I'm so sorry."

"Still just coffee friends I'm afraid. I did kiss him on the cheek and we briefly touched hands, but it was almost as if he'd had a shock because he snatched back. We do walk though, and we talk. Well, I talk. I still don't know much more about him than what Sam told us. I would love to hold his hand. But what I really want to... "

Cristi smirked. "I know what you want to hold!"

"Yes," Lucy cut in, and nodded, "but just his hand for now would do. I think it's nerves. He's probably just shy."

"Oh come on, JD nervous?" Cristi was very surprised by that. "From what I've heard he's fearless."

"I don't think it's that sort of nerves, because he's definitely not frightened. It's just for some reason he's holding back. He still writes me those lovely letters you know."

"Really? Even though you see each other nearly every day?"

"Yes, really," Lucy said, nodding, "really... and... oh yes, there is something else and this is very strange. Every so often in conversations about his home, he refers to 'We'. I asked him who 'We' is, and each time he hesitates, it's like he is thinking of an answer, and it's not spontaneous. He said 'We' was him and his cousins. But if it was someone you had grown up with, someone you were close to, surely it would just trip off the tongue. Don't you think?"

Cristi put away her bags and nipped into the wet room to freshen up, then called back through the open door, saying she had just seen Pedrasz. "I don't think he realised it was me. He was just crossing over the road, then he ducked through that gap in the railings."

"I think his parents live somewhere around here," Lucy replied, "other side of the park I think he once said. I've seen him a few times too, but he's always going away and that's how I'd like to keep it, him going away. He gives me the shivers. Why the mejj I went out with him, I don't know."

And that's all she had to say on the subject as she joined Cristi on the sofa, and they opened a bottle of wine. It was a good wine, and as they finished the bottle whilst putting the worlds to rights, they opened another. Lucy said, "I have a Jez-plan."

"You have a Jez-plan?"

"I do," Lucy replied. "I need to get him away from everything and I've seen this advertised," she said, pointing to an ad in a magazine.

Cristi looked down and read. "A gentle, managed walking weekend. We take your luggage between the overnight stops whilst you stroll through the countryside. Three nights' accommodation, meals and transfers included.

All you carry is a day bag." Cristi looked up at Lucy. "Sounds lovely Luce, but how's that going to help your plan?"

"That is my plan. If I can get him somewhere on his own, away from here and from Sam and everyone else, then he might properly relax and maybe we can really, y' know."

"Do you think JD will go for it?"

"I don't know."

Unfortunately, when Lucy made the booking there were only two, four-bed rooms available. "Oh," she groaned, "bugger!" She thought about booking one of the rooms and wondered if JD would share. [-"We could hang a curtain down the middle.-"-] But she very quickly dropped that idea, as it felt tacky and she didn't want to scare him off. [-"I can't afford both rooms though, and I can't expect him to pay for something that he might not want to do."-] "Damn!" So she changed her plan into a couples weekend and invited Cristi and Sam.

Cristi had bumped into Judi who told her that Robbie would be over that weekend. "I told Judi about your Jez-plan. "Judi said book them in too. So that's two more beds filled," said Cristi. Then she said, "How about Mischa and Conner?"

Lucy liked that, so she sent Mischa a text and an hour later the rooms were booked. The girls would have one room and the lads the other. It wasn't what Lucy had wanted, [-"But"-] she thought to herself [-"an opportunity might still arise..."-].

"Hold on a minute though Luce, you still have to invite JD."

"I was hoping we could ask Sam to do that," she replied. "Do you think he would?"

"I'm sure he would."

"I just hope you, me and the girls, and *the* boys too, can manufacture a situation that throws us together."

Lucy needn't have worried though, because the very thing that was needed simply happened, all by itself, on day three.

27

No accounting for taste ...

A few weeks after Lucy booked the 'Walking Package', Sam, JD and most of the LSP Project team, the men *and* the women, were sitting up on the roof of the accommodation and eyeing up the sunbathing students on the campus lawns below. They were marking them out of ten and irreverently discussing their various attributes. It was good old workshop banter and both sexes were fair game. JD passed a beer to Sam; they were the last two bottles from Robbie's collection. They knocked the caps off, chinked the bottles together, and toasted Robbie.

"Robbie, here's to you mate," Jez said then drank and enjoyed the clean fresh taste. "You've got to hand it to him," he added, "Robbie certainly knows his beer... this is excellent."

Sam nodded in agreement. "Sure does, shame these are the last. Any idea where he got them from?"

Jez turned the bottle to look at the label. "Mejjas Minor by the look of the script, and it's certainly not the common tongue. Was he posted out there?"

Sam wasn't sure. "Don't know, but I think he gets his beer by mail-order. Yeah, I seemed to remember that," he said as he drained the bottle.

"The Laxi gets out there sometimes. I'll get in touch with the Jag boys, and maybe next time they go that way they could get us some. Maybe a couple of crates. Leave it with me and I'll see what can be done," he said as he tilted his bottle and savoured the last mouthful. "Very nice."

Sam took a couple of bottles from his own beer stash in his bag, knocked off the caps and passed one to Jez. As he did so he turned and asked, "Have you caught any of the conversations Conner and I have been having about this Walking Weekend, the one that Lucy has organised in the highlands? Has Lucy said anything to you about it?"

Jez shook his head. "No mate, you know I don't pay attention to private conversations." Jez's ethos was to be focused at all times whilst working and never to eavesdrop on his fellow workers, even going to the extent of explaining, very early on in their friendship, of how Sam could inhibit his thoughts. So Sam's mention of Lucy's weekend away came as news to him. "No, and Lucy hasn't said anything either."

"Well it's booked," Sam continued, "three nights, two whole days and two half days."

"Okay, and?" Jez was puzzled. "Should I know something about it?"

"Well, Lucy has asked me to ask you if you would like to join the party."

JD made the slightest acknowledging head inflexion, then put the bottle to his lips and took a sip. After quite a long pause he asked, "Where are you going?"

"What!" Sam was stunned. "Lucy Hettler, the girl of every man's dreams, the coolest girl on the planet, has expressly invited you to be one of her party and all you have to say on the matter is where are you going? Geeze JD, are you for real?" Sam looked at him aghast, then bluntly announced, "The Mecklenburg Highlands."

"When?" he said and took another sip.

Sam couldn't believe him. [-"Is he playing me?"-] he wondered. "Friday week, not this weekend, the next one," said Sam through gritted teeth.

"Eh... don't know."

"What!" Sam gasped again. "For goodness sake Jez. 'Eh, don't know'. Are you winding me up? She's stunningly beautiful, the prettiest girl on campus and for some reason, she's only interested in you," he replied, his voice raising a decibel, and at this point, some of the others on the roof started to take an interest. "She wants you to join us."

"What are you two tarts jabbering about?" asked H-One, an old school mechanic from the other side of Mejjas.

Another was less polite. "Lower your voices you effing idiots. You'll scare off the totty." Others muttered in agreement.

Then Harriet, Harri-Too, leant across. "Like Danny said, you're going to scare off the bits of fluff."

Sam raised both his hands in submission and mouthed an apology. "Sorry. Sorry." Then he turned to both the Hs and in a lower voice, said, "This girl has expressly invited him. Wants him," — he pointed at JD — "to join our weekend party. This girl is stunningly beautiful, and she could have asked anyone. There's a whole host of hopefuls, but she's asked him, and all he's interested in is where and when."

"Do I know the girl?" H-One asked.

"Yeah, do we know this girl?" H-Too repeated.

"Probably by sight. Her name is Lucy."

"Lucy?" Both Hs gasped in stereo. "The girl that meets him after work?"

"Yeah, that one."

"Jeepers JD. Jeepers. Well, I would, wouldn't you Sam?" H-One replied as some very earthy thoughts ran through his head.

"I would too," said H-Too.

Sam said, "Who wouldn't?"

"Didn't she go out with that bloke who exploded in the Bean?"

"She did. For one night."

"And now she wants him?" she said, pointing at JD.

"There's no accounting for taste," said H-One.

But it was as if Jez was in a different conversation. "I've always wanted to visit the Mecklenburg Highlands," he said as he stared down at the comings and goings on the campus lawns.

"What!" Sam turned to his mate, then back to H-One and Harri-Too, then they all looked back to JD. They had been talking about the prettiest girl on campus, lewd thoughts running wild through all their minds, and all JD could think of was wanting to visit the highlands. Sam shook his head in disbelief.

By now their raised voices were annoying the other rooftop voyeurs.

"Oi, move back from the edge will yer," hissed one.

"Cut the jabber," hissed another.

Just then, Sergeant Pete, without saying a word, spread his arms and pointed and ordered everyone away from the edge. After a few minutes, Pete nodded and all those that wanted to, shuffled back and continued their vigil. H-One shuffled back too. H-Too though, moved up closer to Jez and Sam.

"What on mejj are you thinking JD? That girl is gorgeous, and feisty too. Heaven knows what she said to that Pedrasz twat, but... "

"Did you say Pedrasz?" asked H-One, who had shuffled back. "The footballer?"

"Yeah, that's the one. A winger in the college squad. He's a piece of shit he is, deserved all he got."

"It was him in the Bean that caused the ruckus wasn't it?" said H-One. "Threw his drink over everyone because the girl answered him back or something like that. That's what I heard."

"Yeah, he's a trophy hunter," said H-Too, "that's what he is. Thinks he can click his fingers and the girls will come running. He was going out with the younger sister of a friend of mine, pretty thing she is, though maybe not in the same league as your Lucy."

"She's not my Lu —"

"Yeah, whatever," Sam cut in.

H-Too continued. "When her hay fever puffed up her eyes and her nose was red from sniffing, he dumped her and targeted your Lucy instead. It's not Lucy's fault. He's a flatterer, and he's got the physique and all the right words wrapped up in sickly charm. But it's all for show, and that's all Lucy was, just like my friend's sister, a trophy. From what I heard your Lucy gave him what for. Good on her I say, good on her. So what the eff are you doing asking about the hills when you could be up to your armpits in a great looking woman? What's wrong with you JD?"

"She's not *my* Lucy. We just meet for coffee. She's never mentioned this trip to me."

Harri-Too looked at Sam and shrugged. "I tried Sam."

Sam nodded and said, "Thanks H." Then he turned back to JD and tried again. "Last chance Jez. Lucy wants *you* to join us, to join her. So is it a yes or a no?"

JD shrugged. "Well, yes. It sounds like it could be fun. Yes, but I suppose she only asked me because she's short on numbers."

"For fu... I just don't get you mate," Sam replied, shaking his head, "don't understand you at all. The loveliest girl on the planet, the girl with the sweetest temperament and the loveliest legs wants you to join a party that she has organised, and all you can think about is the scenery."

"I told you," Jez mumbled as he put the bottle to his lips, "we're just good friends."

"Oh, of course, silly me, I forgot," Sam said, head still shaking in disbelief. "Drink your beer JD," he said. "Yeah, of course, you *are* just good friends."

28

The Mecklenburg Highlands ...

It was late morning, Sunday, their second full day and they were now enjoying the gradual descent after having spent Friday and most of Saturday climbing up the steep paths into the foothills of the Mecklenburg Highlands. The downward slope was much shallower, which was a blessing as the air was heavy and muggy, and their shirts and blouses were clinging. Robbie and Sam were stripped to the waist, and Judi too had stripped off her blouse, but was regretting that decision. She wished she had opted for her sports-bra now because the straps of her day bag were rubbing over the straps of her strappy vest and irritating her shoulders.

"I could murder another beer," Conner announced as he wiped the sweat from his brow and held out his arms to let his armpits breathe.

"You had one only an hour ago," JD said. "That's the trouble with you townies, you don't know how to pace yourselves. If you think you're thirsty now, you should have done the Jaeger Basic. I used to think I was good at managing thirst, filling a bladder and strolling between waterholes. It didn't help me at all on that Basic"

On OiT Basic JD had amazed them at how long he could go without water, so when Conner heard him talk of the deprivations of the tougher Jaeger Basic and how JD had found it hard work, he didn't know what to say. "Geeze JD, I don't think any of us realised just what it was like. I thought our basic was tough, so what the hell did those bastards put you through?"

But before Jez could spill out the gruesome details the group rounded the next bend, and there below them, randomly scattered on the hillside, were the houses of another pretty alpine village. More importantly, there was another inn.

The route option Lucy had chosen was popular with walkers, and in each of the villages along the trail, as well as an inn, their little group had been overwhelmed by the choice of portable crafts that were on offer. This village was no exception and Jez, as he had done in all the other villages they had passed through today, when the others had gone straight to the inn for a cooling beer, had made a beeline for a woodcarver's shop. By now Sam, Robbie and Judi were more than a little puzzled by his behaviour and they followed him into the low-roofed, wood shaving-strewn workshop.

This time Cristi didn't follow Sam. She was hot and she needed the shade of an umbrella so she went straight to the table and sat down opposite Lucy. Mischa and Conner took seats on the opposite side and when the waiter came they ordered eight large beers.

"Where's Sam?" Lucy asked.

"He followed JD again, into that shop. He's still curious about what he's up to. Robbie and Judi are too. JD is certainly acting out of character," said Conner.

Jez was browsing and had very nearly settled on his purchase, he just needed to know the price. "Excuse me, sir, how much is this?" he asked the elderly craftsman.

Jez had visited every craftsman along today's route, and Sam had gone into all of them with him. At first, he was interested in buying a souvenir for himself and Cristi, and had done so about five villages ago. He had bought his girl a beautifully carved love spoon and an exquisitely carved wooden necklace, which was already adorning her neck. But in all the shops that JD had visited he hadn't bought a thing. Then, in this shop, Sam realised that at last JD was showing some real interest in something. "I don't believe it," he whispered, "he's actually buying something."

"That one, young sir, is seven-fifty," the craftsman replied. Jez then showed him a larger piece, "that one is ten, and the little one, the pocket-sized one, that's five."

Jez held each one in turn, weighing up which would suit his idea the best. He picked them up, put them down, went back to the first, then turned the last one over, and all the time the woodcarver stood patiently, as if Jez was about to provide his biggest sale of the season.

Sam, who was on the other side of the workshop, muttered, "Oh, perhaps not. Here we go, another of his long silences. They'll be screwing the lid down on that old guy's box before JD makes up his mind."

Judi giggled, Robbie smirked and Sam shook his head.

"I'll have this one sir, the seven-fifty, and the little one too."

"Glory be, JD, what's come over you? An instant decision. You ill or something?"

"Cheeky bugger," was JD's reply to Sam. Then he turned to the woodcarver and asked, "What's the price of this shepherd's staff, the crook sir?"

"That my young friend is twenty-five."

Jez weighed it in both hands, balancing it on his fingertips and eyeing its length for trueness, then nodded. "It's good, and the hook is beautifully carved. Your own work?" he asked."

The old man nodded proudly. He could see that this young man knew his crooks. Jez though was certain it was under-priced, so he asked again.

"Twenty-five you say, are you sure? The carving is simple yet beautiful. Is twenty-five correct?"

"Twenty-five."

"Then twenty-five it is," Jez said and put out his hand and they shook. "So that's thirty-seven fifty all told for you," he said and handed over the cash, "and this crook and these two for me." He put the smaller pieces into his bag. "Thank you, sir." Then he took up his staff, smiled at Sam and stepped back into the sunshine.

"What have you got there?" Lucy asked. He had bought something at last, but it wasn't at all what she had expected.

"It's a crook. For sheep."

"For Meeko?" she asked.

"No, it's for me."

"You going to hook us a sheep for tea then JD?" Conner asked.

"I could do Conn," JD replied, "I've got all we need in my bag. Catch, cook and eat before the shepherd has an inkling."

Lucy was horrified, "Oh, you wouldn't!"

Jez quickly backtracked. "Eh, no. No I wouldn't," he assured her, and looked her square in the eyes and smiled. "No." [>"And Conner knows I wouldn't too."<] he said with his fingers crossed behind his back, [>"just soldier banter, that's all."<] Then to Conner, he pulsed, [>"Another time Conn, when it's just us guys,"<] and he nodded and Conner nodded in reply.

"What's the commotion?" Robbie asked as he walked into the middle of Lucy's raised reply. "Who wouldn't?"

"We were just contemplating hooking a sheep with JD's new staff, 'hook, cook and eat', as JD so succinctly puts it," said Conner.

"No," Lucy squealed again.

"Now there's an idea... could you do that JD?" Robbie asked.

"I could," he said, smiling, "but not today, not in present company."

"Not in any company or at any time," Lucy scolded.

"No. No. No. You mustn't," Mischa joined in. "No."

"It's okay Mischa, Jez won't do that." [>"Will you? You won't."<]

[>"No, I won't."<] he said, then shook his head and winked.

"No he will not, don't worry yourself, Mischa, it's just soldier bravado that's all."

"Those fluffy things are quite, quite safe... " Jez reassured her.

Then to change the subject, Robbie said, "Where's that beer?"

But as they settled at the table, Lucy heard Jez mutter, "... safe for now, that is." The lads thought it hilarious, but Lucy wasn't so impressed and she punched him hard in the ribs.

"That's not funny Jez," she snapped. Jez smiled.

The drinks were served and Cristi moved and pulled up a chair between Jez and Lucy and whispered, "Do you think he's showing off to be one of the crowd?"

"No, I've been watching them," Lucy replied in a hushed voice, "and if anything I'd say it was the other way around, perhaps not with Sam but definitely Robbie and Conner. I'd say they're in awe of him. They're the followers."

"Just like you," said Cristi.

"Yeah, just like me," said Lucy. "It's just not working is it, Cris," she muttered as she stared into her drink. "We walk and we talk together, we laugh and we joke, but there's no spark; it's almost as if there's a barrier that he just won't cross. What have I got to do? Why did he send me those lovely letters? They were so personal and so... he gave so much away in those words. I fell for him when I read those letters, or did I just fall for an idea? That was it, wasn't it? Have I got it all wrong again Cris, did I read something that wasn't there? Or have I said something, that I can't remember saying, and frightened him off?"

Cristi didn't have an answer or know what to say. Her friend had come up with the perfect plan, but all she seemed to have achieved was to make JD the one the other guys followed. It hadn't brought Lucy and JD together at all.

"We're midway through Day Three already," Lucy groaned, "eight kilometres left to walk today, and six tomorrow. Then its home, back to Meckloe, and back to coffee after work." Lucy had hoped that she and Jez would have found themselves alone together by now and that the spark that she hoped was there would have flashed between them. But so far nothing like that had happened and she was losing hope. "What am I supposed to do, Cris?"

"I think it's time we confided in Judi and Mischa, don't you?" said her friend.

Across the table, the lads were chatting. They discussed the walk so far, the scenery, how clean everything was compared to the grime of Meckloe, and obviously, the possibility of nabbing a sheep and general guy stuff. They wondered why none of them had thought of getting into the mountains before.

After about an hour and several beers, they asked for the lunchtime menu. With only eight kilometres left to walk and the promise of a warm evening, they made a joint decision to stretch out their lunchtime break.

"I think tonight's table is booked for eight-thirty," Lucy said as she skimmed through the itinerary. "Yes, eight-thirty. So at five klix an hour we'll get to the hotel in bags of time."

Everyone thought that to be a feasible assessment and nodded in agreement, everyone that is except Jez, who was staring up at the skyline.

"Did you get any of that mate?" Sam asked.

"Get what?"

Sam shook his head in disbelief. "We're going to have a long lunch here, take things easy for an hour or so. Perhaps wander around the village, check out the other shops and crafts, then get ourselves down to the hotel for eight and the table Lucy booked for eight-thirty."

"Oh yeah, I heard all that" he replied, "but I've got my shopping so I might just check out that ruin up there."

"What ruin?"

"There, do you see? Up there, at the skyline. It looks like an old fort to me. Are you up for it?"

"Where? Show me." At the mere mention of 'fort' Sam was interested. "Point it out JD."

"There look, just to the right of that pointed crag and to the left of that... " he aimed with his new crook.

"Yep, got it. I'm up for it mate. I'll get the others, and we'll get out whilst the girls aren't watching. Go now, we'll catch you up," he added and as Sam nipped into the bar area to tell Robbie and Conn, Jez swung his bag onto his back and picked up his crook then set off across the street.

Conn and Robbie were wide-eyed as Sam explained. "Looks like a tower and a couple of slabs with crenulations. Bit of a climb, but much better than craft shops. Interested?" It was 'old' military, so of course they were interested, and they were already gathering their gear, when...

When Mischa said in a loud indignant voice, "Where's JD going?" He was already across the street, and she turned to Conner. "Where's JD going ...?"

Jez was already into the meadow and picking up the pace, but he could hear the raised voices behind and decided he didn't want any part of it. He had been hoping to get some time alone with Lucy, and he'd thought that moment had come as they sat down together at the table. But then Cristi had sat between them. He was crestfallen. It had been the same all morning. There had been moments as they had walked that had felt right, but whenever it had felt right for him she was always talking to someone else. He had tried the mindPlain, but for reasons best known only to her, she had been inhibiting. So when he saw the fort and weighed up the options, he considered the fort to be the better bet.

As he closed the gate to the meadow and started along the path he heard Mischa's shrill voice call out again. "Cris, Judi, where's JD going?"

"I eh, don't know," Cristi replied. She turned to ask Sam, only to find he had picked up his bag — Robbie and Conner were picking up theirs too — and all three were sheepishly sidling between the tables.

"Sam, no. No. Sam!" Cristi shouted. "No!"

"Huh?"

"Sam, have you forgotten why we're all here?"

"What?" said Conner.

"Huh?" added Robbie.

"Sam?" Cristi hissed and dropped her brow then stared at him over the top of her sunglasses.

"Oh shi... yeah, of course," he said and quickly explained to Robbie and Conner.

"Right, yeah, of course," they replied in unison.

"Where's Lucy?" Cristi cried. "Find Lucy, everyone, look. LUCY? LUCY?"

"Who wants me?" Lucy said as they all called out her name again. "Is there a fire or something? What's up?"

Cristi just held up her bag. "Put this on, and run that way... through the gate and up the hill. It's that chance you've been hoping for."

"Huh?"

"JD is going up the hill to check out some old ruin or something, up there on the skyline... alone. The boys *were* set to go with him, but we've stopped them because you're not going to get another chance like this. So don't dally, put on your bag and get running, girl. Go on."

Without a second thought, Lucy shouldered her bag and sprinted across the street, up between the chalets, through the gate and into the meadow. By now Jez was a long way ahead. He was sprinting, and she could only just make out his shape as he dodged in and out of the rocky outcrops. Lucy ran on in pursuit, hoping he would have to stop sometime soon. He was running at a much faster pace than she wanted to maintain; she was quick and often ran ten-ks, but not at this pace. This was sprinting, and uphill, too. But she knew he would have to stop soon, otherwise the others wouldn't have been able to catch him up.

She ran on until she stumbled as the path rose up before her, pitching to almost forty-five degrees. The grass was shiny and slippery, and because of the angle, she had to clamber up nearly fifty meters of slope on her hands and knees. It slowed her a lot and she worried because she had lost sight of her quarry.

Jez stopped to wait for the others. He had found a suitable collection of rock slabs that formed a natural chair. The rocks were warm so he made himself comfortable and settled down to wait, and gazed out over the valley. The rock and the steepness of the climb hid the village and the path, which meant he was looking out over fresh fields and the view was breath-taking. "I don't know which I like the most these days," he was saying, "the endless steppe or," as Lucy's red and sweaty face appeared over the lip of the rock, "Oh!" His heart skipped a beat. "Hello," he said, gasping.

Lucy pulled herself onto the slab and sat down beside him, and shuffled closer until they touched. Jez felt a shiver.

"Sam's not coming," she said.

"Robbie and Conner?"

"Them neither. The girls, you see, they want to look around the village, and they don't want to do it alone. I haven't g... I, eh. So, well, it's just me I'm afraid."

"Okay, yes." Then, "It's a great view, isn't it," he said as he stared away from her across the valley, suddenly aware that he didn't have the right words for being alone with the girl of his dreams.

Lucy realised she had taken him by surprise, hence his nervous response. This wasn't what she had had in mind either. She was nervous too, and kept the questions topical. "If Sam and the others had come," she began, "how long would you have waited?"

"Ten minutes probably."

"And if they hadn't have come, if no one had come?"

He shrugged. "Gone on I suppose."

"You wouldn't have come back down then?"

"Didn't seem much poi… " he started, but stopped short. "No."

Lucy nodded. "Yes." It was clearer now. Had they both been waiting for that spark to flash? Was it too late? Or had she caught it just in time? "And," she ventured, "if you had known it was me coming up to join you, how long would you have waited for then?"

Jez fell quiet and turned and stared into the snowy peaks. There was a very long pause and Lucy kicked herself.

[-"*Damn Lucy, you idiot, too much question, too soon!*"-] she thought and the silence continued. Was he thinking of a polite way to excuse himself and go on alone? But his answer, when it came, surprised her. Unwittingly, with her chanced question Lucy had provided the moment Jez had been looking for.

He hadn't planned it like this and he wasn't ready for that particular moment. Her question had taken him by surprise, and the words he had practised over the last few days were jumbling as he tried to remember what he had wanted to say. But it was now… or never. This was his one chance and he was going to take it, no matter the consequence. He stared straight ahead into the distant mountains, and finally, he said. "For you, Lucy Hettler, I would have waited forever."

"Oh… oh… oh gosh. I wasn't expecting that," she said and gasped.

[-"*I said it. I did it!*"-] he said to himself and a big beaming smile creased his lips. "I told her," he gasped out loud, still staring at the distant mountains. It wasn't what he had planned to say at all, wasn't what he had practised, [-"*Where did that come from, that's not what I planned?*"-]

[-"*He just said my whole name, he's never done that before. And he said he would wait forever. That's so lovely. Ohh, he's so lovely,"-]* and her eyes moistened. "Oh..."

Jez turned to her, just as she turned to him, which was a bit awkward because they were still sitting. Then Lucy leant forward hoping for a kiss, and Jez met her for the briefest of touches, then panicked.

"Eh, the fort," he said, pulling away and scrambling to his feet, "are you coming?" And he was off.

[>"Gosh, that was a whirlwind romance!"<] "Eh, yeah right," she said.

Jez was several strides away from where Lucy was still sitting when he heard her comment across the mindPlain, and he scolded himself. *[-"Idiot. You just said you would wait forever, so wait,"-]* and he stopped and turned back to her.

"Sorry Lucy Hettler," he said and he fessed-up. "I panicked. I said I would wait for you, forever, and I didn't." He walked back to the rock and held out his hand. "Will you come with me?" he asked.

She put her hand in his and got to her feet. "You are silly, you know," she said and smiled, and he nodded sheepishly. "Why did you panic? Hmm? Am I that scary?" she asked and she could see that he was embarrassed, so she just said, "Come on then, let's go and look at that fort."

29

But your eyes are closed ...

They climbed, both conscious of the nervous tension still between them. They had only managed to hold hands briefly because now the narrowness of the track had forced them to walk in single file. The path was well-worn and very old, and Jez reckoned it was a sheep path. There were some sections so steep that only hooves could have found grip. After a couple of slips Jez held out his hand, which Lucy took, and this time she didn't let go even when it was narrow. And they walked together like that, hand in hand, until they reached the fort.

It was quite a climb, a lot more of a climb than even Jez had anticipated, and there were moments when he literally had to pull Lucy up the steep bits. On those really steep sections it was easier to carry her, but she still held onto his hand. She had caught him now and she wasn't going to let go.

As they climbed, and the afternoon wore on, they talked endlessly about this, that and everything, and Lucy was fascinated by his extensive knowledge of plants and trees and the land.

He told her it was fifty-fifty due to his nomadic heritage and his Jaeger Corps training. They talked too about her degree and post-grad studies, about how when she was a fully qualified lawyer she wanted to practice on Mii'een, and she talked too about the small part she played on that important government trip to his home planet. They had talked about this many times at the 'Bean' but Jez never tired of her memories of his homeland.

They climbed onwards and upwards, laughing and joking, at last comfortable in each other's company, seemingly oblivious to the time and the darkening clouds that were creeping up behind them.

After another hour, as they crested another very steep slope, they found their way barred by a rusting fence that stretched right across the meadow from left to right. "Oh?" said Jez. "That's annoying, I didn't expect that, couldn't see it from the village."

"Oh!" said Lucy, "that's a shame. I so wanted to see the fort. Oh well, never mind," she added and turned and started back, still holding his hand. But he didn't budge. "Jez, are you coming?"

"Nope." He was staring at the fence.

"What're you looking at?" she asked, and noticed his eyes were closed. "What are you doing?"

"Looking for a gap in the fence."

"But your eyes are closed," she said.

"Yep." Jez had stepped onto the mindPlain and projected his thoughts forward towards the fence. It was an old fence that hadn't been cared for in a long time, and there were a lot of bramble briars and ferns and scrubby bushes growing up at least half its height, plus a lot of tall grass too. He pushed his thoughts this way and that, looking for a gap, and before long he found a rabbit-run below a bush and followed it to the rusting chain link. Once at the fence, Jez steered his thoughts, first to the left, and after finding nothing he turned them to the right.

Lucy was fascinated and recalled Jez leaving the refectory with his eyes tightly shut and wondering then what he was doing. Now he was doing it again and she was truly in awe. She watched as he turned his head, first to his left, then a few moments later he shook his head and mumbled "No." Then he turned his eyeless gaze to the right, and after a few minutes, he smiled.

"That'll do," he said. Then he put his head to one side and a few seconds later chuckled, and smiled again and said, "Claude, you old goat." Jez then turned to Lucy. "There's a hole over there under that tree, and a track too. Come on, let's check it out," he said, and led the way.

There wasn't much of a track left, just a line through the vegetation that was slowly being reclaimed. But there was a hole in the fence that had been there for quite some time. "There we go... shall we?" he said, and was about to step through when Lucy stopped him.

"I'm not sure about this Jez."

"What?"

"The sign, it says KEEP OUT." She wasn't happy.

PRIVATE PROPERTY - KEEP OUT

By ORDER

Claude Atkins CEO – The Praes~Eedan Corporation

"It's an old sign Luce, an old fence too, and look at all these bushes. I'd be very surprised if Claude actually knows there's a fence here, or an old fort for that matter."

"But it says by ORDER, so what if someone from security comes?" Lucy wasn't convinced.

"If Praes~Eedan and Claude can't be bothered to rehang the sign, then they can't be that bothered about keeping people out, so I'm going in." The sign was only held in place by one fastener and it had swung down so that the horizontal words were now vertical. "The sign has slipped, and it's been like that for a very long time, so long that I'm surprised the words haven't slid off the board."

Lucy still wasn't sure. "But what if we're caught?"

"We won't be caught. No one has been this way for a very long time, but to reassure you I'll check. I'm going to do a bit more closed eye searching, okay?"

Lucy nodded, nervously looking about her, worried that someone in uniform was going to jump out any moment and shout at them.

A few moments later Jez opened his eyes and announced, "The last people to come this way were a teenage boy and his teenage girlfriend. They went through the hole and up to the fort. They were there for about half an hour and then they came back out. And that was three years ago, give or take."

"Oh. Are you sure?" He nodded. "Can you see anyone up there now?" He shook his head. "Has anyone followed us?" Again he shook his head. "Oh, then I suppose it will be okay," she said while looking nervously about her.

30

A great place to live ...

The tower was a lot bigger than either of them had imagined. Lucy paced it out; it was seven paces, so a diameter of roughly six meters. Jez nipped back outside and did a quick bit of approximation and came up with twenty meters for the height. The tower was perfectly round and open to the sky. A rope hung from a beam and around the wall ran a spiral staircase with three landings. On each of the landings was an empty doorway that led to each of the slabbed levels. The fort had to be at least a thousand years old, though the rope looked like a recent addition and so did the beam.

"This would be a great place to live," Jez said as they stood together on the top level and gazed out over the valley to the village below. Then they turned to face the view the other way. There was another village about one kilometre down the back slope, and quite a few little tracks leading from there to the fort. "That would account for the new rope then," he said, then added, "and those teenagers."

They spent the next couple of hours exploring. Jez didn't think there was much to see other than the amazing view, and he was ready to start down after about half an hour. But Lucy surprised him. She seemed to be interested in everything and looked into every nook and cranny, and every time Jez thought they had seen all there was to see Lucy surprised him with something else. If it meant another moment in her company though, then he was happy to see what she had found. He was conscious of the darkening clouds and the rising clammy temperature; there was a thunderstorm on the way and a walk back down in that sort of weather, even if they were holding hands, wouldn't be very nice.

They were up on the top level when the first big drops splattered the dusty floors. Lucy had just worked her way to the furthest corner from the tower, but when Jez called to her to get under cover she appeared not to hear. So he pulsed across the mindPlain. [>*"Luce, it's going to piss down I'll see you down on the middle level."*<] He was already running to the tower and down the stairs, as he knew what it was like to be soaked through and he didn't want that today. By the time Lucy arrived though, it was teeming down and she was soaked to the skin. Her vest and shorts were translucent and rivers ran from her long dark hair over the contours of her body. There wasn't much left for Jez's imagination.

"I think we're stuck here for a while," she said.

"Oh, and you're soaked through too," he said, pretending to have just noticed, eyes wide and taking in her beauty. "You can't walk down in those wet clothes, they'll rub. Oh no, this won't do."

[-*"Damn, this wasn't supposed to happen"*-] It *was* one of his imagined scenarios, but they were just dreams, and weren't real. How was he going to explain this to everyone?

"Hold on, I've got a coat you can put on while your clothes dry. Hold on." Strapped to his backpack was his shepherd's cape, and rolled up in the cape was a striped silk coat with a hood. "Put this on," he said, "it has a thermal fleece lining and it's very warm."

"Thermal fleece?"

"And why not?" He sounded indignant.

Lucy reeled back, her eyes widening and a smile on her lips. [-*"Oh, he's so nervous,"*-] she thought.

"We might wander the steppe following our sheep, but we do move with the times too y' know, and we're not backward. Here, put this on." Then he dropped his bag and ran to the stairs.

[-*"Oh no, where's he gone? I've done it again... Ohh!"*-]

But he was back a few minutes later with armfuls of bracken. He put them against the rock wall then went again to the stairs. A few minutes later he was back again, repeated the process, and again returned to the stairs. And this he did until he had brought up enough to make a mattress. He spread his cape over the vegetation. "We might have to stay here tonight. I'm so sorry, I didn't mean for this to happen...."

[-"I did..."-]

"... but you can sleep here, and I'll just get some more bracken and sleep over there. The lower level is clogged with bracken, but you'll be okay as it's very dry."

Lightning flashed over the distant mountains, and the rumble of thunder sounded fainter now. *[-"Is it moving away?"-]* he wondered. "We might be lucky," he said, "it sounds like it's moving away," but if anything the rain fell harder. "There's something else I need to do," he added and he ran over to the stairs, then stopped. "Eh, no." He turned and went a few paces, then stopped, and turned again for the stairs.

"What are doing Jez?" Lucy asked, "running this way and that way, and not getting anywhere. You're like a cat on a hot tin roof. Why don't you just come here, hmm? I'm not going to bite *[-"Yet"-].*"

He did as he was told and obediently moved beside her. "I'm so sorry," he said again, "this isn't how it was supposed to be. I knew it was going to rain, but I thought we would have been back with the others by the time the first drops fell. But the climb up took a lot longer than I thought it would. I forgot how much fitter I am than you."

They had taken several rest-stops on the way up. Jez would have taken only a few minutes to catch his breath, but Lucy needed longer and those stops had added at least thirty minutes, maybe an hour. It had been further than he'd anticipated too. All in all, they shouldn't have stayed so long exploring the fort, but Lucy was so interested in everything and the rain had caught them out.

"I'm sorry," he said again, as over the mountains more lightning flashed, followed by very distant thunder. "The rain will stop soon," he reassured her, "and we can make our way down. You won't need that mattress, and we can leave it for that teenage couple."

[-"*Oh, he's so sweet and so very nervous, and he's not going to make a move is he, so I suppose it's down to me.*"-] "Look," she said.

"Huh?" Jez turned and looked out into the rain-swept valley.

"No, you silly thing, here," and she let the coat fall open.

"Oh," he said and swallowed, "yes."

"Well?"

"Hmm, yeah it wasn't... I erm, want."

Lucy smiled and put her head to one side. "What's up sweetie?" she asked. [-"*Gosh he's so nervous. It's so sweet.*"-]

"I didn't... it wasn't ... I erm. I..." He stumbled over his words and Lucy was surprised at how reticent he was. But then he gingerly slipped his hand inside the open coat and gently touched his fingertips to her back. Lucy shivered.

"This is my dream," he whispered. "I've dreamt of touching you for so long, but you said," and his voice trailed off when she put her finger to his lips.

"Shush," she whispered as she unbuttoned his shirt and bent forward and kissed his chest, and he kissed the top of her head. But when she started to unbuckle his belt and unfasten the top button of his shorts, he pulled away.

"Ah... I um," he managed, then frantically thrust his hands into his pockets and looked anxiously for his backpack.

"Hey, what's up?" she cried, not wanting to let go but concerned none the less. "What's wrong Jez?"

Jez was all of a fluster. "I need... I need... need, erm!"

"One of these?"

"Yes," he said and breathed a startled sigh. "Yes, one of those."

"Well I brought a few," she said, "so can I unbutton your shorts now?"

He nodded, then grimaced. "Ah but, eh..." he said as his shorts dropped to the floor. "Highlighter ink," he groaned, "doesn't wash out."

Lucy looked down to admire the Jaeger handiwork, and everything else, and at that moment lightning rent the sky overhead. The immediate thunderclap shook the fort, dust fell from the rock above, and Jez seized the moment and pulled her to him. "I love you, Lucy Hettler, I always have."

31

I got a dusty bum ...

The rain had stopped, the storm had passed over and now the thunder was no more than a faint and distant purr. Lucy lay in the inky black darkness listening to the trickling timpani of raindrops, the faint breathing of the man beside her and the noises of the night. Something had caused her to stir. Something out there in the darkness. There it was again, a whimper, a cry. An injured animal? Was it close, was it far away? She wasn't certain. Lucy was a city girl and the noises of the dark were new to her.

Jez was lying on his side with his back to her and breathing softly. Whatever it was, it hadn't disturbed him, and as she lay there listening to his gentle breathing he rolled over onto his back, tipping off his part of their shepherd's coat covering. Lucy snuggled up to his warm body, put her arm and leg over him so she could get as close as she could, and rested her head on his chest. He had been all she had hoped he would be, and their lovemaking she would remember forever. She pulled back and rested on her shoulder, her leg still over his and traced her fingertip over his glistening body, from his chest to his loins, trying to coax a little more, but he'd given his all and all of him was exhausted. So she pulled the coat over them, and with her ear over his heart she let his steady heartbeat guide her back into her dreams.

"No... No!"

Lucy was thrown off the mattress and landed in a tangle of coat, dust and bracken.

"CAN'T BREATHE!" Jez screamed. Lucy was startled, yet *he* was still fast asleep. She *had* heard him shout 'NO' and was reacting just as he had lashed out, sending her tumbling onto the hard floor.

"Jez sweetheart, are you okay?" But he didn't stir. [-*"A nightmare? Or was it a comment about me?"-*] He just rolled over as if nothing had happened. Carefully she moved back. [-*"Was that whimpering him?"-*] she wondered as she wrapped her body around his contours and getting as close as she could without disturbing him. [-*"It seems to have stopped now."-*]

A few moments later the tension in his body eased. But *she* couldn't get back to sleep, as it had been a bit of a shock and her adrenalin was still pumping. So she rolled off the mattress and slipped on her blouse, then tiptoed over to the wall and stared out into the darkness. The clouds were thinning now and the sky behind was black. Beyond the mountains, she could just make out the faintest glow of dawn and down in the village, the lights of the early risers were starting to burn. This whole place felt magical.

[-*"Jez had said this would be a great place to live,"-*] she thought to herself. [-*"It would too,"-*] she agreed, [-*"but only if I could live here with him."-*] She smiled and thought of that moment when the lightning had flashed and they had pulled together. [-*"That was the spark I'd been waiting for, and what a spark it was. Don't they always ask 'did the ground move for you?' Well it certainly moved for me, the whole mountain shook! I've never been loved so passionately before, never. It was fantastic."-*]

As she reminisced over their evening of love she felt his warm breath on the back of her neck.

"You're cold," he said, moving close and wrapping his coat around them both. "I rolled over and you weren't there. I thought you'd left me."

Lucy pulled the coat about her, pulling his body close. "I'll never leave you," she whispered, and he kissed her neck, and as she rolled her head so he could kiss her lips she reached behind. "Oh, you've got your shorts on!"

"I was cold."

"So that's it is it, one night? Wham bam, thank you, mam."

"Noo, I'm not li..."

"Shush," she said, looking into his hurt eyes, "I'm only teasing."

"Oh, sorry. It's just that it was so special," he mumbled. "Do you mind, and I don't want to disappoint you, I just want to remember how wonderful it was, how wonderful you were."

"Don't be silly," she said as she turned around in the circle of his arms, "you could never disappoint me," and this time when she offered her mouth he kissed her, long and slow as he pulled her into his chest. "You could never disappoint me," she repeated as they parted. "I want to love you forever, and we have years for that, so when you're ready you just have to ask. [>"But don't leave it too long."<].

[>"I won't,"<] he replied. Then she turned again and together they watched the sun rise over the distant mountains.

"You called out in your sleep you know. That's why I got up. You startled me. You shouted 'No! No!' and 'Can't breathe', and you flung out your arms, throwing off your coat and me too. I rolled off the mattress."

"No, oh no. I didn't! Did I? Did I? Oh, I'm so sorry, are you hurt? I didn't hurt you did I? Oh, I'm so sorry. What must you think? Ohh... "

"I got a dusty bum but I'm alright," she said and chuckled. "You were just pumped up, [-"And how."-] that's all, and my head was on your chest, so perhaps I was lying too heavily and you couldn't breathe." She knew the moment those words left her lips how stupid they sounded. How would her light head stop his strong chest from rising? But she *was* trying her best to reassure him because she could see that he was upset. She recalled the whimpering too, but kept that to herself. "You're okay now though, aren't you?" Jez nodded. "It didn't spoil anything for me," she said.

[>"That was my first time,"<] he let slip across the mindPlain, his thoughts running free; he was obviously elated. [-"Damn! Peripherals, concentrate you twat,"-] he thought and he quickly shut down, but not before Lucy had overheard.

[-"Huh, no?"-] she thought. "Well, it was still the most fantastic night I have ever experienced." Then quickly changing the subject, realizing he was embarrassed, she said: "I really love your coat, it smells of you and... "

"Home," he said. "I bought it last summer, when I went home for the Drove. I bought it in the souk. It's traditional."

"Oh of course, yes, a traditional thermal fleece?" she teased.

"Yes, a traditional thermal fleece," and even *he* was laughing now. "Stop mocking me. The design is traditional, and as I told you we move with the times. The design is traditional, it's a traditional shepherd's coat. I had one when I was a teenager. That one was lined with wool and made in the old *traditional* way, and I've still got it. It's a bit patched and stitched here and there. I used to wear it all the time until I got broader."

"This traditional one is lovely. I want one, so will you take me to the souk."

"You know," he said, stepping back and sizing her up, "I reckon my old coat would fit you. It was always too long for me, so if it fits would you like it?"

"Oh yes please."

"And some breakfast perhaps?"

"You have food?" He nodded and smiled. "Are you going to cook for me?"

"Well, I'm going to boil some water. You had better get dressed; those warm rocks should have dried your clothes by now." He paused and thought for a moment, then asked, "Did you wait on the stairs, in the rain, deliberately?"

"Eh..."

"And maybe take longer than you needed each time we stopped on the way up?"

"Maybe..."

"You little sneaker... I was starting to wonder. Oh you schemer, I bet that was your plan for this whole weekend, and you got wet deliberately," he said, lifting her up. "Forget what I just said, I reckon your clothes need a little bit longer to dry?" he added and carried her back to their bracken bed.

32

I bet they were soaked ...

"Good morning. Looks like we're in for another good one, but did you hear the storm?" Sam said to Robbie.

"Storms more like, there was lightning everywhere, and some of those thunderclaps."

"I thought the roof was going to come in," Judi added.

Robbie said, "Didn't hear it mate, legs wrapped around my ears," he said through a smirk and Judi planted a well-aimed slap to the side of his head.

"What time did our lovers get in?" Robbie asked, quickly changing the subject. "I bet they were soaked."

"Morning," said Cristi. "Did you sleep well?"

"Didn't get any... " Robbie tried again, and again was slapped.

"Don't mind him, Cris, he's having one of his wishful dreams again. Yes, we both slept very well. He was asleep before me, too much beer at lunchtime. How about you two?"

"Sam was the same, and me too."

"Good morning everyone," Mischa and Conner said as they greeted the others already at the table.

"Did you sleep well?" Judi asked.

"Eventually, Jude," she replied, smiling. "That was a stroke of luck wasn't it, them mixing up the booking and giving us the double rooms."

The booking agents had messed up their paperwork and instead of giving their party the two, four-bed rooms, they had given them four, two-bed rooms. So the couples had rooms to themselves, albeit in different parts of the hotel and on different floors.

"Does anyone know which room they got? Should we give them a knock?"

"Who?" asked Judi.

"Lucy and Jez," said Robbie.

"Are they back then?" asked Conner.

"I'm assuming they are," said Sam. "Hold on, let's ask Jenny here," he said just as the waitress brought the breakfast coffee. "Jenny, can you tell us what room the other couple, our other friends, are in please?"

She shook her head. "We locked up after you left the bar last night. There's no other couple sir, just you guys."

"Ooo!" they said as one.

33

I thought you were joking ...

Jez had boiled up some water and made them coffee, and they sat on the edge of the slab sharing his one cup and eating the cooked meats he had kept from yesterday's breakfast. Dawn had come early; it was still only five-thirty, and they had decided to start down soon. But for the next few minutes they just wanted to enjoy being together and alone. They sat in silence and enjoyed the moment.

It was Lucy who broke the spell. "Would you like to meet my parents?"

"That's spooky, I was just about to ask you the same thing. Yes, I would, thank you."

"My parents are closer than yours so it will be easier to arrange," she said.

"Ah well, you say that, but Mumma n' Pop will be here in two weeks' time for our Passing-Out Parade."

"Of course, yes. Can you get me a ticket, I'd love to be there?" she asked hopefully.

"I've already got your ticket. We can each have four guests, so I got you a ticket just in case. I was hoping you would be one of the four."

"Four? So that's your Mumma, Pop, and me and...?"

But Jez was already standing and holding out his hand to help her up. "Shall we go?"

"Yes, but who's the fourth?"

"That'll be Claude. Come on."

They followed the old cart track, walking hand in hand back down the hill to the village where they had left the others, then picked up the walking trail. "What time was breakfast at the hotel this morning?" Jez asked.

"I think it's a late breakfast today followed by a leisurely six k walk to the pick-up. Why, do you think we might get there for the hotel breakfast?"

"If we keep this pace up I'm sure we will. It's only seven-thirty now and you said breakfast wasn't until...?"

"Nine-thirty. Who's Claude?"

"Claude Atkins of course, the one on the bottom of the KEEP OUT sign. I told you I would speak to him and you can too."

"I thought you were joking."

Jez just smiled and shook his head and motioned for them to continue on their way. Which they did for a few more paces, but this last revelation about Claude had brought to mind another of his comments. She turned, and as they were holding hands he had no choice but to stop. "What you said?"

"Huh?"

"Earlier, when we were going to have some breakfast but... eh, you know, you picked me up and we erm, you know. You said something... thought something, I overheard?"

"Oh that, yes..." He nodded, looked at his feet and mumbled in a whisper, "Yes. Yes, it was."

"There's no need to be embarrassed sweetheart, it was lovely... you were lovely. It was fantastic. I would never have guessed. Never. Where, how, did you learn to do the things you did?"

"Erm," he shuffled his feet nervously. "Engineroom Ernie, he got vids," he mumbled. "We all paid a bit, a subscription he called it."

[-"Ah, I see, that would account for some of the moves. Well..."-] "Is that it then, really? You watched vids."

"Y-yes," he stuttered, shuffling his feet. "I just wanted to make you feel good. Did I make you feel good?"

"Oh you were wonderful. It was wonderful. I'll never forget last night, not for as long as I live. Never. Now stop looking at your shoes," she said and put her finger under his chin and lifted his face. There was a nervous smile

146

on his lips. "You really are an intriguing person Jez Devii'rahl, and I am so looking forward to getting to know you better," she said and planted a kiss on his lips. "Come on, let's go meet the others."

A few minutes, Lucy asked, "Are you still in contact with Ernie?"

34

I bought you this ...

Like some stirring animal, the little village was blinking open its bleary shopfront eyes as they walked hand in hand through its narrow streets. Shopkeepers greeted one another, and nodded and smiled at the young couple — so clearly very much in love — as they pulled out their awnings and set out their wares. Lucy and Jez stopped at every stall, both of them seeing each display in a different light, spotting the little things that would have been missed yesterday.

A lady fussing over her display saw how close they were; how they turned as one; stooped over the wares as one; and she smiled and plucked a posy from her window box and presented it to Lucy. "There you are my dear. Hold on to this man. He's good and strong, never let him go," she said with a wink and smile, "and may you both be very happy." She kissed them both, and as they walked away she and the others in that narrow street applauded them.

As soon as they could though, they dodged into a side alley, laughing and happy, and fell into each other's arms. The air was electric; they were so happy and everyone was happy for them. Rather than go back into the clapping street though, they slipped down the alley and found themselves just a stone's throw from the hotel. It was just after nine-thirty.

"Let's get a second breakfast?" But Jez didn't budge. "Er..." Lucy was puzzled.

"I bought you this, but I forgot all about it until a few moments ago. I spent all of yesterday morning trying to find something that you could look at and think of me. I honestly didn't think we would have last night, as we just weren't getting together, so I thought I would buy you a souvenir of the weekend. But now I know that you'll think it a silly thing and just laugh at it."

"Well even if I do, I'll know you bought it for me, won't I?" she replied. "Come on then, what is it?"

He gave her the little package wrapped in tissue paper, and she carefully unwrapped it, then neatly folded the tissue and slipped it into her bag. Jez had bought the love of his life a beautifully carved sheep.

"Oh," she said, and tears welled then trickled down her cheeks. "It's lovely and silly and wonderful and I love it. I love you too. I love you both, both you and the sheep. I will treasure it always, always." Then she wiped away her tears with the corner of her blouse. "Oh you silly shepherd, it's lovely."

"Do you really like it?"

"It's lovely, and so are you," she replied.

[>"Really? You're not just saying that?"<]

[>"Oh, you silly thing. Yes really."<]

Jez heaved a sigh. "Do we have to go in?" he whispered.

"I suppose we should," she answered, but before they moved she wrapped her arms about him and gave him a long and passionate kiss. "Come on, then."

Cristi overheard the waitress say, "Good morning sir, madam. Yes of course, they are in there, by the window. Go on in, and I will get you some coffee."

And as Cristi and the others were just pushing back their seats Lucy and Jez entered the dining room.

"What have you two been up to? As if we didn't know," Robbie said through a smirk, and once again Judi gave him a slap.

"Shush," she said, "don't be such an ars…" But the rest of her words were lost amid the general congratulations and hugs and hand-shakes. The girls barraged Lucy with questions, and the couple's hands were dragged apart as the lads slapped JD on the back and shook his hand.

When Lucy answered, "Three!" the girls whooped and giggled.

35

There are whispers ...

"Well lads, next week we have your big day. I bet it feels like only yesterday when you fell into your first parade? And now, in ten days' time you will be fully-fledged Fleet Officers. Are you excited?" Jimi the Skip asked Sam, JD, Conner and Robbie.

As one they nodded and replied, "Yes, Skipper."

"I'd be surprised if you weren't, it's been a long journey for you all and I know that in postings other than LSP, OiTs get the shit end of the stick. How the hell did you get on in the Jaeger Corps, JD?" But she remembered before he answered and answered for him. "You got on okay, didn't you, on account of that incident upon the Star-Link."

Jez nodded, and shook his head.

"Ah, not okay?" Jez made a slight upward nod. "Right, hold on," she said as she thumbed through her notes. "Yes I jotted it down, a bit of hearsay. Hold on, here it is. Would I be right if I said you were set upon by a gang on Jaeger Basic or something like that? Is that right?"

Jez nodded again.

"A few bruises I was told," she said, hoping for a sign of emotion, though none came. "Are you okay now though, no lasting effects?" she asked. From what she had been told the RSM and his friends got there in the nick of time; one or two seconds more and JD could have been crippled.

"No lasting effects, Skipper." He knew she was fishing and he wasn't in the mood to give anything away, so he just said, "I was tired and focusing on Sergeant Garrard."

She had hoped he would say more than that, but if he didn't want to talk about it, well, she couldn't force him, could she? She hadn't got a clue who Garrard was, but realizing this was all he was going to give she turned back to the job in hand.

"Well then, this is the bit I dread. I have to ask you what your intentions are after you Pass-Out. Do you want to go on to pastures new? It's the prerogative of a newly-badged officer to choose a new posting. Of course, I would prefer you all to stay here, as you have all slotted into the team and we all like working with you."

Robbie raised his hand. "I need to talk to you about that Skipper," he said.

"I thought that might be the case, Robbie. I have already pencilled you in for a chat this afternoon at two pm. Is that okay?" Robbie nodded.

Then just as she was about to ask the other three, there was a knock on the door and another Captain stuck his head into the office.

"Ah, Raef, yes come on in. This is Robbie, JD, Sam, and Conner. Lads, let me introduce Captain Jaxton who will be joining us at LSP. He has the 'honour' of commanding the first craft to get the prototype LSP generators. The lads all pass-out in ten days' time."

Raef nodded and smiled. Raef Jaxton was thirty, had gone through the same OiT process as they had, and was between commands. His last craft, in fact, his first craft, had been an Inter-Planetary Patrol Craft, an IPPC. It had been his first full command, and now, after patrolling the outer reaches of the Endecca System for three years Jaxton was anxious to try something completely different. He shook hands with each of them.

"I don't know if it's an honour getting the first LSP command," he muttered as he congratulated them on getting to the end of the OiT process and their forthcoming Passing-Out. "Time alone will tell I suppose."

Shallop then said, "I've just got to wrap this up, Raef. Get yourself a drink and I'll pop out in a little while and show you around." As he left she turned back to Sam, JD and Conner and asked each their intentions, and was more than pleased when they all said they wanted to stay. As they filed out, she asked Jez to hold back for a few minutes.

"Nothing sinister JD. Just a bit of curiosity really."

"Skipper?"

"I was booking in your guests for the Passing-Out, and well, I'd expect to see your parents on the list. I'm assuming Alloocea Hettler is the young lady who meets you after shift?" The mention of Lucy's full name sent a shiver down his spine and he blushed, but Jimi Shallop had the good grace not to comment. "Is that *the* Claude Atkins?" she added.

"I'm sure he's not the only one, Skipper, but if you mean is he the Atkins that's the CEO of Praes~Eedan? Yes, he is."

"Wow. You know that I worked on the AtomSpheres for nearly two years, on an engineering exchange, and I never met him. Yet he's coming as one of your guests. Wow."

"Claude has been a family friend since... well you know, then. He and Mumma spent that afternoon, before... talking. He sorted everything out for us, and the rest of the Rahls. Claude organised our transport, everything, and he has stayed in touch with Mumma n' Pop ever since. When I joined up he kept an eye on me and my progress, and he even offered his address so I wouldn't stand out and get labelled. I didn't use it, and I sorted something myself, but it was a kind offer. I call on him about once a month. He's a really nice person."

"I don't doubt it. Wow. I don't know what to say JD, I'm so envious." Jimi Shallop was stunned. "Well thanks for that JD. Perhaps you can tell Capt. Jaxton that I'm free now. I'm sorry that I pried."

"No probs, Skip."

Shallop watched JD through the open doorway as he found Jaxton. A few words were exchanged, then JD went back to the workshop.

"Wow, who'd have believed it? A roaming nomad from the steppe of Mii'een counting the wealthiest man in the galaxy as a family friend. That's a-ma-zing!"

Raef joined her and they went back into her office and closed the door. "A nice bunch of lads," he commented.

"I have a very strong feeling Robbie will be asking for a permanent transfer when I see him this afternoon. His father is seriously ill, and he's been on secondment for the last six weeks. I think he will be making that permanent. But the other three want to stay."

"That's a shame, for him and his family. That lad I just spoke to though, was it JD?" Shallop confirmed his question. "Seems like a nice guy... is he?"

"Probably the very best of the bunch. When you start putting your crew together you won't go far wrong in selecting him. He's conscientious and single-minded when it comes to LSP, though he's only been with us for six weeks; started the same day Robbie left, and he's already the go-to guy for anyone with a problem. New-hands and old-hands alike. He studies all the time, perhaps not quite so much these days as he's just hooked up with the prettiest girl on campus, if you get my drift?" She smiled and Raef smiled back knowingly. "But he's willing to have a go at anything LSP. He's tough too, a Jaeger..." she said.

"Really? A Jag. Now that does surprise me, as those thugs don't usually go in for this sort of thing. I wouldn't have put that label on him. He doesn't look like a thug to me. Surely he's too short, the wrong build."

"JD's no thug, but I wouldn't like to get on the wrong side of him though."

"J D? Is that D for Deverow?"

"Devii'rahl," Shallop corrected him, "and yes, before you ask, he's the one who was centre stage in that ruckus at the Memorial Stone up on the Hub."

"No wonder he got on well in the Corps. An interesting chap by the sound of it."

"JD's an enigma. He's into anything and everything. He takes on any job I give him with a smile. Will help anyone. Yet he's shy and secretive, and never talks about his home life or his young lady. He rides a hoverboard for relaxation, and apparently he and his cousin have some sort of partnership?" She shrugged. "But that's all I know about him." She turned to Raef and smiled.

"Ah, the *'floating Jaeger'*, that's him is it, who'd have thought?" he replied.

"And yes," she continued, "you're right, he doesn't look like a thug, but then he doesn't have to because he has the full-blown Homid gene. There are whispers that he's one of those Mii'een Smoke Dancers."

"I see, that would do it then. Thanks for the heads-up," Raef acknowledged, and as they watched JD walk across the workshop, he added, "It seems you mess with Jez Devii'rahl at your peril."

36

Not the Devii'rahl way ...

The bus dropped Lucy and Jez opposite the end of the lane, and as they waited for the bus to pull away and the road to clear so they could cross, Lucy asked. "Do you see that blue letterbox, just before the bend?"

Jez pushed his glasses to the top of his head and gazed into the distance. "No."

"Look, just there," she said, pointing with her finger. "Follow my finger, there, do you see?"

"Blue, er no. I think I can see a blue gate."

"No, that's next door."

"Are you sure it's blue? I think you'll find the box has been painted and you only thought you saw it," he said, grinning as they crossed the road.

"Oh you sneak," she squealed and thumped his shoulder when she noticed his eyes were closed, "stop doing that. You've already pushed up the lane, haven't you?"

Jez had indeed pushed out his thoughts, and by stepping onto the mindPlain he had been able to move up the lane and see that the once blue letterbox was now red with a bit of blue on the hinge, and so was the gate.

"How can you push out so far?" she asked, putting her hand in his.

"Born with the knack I suppose," he said and squeezed her hand. "Give it twenty years and you'll be able to as well," he said and chuckled.

The freshly-painted *red* gate swung shut behind them and Jez followed, a little apprehensively, towards the house. Lucy had told him that the house was about a hundred and thirty years old, and was a good example of a mid-period cottage. Apparently, such houses were much sought after, but for a boy from the steppe, who had lived in a tent until he was nineteen, their mid-period example was nothing more than an old house that was probably in dire need of repair.

Jez didn't understand houses. [-"*It's probably only held together by the ivy over the door,*"-] he thought. He just couldn't see the attraction at all. True, the ivy was a flowering variety and very pretty, but such flowering plants were never seen on the steppe and if they were to be found they had no value. They weren't medicinal, and you couldn't eat them either. So what was the point? [-"*Unless perhaps the ivy is holding the brickwork together, that must be it,*"-] he thought.

The garden he did approve of though. [-"*Mumma would love something like this.*"-] It had a much loved and well-tended feel to it. Lucy had told him that when her parents had bought the house, just a year after getting the posting to Meckloe, the garden was a wilderness and the ivy had completely hidden the door. But he still couldn't understand why her parents would want to buy this old pile in favour of the one that came with the job, and it didn't make sense to him at all. But for Lucy's sake he had remembered everything she had told him, just in case it came up in conversation. He was worried that he would let her down.

He needn't have worried though and soon realised that the barrage of information was Lucy's way of calming her own nerves. This was a big occasion for her; the Hettlers had invited Jez to Sunday lunch, a meal reserved strictly for family, and of course, Lucy wanted everything to be perfect.

As they approached on the house, Jez heard a deep baying sound, and when her parents opened the door two hounds burst from either side and raced down the path to greet them. "Dogs?"

"Oh no, didn't I mention them?" asked Lucy.

"No, everything else, not dogs," he said as he held out his hands and backed off a little whilst the hounds jumped and fussed around Lucy.

"Oh dear, will you be okay?" she asked, pulling a face and hoping she hadn't messed things up between them.

"I've got no problems with dogs, we have bigger nastier dogs than these soppy mutts to fend off the wolves and kats," he replied, "I just don't like dogs that jump up, that's all."

Then, as the dogs turned their attention from Lucy to him, her father shouted from the doorway, "It's alright, they won't bite, they're just being friendly," and they both jumped at him at the same time, then landed and turned full circle, looking; he wasn't there. He was back at the gate. Unperturbed the dogs tried again and bounded down the path and jumped, but again he wasn't there either. And again they turned full circle looking for him, but he was behind and between them and Lucy. Before they could mount another attack Jez stepped quietly up to them, crouched and put the flat of his palms on each of their heads, muttering something only they could hear, and they sat quietly waiting for instruction.

Jez then stood and joined Lucy, who looked on questioningly. "Daddy has been trying to calm them for years. How did you do that? And you moved so quickly too, I didn't see you move at all. You were there, now you are here... how?"

[>"Secret,"<] he told her, and winked as the two hounds waited quietly whilst they continued down the path toward the awaiting Hettlers.

Colonel Kurt and Mrs Hettler welcomed them both with open arms. Introductions were made. "Mummy, Daddy, this is My Jez," Lucy proudly announced. The two men shook hands and the Colonel ushered him into the house. Then he noticed the hounds were still sitting patiently on the path.

"Ah, the boys... here boys," he called but they took no notice. "Come on," the Colonel growled, and he was about to go to them.

Then, [>"Come on,"<] Jez called across the mindPlain, and they obediently trotted through the doorway to their basket. [>"Lie down,"<] he added, and they did just that.

"Oh, you've decided to come in now have you?" said the Colonel. "I just can't get them to do anything y' know."

Jez crouched down beside the dogs and fussed and ruffled them, then spoke directly into their thoughts. "I think they will be good boys now sir," he said.

Lucy gave him another questioning look. *[>"What did you say to them?"<]* she asked, *[>"Or is that another secret?"<]*.

[>"I told them to be good boys."<] Jez smiled as Lucy followed her mum into the kitchen to organise some nibbles, and the Colonel suggested that the men go into his study.

"While the ladies sort things out in the kitchen shall we get down to business?"

[-"Huh! Business?"-] Jez was puzzled, and it very soon became plain that he should be, because out of the blue Lucy's father said, "So you want to marry my daughter do you?"

Jez swallowed. "Eh?" *[-"WTF!"-]*

"And what do you have to offer, might I ask? Alloocea has said you have some sheep, so how many, and is that a serious proposition? I ask you, sheep, really? Are you expecting me to barter for my daughter's hand? I have no need of sheep."

[>"WTF! Lucy, help."<]

In the kitchen, Lucy felt his nervous plea. *[>"What's up?"<]* she pulsed.

[>"You dad thinks I've come here to ask to marry you!"-]

"Marry!" She gasped. *[-"WTF?"-]*

"Is your father at it again?" her mother asked. Then after a couple of seconds she looked up and said, "But how did you...? I didn't hear anything."

"We use the mindPlain mummy."

"Oh, that's nice...," Lucy's mum had a vague idea about the mindPlain, but didn't really understand it so she returned to safer ground. "Last weekend your father confronted Hanzii's latest boyfriend. The poor lad was halfway down the garden path before she could stop him."

"Hanzii has another boyfriend? Since when?"

"Just a couple of weeks, though I don't think it's anything serious, so you can imagine why he was running. Anyway, you had better nip in there and stop your father. He'll pick on the wrong one, one day," her mother said, sighing and shaking her head as she checked the oven.

"Daddy, stop it," Lucy snapped as she flung open the office door.

"Well he hasn't run off like the other one, I'll give him that."

[>"Other one?"<]

[>"My sister's new man. He was halfway down the garden path before she could stop him. They've only been going out for a few weeks."<] "Daddy, you must stop this, it's not funny anymore," she scolded.

"It's just my little joke... call it a test. No harm done my, boy," he said and put out his hand, "hey?"

Jez took it and they shook. "No harm done, sir," he replied and smiled. [>"Shit! I don't know... I wasn't expecting that Luce. You know I w..."<]

[>"Shush,"<] she said, then for all to hear, she asked, "Are you alright?"

"Took me by surprise, that's all," Jez said.

"Take no notice of that silly old fool," Mrs Hettler said, "he'll bite off more than he can chew one day, and then we'll see who's laughing. Now, you two sit yourselves down in the lounge and Kurt, you come with me."

There were mutterings coming from the kitchen and Jez listened in. *"If he's anything like the lad you described to me, then I'd go carefully. It's plain to see that Lucy loves him, and that should be good enough for you, so don't go scaring him off. Now take these in."*

Lunch was a convivial affair of small talk and polite questions, and Jez sensed by what they were asking that they were concerned whether someone with his perceived reputation, and possibly his background too, was right for their daughter. He did his utmost to reassure them. Lucy had primed him on their likes and loathes, so he was able to ask all the right questions and give all the right answers. If he stumbled then Lucy was in his head to help him out.

After lunch, after helping to clear up, he asked Lucy's mum if she would show him around the garden, and he spent a very happy hour chatting and learning about her flowers and shrubs, and the family, and about Lucy and her sister when they were growing up.

"What do you think Daddy?" Lucy asked her father as they stood in the window and watched their respective partners wander aimlessly about the garden with the dogs trotting obediently behind.

"Is he right for you Lucy? He's a Jaeger, and they have a reputation you know. They work hard and play harder."

"He's the only one for me, Daddy. No one else will do."

"Well if you're one hundred per cent sure... "

"Two hundred per cent," she replied. "No one else comes close."

Just before teatime Annie, Mrs Hettler, brought out the family albums and showed Jez all the embarrassing pictures of the twins growing up. Jez dutifully listened to all of the childhood tales told by both parents. Most of Kurt's tales were those that his girls had related to him in their letters, and he added that Lucy had never lost the letter writing bug.

"We knew all about you long ago, as Lucy writes about you all the time."

Lucy blushed. "Daddy, don't," she pleaded.

[>"Do you?"<] Jez asked.

[>"Yes I do, do you mind?"<]

[>"Of course not,"<] he said and put his arm around her, then kissed her cheek. Across the table, Annie nudged her knee against Kurt's and nodded, and they both smiled.

"Jez still writes to me too, y'know. His letters are much better than mine. He wrote to me all the time he was away, and told me about all the places his ship had been too... ah... " She paused a moment and thought about what she had just said to a Colonel of the Fleet, then added, "but only the places he was allowed to tell me about, that is." Her father said nothing; he knew what went on. He just smiled and winked.

Teatime soon came around, and whilst Lucy and her mum were preparing it, Lucy commented, "We've made enough sandwiches for an army, Mummy," as she arranged them on the plate. Then she asked, "Do you like him, Mummy? Do you like my Jez?"

"He's lovely, but maybe a little shy... perhaps overwhelmed? I'll have words with your father about that later, he's got to stop doing that. He frightens boys off. Hanzii has had no end of trouble, and only on very rare occasions will she bring a boy home." She shook her head in disbelief and tutted, "Silly old fool. Anyway, Jez and I had a very nice walk around the garden," she added as she cut the cake into wedges. "He told me that his mumma would love a garden like this. That she sows seeds and plants cuttings wherever they pitch up, then they move on so they never stay in one place long enough to see them germinate. It could be years before they pitch in the same place again. I got the impression he was a little bit sad for his mumma, as the note of his voice changed," she said as she poured the hot water into the teapot. "He asked about you and what you were like when you were little," Annie said with a smile, "and I asked him about his childhood and his family, but he didn't say much. I did manage though to get the names of his mumma and pop; it's Mae and Rynn. But I got little else."

"I don't know much more than that myself," Lucy said as she filled the milk jug. "He talks in his sleep... "

Her mother gave her a sideways glance.

Lucy blushed when she realised what she had said, and to whom. But her mother just patted her gently on the back of the hand and smiled. "Just be careful, that's all I ask," she said as she took four plates from the dresser. "So what does he say in his sleep?"

"He cries and he whimpers and sometimes he shouts out. He's holding something back Mummy, he's hurting, and he won't say why or what."

"But you love him, don't you?"

"I do."

"Then you will just have to wait. When he's good and ready he'll tell you. Now then, you take that tray and I'll bring these."

They stayed for just an hour after tea was finished before they excused themselves, as they didn't want to miss the bus back to town.

As they made their goodbyes, after the parental hugs and fatherly advice, Jez and Kurt shook hands. Jez's grip was firm and he fixed Kurt with his coal-black eyes and fathomless stare. After a few seconds, he said, "There aren't enough sheep on the whole of Mii'een to match Lucy's worth. If she would have me, I hope it's because she loves me and knows that I love her. *If she would have me, I would hope it was for the love and commitment that I can give her. I would never barter for her, not with you, nor anyone else. It might be the way of some of my people, it might be the way of your people, but it's not the Devii'rahl way and it's certainly not my way, and it never will be!*" He held Kurt in his icy stare and only released their handshake when Kurt nodded.

"Thank you," Kurt said, choking up a little on his words. "That's all a father wants to hear. Thank you."

Jez's newfound canine friends followed them to the garden gate, where the couple stopped, turned and waved before patting and sending the dogs back. Then they set off down the lane to catch their bus.

Annie then turned to her husband and said, "I think you've met your match, don't you?"

"Oh yes, he certainly put me in my place. I couldn't wish her a better man."

37

This is our moment...

"Just one more photo gents," the official snapper announced. "If you could line up either side of the flag. A little bit tighter, come on gents. Right now, hold that. Got it, thanks."

This was their afternoon, the end to their three-year journey; in a couple of hours' time they would be proper officers. They were dressed in their best blues and constantly fussing. Jez hated high collars and kept running his finger between the collar and his neck.

Sam slapped him. "Stop that you twat, it's going to get grubby. You've got to look your best, mate. Here, let's see if I can loosen your collar." Sam fiddled for a few minutes, then asked, "How's that, is it better?"

"Yeah, thanks. Do I look okay?"

"Very smart JD. How about me, will I do?" Sam asked.

"You look great, Sam."

"Okay you lot, fall in," the Parade Master barked. "Smart as you can ladies and gentlemen, this is your moment, the one you have worked for the last three years. Show them what you are made of, and get out there and shine."

They fell in, dressed the line and came smartly to attention. The command was given and as one, they moved off by the left and marched onto the parade ground as OiTs, Officers in Training; the lowest of the low. They would *'fall out'* as fully trained, fully qualified and fully badged officers. This was their day.

[>"This is our moment, Peiite – Miike, we've done it."<]

There were five training squads on parade that afternoon, from all wings of the service. Eighty-seven men and women, a good finishing number, of the hundred that had signed up. The three-year officer apprenticeship was long and arduous, and to lose only thirteen along the way was considered quite an achievement. Today the OiTs would demonstrate their marching prowess to the gathered dignitaries and guests. Marching wasn't something that the Technical Squads did on a regular basis. Parade Ground Practice — or PGP — certainly wasn't top of the list of daily activities for the LSP Project. Sam, JD, Conner and Robbie were not looking forward to the next two hours.

To prepare for this afternoon the boys from the project had been back with the rest of Tech2 for a week's intense PGP refresher, and they'd gone home each evening exhausted, which hadn't gone down too well. But this was what they had been working towards, and was one climax that they had to get right.

So, they marched back and forth across the parade ground, wheeling and countering, dressed in their finest high collars and caps and sweltering whilst their guests enjoyed the cool shade. It was an exceptionally hot day, and there was no place to hide on the parade ground. Eventually though, after what seemed an eternity, they wheeled once more to form up in front of the saluting dais to salute the Admiral of the Fleet, to take the oath and to receive their badges.

The five squads looked mismatched; they were a uniform height within their squads, heights that suited their calling. Techies tended to be a couple of hands short of two metres, tall, and thin; Maintenance and Ground Support were usually about the same, maybe a little taller and perhaps a little broader. The Jaegers, though, well they towered above the rest of the fleet personnel; they were taller and wider, and built like brick-outhouses.

And that's how the five squads lined up on that blisteringly hot summer afternoon; two Technical squads, one from Maintenance, another from

Ground Support, and fifteen men and women from the Jaegers forming the fifth squad.

The Parade Master called them to attention, and once again they dressed the line as the Admiral got to his feet.

"Good afternoon ladies and gentlemen," he said, turning and encompassing everyone in attendance, "and welcome to this very important event in the lives and careers of these," — he swept his arm across the squads — "young officers. But before they take the oath and throw their caps in the air, I have the pleasure of awarding Certificates and Citations to an OiT from each Training Squad, and in one case a perpetual Merit insignia for Outstanding Achievement. These certificates are given to those who have excelled during training, and these Citations go on their Service Records, and their uniforms, and will raise their commission status."

The OiT from Jez's Tech2 was last to be called. "Now then, the acclamation for the most outstanding Officer in Training across the entire intake is awarded to Devii'rahl J."

Jez gulped, this was totally unexpected, and as he mounted the steps, he thought [>"This is for the three of us."<]

"An interesting training record Devii'rahl, two Basics; Technical *and* Jaeger! That's very interesting indeed. I see you excelled at everything academic throughout the whole of your three-year training, but only came to the fore in physical disciplines when you were on your second Basic, JB316." He turned the page. "Ah, that was you, was it?" he said turning, away from the mic. "Well, that probably helped push you to the top. It's a shame we can't make more of it, but if we did we would have to make mention of the other outcome, but we're not going to do that, are we? Nevertheless, you've done more than enough to deserve this honour. Congratulations," he said as pinned the medal to Jez's chest.

Jez then moved down the line of dignitaries. Those in uniform saluted, while the others just shook his hand. The General Commander of the Jaeger Corps did both, and held Jez's hand and smiled whilst he quietly spoke.

"It was my recommendation that you be posted to the Jaeger Corps, though

I didn't think you would make it," he said and smiled as he squeezed his hand. "I admit I thought we would break you," he added, still smiling. "I couldn't have it known that a scrawny shepherd boy from the steppe could better nine of my officers. Even that arsehole Garrard couldn't break you on his own. He wasn't my idea, please understand that." Jez nodded and the General continued, still smiling and squeezing. "But you proved us all wrong, and I underestimated the men and women in the Corps too. Their idea of caring and mine seem poles apart, but I'm so glad I was wrong. We need people like you. You really are outstanding. Keep it up."

As Jez returned to his place in the line the Admiral addressed everyone present. "Ladies and Gentlemen, would you please be upstanding for the Solemn Oath."

"We did it," cried Conner as the new officers turned crisply to their right and tossed their caps skyward. "I'm an officer now, and those oiks will have to call me sir. Well done guys," he said as he shook Sam's and Robbie's hands. "We've made it," he added as he shook Jez's. "I'm off to find Misch, so I'll catch you all later."

[-"I better find…"-] JD thought, but Sam interrupted him.,

"Well done JD," he said. "I was wrong about you, we all were. I fell in with the others and we treated you like dirt, but you were different that's all. Yet, you didn't care what we thought, did you, you just did things in a different way and proved us all wrong in the end. You came out the strongest of all of us. No one should have to do two Basics… they were trying to break you. I caught a bit of what the General said. But you *are* unbreakable. You stayed the course and you proved everybody wrong. I'm proud to be your friend."

"Thanks Sam," Jez whispered as he clutched the medal on his chest. "Thanks. I didn't expect this, not at all, and I don't know what I did that was any different to what you guys did?"

"Are you kidding? I wouldn't have stepped in and stood up to that mob, and you were top of every class. You deserve it, so don't put yourself down.

"Here's your cap mate," said Robbie, who had gathered his own, Sam's, Conner's and JD's, and a couple of others too. "Open your hand mate, let's have a look."

Jez did so, and Robbie reverently rested the simple star in the palm of his hand. "You certainly deserve this. I couldn't have done it. They say it's for academic and physical prowess, but we all know what it's really for. Wear it with pride." Then he asked, "Have you seen Conn?"

Sam pointed across the parade ground and Robbie went to find him to return his cap.

Now that the parade had fallen out and the newly badged officers were milling about and congratulating each other, and guests were venturing onto the hallowed parade ground, Lucy and Cris left their seats to join Sam and JD. They walked as quickly as their heels would allow until Lucy slipped hers off and, with her shoes in one hand and her hat in the other, she sprinted to Jez and arrived just as the official photographer was about to snap.

"Hi Luce," Sam said, chuckling. "Couldn't you wait? Where's Cris? Obviously I don't shine so bright these days. Give it a year JD, and Lucy will walk as well."

"You got a medal, that's fantastic. I'm so proud of you," she said, planting a kiss on his cheek, and leaving a lovely red smudge and frustrating the photographer. "I'm so proud of you," she said again as she wiped his face and smeared the smudge. Then she dabbed her hanky on her tongue and wiped his cheek clean.

"Miss, if you don't mind," the snapper pleaded.

"Will you take one of us," Lucy asked, smiling sweetly.

"Oh miss, I don't know," he said, and shook his head and looked at his watch.

"Please," she persisted, still smiling.

[-"*Oh you lucky man*,"-] he thought, [-"*oh there's so much promise behind that smile.*"-] "Yes okay, but just the one miss, I have a lot to take this afternoon."

"Oh, I'm so proud of you," she said once again as the photographer, having exchanged details, set off in search of another photo.

Jez just shrugged. "Thanks Luce, it's all a bit too much at the moment, and

I've not taken it in yet." He didn't seem to want to talk about it and changed the subject. "Did you enjoy it?"

Lucy nodded but her thoughts gave her away.

"Yeah me too, marching's not for me either. Did you have good seats, did Mumma n' Pop and Claude look after you?"

"Yes, they were lovely," she said, still holding him close, "I love your Mumma."

Jez smiled. "Mumma's lovely, I just knew you would like her," he whispered.

Then Lucy asked, "How the mejj do Mumma n' Pop know Claude? They're so close."

But sensing his parents were near, he just smiled. [>"Later."<] he pulsed and turned to greet them. Claude, although very fit for his age — he was seventy-nine — preferred a slower pace to Lucy's and the three of them had strolled sedately from the seats because of the heat. And because of the heat Mumma n' Pop were glad to have opted to wear the loose and flowing robes of the steppe. Claude, who had been born and had lived most of his life on the AtomSpheres, was a bit more conservative and wore a silk suit with a wide-brimmed hat. The girls, Cristi and Lucy, both wore mid-calf summer dresses, with hats and heels.

Sam exchanged greetings with the Devii'rahls, but he was anxious to meet up with his own guests. He and Cristi were about to go and find them just as Jimi the Skip, Raef Jaxton and Andy Hobbins greeted them and added their congratulations.

"Well done lads," said the Skipper. "Marching in this heat is a right pain and a bit pointless if you're in a technical trade. But you both looked good and you did LSP proud. And you JD, you dark horse, well done you. This must be the Lucy that you are so proud of?"

Jez smiled, and Lucy, who had been looking the other way, turned as Jez introduced the two Captains and Professor Hobbins.

Lucy gasped. "Huh?" [-"That's the face in the dream!"-] Jez felt her start and turned to her, but she shook her head. "Pleased to meet you all," she said. But she *was* puzzled. *[-"Why would that man be in Jez's dream?"-]*

"Are you okay?" he whispered.

"Of course, my shoe caught as I turned, that's all. I shouldn't have taken them off earlier," she said and playfully kissed his ear and tugged the lobe between her teeth. But she *was* puzzled. *[-"Why him?"-]*

"Can I see the citation?" Captain Shallop asked.

"Eh, it's here somewhere Skipper," Jez replied. "Who's got the scroll, Sam?"

"I think Claude has it at the moment."

"Ah, I'll not disturb your guest, though perhaps you could make a copy and we could put it up in the Crew Room. Would that be okay?" JD hesitated. "But only if that's okay with you JD?"

Sam could see his mate wasn't certain, and showing off wasn't his thing. Experience had taught him that Jez'iiah Devii'rahl was a very modest man.

"Can I think about it, Skipper?" Jez asked, then he nodded to her and turned his attention back to Lucy, leaving Sam and Cristi to chat with the LSP Captain.

Jez wrapped his arm about her and kissed her cheek. "I'm so glad you were here, it means so much to me you know."

"Oh sweetheart," she murmured and returned his kiss.

He was about to suggest they move into the shade when Raef Jaxton tapped him on the shoulder. "I'm at a bit of a disadvantage JD. Andy here seems to know everybody in your party. I don't know anyone. Would introduce me to your guests?"

"Oh, I'm sorry sir, of course. This is Lucy." Lucy smiled and Raef nodded politely. "And this is my Mumma - Madam Mae Devii'rahl, and Mumma, this is Captain Raef Jaxton."

"Madam Devii'rahl," Raef said and snapped to attention, then kissed the back of her hand.

[-"Just like Claude,"-] she thought, and smiled. *[-"You can't beat a bit of old fashioned charm."-]*

Jez then turned to his father. "Captain Jaxton, may I present my father Mineer Devii'r..."

But Mae, seeing a group of combat-clad soldiers bearing down on them, with the photographer in tow, turned to her son and said, "It's okay dear, I'll do the necessary, as it looks like you are just about to get busy again." She pointed over his shoulder. "We'll move into the shade, it's a little bit too bright out here for Claude. We'll be over there," she added and nodded in the direction of a free table and smiled. Then she leant forward and kissed him on the forehead. "I'm so very proud of you," she whispered.

"Look at my sweet boy, he looks so tiny amongst those hulks," Mae exclaimed as he lined up for a photo with the group of Jaegers. "Even the women are taller than him!"

"I'm taller than him too," said Lucy.

Mae turned to her and smiled. "Yes, but so pretty." Lucy blushed and Mae winked, then turned back and said, "Those girls out there are fearsome. I'm assuming they're girls, they seem to have the right bumps, but... well? Have you any idea what their connection is to our boy?"

"Eh no, I don't," Lucy replied.

Raef Jaxton, who had stayed with them when they moved to the shade, overheard Mae's question. "Crew from Laximus IV perhaps, the assault craft he was on," he offered, but he wasn't sure. "Don't quote me on that though."

"Those Jaeger girls are huge, and Jez, well he isn't. He's..." Lucy then paused as she thought fondly of his stature, whilst Mae commented.

"They'd make an awesome date. You'd certainly know if you'd spent a night with those girls," she said and roared with laughter, and Lucy laughed with her. Mae's sonorous tones were infectious and Rynn, always loving her laugh, looked across to see what it was all about. But Mae just waved him off as she dabbed her eyes and took a deep breath.

"Aaaand, calm," she said, sighing, but when Lucy looked at her and giggled, Mae lost it and burst out again and the two of them laughed together, comfortable in each other's company.

When they had calmed down and were once again sitting prim and proper, Lucy gathered her thoughts together and decided to ask something that had been puzzling her since she had first met Mumma n' Pop a few days ago. But although she was comfortable in Mae's company she wasn't really certain if she should ask at all. "Mae...?"

Mae had felt her thoughts. "It's alright my dear, don't be afraid."

"But?"

"It's okay," she said, squeezing her hand. She had sensed when they'd met the other day that Lucy was surprised, even though life on the steppe had worn her down, at how youthful she and Rynn were. "I'm thirty-eight, going on thirty-nine, or perhaps I'm thirty-nine going on forty. I've never been that sure because we have a funny way of recording things on Mii'een. I was fifteen and Rynn was fifteen and a half when we were 'handfast'. My birth-day falls in the spring. The first of our boys were born the following winter."

"So young!" [-"Boys?"-] "My father must be twenty years older than Pop. My Mum..." [-"Jez has brothers!?"-]

"We were both adults, Lucy, and we had been an 'item', so there was an understanding between our families," — Mae wagged her index fingers — "for a couple of years. We waited until I was fifteen, the year the children of our people step from childhood to adulthood, and we were in love..." — she looked up at her man, who had turned briefly from his conversation, and they shared a nod — then she added, "and we still are. But... " and she gave a mischievous wink, "... when we could, we did."

"Oh, Mumma!" Mae chuckled at Lucy's shocked face and shook her head.

Then Rynn leant over, kissed his wife on the cheek, and said, "Claude's going to take his leave now... it's the heat."

"Oh, of course, you must be finding it too much my darling," Mae said as she stood and moved around the table. "Have you enjoyed it?"

"It was just perfect my dear. Didn't he do you proud?" Then he reached out and Mae stepped between his arms. Behind him, Rynn smiled as Claude kissed Mae on the forehead. "Stay out as long as you want," he said, "you have your key and Mathers will be on call should there be anything extra you require." Claude took Lucy's hand in his. "It's been a pleasure meeting you, my dear. Tell that young man of yours to bring you to see me soon. Tell him not to leave it too long, I'm not getting any younger y'know," he added and winked. Then Claude and Rynn strolled arm in arm to the waiting car, with the ever-patient Mathers in tow.

Mae looked on fondly and waved as car drove away. "Isn't he lovely," she said, "and so kind and thoughtful. We met Claude on our holiday," she said, "and we've been friends ever since."

Jez wanted to mix and catch up with old friends. He excused himself, and knowing that Lucy was enjoying his mumma's company, he set off across the parade ground to mingle. Everybody wanted to say 'Hi', to shake his hand and to see his medal or get a selfie. Mae and Lucy, watching from their shaded table, discussed his movements, laughing every time he thought he had seen everyone and was free to return, only to be grabbed by someone else.

Rynn was mingling too, being introduced by Raef and Andy, who also seemed to know everybody. He had called back after seeing Claude on his way, and asked Lucy and Mae if they would like to join them too, only for Mae to guffaw, "In this heat, are you having a giraffe?"

Rynn smiled, kissed her on the top of her head and went off with the others. "We're going to see if we can catch up with our boy," he called back over his shoulder.

"Jez is going to be so worn out by the time the day is over," Lucy groaned. [-"He'll be too tired. I had it all planned, too. Candles, soft music. That lovely silk nighty,"-] and Mae smiled at Lucy's disappointment.

"You must cover your thoughts, dear Lucy."

"Oh no, what must you think of me, oh no. Jez taught me how to shield, but the occasion has been overwhelming and I forgot. It's not second nature yet. What must you think of me?"

"I think you're lovely, that's what I think of you," said Mae, reassuring her.

They sipped their drinks and watched the *toing and froing* out on the square, then Mae ordered them both an Atom Cocktail. "I bought myself one of these on our holiday," she said, "whilst I was watching Rynn and the boys on their boards. These cocktails were so decadently expensive back then, but it was my holiday treat to myself. Claude bumped into the back of my chair and I spilt my drink, but he was such a gentleman. He ordered another Atom cocktail without a second thought, despite my protestations. Then he bought one for himself, turned his chair so we could chat, and we've been chatting friends ever since." She smiled and sipped.

A few more moments passed, then...

"Mae, sorry, I mean Mumma, I saw you, nearly a year ago with Prof Beske'haht outside his rooms at Uni. Professor Hobbins was there too."

"That's right! Gosh, you do have a good memory. And if *my* memory serves me right, I recall it was the briefest of encounters, and we didn't actually speak, did we? Yes, we were with Andy, we met him on that holiday too. Tomasz's parents are friends of my parents. Fancy you remembering that?"

"I remembered your lovely smile. Your whole face lights up."

"Oh, thank you," Mae said, and she took Lucy's hand in hers and rested it on her lap, "you're so sweet."

But then Lucy shocked Mae when she said, "I saw Andy's face in a dream."

"Really?"

"Oh no, not my dream. No," Lucy said, blushing. "It was Jez's dream. *I wasn't* dreaming about Professor Hobbins, it was Jez. Our thoughts were open you see, we'd just... Oh no, there I go again. I'm giving a terrible impression of myself. What must you think of me?"

"Don't be silly," Mae said, putting her arm around her shoulder, "I think nothing of the sort. Why don't you tell me about this dream you shared?"

"Oh, okay. Erm, are you sure, it's... well, you know, and you're his mumma and all..." Mae said nothing, just smiled. "We were in the attic apartment that Cristi and I share, in my bed. It's a bit of a squeeze. Jez was fitful and his dream was everywhere... it filled the room. I wasn't certain if I was awake or dreaming when suddenly the professor's face was there pleading at me, shouting at me, and there were other voices too, younger voices calling out 'Tomii', 'Tomii', and I jumped out of bed. The bedclothes were scattered about my tiny room and Jez was curled up and crying. Why does he cry in his sleep Mumma? Who is Tomii, and why was Andy there too?"

Mae frowned. "So he still talks in his sleep then?"

THIS IS OUR MOMENT...

"Yes... "

She looked at Lucy, hoping more was forthcoming, but that was it. "I'm afraid that's something only your Jez knows the answer to. Rynn and I, even Jixa-Vo and Meeko, have tried, but he just clams up. It's something buried deep... we think we know what it is, but we just don't have the key to unlock it for him. He must do that himself. But at least he's sharing with you, albeit whimpers and screams, though that fills me with hope. He's not alone anymore." Mae didn't dwell on it though and quickly changed the subject, asking, "Shall we walk around the camp? I believe we have leave to do that today. Shall we?"

As they strolled, they chatted, wandering aimlessly between the huts, neither of them taking any notice of what was in front of them or behind or where they were going. They were just sauntering about, happy in each other's company. As they stepped from between a couple of huts they were confronted by the sergeant of the 'fearsome five', the group that had made them laugh earlier in the afternoon.

Mae seized the moment. She offered her hand and said, "Hello, I'm JD's Mumma."

"I'm sure you don't call him JD at home ma'am," he said, flashing a smile that lightened the moment, and before Mae could ask where he fitted into all this, he said, "Your boy saved my life. But I don't think he did what he did just because I was on the floor and defenceless. Those animals that set on me had poured coffee over the Memorial Stone and names of people special to him, and special to you too, I think. I didn't see what he did, I was only told later. They said he was a man possessed, and that he moved like smoke. I will be eternally grateful to those names, because if he hadn't been so incensed at that moment, at best I'd be a cripple. I don't like to think of the other possibility." Then the sergeant snapped smartly to attention, saluted and marched away."

"Golly!" they said together, and as he strode away from them, he brushed something from his face. Mae even thought she heard him sniff.

38

Dove-tailed perfectly ...

Over the following weeks, life got back to normal. Mae and Rynn stayed on a few more days with Claude, then took the shuttle back to Mii'een, and onto the Drove School where they taught. Claude shut up his town apartment and moved back to his country estate.

Jez was promoted to Tech-Lead of the Installation Team, and he and Raef Jaxton spent many hours planning how they would install the prototype LSP Power Generators to a previously decommissioned cargo carrier. Lucy was invited to join a team of Beadles' lawyers, who were going to the green planet of Mii'een to finalise the Supply Chain contract. The timing for this trip dove-tailed perfectly into Jez and Lucy's calendar because they would both be away at the same time, which meant neither would be at a loose end. And Sam, now an officer with a promising career, proposed to Cristi, who accepted without a moment's hesitation, after which the couple spent a very pleasant week at her parents.

39

And a lot of Claudias too...

Cristi's parents, Bob and Marcia Derrent, were thrilled with the news and the Derrents spent the whole week showing off their prospective son-in-law. It wasn't all family visits and friends for dinner though. They did take Sam and Cristi out for one day to the tourist sites on the little island where they lived, but only those that were on the way to the golf club and/or Marcia's Ladies Club. In fact, they went anywhere her mother thought there would be someone she knew in order to show-off her handsome soon to be son-in-law and Cristi's sparkly engagement ring. By the end of the week, however, even Marcia had to admit she was all *show-offed* out, and was more than happy to spend a quiet night in.

After dinner, they took their drinks out onto the terrace and relaxed at the end of their hectic week. It was a balmy evening filled with the songs of nocturnal insects.

"Tssszzzz," hissed Cristi.

"What was that?" asked Sam.

"That's the sound of the setting sun," said Marcia.

"Huh?"

"As it slips below the waves," Bob chimed in. "Look, do you see? It looks like the sea is bubbling, but it's just blowing up a bit out there. It always does just beyond the point. The girls used to say the water was boiling. How did it go, Cris?"

"Tssszzzz," she hissed again.

Then Bob raised his glass. "Farewell sun, see you tomorrow. To the setting sun," he said, toasting, "we look forward to your rise." Then, still with his glass raised, he turned to Cristi and Sam. "And to you two, too, congratulations on your engagement. May you have a long and happy marriage, just like us."

"Cristi and Sam," said Marcia.

"Cristi and Sam," repeated Bob as he leant forward to shake Sam's hand and kiss his daughter. "Welcome to the family, Sam."

Bob brought out the cigars, offered the open box to Sam, who declined. Bob nodded. "Very wise Sam," he said.

Then Marcia said, "I don't like smoking either, but I do enjoy the smell of cigar smoke on an evening like this. I don't know, it just seems to round things off. My father smoked cigars, so I suppose it reminds me of him."

Sam stared at the glowing ball as it slipped into the sea. "Tssszzzz," he gently whistled. "I'll always think of sunset like that now," he whispered and Cristi leant across and kissed his cheek.

"Tssszzzz," she hissed into his ear.

Bob and Marcia smiled.

The last rays of the sun streamed over the horizon. "I love this moment," said Marcia, "I love the way the light throws the moon rise into a silhouette for just the briefest of moments before they rise in their own reflective glory. And then there's always that extra flash. There look, that twinkle. We never did find out what it was, did we?" she asked her husband.

"That's the Star-Link Hub, Mrs Derrent," Sam said, "it's the Fleet base for this sector. I hope that one day I'll have a command that's moored there. From next week our team, me included, will be up there for a month fitting a prototype propulsion unit."

"Is that the same Star-Link that the sphere vanished from?" Bob Derrent asked.

"Yes, sir, it is. There's a Memorial Stone near where the sphere was attached."

"Sam and his Tech2 intake, built the Memorial plaza, didn't you?"

"Yes sir, we did," he said and nodded and smiled to Cristi.

"That was a terrible business," said Marcia. "The Bleakdales, friends of ours at the golf club, were in Spher'rios when it disappeared."

"I didn't know that Mummy, I just thought they had moved away."

"No dear," Marcia said, wiping away a tear. "And then there was Mickey... Mickey, uh, who was it? You know Bob, the lad who worked at the tackle shop on the bay."

"Mickey Ribertz, Marci. He had just landed himself a job on the Atom-Spheres in the Aquapark, on the new sphere — Spher'rios. He was so excited, I remember his dad, Seb, driving him to the shuttle. So full of hope. Seb couldn't cope, said he drove his son to his death. Took his boat out into the bay and never came back! It was a terrible time."

"But no one talks about it, Daddy."

"You're right, no one does."

"Sam showed us a magazine, that had the whole story, everything right down to the tiniest detail, yet both Lucy and I knew nothing about it. You've never talked about it and Lucy's parents don't either. I've even searched the records at the museum and there's very little about it," said Cristi.

"It was too big you see," said Bob, "and it happened so fast. One second there, the next second gone," he added as he snapped his fingers. "Disintegrated without a trace."

"What was the name of that man who was always on the TV and in the newspapers, you know, the Praes~Eedan executive?" Marcia asked as she set down her glass. "He worked tirelessly to see that everyone was looked after. Wasn't it Atkins or something like that?"

"Claude Atkins. The man's a legend," said Bob.

Sam and Cristi spoke together, "JD's family know a Claude Atkins."

"I doubt it's the same one," said Marcia, "there must be thousands of Claude Atkins. I doubt shepherds from Mii'een know *the* Claude Atkins?" She chuckled at the thought.

"It's not a common name though is it? Hold on, have you got a picture of him, Sam," Cristi asked as her mother asked if they would like their drinks topped up.

"Maybe not that common amongst our age range," Marcia admitted, "but there's an awful lot of ten-year-old boys called Claude," she added as she poured the wine.

"And a lot of Claudias too," Bob added.

"Here you go Bob, is that him?" Sam asked.

"Crikey!" gasped Cristi's dad, "that's him alright. That's *the* Claude Atkins. Take a look Marci, seems that shepherds can know very influential people."

"Well, what can I say? Please accept my apologies you two. Who'd have thought?" she said. "Hadn't he just retired or something?"

Bob nodded. "I think you're right. I'm sure I read somewhere that he'd been ousted from the board, got outvoted, as they were trying to push through a new initiative, and he was outmanoeuvred. It was that very afternoon, and all the people driving this new plan were on Spher'rios when it vanished. Atkins was the only one left with an air of authority, so he took back the reins and got organising. He started by getting everybody off in a controlled evacuation. I think it was reported there were just shy of a million people on the Atom at that time. It took them a week to get everybody off. The bereaved relatives, of course, were given priority and allotted the superfast shuttles. Then over the next year, Atkins set about dismantling the AtomSpheres. But nothing went to waste, hence your Star-Link Hub."

"Were the other bits scrapped Daddy?"

"No, oh no, heaven forbid. Praes~Eedan and Claude Atkins are in it for the money. He might be a philanthropist and a sponsor of good causes, but he also knows how to turn a quick buck. No, the spheres are still up there in orbit, they're just separate units now."

"Did you say that this JD and your Lucy are an item now, Cris?" her mother interjected. She thought they had dwelt a little too long on the subject of the Atom. After all, she had lost some very good friends and didn't want to think about it. But her change of tack didn't quite work out as she had hoped.

"Yes, they've been getting close for over a year now, well longer than that really. It started as part of her college assignment, which led to them meeting for coffee. But they only really got it together on that walking weekend Lucy organized, you know, that weekend I told you about last time I was here. One thing led to another and Bob's your uncle, but not Dad Bob if you know what I mean. It was all a bit of a ploy by Lucy, and they ended up spending the night out together under the stars. It was very romantic Mummy... "

"Except when he threw her out of bed!" Sam added.

"He did what?!" Marcia gasped.

"He was having one of his nightmares... he has lots of them. Lucy says he talks in his sleep and sometimes shouts and cries. What do you think that is, Daddy?"

"It sounds to me like he has something buried deep in his psyche. Has he had a shock, do you know?" Bob Derrent asked, putting on his professional psychiatrist head. "It could be PTSD; you guys call it Battlefield Fatigue. It could be something like that. Does he talk about it?"

"No, and we weren't very sympathetic on Basic either. He used to whimper in his sleep and wake everybody up and we would rag him about it. I remember we even threw water over him once to shut him up after a long hard day. Yet he just shrugged it off and got on with it. We were bast — we weren't very nice Mrs Derrent," he quickly corrected.

"He only ever talks to Lucy. They share thoughts at night you see, and that's why she hears all his hidden pain."

"Can we change the subject, sweet pea? I don't think I want to hear about their bedtime activities!" Marcia said. She was sympathetic, she liked Lucy a lot, but this was Cristi's week and she wanted to know more about Sam and his family.

"Okay dear, professional head is off and relaxing head back on. Sorry Marci," he said and touched his hand to his lips and blew her a kiss that was reciprocated.

"Mae said they met Claude when they were on holiday."

"What's that, Sam?" Cristi asked

"Oh no. I'm sorry Mrs Derrent, I'm sorry, you wanted to let the subject lie. Forget I said it. Leave it, Cris." Sam felt a little awkward.

But Cristi picked up the thread, much to her mother's displeasure. "Yes, that's right. Mae, that's JD's mumma, well I remember her saying that when we were sitting watching you lot marching up and down. They met Mr Atkins on the AtomSpheres."

"JD has only ever had one holiday," said Sam, "and that was on the AtomSpheres. There was a big party of them. He told me once that there were five or six in the family, the larger family, who all had their fifteenth birthday in the same year. And that they had somehow managed to find the money to go to the AtomSpheres to celebrate all the birthdays. There are the names of an aunt, an uncle and a cousin of JD's on the Memorial Stone, and two brothers as well."

"JD's brothers?" Cristi asked.

Sam just shrugged.

"Fifteen is an important age for the people of the Mii'een culture, the step from childhood to adulthood, the rite of passage for both boys and girls. You said they were shepherds, so is this JD from the Nomad tribes?" Bob asked.

"Yes he is, Bob. Is there some significance?"

But Marcia interrupted before Bob could expand on his question. "The poor lad!" she exclaimed.

"Huh?" Cristi was taken aback by her mother's change of tune. "You've changed suddenly, Mummy? A few moments ago, you swept JD and Lucy under the carpet, so what's changed?

"I'm not a heartless woman sweet pea, it's just that I'm excited for you and Sam that's all. This is your week and I've put everything on hold so I can share your fantastic news with you and find out what's going on in your lives. But when I hear about someone having that happen on their once-in-a-lifetime holiday, well I can't help but feel sorry for them. The AtomSpheres disaster was truly horrendous, it was one of the saddest events I've ever had the misfortune to witness. That's right, isn't it Bob? We lost neighbours and close friends and we lived through their heartbreak. If he lost close family members in that disaster, then I'm not surprised there's something hidden deep inside. Are you Bob? It all makes sense to me." Bob nodded in agreement.

Sam then followed up with something he'd heard from one of the Jags who was on JD's Jaeger Basic. "You asked if they were JD's brothers Cris. Well a Jag told me that JD's brothers died in an accident, though he never said where the accident occurred. Up 'till then I didn't even know he had brothers. But now, tying two and two together, it's very probable these brothers *were* lost in that sphere. They could well be the two Devii'rahls, the brothers named on the stone. No wonder he doesn't talk about it, and if they were his brothers then it certainly explains what was driving him when he stepped into the thick of that fight. Was it the names of his brothers that those bastards poured coffee over?" This time he didn't pull his words.

"Wait a minute, did you say, Jaeger? Jaegers are dangerous people!" Marcia exclaimed to no one in particular. "And you just said he can get violent. Is Lucy safe to be with him?"

"Oh, Mummy, he didn't get violent, he's a gentle gentleman. He just thrashed out in his sleep. I've never seen him fired up like when Sam saw him. I'm sure there were reasons, didn't Sam just say."

"But you said he threw her out of bed. Nobody knows what they're doing when they're asleep." Marcia was concerned now. "Just tell your Lucy to be careful, that's all."

Bob moved in quick and changed the subject, "I think you need to do a bit more digging Cris. Try using a different approach... look under the name of Atkins and see where that gets you. There must be some footage somewhere. Anywhere the public goes, if it's recorded, then by law it must be on record for a number of years, just in case there's a litigation case as there would have been for the AtomSpheres disaster. There's a little project for you, just keep looking and report back. We would both be interested, wouldn't we Marci?"

"Yes, we would sweet pea."

"I wish she wouldn't keep calling me sweet pea," Cristi said to Sam as they kissed good night outside Cristi's bedroom. This week they were playing by Bob and Marcia's rules; no sex before marriage, and separate rooms until they were an official couple. But it didn't stop them having a quick knee-trembler in the bathroom.

40

Not as farfetched as you might think ...

Cristi checked her watch, again. It was two minutes closer to home time than it was two minutes ago. To fill her time she marshalled her pens and restacked her paperwork, ready for picking up again tomorrow. Then she checked her watch; one minute closer to home time.

In three minutes she would pick up her bag and walk to the coat stand, unhook her coat and scarf and walk quickly past Jennie's office, just as Jennie was unhooking her coat and scarf. Together they would walk through the museum and out through the main doors, nodding to Danny in reception. At the top of the steps, they would idly chat whilst they looked — Jennie standing on the right looking to the left and Cristi on the left looking to the right — in the directions their buses would come from. Same as yesterday, same as the day before, and probably the same as tomorrow. Then they would see their buses, give each other a quick peck on the cheek and go their separate ways.

Except tonight. Just like last night and every night for the next three weeks, Cristi had no one to go home to. Lucy was on Mii'een, the green planet, with the Beadles' lawyers, Sam and JD were up on the Star-Link Hub installing their two propulsion units, and there wasn't anything worth watching on the box. And whilst she sat there thinking about what did or didn't lie in store for her tonight, the time ticked past home time and Jennie was halfway down the hallway before she realised Cristi wasn't with her.

"Cris, are you going home tonight?" Jennie called from the doorway.

"Oh sugar, sorry Jen." Cristi was in a world of her own. "I'm coming now," she called as she gathered her belongings and skipped down the hallway. "Eh, Jen, would you mind if I came in on Saturday and maybe stayed later during the week?"

"Eh... what?"

"It's only that Sam and Lucy are away, so I've no real need to rush home, and I want to do a bit of research. Would it be okay?"

"What sort of research?" Jennie asked as they passed Danny at his desk and went through the main doors.

"I want to find out all I can about the AtomSpheres disaster. Lucy's boyfriend, Jez, has nightmares, and we think it might be connected to the AtomSpheres. He lost family members and I was hoping to be able to find out something, anything that might help Lucy understand what's going on inside his head. He cries in his sleep. Could I do a bit of research? In my own time of course."

"I don't see why not, but let's have a chat about it tomorrow. I've got to dash now, there's my bus. Tomorrow, when we have coffee, ask me about it then. See you tomorrow," she said and was halfway down the steps when she turned, ran back up, kissed Cristi on the cheek then sped off to the bus stop."

"So Cris, what were you saying yesterday about the AtomSpheres? Did you say something about staying after hours and coming in at the weekend?"

"Yes, would that be alright?"

"I don't see why not. I've no objection. But why don't you do a bit now, while we're slack? I'd rather that than have you wandering about after hours, not certain where you should be and security finding you, a gibbering wreck at three in the morning because you took a load of wrong turnings. Because I know you, you'll get lost or find something obscure and forget the time. So, start your searching now, and if I can help I will. Then if you need to know more, why not go to the library at the weekend, or once you have some leads use the PC at home? You don't want to be in here late at night... or do you?"

"Not really."

"Then start now. But before you go looking down blind alleys, there are a couple of places where I know you won't find anything. I know, because I've looked in the past, occasionally out of curiosity and once or twice for people who wrote in with questions. The obvious one to avoid is the 'AtomSpheres'. You won't get a lot following that lead. The other is 'Atkins', that's another avenue that's closed, but your dad's right about recordings made of people having to be kept on file for so many years. If I were you I would look for relevant videos by typing in the names of the people that disappeared. That might be the quickest route."

"Just random names? That would take forever."

"Use your head, Cris. Think. How did people get onto Spher'rios? They went down the Star-Link, that's how. So, look for the video files of people moving back and forth along the Star-Link on the day it went missing."

"Yeah, I get that Jen," said Cristi, "but unless their names are pinned to their chest how will I know who they are?"

"Well, we have a record of the names of everybody that was on Spher'rios at the time it disappeared, because we have the transcript of all the names on the Memorial Stone, don't we?"

"Of course, we do. Of course. Oh, I could... " Then Cristi leant across to hug Jennie.

Jennie said, "But your idea about notes pinned to chests is not as farfetched as you might think. Every visitor carried a token that had all their details, and every time they went through a sensor loop all their details were recorded. That's how we can be certain about who was actually on the sphere when it disappeared. It's the way that Praes~Eedan gathered all of their statistics. So if you can get the right video file then you might be able to pinpoint Lucy's boyfriend and the reason why he cries out at night."

"Oh Jennie, you're so clever."

Cristi settled down in front of her screen and scrolled through the files that Jennie had suggested. "Right then," she said as she intertwined her fingers and bent them back until they cracked. "Let's see what we can find out."

It didn't take her very long at all to find the video footage for the Star-Link for the day that Spher'rios disappeared, and of course the time was precisely documented, so she typed in Jez's full name. 'Jeziiah Devii'rahl.' Then she hit ENTER, and sat back and waited and waited. Nothing!

"That's weird," she muttered as she picked up her notes and read through them. "His name is Jeziiah, Jez, JD for short. Okay, so what about J Devii'rahl?" She punched that in, hit ENTER and waited. Still nothing. "Devii'rahl J: Nothing." Cristi was puzzled. "Oh? Okay, let's just try Rahl."

This time when she hit ENTER a whole host of entries popped up on the screen, but there was no J Devii'rahl. There was a P, an M and a T Devii'rahl in one group. An M, and an R Devii'rahl in another, and a Y, a Z and a J Beske'rahl, but no J Devii'rahl. "Perhaps he wasn't there, perhaps these dreams have nothing to do with the AtomSpheres. Maybe the P, Ms, R and Ts were the ones that went, and Jez is the one who stayed behind to tend the flocks. Maybe he's suffering from guilt because he wasn't there and wished he had been... wished that he was the one that went and not the others."

The footage continued to roll on as she pondered these theories, when something caught her eye: Three boarders sped past the camera, and disappeared through the gateway into the entrance hall of Spher'rios just as the power seemed to fail. The screen blacked out for a few moments, and when it came back on, one of the boarders sped back the way they had just come, passing two men in coveralls who shouted something which Cristi thought wasn't too polite. Then that video stopped, so she ran another search for the next time slot. Whilst she did that she scanned through the *five thousand eight hundred and six* names on the other screen.

[-"Oh, there's only P and M Devii'rahl amongst the missing."-] She thought for a moment, then pulled up the list for a few minutes before the sphere disappeared, and this time there were P, M and T Devii'rahls. [-"Is that solo boarder T Devii'rahl? Perhaps I can narrow it down... Is he recorded further up the Star-Link conduit?"-]

She needed a location number, so she opened up the 3D model for the Star-Link conduits and traced the one she wanted as it spiralled back towards Nucleo.

"There, what's that location ref? ST-395467124. Okay," she said to herself, and she keyed that in. After an hour she found a video and statistics for ST-395467124, and T Devii'rahl showed three times in less than five minutes. *[-"Right then, that accounts for T Devii'rahl."-]* she thought, then she whispered, "And does he have a full name? Yep, there it is – Tomii? Tomii? Didn't Lucy say that he shouts out Tomii in his sleep?"

Cristi then managed to track this Tomii from location ST-395467124 into Spher'rios, then back up past the sensor, then back to within a meter of the closed emergency doors. "Wow!"

So she went back to the cameras that were focused on the doorway. Fortunately they were set back about ten meters so Cristi was able to see Tomii talking to the two men in coveralls. She heard him ask, *"Excuse me, sir, my brothers wondered if you can you tell us how long the doors will be closed?"*

This Tomii character, who was holding a hoverboard and wearing long shorts and a stripy, ethnic coat, and who had been looking intently through the transparent door at the other two boys, then trotted up to the men in coveralls.

One of the men in coveralls replied, *"Don't know, nipper. Doubt it'll be long though."*

Then the whole doorway turned the brightest neon pink that Cristi had ever seen, so bright and so vivid that it hurt her eyes. Then the voices were drowned out by a high-pitched hiss as the boy started running away from the doorway. But he wasn't getting anywhere, and that's where the video finished.

"His coat! That's...!" But that's where the video suddenly stopped. "Of course, it's the coat in the magazine. Did that video show his face?" She had been concentrating so much on the coat that she wasn't sure if she had seen the boy's face, so she played the video again. But the man in the coveralls blocked him out every time. The workman's voice sounded familiar, though the boy's voice was squeaky, as if it were just breaking. But she was certain she had heard the older voice somewhere recently, but couldn't think where.

[-"This gets spookier by the minute,"-] Cristi thought, "And that coat is just like the one Jez gave to Lucy. I wonder if I can get a clearer view of it?" And that's just what she was doing when Jennie brought her afternoon tea and

biscuits and asked how she was getting on.

"It's this coat," she said and showed Jennie. "Lucy has a coat just like it. Yeah, I know there must be thousands, but you have to admit there are some pretty remarkable coincidences; the coat; the Devii'rahls; Tomii. Or they could *just* be coincidences. But I'm going to try and get a better picture before I finish tonight."

"So what are you going to do tomorrow, or even this evening?"

"Huh?" Cristi was puzzled by Jennie's question.

"Well, you seem to have your conclusion and there's still a couple of hours until home time, and you've found out all of this on your first day of research. So, what will you be doing this evening with no one to talk to?"

"Oh yes, I see what you mean. I don't know."

"Would you like to join me and Ed for dinner? Then we'll drop you home afterwards, and perhaps you can entertain us sometime next week. Shall I get Ed to set a table for three?"

"That would be lovely Jen, yes please, I would love to join you. Yes, I'll cook something for you guys next week. It's a deal. Thank you."

41

It's only a hard hat area ...

"Okay, listen up," Jimi the Skip called above the hubbub of chatter to bring her crew to order. "I'll be blunt with you, guys, the brass still don't consider LSP a worthy cause. But you knew that, didn't you?" A sea of nodding faces gave her the answer she was expecting. "Therefore, it won't surprise you at all when I tell you that they've only granted us a month to get our job done."

A chorus of disbelief followed, with rumbles of 'Geezes,' 'for fff sakes' and 'shit really?' rippling through the team.

"That's right, just one month. Got any ideas why? Go on, have a guess," she said and pulled back and stared at the blank faces. "No, I didn't think you would. We have to clear up and clear out for a minor service on a twenty-seater shuttle."

"What the...!"

"Exactly, my thoughts too," she replied, shrugging. "But that's how it is I'm afraid."

"Geeze, boss, that hangar's huge. You could fit a dozen twenty-seaters in one corner and put our job diagonally opposite, and there would still be enough room in between for a couple of Star Class Frigates."

"I know, I know. But it seems an oil change and screen wash are worth disrupting our insignificant install project for. Apparently, it's more important. So we have to prove these doubters wrong. We must show them that LSP does have a place in the Void Fleet, and that it's the way forward," she added and shook her head, still smiling. "Anyway, that's enough from me, over to you Raef. I'll leave it to you and JD to sort out the shift rosters, whilst I'll have another jab at getting us more time." She turned and faced the team. "I know you guys always do your best, but this build is going to need more than that. It's going to be a tough month of twenty-four-hour working, twelve on six off. But we can do it." Then she handed over to Jaxton. "All yours Raef, JD."

Raef Jaxton stepped forward. "Like the Skip says, that's the situation. There's no point us mithering about it. Just be prepared to hit the deck running, because every minute we stand around muttering is a minute less on the build."

JD gave everyone a roster sheet that detailed the teams they would be in.

Then Jaxton said, "We dock in just over an hour, so leave your personal kit here and get straight to work unloading the equipment. That's how tight time is. We have to get everything in place before they suck out the hangar and bring in the *old tub*."

It was an old tub too, at least seventy years old, and had been moth-balled for the last twenty. It seemed that as far as the General Staff were concerned the Void Fleet worked, so why try to improve something that didn't need improving? *'Why waste money and time on untried technology?'* Which is exactly why the only craft on offer to Shallop and Hobbins for their prototype generators was an ancient ore carrier that had been bobbing around in the junk pound for the last twenty years. So old in fact, that none of the modern mountings fitted and the LSP engineers had had to put a lot of effort into getting parts specially made, which was something else the brass weren't happy about.

"Right then, we've got just a little under an hour before we dock, so to fill in, Andy is going to give you a little background refresher regarding the physics behind Linear Spheric Propulsion or LSP, and how it all came about in the first place. Over to you mate."

"Thanks, Raef. Hi guys. So, this month lark is a joke, isn't it? But don't worry, the Skipper is working on it. So then, LSP. Are you familiar with the real explanation of the AtomSpheres disaster? I know you are JD." Jez nodded then slipped out into the cargo space. "Is there anybody else?" But no one was prepared to offer their understanding and possibly make a fool of themselves.

"Okay, never mind, it doesn't matter. Right then, LSP, or Linear Spheric Propulsion, literally means, all the balls lined up. And it was a line of balls, huge balls, spheres, that fuelled the AtomSpheres disaster. A line shouldn't have been possible. The AtomSpheres was supposed to resemble a textbook atom, you know, it's the diagram that they stamp onto nuclear devices." There was a lot of nodding. "Good, you get the idea. One ball with a lot of smaller balls orbiting. The AtomSpheres started as a nucleus — Nucleo, with an encircling hoop — Taurus, onto which was attached a second sphere —Dominion. And before you ask, I don't know why it was called Dominion, that's one of those mysteries that's lost in time I'm afraid. Anyway, it started as two balls or spheres, and a hoop, which eventually grew to become one central sphere, three hoops and six orbiting spheres."

"Then the planners went berserk and filled all the spaces between the hoops with floating hotels, conference centres, night clubs and advertising spheres, and then, for good measure, they bolted on the Star-Link with another sphere on its end. That was Spher'rios, the newest and most technologically advanced piece of space hardware at that moment in time."

"But it was those innocent little free-floating AdSpheres that were to cause the problem. Why? Because they had random orbits. Random and scheduled doesn't work, does it?" There came a ripple of murmured agreement whilst Andy thought of his next move, and he glanced at the doorway to the cargo bay.

"Hmm?" He returned to his explanation. "At LSP we project a power source over and along a series of spheres which we move in and out of line or stretch/close-up the line to increase or decrease the power output. We know to within a gnat's when it's in drive or when it's out. But on the AtomSpheres we kept getting power surges and power outages and we couldn't fathom why. And don't forget, those balls were much, much bigger. Jimi the Skip was there, she was the Chief Engineers assistant. I was there too on a year's placement with the Peripheral Maintenance Teams, for one awesome year I was one of the legendary Skin-Skippers bouncing around on the outer surfaces of the spheres, and it was a fantastic job. But that's another story."

"I was actually in the Star-Link conduit, I'd say roughly where the Memorial is now, and I witnessed the power surge in action as the spheres lined up. I saw the knife-edge cut through the tubes and set Spher'rios adrift, and that would have been okay if we could have pulled it back and anchored it. Spher'rios sat there for about fifteen seconds, then *poof* and it was gone and the whole area was a mass of scattered debris. They said it was the disintegrated sphere! Not that I had much time to look at it, as I was doing my best to save my team-lead and myself and... "

"See. Told you," said Renton, an LSP Tech-Fitter, to a mate over his shoulder, "the whole 'boy on the rope' thing is just a bit of dramatic hype. The Prof was there."

"It's not dramatic hype Ren, the boy was there and yes, so was I. It's my hand you see in all the pictures."

Renton's mate put his hand over the shoulder and said, "That's five you owe me, Ren."

"The boy was a boarder with a rope around his ankle, so I grabbed that ankle rope, *the* rope. If I hadn't, then he would have been sucked into oblivion. We found out later that the debris was all that was left of an AdSphere. But we didn't find that out until much later. I was on my way to Spher'rios. I'd been going over some calculations and had worked out what was going on. I had just been to the Chief Engineer's office hoping to catch Ted Rawlins, that's when I first met Jimi, she told me Rawlins was meeting the other directors in Spher'rios. And that's why I was where I was, as I was hoping to compare notes. Luckily for me, the emergency doors closed, and I couldn't get into Spher'rios. Ted Rawlins and the CEO and a lot of other important Atom people vanished with the sphere. Five-thousand eight-hundred and six to be exact; that's how many people were in Spher'rios at the time it disappeared. Let's not dwell on that though. It's gone and it's not coming back.

"But we, you included, have managed to harness that power source, and with just two units, each the size of a very small car, we can push that *old tub* they have given us at speeds up to Light. If we can do that with these tiny generators just imagine the magnitude that was generated to fire a sphere two klix in diameter beyond the range of the human eye in a nanosecond. That's a distance of the dockyard waterfront to Fleet HQ."

Andy waited as his wide-eyed audience took it all in, and he snatched a few moments to remember his skin-skipper friends who were lost with the sphere.

"Okay then," he said, getting their attention back, "we will be docking soon so you'd better get yourselves ready. Don't forget, we must hit the ground running." As the teams assembled ready for the off, Andy went into the cargo hold to find Jez. "You okay, JD?"

"Yeah, cheers Andy, I'm fine thanks. There are just some things I don't like to listen to. I need to keep a clear head for the install and don't want to be thinking about... *that*, just now."

The build went well. They had planned for it for months, and because the brass had done their best to hamper it, they had come up with some very ingenious thinking to counter those negative thoughts. The actual power generator units *were* tiny, they literally were the size of a small car and a very small car at that. Each unit was just two metres in length and about a metre high. Andy had known that when he put his case to the brass, if they had seen the unit size, they wouldn't have given him cupboard space, let alone the use of a hangar. He had needed an outflanking manoeuver, he needed size and flashing lights: People were always impressed by flashing lights, generals included. So he designed two purpose-built box-housings and into those housings he and the team built the LSP power plants. The housings were each the size of small truck containers. The generators were centrally mounted and there was at least a metre and a half free space all around that gave the fitters plenty of space in which to work. Andy had designed each housing as a self-contained workshop. Which meant they had familiar working space from the word go. It also meant they were able to have all the necessary tooling on hand if any of the couplings, attaching parts, switchgear and the obligatory flashing lights' connections needed a tweak. Planning the build this way they were able get everything in place before they left their base at

Mech-U. So when they got to the Star-Link Hub it would be a simple matter of clamping each boxed unit into position and hooking up the necessary connections. Andy also hoped that any sudden unexpected visitor would be distracted by the neat and clean lines of the housing and the already installed switchgear and dials. Each unit-housing also had a solid door that could shut and only opened by those that knew the combination.

Building the units at the Meck-U base had many advantages. It was comfortable and the crews could work in relaxed and familiar surroundings. And importantly they could go home after each shift. A happy home life meant happy work life. Andy was also thinking ahead though. If this prefabricated unit installation worked and the brass were impressed, and hopefully adopted LSP to power other craft then they already had two prototypes they could enhance and improve. For now though, Andy and Jimi's two main considerations were ease of installation and keeping tempers on an even level when the pressure was on. The flashing lights though had nothing to do with the power unit, they were simply there to impress the casual visitor, and were operated by a key fob hanging around the shift manager's neck.

The installation started well. The power units were in place and hooked up by the end of week one. It was establishing the connectivity of the old tub's power banks that took the most time. Without those power banks, they wouldn't be able to start testing proper. JD was running that part of the installation, so whilst they waited for his team to prove the connectivity, the build teams hooked up the 'Edward Rawlins' — Jimi's tribute to her old AtomSpheres boss — to the hangar mains feed. That took quite a bit of pressure off of JD's teams, but even then it wasn't until the end of week three that he was able to report that all the solar storage units were connected and charged, and there was enough electrical supply to power the generators.

Andy, Raef and Jimi, though, weren't happy at the speed they had been forced to work at, and now they only had one week left of that time. The teams were tired, mistakes were being made and the schedule was starting to roll back. They needed a miracle.

195

"Excuse me, is Captain Shallop nearby?"

"Eh, Captain? Oh yeah, sorry sir, you mean Jimi the Skip." It had been a long time since anyone had called the Skipper by her rank and Trooper Renton was thrown a bit. "She's down in the bowels at the moment I'm afraid. It's Colonel Henish, is that right sir?"

The colonel nodded and smiled at the recognition. "It is," he said.

Renton continued. "Would Professor Hobbins do? Eh, or Raef, I mean... No, Captain Jaxton is on the opposite shift, so he's probably in bed."

"Thanks, but no, I particularly wanted to speak with Captain Shallop, so could I go down?"

"I don't see why not sir, but you'll need a hard hat and someone to take you. Let's get you the necessary PPE and I'll take you myself."

The teams were under strict instructions to show all unexpected visitors everything. There were to be no secrets. Renton was well aware that this colonel was the Star-Link Maintenance Director, and he was looking forward to showing the maintenance chief all the switches and flashing lights.

Renton was just guiding Colonel Henish the towards the equipment store when Jimi the Skip poked her head out of the hatchway. "Ah, Skipper, [-"*Damn!*"-], the Colonel here wants a word."

"Thanks," said the Colonel, who was equally excited, "I nearly got down there. Another time perhaps. Thanks."

Renton smiled and nodded. "Next time, sir."

Then Shallop asked, "How can I help Colonel?" Then to Renton, she said, "Wait a mo Ren, you can take the Colonel down if he wants."

"I'd like that, thanks Captain," the Colonel said and smiled, "but first I have a favour to ask. I'm hoping we can help each other. I need your accommodation, and in exchange, I'm happy to extend your hangar time by three months. What do you think?" the Colonel asked. "Can we do business?"

"Eh... well, yeah. Absolutely. My team need a break, they've been on a continuous twenty-four-hour work pattern for three weeks now, twelve hours on, six off. As you can imagine, they're getting a bit tired and we're getting mistakes. When do you want the accommodation, sir?" Jimi was cock-a-hoop. Then she wondered, "And why... sir?"

"Well, you know how those in power have great ideas but don't plan or factor things in?" Jimi nodded, and the Colonel continued, "Well we've got this tenth-anniversary event of the AtomSpheres disaster happening in just over a week, and of course, this is where it all happened and everyone that's had a passing interest in it wants to attend. They all want somewhere to stay. The Platform for the Bereaved Survivors is obviously out of the question, as that's for the families only, and we always get thousands of those coming every year. But now I have to cater for 'special dignitaries' too, hence I need your accommodation, and I will need it for two weeks. Would that be okay with you, Captain?"

"Like I said, sir, we could do with a break. Two weeks would be just right, I reckon. When do you want us out?"

"How long will it take you to close everything down in the hangar? Sensibly, I don't expect you to rush, as I can see your teams have put a lot of effort into the build and there are a lot of little jobs going on. And whilst we're on the subject of your install, I just want you to know how impressed I am with the professional attitude of your teams." He paused a moment, then, "Hmm, how can I put this without erm..." The Colonel thought for a while, then said, "I'm guessing you experienced a lot of negativity when you were setting up...?" He gave Jimi a sideways glance, with a little twitch and bob of the head. "Huh?"

"Possibly, sir," Jimi replied.

"Well let's just say there won't be any more of that. I'm impressed, and those impressions have been passed back up the chain." The Colonel waited a few seconds, then asked again. "So how long Captain? Comfortably, that is, how long do you need to close up your operations and vacate the accommodation?"

"Can you give me twenty-four hours sir?"

"Twenty-four it is. Enjoy your break."

They shook hands, then Jimi signalled to Renton. "If you'd still like to see what we've been up to sir, then I'm sure Ren here will be happy to give you the guided tour." Colonel Henish nodded, and Jimi said, "Thanks again, Colonel."

Jimi needed a drink and a little time to think before she broke the news to the teams, so she went straight from her meeting with Colonel Henish to the Crew Room. But she was surprised when she found a complete team sitting around on the floor, chatting and drinking coffee.

"What are you sitting out here for?" she asked. "Why aren't you in there?" she said, pointing at the Crew Room door.

"Tech Sam's in there, Skipper, catching up on his sleep."

"Oh?"

"Yeah, he mumbled something about JD having a nightmare, talking in his sleep or something like that. Said he couldn't get to sleep, so he's catching up in there. We didn't want to disturb him."

"Right... damn, I was so looking forward to a coffee, bugger... Where's the closest machine?"

"Halfway down the Star-Link ma'am, there's a crew area."

"Damn, it'll take too long."

"I could get you one, Skipper."

"Thanks, but I need to wet my throat now, as there's something I want to say to all those on shift. Sorry Sam, but it looks like I've got to disturb you.." She turned to the sitters. "Gather up everyone who's awake and meet me in the hanger in five minutes. Don't worry, it's nothing sinister. Five minutes. Oh well, here goes," she said and she carefully opened the door, slipped through, and went as quietly as she could to the coffee machine.

But not quietly enough. Sam stirred and looked up at her, bleary-eyed.

"Oh, sorry Skipper, I was just catching up with a bit of shut-eye. It's a bit noisy in my room."

"Yeah, the guys outside said as much. Is JD often like this?"

"Only at this time of year ma'am. Usually lasts a couple of weeks, then he's right as rain. Don't know why, but he cries and whimpers and shouts out. It's something deep, but I don't know what."

Jimi nodded. "And it's always around this time of year?"

"Yes, ma'am."

Jimi thought a while, covered her top lip with the bottom and nodded again. "Yeah, it would be," she whispered, nodded some more and fell quiet, thinking to herself. *[-"I know how he feels."-]* Then she said, "I know you're trying to catch up with some sleep Sam, but as you're awake now you might want to hear what I've got to tell everyone else. Would you mind popping down to the hangar for a few minutes, then maybe you can borrow a bed in a quiet room and do a proper bit of catching up. Would you mind?"

"Eh, no ma'am, but I've only got my shorts on."

"Well, I don't mind if you don't mind. I'm sure the girls won't mind either... it might be a thrill for a couple of the guys too."

"That's what I'm afraid of," he said as he clambered out of his sleeping bag and slipped on his flip-flops. Behind him Jimi smiled. She loved her team and all its different facets; gay or straight, she didn't care, as long as they were happy.

"Here's a coffee Sam," she said as he stood. "I don't mind you just wearing shorts at all." There was an admiring tone to her voice, to which she added, "Your young lady is a very lucky girl," but before he could reply she added, "Come on, let's get to the hanger."

Sam, now draped in his sleeping bag and clutching his coffee, was greeted by a chorus of wolf whistles by both the women and the men.

"Okay, okay, calm down," said the Skipper as she called them to order. Then she turned to Sam, and with a sly grin, said, "It's only a *hard hat* area, Sam."

Her cheeky comment was met with a ripple of laughter whilst Sam blushed and quickly wrapped the sleeping bag about his loins.

"Okay, Okay, right. I have some good news. It's a double whammy as far as I'm concerned, and I think you guys will welcome it too. We've been given a three-month extension on our hanger time."

There followed a chorus of "Fantastic," and "at last," and "that's great" and "about bloody time" and "oh wow" rippling through the team. Then someone asked, "What's the catch?"

"They want our accommodation for two weeks, to house the many dignitaries that have been invited to the tenth-anniversary event to mark the AtomSpheres disaster. So I'm giving you all a fortnight's holiday." That went down well too, and it was greeted by cheers and whoops. "So," she continued, "over the next twenty-four hours we will pack everything into our secure containers and do an inventory of all the work we've done so far, so that when we return in two weeks we'll be able to hit the ground running. The first thing that we must do on our return is to check through everything top to bottom, side to side, in case we missed anything in the first three weeks. It's been a bit of rush, so I'm sure we've missed something. Now was there anything else?"

She paused, then said, "Oh yes, there's one other thing that makes it a triple whammy for me. Colonel Henish, the Hub Maintenance Director, has been impressed by the whole team's professional approach and has made a point of passing his impressions back up the chain of command. I want to add to the Colonel's plaudits my heartfelt congratulations and thanks. Well done guys, you totally deserve a good break."

She was just turning around, looking for Andy and Raef, when she bumped into Sam. "Ah yes. Hold on a minute everyone," she called to the teams. "Can someone let Sam use their bed so he can catch up on his beauty sleep?"

Sam got a lot of offers, but settled for Sergeant Pete's as it felt like the safest option.

42

You really are a lucky boy ...

"Hey girl, I wasn't expecting you 'till next week," Cristi said as Lucy staggered up the stair from the front door. "Here, give me that." Cristi took one of Lucy's bags. "How come you're back early? I was just turning in."

"We wrapped it all up in less than three weeks, even with a trip out to the... what do you mean you're just about to turn in. Why?"

"Nothing to do, you're not here and Sam's still up at the Star-Link, and nothing on the box. So I might as well go to bed," Cristi replied.

"Well I'm here now," Lucy said as she dropped her bags in the middle of the lounge. "Is there room for me in your early night?"

"Your bed is bigger, and tomorrow's the weekend, so we could lie in. Shall I turn your covers back?"

"I need a shower first though, it was a long flight, dodgy air-con too and a lot of sweaty bodies," she called as she nipped into the wet-room. "We had a trip out to the drovers," Lucy yelled through the open door. "Met up with Mumma Mae and Rynn. I spent a couple of days with them at their school tent whilst the others from Beadles were introduced and spent time with the drovers. I learnt a lot about Jez's family, and Jez too. Mae made sure I was welcomed by everyone and stayed close so I didn't feel alone. I even did some teaching," Lucy added as she towelled herself down and stepped back into the passageway.

Cristi was dressed in her p-jays and waiting for her with two glasses and a bottle of wine. "I've been thinking about this all the way home," Lucy said. "I was hoping we could have a bit of time together before the boys got back. Just like it was before the boys."

Lucy always seemed to wake first. Her instinct was to straighten her legs, but the covers were twisted around their feet. It had been a warm night. So, whilst her eyes cleared, she listened to the gentle sighs and puffs of Cristi's breathing before she carefully lifted Cristi's outstretched arm and rolled herself out of bed.

She was going to lay breakfast. "Oh ah, perhaps elevenses," she said and chuckled as she checked her watch and slipped on her stripy coat. Then, as she pulled the sheets up to cover her friend, she whispered, "Oh you are a lucky boy, Sam."

43

I've just had a dreadful thought...

"What were the sheep, like? Were there lots, and did you see Jez's, and meet Meeko?" asked Cristi, her hair in a towelling turban as she carefully applied a different colour varnish to each of Lucy's toes. "I like this colour," she muttered as she feathered out the brush lines, "and how about neon green on the next one?" she lisped over a dry tongue that was poking between her teeth as she concentrated.

"They were woolly, there were easily a couple of thousand, and they hummed a bit too. Hmm yes, I like neon green," Lucy said, craning forward to examine Cristi's handiwork. "I did meet Meeko, but not his sheep, as they were mixed amongst the rest. He said that he and Jez had six hundred this year. Last year's market had been good for them, and they were getting well known for producing quality even with such a small flock. He said they had sold well and they were able to buy more than they had expected. It had been a good lambing year too. Meeko said the partnership was doing well, and now that Jez was a fully badged officer, he had been making some hefty investments. I liked Meeko a lot, and An'gea his handfast-lady. They're expecting their..."

"Handfast? What's that?" Cristi asked.

"It means the same as engaged," Lucy told her friend.

"Gotcha," said Cristi.

Lucy resumed. "Meeko and An'gea are expecting their first child or children. They're both pureblood nomads, so a triple birth is always a possibility. But they're not officially married yet, as Meeko wants Jez to be at his side, to be his best-man and share his joy. So they're waiting for Jez to finish fitting this engine thingy before they finalise a date. But no one seems at all bothered. An'gea told me that there was an understanding and that both families were quite happy about it."

"Ooh, but carrying three, that doesn't sound very comfortable for walking people!" Cristi exclaimed.

"Apparently it's the norm. Mae confided that Jez and his brothers were all from multiple births." Cristi's jaw dropped as Lucy continued. "Yes that's right, he has, or had, brothers. Mae didn't say much more about them though. But she did say 'Your Jez'. Oh, I think it's so sweet how she refers to Jez being, My or Your Jez. Anyway, My Jez was one of three and the only survivor. I thought it was sad, but Mae just shrugged it off as one of those things that happened to her people out on the steppe. She said that the survivor always comes out stronger and showered in gifts. And you have to admit that My Jez is certainly gifted. He walks about with his eyes closed for goodness sake!"

"Well I've been doing a bit of research too," Cristi announced. "Jennie let me do some when we were a bit slack the other week. I thought it would take forever but she pointed me in the right direction, and I got this snap after a couple of hours. Look, it's your coat."

"It could be…" Lucy replied and peered closer. "It certainly looks similar. Where was this taken?"

"In the Star-Link conduit, the walkway, a few minutes before the sphere disappeared. And that boy's name is Devii'rahl."

"Really? Devii'rahl? How do you know that?" Lucy was gobsmacked.

"Because, and you have Jennie to thank for this bit of vital info, because every visitor to the AtomSpheres carried a token with all their details recorded onto it. These tokens were read constantly by the sensor loops that encircled every walkway. This is Tomii Devii'rahl…"

"Tomii! Jez cries that name in his sleep. Are you sure it's Tomii?" Lucy asked.

"Oh yes, positive. The sensor in the conduit recorded him passing three times in five minutes. He went down the conduit with two other Devii'rahls, on their boards, and a few minutes later he was back up through the sensor loop, and back again a few minutes after that. Here, I've got a recording. I'll play it. He speaks to someone. Tomii's voice is croaky, as if his voice is breaking, but the person he talks to, his voice is familiar. Here, watch..." Cristi played the video.

Lucy watched enthralled as the three Devii'rahl boarders sped past the camera and disappeared through the gateway into the entrance hall of Spher'rios, just as the power seemed to fail. She turned to Cristi as the screen blacked out for a few moments, but her friend said, "Patience sweetheart." The video sprang back into life and one of the boarders sped back the way they had just come from, passing two men in coveralls who shouted something.

"I don't think it was very polite what the man shouted." Cristi said, chuckling. "That's the end of that vid. But there's another, hold on... ah, here we go."

Cristi played the next clip. There had been a break of a few minutes since the other one, and this one showed Tomii talking to the two men in coveralls and asking, *"Excuse me, sir, my brothers wondered if you can you tell us how long the doors will be closed?"*

"Don't know, nipper. Doubt it'll be long though," the man had replied.

"There Luce, that voice, it's familiar. Do you recognise it, it's... "

"Andy Hobbins."

"Yes, you're right, it's Andy Hobbins. It is... yeah, it is. Wow."

The video was still rolling. The boy had returned to the closed doorway, and Lucy gasped as the whole doorway turned the brightest neon pink, so bright, so vivid that it hurt her eyes! "Gosh, that hurts!"

"It hurt my eyes too when I first saw it. I've done a bit of reading about that pink flare and that was the moment the knife-edged beam cut through the Star-Link conduit and separated Spher'rios from the rest of the AtomSpheres. You can hear the hiss of escaping air and see the boy fighting against its pull. Listen... Look." As they watched open-mouthed the voices in the video were drowned out by the high-pitched hiss and the boy, a black outline against the pink, was slowly floundering and losing his fight against the pull of the escaping air. That's where that video finished.

"Oh! No! Oh, is that it? Play the next one Cris, I've got to see what happens to Tomii."

"That's it, Luce, there isn't anymore. I've searched and scanned, and read and read, and there's no more on record. Jennie does think that there's one more somewhere, and maybe even a copy, but no one knows of its whereabouts, or if it actually exists at all."

"That poor boy. That's *the Boy on the Rope*, isn't it? The horror of it, it's difficult to imagine what it did to him. I mean, the mental scarring." Lucy was visibly shocked. "And to think I kept wearing that t-shirt, and somehow thought it made me feel connected. Oh Cris, what was I thinking?!"

"I found out more as well. I found out that there was no Jez Devii'rahl on the AtomSpheres at the time of the disaster. There was an R, which I think was Rynn, two Ms, possibly Mae and a Miike, a P who I think was Peiiter, and a T, Tomii. The names of Mike and Peiiter are recorded on the Memorial Stone, but there's no Jez. I was wondering if his nightmares are fuelled by the guilt of not being there. Was he left behind to tend the flocks? Did he pull the short straw?"

"Oh Cris, this is much too heavy for a girly day. I need wine and ice-cream. I'll get that ice-cream from the freezer. You get the wine and the glasses. I need a break from this. It's too intense." Lucy unwrapped her legs, which had gone to sleep, and clambered most inelegantly across to the freezer, then she stood tall and winced as the feeling returned. "Ooh that tingles," she gasped. "It was horrible seeing that poor boy struggling against the rushing air," she said as she peered into the freezer. "He looked so hopeless. Can you see his face at all, Cris?"

"No, when he's facing the camera his cap or Andy are obscuring it. It is Andy isn't it?"

"Yeah, without a doubt. I caught the side of his face when he turned to talk to his mate. It's the face I've seen in Jez's dreams. It's definitely him. I've no doubt at all."

"Oh no, I've just had a dreadful thought, Luce." They were back on the settee.

Lucy was leaning back on the armrest, and Cristi was between her legs with her head in Lucy's lap. Lucy was spoon-feeding her the choc-chip ice-cream whilst sipping her wine.

"You said Jez is one of three," Cristi said through a mouthful of choc-chip, "and you are one of two, so if you and Jez tie the knot you could be carrying five!"

Lucy winced at the thought, jerking her arms and spilling her wine, missing Cris's mouth with the spoon and smearing ice cream across her friend's nose. "Shit I hadn't thought of that. Oh no!" she groaned and squeezed her thighs together as she thought of the consequences. "My lovely tight... oh no, it'll be like an old boot," she shrieked, "and my hips... Oh no."

"It's just a thought, Luce, and I'm sure it won't be like that at all. It's all down to genes. It either will or it won't."

"And I'd rather not think about it either, but oh, Cris. No, let's think positive, let's think of something else. Is there anything else about the AtomSpheres and Spher'rios?"

"I did find a short promotional animation online that was done when Praes~Eedan were doing their initial marketing. I'll get it up," she said as she wiped the chocolate chips from her nose and cheek. "Here you are, there's a bit of sound too. It's short but it shows what they intended."

They watched together as the giant intertwined satellite worlds swept across the screen high above the planet of Mejjas Major and the narrator proudly announced...

"The AtomSpheres, the future 'go-to-holiday-resort'. Imagine a holiday amongst the stars. One day very soon that will be the reality. One day soon the AtomSpheres will be the go-to-holiday destination that everyone will want to say they visited."

The animation then changed to Nucleo, Taurus and Dominion,

"We shall start small with just two spheres, but other exciting new worlds will be added, worlds that will reflect the cultures and lifestyles of the real worlds in the Endecca Solar System. The AtomSpheres will be the Endecca in miniature."

Other spheres appeared and were added to the graphic until the animation resembled the classic laboratory emblem that had inspired the AtomSpheres in the first place.

"Wow, it was massive, I never really took on board just how big it was. I know Sam said it was big, but it's not until you see it like that with an area pinpointed and the camera panning back and the 3D modelling. It was huge." Lucy gasped, then asked, "Which one was Spher'rios?"

"Eh... " Cristi froze the video, "I think it was that one, the orange one. Hey! Twiddle your own hair."

"Oh sorry Cris, I'm trying to stop. I've stopped twiddling mine, and Jez only has stubble. I..., just, sorry..."

"Don't be silly, I love what you do Luce, it gives me shivers, just don't twiddle that's all. It gets all knotted. Now, where were we?"

"We were shocked at Spher'rios' size and how it just vanished," Lucy said as she clicked her fingers. "Vanished just like that. Click and it was gone." Lucy said as she resumed her position on the settee and opened her legs for Cris to snuggle back in. Then for the next few minutes, they both sat in silent contemplation just thinking about what they knew and what they had just seen.

Finally, Lucy asked, "But who is Tomii and where does Jez fit into all of this?" Then she yelped. "Oh Cris, I forgot, I bought something for you, for your wedding," she said as she lifted her leg over Cristi's head and rolled onto the floor. "Stay right there," she cried as she ran from the room. She was back a few moments later with a neatly wrapped package. "Here sweetheart, this is for you."

"Silk...oh Luce, they're beautiful, it's all beautiful. This isn't from Mii'een is it? This is from... "

"They only do rough silk and wool on Mii'een. I got these in Mejjas Minor, as we stopped off there on the way home. Its orbit put it directly in the line of our route, and we had a five-hour layover so Maesi and I... she was one of the lawyers... we got on really well," [>"But not like you and me,"<] she whispered across the mindPlain. "We went shopping and as you know, Mejj Minor is the place for silk, so I got you these. They are for you with all my love. I hope you like them."

"What's not to like Luce? They're lovely, and I'm sure Sam will love them as well. [-"*Love taking them off more.*"-] She smiled as Lucy dipped into Cristi's thoughts and they shared the moment. "And I know you, Lucy, you can't resist silk, did you get something Jez might like?"

Lucy didn't say anything, she just smiled, and Cristi held out her hand... "Come on, show me?"

"I feel rotten Luce. I got really upset. Do you remember, under the Hoof, I was frightened that you would leave, and I would be left all on my own. Do you remember?"

"Uh-huh, I do?"

"But it looks like I might leave you."

They were looking at each other, sharing the pillow in Lucy's bed. Cristi was gently brushing hair from her friend's face with her fingertip. "I don't want to leave you, I love being with you, I always have from that very first moment when they were allocating the rooms."

"Shush Cris. Shush, you'll make me cry. You're not going anywhere just yet are you? You never know, I might still be the one to go first. But whatever happens, it's not going to happen for a few more months at least, and certainly not until they get that engine thingy fitted and tested. So shush, just enjoy this moment and stop fretting over what might not happen."

Then Lucy rolled onto her back and stared up at her map, Jez's map. "He still writes to me you know, not every day but at least a couple of times a week. Although I did check the cubby on the way up. The door sticks now, so I had to thump it with the flat of my hand to get it to shut. I thought there might have been a few, but there's been nothing recently. He's probably very busy. I really love him Cris, but the more I know about him the less I seem to understand. I had a lovely time with his mumma, and she's such a lovely person." Lucy stretched, put out her arm, and pulled Cristi close.

"I know you do Luce, and I love seeing you two together and seeing you so happy. There's definitely a spark between you. Did his mumma tell you anything?"

"Well, she did and she didn't. Well, nothing that I didn't already know, though I did learn quite a lot from An'gea. She told me about all sorts of things Meeko had told her about them growing up out on the steppe. I met his other cousin Jixa-Vo, he's a little bit older than Jez and Meeko, about my age, maybe a little older. He was very nice too. Mae did let me in on one secret though. Well, perhaps not so much of a secret, as it was to do with that time I met them outside the Prof's rooms last year, when I was desperately trying to make contact with 'the boy'. It seems that the Prof had told Rynn and Mae about me and what I was trying to do and that the Prof was hopeful I might be able to get inside Jez's mind."

"Mae said that she and Rynn liked me from that very moment. But I had to own up to her that it was always the other way around, and that as much as I tried to find a way into Jez's psyche, he was always one jump ahead and knew exactly what was going on in mine."

"Didn't that make you feel awkward, that you were being used? Don't you think it was a bit underhand?"

"Well not really, and if anything the Random Target project was more intrusive if you think about it. We were prying into someone else's thoughts, going in uninvited. I just happened to choose someone who was several leagues above me, so I was out of my depth from the word go. I feel honoured that Mae and Rynn trusted me to do it. I told her the other day when we were walking away from the school tent. We took some food and spent the afternoon on a little rocky outcrop, just chatting. I told her then how my attempts had failed over and over, and how when he finally responded that I vented my spleen and gave him what for. She thought that was very brave and very funny and we laughed a lot.

"I do so want to be part of their family, Cris. Mae is so lovely and so genuine, so is Rynn, but they both look so careworn. Something major has happened in their lives, and it's etched in their faces. Meeko, An'gea and Jixa are all very protective of them, and so are the rest of the Rahl people. But before I forget, I'm sure I saw that creep Pedrasz leaning against the railings across the street. He was there when the taxi dropped me and I'm sure he's still there now. I'm certain I just saw him through the kitchen window when I got the glasses."

"I've seen him around here a few times too whilst you've been away," said

Cristi.

"Have you?" Lucy was a little surprised, and a little anxious.

"I checked with one of his nicer friends. I remember you saying you thought his parents lived around here. They used to, but they moved across town a couple of years ago."

"Enough of him," said Lucy, "he's someone I would rather forget. He gives me the creeps," she added, shuddering as she asked, "More wine?"

44

He's messing with our girl ...

"Whoo-hoo the boys are back," Cristi squealed as she sprinted two steps at a time from the front door, tripping on the last step and face planting the carpet in her haste to break the news.

"You silly thing Cris," Lucy scolded as she dabbed antiseptic cream onto Cristi's chin. "You've scuffed your pretty chin, but it'll have to do. Where are you meeting Sam?"

"He said he'd be at the Bean at six. He told me to tell you that JD and Conner were going to be there too. We both better tart ourselves up," she said and before Lucy had finished smoothing the cream Cristi was up and rushing into her room. "Have you seen my blue top Luce?"

"Washed it this morning."

"Damn, it'll have to be the green one then. Now which earrings shall I wear? And I think a skirt, yes, a skirt. What are you going to wear Luce?"

"I'm going to go like this, what do you think?" she asked as she stood naked in the doorway."

"Hmm," Cristi replied, rocking her head from side to side, "it has merit, but do you want to sit like that on the bus? The seats can be cold and... sticky. I'd wear that little summer dress if I were you, and maybe something underneath just in case it's windy."

"I hadn't thought of that, good point. Okay, I'll be ready in five... ish." Lucy disappeared into her room, made herself decent and called out through the open door, "Have they finished their mission already? I thought it would take them longer than three weeks? Didn't Jez say it was a month's job at least? I'm sure I read that in a letter he sent to his mumma."

"Sam says there's some big function on and they need the accommodation that they were using, so the Skipper has given them the best part of two weeks' holiday. Two weeks Luce, I'm going all, *you know*, just thinking of it. Are you ready? Let's go?"

And Cristi was halfway to the door when Lucy said, "Skirt?"

"Oh yeah," Cris said looking down. "Ooops."

"Has she told you what she forgot?" Lucy asked Sam, who had Cristi hanging on his arm, her head against his chest. Cristi had virtually leapt off the bus and sprinted to the Coffee Bean, leaving Lucy to pick up both their jackets and the scarf Cristi had dropped on the path in her rush to get to her man.

"No," said Sam. "What did you forget, besides these?" He held up her belongings that Lucy had carried. "What was it?"

"Oh Luce," she said, squirming, now all coy and bashful, "you weren't going to tell... that was supposed to be a secret."

"I'm intrigued now?" Sam said looking down at her.

"Shall I tell him then?"

"No Luce," said Cristi, and she stood on tiptoes and whispered so only Sam could hear.

"I wouldn't have minded," he said, "so perhaps you can show me later."

Lucy though was peering through the open door of the Bean. "Where's...?"

"Sorry Lucy, he's on his board, usual place, beyond the fallen log."

"Thanks, Sam," she replied, already walking across the campus lawn towards Jez's favourite perch.

[>"*Can you hear me?*"<] she pulsed across the mindPlain.

[>"*I can, and I can see you too. You look gorgeous. I've missed you so much,*"<] Jez replied. His thoughts were roaming, and he was boarding with his eyes closed and watching for her.

As soon as she came into view, although she was still beyond the fallen log and the slope, he turned his board and skated in her direction, getting faster with each sweep of his leg, driven by anticipation. All the while they continued to chat.

[>"*I saw your mumma last week. I have something to show you later.*"-] Lucy was excited too, speaking without thinking and saying the first things that came into her head and getting into a right muddle.

[>"*Mumma sent something for me?*"<]

[>"*Eh, did I say that? No, no. Oh no. I have something to show you later. Mumma just sent her love.*"-]

Lucy was walking without paying attention, bumping into others on the lawns, apologizing as she went. She was talking across the mindPlain as if she were chatting on her cellfone, totally oblivious to her surroundings. Which is why she walked right through a football training session without even noticing the chaos she caused. The players, realising who she was, cleared a path to ease her passage. After all, she was the college pin-up and adorned every locker on campus. They stared, standing proud and drooling, undressing her with their eyes as she walked unknowingly through their game.

"Oh she's gorgeous," one of them was heard to say.

"Miss Horny Babe, and she's just walked across our pitch. I've got to get a bit of that turf."

"What I could do for you," said another.

"She's already doing it for me," said the first as he glanced down at his shorts. "Oh my God, she's gorgeous."

"That's *my* girl. We've dated."

"Oh yeah, in your dreams Pedz. I've heard the talk."

"You've heard wrong mate. I just have to snap my fingers and she'll be hanging off my arm."

"Can you still do that?" asked another and the others chuckled. "I thought those soldier-boys broke them. It must hurt to snap them these days."

"She blew you out Pedz, we all know the story. We know about the blue drink in the Coffee Bean café, too."

"Come on you lot, snap to it, we've got a game to train for," the coach called, as he too followed her progress across the pitch, as he shook his head.

[-"If I were twenty years.... No, snap out of it you old letch."-] Then he turned back to his players.

But Pedrasz kept his eyes on Lucy, ignoring the coach, and as Jez leapt the fallen log and landed beside her, he said in a voice loud enough to be heard by the rest of the squad, "The board-nerd is bothering her again. Look at him, he's got his grubby little hands all over her. Hey, that's my girl. Fellas he's messing with my... our girl!"

He started walking towards the couple. "Oi, get your hands off her you little shit."

The rest of the squad, upon hearing him say *'he's messing with* our *girl'*, turned to see what Pedrasz was wittering on about and, sensing the concern in their team-mate's tone, they started to follow.

[-"My turn now, soldier-boy. I'll fix you, you bastard,"-] thought Pedrasz

Jez cartwheeled over the fallen log and landed gracefully in front of her, and the little audience that his boarding always attracted rewarded him with a ripple of applause and a chorus of whoops. "Not quite what I intended, not enough speed," he said, flashing a smile and a nod to the watchers, "but it felt pretty good. I've missed you, Lucy Hettler," he said as he scooted forward.

"I've missed you too, missed you so much," she said, pulling him to her and kissing his lips. She liked it when he stood with her on his board, because it meant they were the same height. "Are you finished up there?" she asked.

"No, sorry. Just a two-week break, that's all. They need our rooms for guests." As they embraced, someone shouted something about a girl and Jez thought he saw Pedrasz run behind Lucy. "Huh, is that Pedrasz?"

"Where?" she yelped, turning around, "Where Jez?" she asked as she turned back.

"What's up, Luce?" Jez asked, as he could see she was anxious. "What's up?"

"Did you really see him, did you? He's everywhere I look these days, on the bus, in the street, everywhere. He follows me. Did you see him, Jez?" Lucy was shaking. "Is he there now?"

"No, he's... er no, I can't see him now, but it *was* definitely him. He's following you? I'll fix him if you want."

"Stop him for me, Jez, please, he's... argh, no!" she squealed as Pedrasz wrapped his arms around her and kicked the board.

Jez, who had been concentrating on Lucy and her fears, felt too late the tremor of the charging footballers. "WTF?" he gasped, "WTF?" as the kick sent him spiralling into the path of the charging squad.

"It's alright my darling, you're safe now," Pedrasz whispered in her ear as he pulled her clear and Jez disappeared under a deluge of fists.

"Get off me you creep," she shouted. "I'm not your darling. I never was. We went out once. Once. You spent the night talking to your mates."

"Shush, Lucy."

"Leave me alone," she cried, twisting in his grip.

"Shush, you're hysterical, though it's understandable. Shush."

"Let me go," she squealed, trying hard to pull away.

"Shush. Stop struggling. You're safe now. I promise. That nerd won't bother you anymore."

"What?" Lucy stopped struggling and looked him in the eye. "WHAT?" she shouted again.

"The guys will fix him. You're safe now. Oh, I've missed you so much Luce," he said as he pulled her close. "We are so good together. Everyone says so," he added as leant towards her and made to kiss.

"NO!" she shouted, pushing him away. "I'm not *your* Luce. There never was an us. We went out once. You just wanted to show me to your mates. I had to get a bus home. Leave me alone Pedrasz. Let me go."

Lucy twisted and turned, trying hard to pull herself free. "I've just saved you, you ungrateful bitch," Pedrasz screamed in her face, then he slapped her hard across the cheek. Lucy shrieked! This wasn't going to plan. Girls didn't do this to him. "I've been watching over you," he shouted. "Is this all the thanks I get for keeping an eye on you and making sure you're safe?"

"Stalking me more like. I've seen you, and so has Cris, on the bus, hanging about in the street under our window, following me around college. You're a creep Pedrasz. Let me go," she spat, but as she put her hands on his shoulders to push him away, he knocked her hands aside and backhanded her, grazing her cheek with one of his gaudy rings and drawing blood.

At the tables outside the Coffee Bean café, someone commented, "Don't you just love the sound of the crèche, all those squeals and yelps? It's the sound of summer."

Sam and Conner heard the screams too and sat up and listened. "That wasn't an excited child," said Conner.

"What's she on? The crèche is the far side of the college," said Sam, pushing back his chair and standing.

Lucy screamed again as the ring bit!

"Sounds like someone's burnt themselves at that BBQ," said another at the tables. "I could never see the attraction of burnt smoky food. Each to their own I suppose."

"BBQ?" asked her friend. "On the lawns? Are they allowed?"

"Well yeah, look. There's some sort of fire, and look at all that swirling smoke."

Sam and Conner had heard the screams. "That's not kids, that's a cry for help," Conner gasped, and he was standing now and scanning the lawns. "It's Lucy!" he shouted, and in an instant both he and Sam were sprinting towards her, leaving their chairs to topple and their drinks to spill.

But a few strides into his sprint Sam faltered. "Smoke? What smoke? No, she's right, they don't have barbies on the lawns. Hold up, Conn. Stop mate."

"What's that?"

"Look at the smoke Conn."

"Oh yeah, of course, *that* smoke," he said and he stopped too.

The charging footballers realised, too late, that Pedrasz had used them. They were a distraction, and the guy on the board wasn't a nerd with grubby paws at all.

"That's her boyfriend, shit! Isn't... he's a... Jaeger!" one of them shouted, but the momentum pushed them on and it was too late to pull back so they just had to keep going and hope they could hit him hard enough.

But Jez was more than a match for this lot, and even though he was right in front of them as they launched their attack, he sidestepped and was now attacking them. And his attack was ferocious.

He was lightning fast, moving between them in a blur of fists and kicks. They found out the hard way why the Jaegers were elite, and he was enjoying every second. But when Pedrasz grabbed the shoulder straps of Lucy's summer dress as she tried to push him away, as he yanked her forward the material tore, leaving her exposed, embarrassed, and screaming, everything changed.

Lucy's distress triggered a deep primal response in Jez, and his breathing accelerated. The speed of his actions increased too, whilst his surroundings slowed. He was on fast forward. His opponents were on pause and he wafted amongst them like smoke through the tall grass. The footballers were in the way. He brushed them aside, throwing them left and right, casting them like chaff on the breeze. They didn't know or see what hit them. Jez then turned and slammed his knee into Pedrasz's groin and clamped his hand around his throat, lifting him off his feet and squeezing so tight he could hardly breathe. Then he fixed him with his piercing black-eyed stare and looked directly into his thoughts.

Pedrasz was terrified. Everything happened in an instant. The pain was intense and there was just that grin and those black penetrating eyes. This was Jez's moment. Pedraz's mind and thoughts were an open book, and Jez poured all his haunting nightmares into every corner. Then, still clutching him by the throat and swinging Pedrasz like a flail, he waded amongst the scattered squad, pushing out his thoughts at the same time and fixing them all with a mindLock. They might have been duped, but at that moment Jez didn't care. He was angry, and even though he was feeling the strain that the smoke dance took out of the dancer, he charged into the players thoughts too, twisting their nervous systems until they were screwed up and rigid. Then his energy failed him, and he stopped.

"Yeah, okay. No more," he mumbled and nodded, then dropped Pedrasz and released his grip on the players' minds, letting them all slump to the ground in their own mess.

"Why have you stopped?" Cristi screamed. "Why aren't you running to help her?" she screamed. "Sam, Conner? It's Lucy. Why?" Cristi couldn't understand why both Sam and Conner had stopped. "Help her," she pleaded, looking up at Sam. "Sam, please," she implored. "Please."

But Sam just touched her shoulder. "Look, Cris," he said.

Lucy was wearing Jez's shirt, whilst he gently kissed the graze on her cheek and wiped it clean with his handkerchief.

"Huh?" Cristi said, gasping. "How?"

Conner had snatched a coffee from the closest table. "You'll need this mate," he said, holding the cup out, but he dropped it as Jez's knees buckled and the two friends caught him under the arms and helped him to the nearest seat. "Sorry, let me get you another," he said to placate the drink's owner.

Most of the LSP Engineers were in the Bean, and when they heard those painful screams and saw their mates running towards the sound, they'd left their tables to lend a hand. They were too late to help, nevertheless, they weren't going to let Pedrasz and his friends go without a little bit of Fleet retribution. Yet, when they got to them the smell put them off.

"Urgh, shhhh, urgh, no way. I'm not getting involved in that," said Sgt. Pete. "Those idiots have got more trouble than we can give them."

"Have they sh...?"

"Yeah, they have," said Pete. "They've dropped the lot. Leave 'em. Let's check on our boy instead."

But H-One and a couple of the others weren't going to let a bit of poop get in the way of a good hiding, and delivered a couple of carefully-planted kicks to add to the players' discomfort.

"I'll get him a strong coffee," Conner said to Lucy as she sat down beside Jez.

"See if they do ziirt, he needs something strong," she called after him.

Conner put up his thumb, then to the person whose drink he's snatched, he asked, "So sorry, what can I get you? What do I owe you?"

"Same again mate will be fine. I'd have paid to watch that, so just get us a coffee."

As Conner turned, Pete asked, "Was that how it was up at the Memorial?" The sergeant couldn't quite believe what he'd just witnessed.

"Yes, Sarge, and no. This was something else," Conner replied. "What he just did had clinical efficiency, and the Mem Stone was clumsy by comparison."

"That was more than the Mem Stone, Pete," Sam chimed in. "My god he was on fire. If he'd been like that up there, then hell's teeth, what would have happened?

"Really?" Pete was stunned. "I suppose the cat's out of the bag now 'coz of this?" he muttered. "I'll see if I can put a cap on it, but too many of our LSP guys saw something. The cellfones will be buzzing, and it'll be all across the Fleet by the morning."

"You're right Sarge," Sam agreed, "it'll be difficult to keep this quiet. The Mem Stone story is bound to surface, so we'll just have to do our best to play it down."

"I heard the lass scream, but by the time we'd turned he was mopping it up," said Pete. Then he thought about what he had just seen and asked, "I suppose he's a different man to how he was a couple of years ago? He's a Jag now after all; done the training, done the tour, got the tatt, and works out every day. Those dumb klutz' didn't know what they were taking on."

"Aye, that and the mind-stuff, Pete," said H-One. "That Pedrasz was gibbering something about screaming voices. He kept saying over and over, 'Pink, it's pink', and slapping the side of his head as if to shift something. And the footballers, bloody'ell, they're going to have the *worst* dreams. You've got to feel sorry for them I 'spose. They followed like sheep. Their coach is beside himself, and his team is in bits. But he says it's their own fault. Pedrasz though, that arsehole, he got all he deserved, sounds like JD offloaded some of his terrors. This might ease things for our boy, d'you think? Now that he's shared them out?"

"It would be great if it did Pete, as he suffers real pain in those dreams of his. It wasn't because of the noise that I slept in the Crew Room... you get used to night time noises when you share a billet. No, it was the pain that drove me out! I sat and listened to him one night. He never really screamed aloud, and I think he only ever shouts out when he's with Lucy because he can relax when he's with her. No, he would grind his teeth, and moan and whimper. And mutter. There were silent screams too. And he would recite numbers and names. But it was the pain behind those words that made me sleep somewhere else. It would be so lovely for him if those dumb shits had taken away his nightmares."

"Fingers crossed then," said H-One.

They were standing a little way away from the tables, talking in hushed voices and looking down at Jez, who was sipping a cup of ziirt; the café owner had made one for him from her private stash. He was holding Lucy's hand and staring at the sky.

"He looks wasted," Pete commented, "and *he's* probably the fittest of us all."

"And you say he was more fired up just then than he was at the Memorial?" H-One asked.

"He was," said Conner. "I mean, at the Memorial he was phenomenal; he took out nine, and he was nowhere near as fit as he is now. He was just angry because they poured coffee over some names. But this afternoon he was deadly. That Pedrasz has been stalking Lucy. And the footballers? Well, they thought they were defending her from Jez. I reckon those guys are lucky he *is* a different man."

"He's matured," said Sam. "He knows when to stop. This afternoon, if he had been the boy he was before, but with all the physical training he has now, he would've killed them, and I've got no doubt about that at all."

"Sam sweetie," Cristi interrupted, "we're going to go now. Lucy wants to get changed and she's worried about Jez, as he looks so tired. She wants to get him to our apartment, and the bus goes in about ten minutes. Are you going to come with us? *Please?*"

"Of course, Cris." He said his goodbyes and followed them to the bus stop.

45

Does your bed do that? ...

As soon as they got back to their attic apartment the girls disappeared into Lucy's room. Sam went straight to the fridge and cracked open a couple of bottles of beer. "Are you okay mate?" he asked as he handed a bottle to Jez. "You look like shit and you haven't strung more than a few words together all the way here. Is there anything I can get you?" Sam asked.

"No, you're alright. MindLocks, they just sap the life out of you."

"Gotcha. Is that why they all appeared to be standing like dress-shop dummies?"

Jez nodded. "Uh-huh, that would have been it. I had to stop them, they were attacking us. I had to make sure it wouldn't happen again."

Sam could sense Jez was still very angry, but fatigue had drained the conviction from his voice, and he slumped down onto the settee.

The girls joined them a little while later. Lucy had changed out of her ripped dress and was wearing baggy joggers, a loose blouse and her stripy coat. Cristi wanted to get out of her clothes too, and bent forward, taking Sam by the hand.

She whispered, "Lucy wants to spend a little time with Jez on the settee. I said we would go to my room, if that's okay? I need to change."

Sam smiled. "Of course, Miss Derrent, perhaps I can help you with that," he said, but he let her fingers slip from his and turned, then gently put his hands on Lucy's shoulders. "Are you okay, Luce?" he asked.

She smiled. "Yes, thank you, Sam. Thanks for running to my aid, you and Conner, thank you so much," she said, and she put her arms around his neck and kissed him. Then she winked and added, "You'd better not keep her waiting Sam, off you go." He returned her wink and disappeared into Cristi's room.

Lucy sat down and Jez turned to her, smiling a weak smile. His eyes were distant, and he hadn't even taken a sip from the bottle.

"You rescued me," she said, snuggling beside him.

[>"I always will..."<] he told her and kissed her bruised cheek.

"Ow! Ooo, ouch."

"Sorry Luce, does that hurt? Let me kiss the other cheek then," he offered, but that was red too, so he just pulled her close. He was drained and his actions were clumsy, and again she squeaked. "What's up?"

"That creep mauled me. I feel like I'm bruised all over. Everywhere hurts," she muttered and let out a little sob.

Jez brushed aside her tears as gently as his fatigued arms would allow. Then, as he carefully pulled her close and their lips met, a familiar noise rattled the plates on the kitchen wall. *Bonk bonk.* "Huh?" *Bonk bonk.*

"Oh Cris," Lucy sighed as her giggles killed the moment, and soon they were both laughing.

Between sobs, squeaks and chortles Jez managed, "I thought you moved her bed?"

"I did, I move it every morning, and they just jerk it back across the room every night," she said and they both roared again.

"Does your bed do that?"

"It might. But I've always been in it, so I wouldn't know," Lucy said, and chuckled.

"Does the old couple downstairs still knock on the ceiling?"

"They're away for the week," she said through a smirk, then suddenly changed the subject. "Did you write to me when you were away?"

"Of course. Every day. At the end of each shift before I hit the sack. Why?"

"I didn't get them!"

"None of them?"

"None of them."

"Are you saying that little shit got into your cubby too?"

"Yes, I think he must have, as the door's been tricky for the last few weeks."

"It's a good job I kept copies then," he said. "But they weren't that interesting, not really. A couple of times I even fell asleep with my finger on a key. One of my letters went on for fifty-odd pages, each filled with an 'O'."

"Oh Jez, you silly thing," she said and kissed him.

"I tell you what, I'll print off the shorter letters, so you can see what we were doing, and I'll bring round some tools and fix the cubby door," he said as he nibbled her neck and flicked the lobe of her ear with his tongue.

Lucy smiled. "That would be nice," she replied as she ran her fingers through his stubbly hair.

"They've certainly missed one another haven't they," said Jez as the banging on the wall got louder and louder. "It'll get louder still before they're finished," he added as he kissed her ear, but their moment had gone. "It's not working for me, Luce. I don't have the energy to compete with that. Do you fancy a walk? It's still quite early, how about we go back to the Bean?" he grinned, then said, "You can breakfast at mine if you like."

She pulled back. "Really? Oh, yes, please. Are you sure that will be okay? You wouldn't be breaking any rules, would you?"

"It'll be fine. You just grab some things and I'll let the lovers know we're going." He closed his eyes and pushed his thoughts out across the mindPlain, and as Lucy sat down beside him with her overnight bag on her lap, he burst out laughing. [-"That surprised them,"-] he thought, chuckling.

Lucy put her head on one side. "What are you laughing about?" she asked.

"Sam completely missed his stroke. I spoke straight into his thoughts and he almost spun out of the bed, he thought I was behind him." [-"Well I suppose I was,"-] he smiled. "Come on, let's see if we can get the next bus."

As they passed Cristi's door, Jez hammered the woodwork and shouted. "Nice action mate."

They sat at their usual table. The café was empty except for the two of them and the staff were starting to tidy up. As they finished their drinks Lucy asked, "How did you do that... thing?"

"I don't know, it's just something that I've always been able to do."

"Does it just happen?"

"Eh, no. No, I have to summon it up. I have to make it happen. I heard your scream and it just made me angry."

Lucy thought for a while. "But what about those footballers, weren't you angry then? They attacked you!"

"I was annoyed, yes," he replied. "But once I got the upper hand, I enjoyed it. It's not often I get to do what I've been trained to do. It's just when I heard your scream, and saw you torn dress, I just had to do something about it."

"Can everybody in your family do it... " She paused, thoughtful. "Would our children be...?"

But Jez was already answering the first part of her sentence and missed the rest... or chose to miss it. "I only know of one other, Jixa's great great great great great," he counted on his fingers. Then counted again, "Yes, that's right, Jixa-Vo's five times maternal great grandmother. It's said that it's one in ten million, but I reckon it's more like a hundred million. It can burn you out, as it burnt her out. They say she died young, worn out by the phenomenon. I dabbled when I was younger, used to surprise the others by just appearing, tapping them on the shoulder then vanishing again. But it's only on rare occasions that I do it now. It really tires you. The last time was up on the Star-Link."

"What does it feel like?"

"It feels normal to me, nothing different. But it must be different, because, well, it's been explained as smoke wafting through the long grass. Out on the steppe, they call it the Smoke Dance, and those who do it are known as Smoke Dancers. I didn't feel like I got any faster, but you were just like a statue, so too were the footballers." He deliberately didn't refer to Pedrasz as he didn't want to trigger alarm bells. "I can't explain it, Luce, because what I felt and what you saw were two different things. I'll tell you this though, I can see why it destroyed Jixa's great-great-granny. I'm very fit and I could feel the drain. If I kept doing it, like she did, and didn't have the deep-down stamina that I've got now, well it would certainly take its toll."

"Huh hmm." A cough sounded behind them, and they both looked up as the café owner asked if they were finished. She wanted to lock up.

"Sorry, is that the time?" Lucy gasped. "Oh sorry, yes." Together they gathered the cups.

"Can we go to the bench?"

"Err... yes, okay. Of course." Jez sensed an edge to her question. "What's up, sweetheart?

"I want to just sit there. I want to know what it feels like without that creep watching me. He was always there Jez, just on the edge of my eye line. He didn't scare me at first, and then later I had to pretend that he didn't. It was so tiring, it was wearing me down."

"But you never said."

"You were away on the Laxi. It was only your letters that kept me sane." Jez was only just realizing just how much Pedrasz had affected her.

"That's our bench and there's your log, and the ground in between is where we walked together hand in hand. That bench is where I sat when I was trying to get you to listen. It was where we sat after the *Bean blue dye* incident. It's where we have sat together and shared a coffee and a snack, and had our deep conversations. That's where I gave you that awful telling off. That's our ground, and it's our bench, and it's full of our memories... and I don't want this bad memory to spoil the good ones. Will you come with me and hold my hand?" she asked. "I can do it if you hold my hand."

Jez stood and looked at her. He had fallen quiet, and Lucy could see he was pensive and thinking deeply about something. "Of course, I will," he finally said. "Just mind where you tread."

"Why?"

"Because, when I let them go, they let go," he said and chuckled at the thought.

"Really?"

"Uh-huh, really," he confirmed and held his nose. "Really."

She held out her hand. "Come on then, you'll have to guide me."

"Before we do though, I want to ask you something. I've got a few demons of my own. Could you take some time off?" he asked.

"Well I'm not due in until the middle of next week, would that be okay?" Lucy replied.

"Yes. The day after tomorrow, I want to go up to the Star-Link. I want to go up to the Memorial and pay my respects. Would you come with me and hold my hand and help me face *my* demons?"

[–"His demons!?"–] "Of course I will," she answered. "I want to be a part of everything important to you, whether it's good or bad. And I'd love to go to the Star-Link and see where you've been working for the last three weeks. Will you be wearing your best blue uniform? I love that uniform and that stiff high collar, it's so sexy."

"Really! Really?"

"Uh-huh, oh yeah, perhaps we could erm... you know, [>"mile high,"<], later, on the shuttle?"

[>"You are weird Miss Hettler,"<] but Jez knew a good offer when he heard one. "Bench first."

"Yes, bench," she replied, and they linked arms and set off, carefully, across the lawns.

46

Why the mejj did he come here today ...

It was a lot busier than Jez had imagined it would be. There were usually a lot of attendees, people spending quiet time around the Memorial, but that would be spread over the five days the Fleet and the Star-Link commanders opened the Hub to the relatives. So why, this year, were there banks of chairs and great gaggles of people gathered around the stone? Then it dawned on him.

"Idiot, it's the tenth anniversary. Of course," he muttered and pushed back his cap. [-"Why do people only mark the big numbers?"-] he said to himself, [-"when every year is a big number for someone who's been bereaved?"-]

"What was that Jez?" Lucy had heard him say 'Of course', and was puzzled.

"Just me thinking out loud, Luce. It's not usually like this. A lot of the relatives come on the days either side, and that's what we usually do, as it's quieter then, with more time for reflection. There're a lot of people here this year that I don't recognize. Yes, I know that the relatives run into the millions, but you always tend to bump into the same people at roughly the same times. I think this lot are hangers-on. But I suppose, well, we stopped coming on the anniversary so maybe the people that I know were here yesterday."

"Is this where you've been working for the last three weeks?" Lucy asked, trying to change the subject and steer his mind away from the differences he was seeing. "Where's the *old tub*, the *Edward Rawlins*, Jez, can I see it?"

"The workshops are right down the other end, but I don't think I will be able to show you. The public is only allowed to wander freely in the area around the stone. I think the workshops will be off-limits."

"Oh well, never mind, just being up here with you is nice. Is this the walkway conduit that led to Spher'rios?" she asked.

But as soon as she mentioned the sphere, she noticed a change in his demeanour, and when he answered there was a tremor in his voice. Lucy sensed an edginess, a nervousness. "Yes, this is the walkway, and just beyond the stone is where the sphere was attached. We can walk down to it if you like?" he said in a shaky voice, and before Lucy answered he took her hand in his and set off towards the Memorial Stone. He was staring straight ahead, ignoring everything either side, focused only on the glass at the end of the conduit as he walked straight into a uniformed soldier with a sidearm.

"You can't go that way mate. The Memorial is closed to visitors until four forty-five."

"Since when, Trooper?" Jez was blunt. He was an officer, and regardless of what was closed and what was out of bounds, his rank demanded respect.

The trooper realised his error when Jez turned, showing his collar tags and his Jaeger insignia. "I'm sorry, sir." The trooper swallowed and quickly apologized, but orders were orders. "But I can't let you pass. It's for the Tenth Anniversary dedications. It will be open to all at four forty-five."

[-"Four-forty-five! Shit!"-] Jez wasn't happy.

Lucy could see he wasn't happy and was worried about what he might do. The trooper wasn't standing in a good place, and she could tell by his loose thoughts that Jez *was getting* very agitated indeed. Fortunately, the trooper and Jez stepped away from one another and the moment passed.

"Is there somewhere we can get a drink, JD?" she asked. Jez didn't answer, just stared straight ahead to the Glass Screen.

"I don't want to be here at four forty-five. I want to be back down there," he said, pointing through the observation window at Mejjas Major below. "I want to be back there a long time before then."

Lucy looked around and attracted a passing steward. "Excuse me, is there somewhere can we get something to drink, please?" she asked, flashing a smile.

"Just off to the right miss, just around that corner and through the entrance to the Relatives Platform. There's a little café," he said, as he touched his forehead and continued on his way. "Come on sweetheart, let's go and get some refreshments, I'm parched and I need water." This time, before he had a chance to answer, she took him by the hand and led him to the café. It was ten-thirty.

[>"*I don't want to be here at that time. Got to be away before then. Can't stay. Got to go. Got to show Lucy, so much to tell.*"<] He was rambling, muttering incoherently and fiddling with his glasses. And his thoughts were wide-open, so many, Lucy couldn't keep up, was able to read them all.

Jez wasn't thinking straight, and she wondered why it was so important for him to be away from the Star-Link before four forty-five. The more he muttered in his thoughts the more agitated he became. Lucy was getting nervous herself now. She had seen him in action and knew what he was capable of. She was right to be worried. Then she saw someone she recognised. It was the sergeant that had confronted her and Mumma on Badging Day.

"I'll be back in a moment, sweetheart," she whispered. "Keep my seat will you? I'll leave my bag on it, okay?"

"Sergeant," Lucy called as she skipped across to a group of NCOs that were standing close to the coloured rope that fenced off the Memorial Stone. She tapped him on the shoulder. "Hello there. We met at the Badging Ceremony. I need your help."

Reeble turned at feeling the touch, and he smiled. Behind him, a whole stream of muttered ribald comments spilt forth. "Steady, careful now, this is JD Devii'rahl's lady."

Instantly, and without even the tiniest hesitation, each of them apologised.

"Sorry miss," they chorused.

"That's okay," she said, smiling sweetly.

"It's Lucy, isn't it?"

Lucy nodded. "And you're the Fearsome Five," she said.

"Huh, what's that?"

"Me and Mumma Mae, JD's mumma, that's what we called you when you were standing next to him at the Badging Ceremony. You all looked so big, so huge, next to him, and there were five of you."

"I like that, Reebs, the Fearsome Five," said Bella Morton.

"I like that too," Maisie Thorpe added.

Reeble smiled. "Got a nice ring to it. Yeah, I like that. So Lucy, what —"

But before he could get his question out RSM Tomsen pushed his way forward from the back of the little group. "Did I just hear you ladies mention JD Devii'rahl's name?" Then he noticed Lucy, and nodded. "Well hello," he said with an admiring purr. "Who do we have here?" he asked, taking Lucy's hand. "Are you going to introduce me Reebs, or should I do it myself?"

"Before you blundered in boss, I was just about to ask this young lady how we," — he motioned around the whole group — "including you, could be of assistance."

"That's very commendable Sergeant, but you still haven't introduced me."

So Senior Sgt. Reeble turned back to Lucy and said, "Boss, this is Lucy. She is the young lady that JD used to write to."

When Lucy's eyes widened, he paused and put his head on one side, and glanced at her. "Still writes to?" Lucy nodded. "This is the young lady that JD still writes to. And Lucy, this blustering old gentleman," he said with a wry smile on his lips, "is Regimental Sergeant Major Tomsen. Happy now?"

"Hey, less of the old, Sergeant." The RSM couldn't have been more than forty; was probably younger.

The sergeant turned, looked him the eye and shook his head. "Are you quite finished?" The RSM nodded. "Can I finish what I was about to ask the young lady?" Again the RSM nodded. "Good. So, how can we be of assistance, miss?"

"It's Jez. I left him in the café looking after my bag. He wants to go to the Memorial Stone and the Glass Screen, but it's cordoned off until four forty-five. He is very adamant that he doesn't want to be on the Star-Link at that time. A soldier is guarding it."

"Of course he wants to be away by then, poor bugger. Is he agitated?"

"Yes he is, very. He's wringing his hands together and his thoughts are loose and straying. He never... he always covers his thoughts, but today they're everywhere. He's on edge and I've seen what he can do when he's angry."

"Me too," Bella Morton agreed.

"Where is he? And why the mejj did he come here today?" Tomsen asked.

"He said he had demons to face," Lucy replied.

"That he does, but why today? He was never great at peripherals. You had better take me to him, miss." They set off together at a pace. "Reebs," he called back over his shoulder, "clear a path. He's going to that stone and I don't give a shit what anybody thinks. And you, my dear girl, you need to get him off the Star-Link as soon as he's been to the stone. You need to..." But he stopped short as he stepped into the café. "Hello, young sir."

Jez leapt to his feet. "RSM Tomsen, how do you do?"

"I'm doing fine, and between you and me, an awful lot better for having met your young lady." Then he leant forward feigning secrecy and whispered loudly, "She's one hell of a cracker you've landed there, sir."

Of course, Lucy heard, as she was supposed to, and she covered her mouth with her hand. Tomsen turned and winked, and was a little concerned when he saw her brush away a tear with her thumb.

"Your young lady tells me you want a few minutes at the stone, but it's cordoned off until four forty-five. Well it isn't at the moment, your old mate Reeble is seeing to that, so you go and do your stuff and I'll worry about the consequences. Go on, sir."

Jez saluted the RSM, then, a little unsteadily left the café and walked purposely towards the cordon.

"Are *you* okay miss?" the RSM asked.

"I'm just touched by the affection everyone has for him," she said and sniffed. "It's lovely."

"He's a lovely guy. Now run along before I get too soppy. He's going to need you, as today is a very important day in his calendar. But to finish what I was saying before, I'm very surprised he's come up here today. You need to get him away from here as quickly as you can, and get him somewhere quiet. Somewhere away from everyone. If you know of such a place then take him there and take him as soon as you get him back to Mejjas, and keep him there until he's cried it out. Now get after him, go on, shoo."

Reeble had cleared a path between the chairs, pushing his way through the gathered dignitaries, and Jez followed, flanked by the rest of the Fearsome Five. Lucy, though, wasn't certain what she should do, so she remained at the outer cordon and watched nervously as the Jaeger party approached the Memorial Stone and the inner cordon.

At that moment the actual stone was out of bounds, and even the invited guests weren't allowed to approach. But Reeble wasn't going to be halted by a bit of thick string, and simply unhooked the cord so Jez could get to where he wanted to be.

It all looked very official. An officer accompanied by his NCOs, and the parted guests, looked on agog as Technical Officer Devii'rahl stepped past the cord and approached the stone. Then Corporals Thorpe, Brakken, Donelson and Morton linked arms and shored up the gap, preventing any of the guests from getting through.

This was to be Jez's moment.

The Spher'rios Memorial, standing at the centre of an area of quiet contemplation, consisted of a waist-high circular slab of black marble surmounted by a ceramic sphere on a needle-fine spindle. At any other time of the year, visitors were welcome to wander around or sit beside the stone and reflect in its reverential calm. It was a sacred place, yet a thoughtless someone, careless of today's occasion and the meaning of the stone, had left a wine glass on the slab as if it were a table in a wine bar. Jez removed the discarded glass and passed it to Reeble, then he wiped away the stain with his cuff. Behind the cord the guests, curious to see what the young officer was doing, pressed forward, so Lucy had to stand on tiptoe to see what they were seeing. She could just see his cap, and guessed he was beside the stone. But as the guests moved this way and that to get themselves into better positions, she too had to hop from side to side to see what was going on. Suddenly Tomsen took Lucy's hand.

"Oh no, no no, no, this won't do at all. Come along miss Lucy, let's get you to your man," he said and waded in amongst the smartly dressed guests. "Move aside please, move aside if you will."

There followed a lot of unhappy mutterings, as none of them wanted to lose their hard-won positions, but those mutterings were soon stifled when they saw the size — and felt the authority — of the man making that polite request. Then the four Jaegers parted and Lucy was able to slip into the quiet area and see what everybody else could see.

The marble slab was ringed with several lines of gold. It was stark and impressive. When Lucy stooped for a closer look, she realised that the gold rings were lines of the names; the names of the missing. Each name had been lasered into the stone and each one was inlaid with gold. By the time Tomsen had reunited Lucy with her man, Jez had already polished away the wine stain, and was now resting his hand over two particular names. As she looked on, he crouched down and rested his head against his hand. Lucy heard him sob. Then he slowly stood, leaving his hand to linger for a few more seconds, before he moved cautiously towards the etched Glass Screen.

Tomsen joined Reeble, and together with the rest of the NCOs watched and commented as JD, followed discretely by Lucy, rested his hand on the Memorial Stone. "He hasn't told her everything, has he? I watched her eyes when I said it was an important day in his calendar, and I sensed a question there."

"No boss," Reeble replied. "I don't think he's told her anything. I don't think he knows how to."

"Did you hear what went on the day before yesterday?"

"What's that Maisie?" Tomsen asked. "What and where?"

"On the campus lawns near that new engine project that JD is working on. Seems that some dumb arse has been stalking that young lady there, and JD had it out with him, just like he did up here. I heard he's faster now, clinical and efficient. Others said deadly, like an avenging angel."

"If someone was stalking my young lady, I'd be doing the same," said Jim Brakken, "but I don't suppose I'd be classed as clinical. My list of adjectives would start with brutal."

Lucy gingerly moved a step closer and was able to find the exact spot where his hand had lingered. He had left a warm print on the cold marble. *[-"Peiite Devii'rahl and Miike Devii'rahl... Brothers?"-]* she wondered.

Then a few lines away she saw the names of Yara, Zimba and Jas Beske'rahl. Beske'rahl? *[-"That's Meeko's family name!"-]*

But she was more concerned with Jez, who was slowly reaching out towards the glass, though not to the figure etched into it. Instead he was reaching over the shoulder of *the Boy on the rope*, and as soon as his hand touched the glass he crumpled and slid to the floor, subsiding into a mess of tears. Lucy went to him and held him as he sobbed, and tried her hardest to console him.

Behind him and around the stone there was a surprised hum of hushed muttering; Jaegers didn't cry in public! Beyond the cordon, the NCOs, with not a dry eye among them, waited quietly until Reeble finally spoke. "That's enough. Come on."

47

That's why..." he said ...

"Now you know what you have to do, Lucy, and you must do it. We've been in touch with his mate, Sam, who'll be waiting. JD has over a week before he's due back, so get him somewhere quiet and get him talking," Reeble told her as he helped them settle on the Hi-Speed shuttle.

Then Tomsen took Lucy to one side. "He needs to get this sorted. He needs to open up, and he needs to share. He needs to figure out, once and for all, just who he is. He's charismatic, and people follow him, but it takes more than charisma to make a good officer and we don't carry people in the Corps." Tomsen put his hands on her shoulders. "I can see that you love him, it's in your eyes, it's in your face... it's in your whole being. But is love enough? I've never had much time for it myself. I don't envy the task ahead of you, Lucy. But I reckon if anyone can sort him out, you can." Then he kissed the back of her hand, and winked. "Now off you go."

Lucy was overwhelmed by the heartfelt support they were all giving, and called after them as they stepped ashore. "Why, Sergeant?"

"Sorry miss, why what?" Jon Reeble asked, confused.

"You are Jaegers, you're supposed to be hard uncaring bastards, yet you all care so much. Why?"

Reeble looked at Tomsen, Tomsen nodded, and Reeble unbuttoned his tunic and took out an old photograph. "That's me on the floor next to the Memorial Stone. That's my blood," he said as he traced around a dark stain with his fingertip. "They broke my nose, broke my jaw, knocked out a few teeth, stamped on me and broke both of my hands and my leg. That's Maisie Thorpe," he said, pointing to one side of the stone, "who was knocked senseless with the flat of a shovel. Crouched beside her is Bella, who they pushed the shovel up under her chin and said they would push further if she tried to intervene. Those... those..." He hesitated, looking for the right word. "Those new officers were trying to kill me, and that slight figure standing defiantly over me and facing up to those baying animals is your Jez. And this," he said, turning the photo over, "is how the scene looked a few seconds later." Reeble was still on the floor, but so were most of the new officers. The plaza was littered with bodies, and there was Jez, centre stage, the last man standing. "That's why..." he whispered. "Safe journey, miss."

48

I can't shake them, the demons ...

"There, that's everything from the car. Is there anything else you think you might need?" Cristi asked Lucy as Sam set up a portable cooker and some lights. "Well you know how to get in touch, and we're only a call away."

Cristi and Sam had been waiting for them at the Shuttle Terminal with a change of clothes and supplies to last a couple of days. On the flight down, Lucy had contacted Claude and he had arranged for them to spend a few days at the alpine fort. The RSM had contacted Jimi the Skip, who had asked Sam to collect them from the terminal and drive them into the mountains. Jimi had also sorted out the necessary supplies. JD was an important cog in her team, and she wanted him back in full working order. It seemed that everyone was more than happy to help.

Sam clicked a folding chair together and told Jez to sit down. "Call us if you need us mate." Jez nodded, not really paying attention, he was staring up at where he knew the Star-Link would be, thoughtlessly sucking on an arm of his old and grubby glasses. It was now three-thirty.

Cristi and Lucy hugged. "Thanks, Cris." They nodded, and Lucy turned to Sam. "Thanks Sam, I really, really do appreciate this." Then to both of them, as they walked arm-in-arm to the car, she said, "I hope a little bit of quiet time away from everything will sort things out. Everyone has been so good, but now the only one who can sort it is Jez."

As they drove off, both looking back at Lucy standing beside the ruin, Lucy waved and called out, "I'll call you when I know."

The kettle was boiling, bubbling and jumping about the stove by the time Lucy got back down to the chamber. Jez, oblivious to all, was still staring into the afternoon sky and constantly checking his watch. It was three forty-five.

"I've brewed you up some ziirt, sweetheart. Donna who owns the Coffee Bean got me a pack from her supplier, just for you. Don't let it get cold."

Lucy sat down in the other chair and watched him and explored the mindPlain, but his thoughts were covered now. This afternoon his thoughts were his own as the time ticked on.

[-"Why does he keep looking at his watch? Why did he want to be away before four forty-five?"-] She flicked on her cellfone and went online. The signal was crisp and sharp and so fast. "Gosh, that's amazing, such a clear signal. You'd have thought the mountains would have blocked it," she said as she scrolled. "Ah, here it is. Oh, of course, it's the tenth anniversary, all those people, of course. No wonder the AtomSpheres is on every front page. [-"Okay, here we are... Of course, four thirty-seven, that's why. Four forty-five would have been too late. Of course it would. And the time now is four twenty-three."-]

The instant her cellfone showed four thirty-seven Lucy felt a wave of sadness sigh across the mindPlain as millions of people remembered. And when she looked up, Jez's eyes were glistening and tears were running down his cheeks.

After a few seconds, he raised his cup and muttered in his Mii'een dialect, which she didn't understand.

[-"What's that in his...?"-] she wondered. [-"It's that old folded photo he's always looking at, but what is it?"-]

Then he put the cup to his lips. "Urgh! It's cold!" he said, almost choking. "Who made this ziirt? It tastes like shit."

"Doesn't it always?" she said, and chuckled. "Shall I brew you another, sweetheart?"

"Yeah, er how did... ?" He turned to her, amazed. "Where are we?" It was as if he was emerging from a deep sleep. "Where did you get the cooker from?"

"Sam set it up."

"Has he been here then? Is he still here?"

"He drove us up here silly, don't you remember?" He shook his head. "Sam and Cristi met us at the terminal with a car and some supplies and they drove us up, and Sam set up the cooker and some lights while Cristi helped me make up a bed." She turned and pointed. "Over there, d'you see, in our special place?"

"Oh, that's where we are. I've been out of it, haven't I? I didn't even realize Sam and Cristi were here, or that we're *here*, in the fort. What must you think of me?"

"I think you're lost," she said, shuffling her chair to be beside him, "and I just want to help you find your way, whichever way it is. Why do you stare into the sky, sweetheart? What are you looking at? What is up there?"

He was quiet for a while, and she didn't press him. Instead, she just let him answer in his own time.

"Memories," he said, "I'm staring at memories, Luce..." [>*"Demons."*<] His voice trembled, and his thoughts were wandering again unchecked, but she didn't butt in or try to soothe him, she just let him talk and think. "Memories that cling... I can't shake them." [>*"Up there. That's where it all went wrong."*<] "Can't shake them," he whispered. "Just want to be free, Luce," he said in a slightly louder voice. "I just don't know how? Don't know..."

"Talk about them then. Talk to me. Tell me about those memories. I'm not going anywhere. Well, tell a fib, I'm actually just popping over there to make you a drink," she said as she rested her hand on his shoulder. Then, as she stood she stole a glance at the paper in his lap. "But I'll be listening," she whispered in his ear. [-*"Club 5eightZero6?"*-] She only managed a quick peep over his shoulder before he turned to give her his cup and obscured the picture, but she was puzzled by what she saw. [-*"Huh? Why has he got a picture of that nightclub logo?"*-]

"This is our place, isn't it?" he said as he turned to peer into all the dark cobwebby corners, suddenly aware of his surroundings. "This place has the loveliest memories for me…" Then in an instant, he changed the subject. Lucy couldn't keep up; one second he was plumbing the depths of despair, all sad and sombre, the next he was upbeat. "Hold on, have a look at this," he said as he pushed his glasses to the top of his head and took out an old dried up fountain pen. He unscrewed the top and set the top down on the floor. Lucy heard something go 'click' and a hologram was projected from the pen top into the shadows.

"Wow Jez, it's the AtomSpheres. Where'd you get that?"

"I bought it when we were there on holiday, and Praes~Eedan were doing a promotion. I bought it ten years ago, a couple of days before… befo —"

But he couldn't finish his sentence. Instead, he adjusted the other part of the pen to manipulate the picture. "It's a throwaway toy, and the pen dried out years ago. I've kept everything that I bought on that holiday… "

[-"I wondered about all those holiday trinkets…"-] she thought. She had commented on them when she had stayed at his place after the campus lawns incident. His shelves had been full of trinkets and mementoes, but as usual, he had changed the subject.

"… well almost everything," he continued. "My Snapshot 3000 went… eh, Peiite had it with him when —" Again he cut short. "That's how the AtomSpheres looked when we were there, you can zoom in and out, see," he said and held out the pen's body for her to have a go. "You can see all the spheres and the other floating bodies, and yes, look, there, d'you see the AdSpheres? Do you see them? I used to think the AdSpheres were cool, the way they bobbed all over the place, like free spirits. But I know different now… "

"It's fantastic Jez. So where did you stay? Where was your hotel?"

"We stayed in Nucleo. We were there to celebrate the birth-days of the boys and girls who were fifteen that year. We didn't have a lot of money, as our money is tied up in sheep and stock, so we had to get the cheapest rooms available. We shared an apartment with the rest of the Rahl families, and each family had a room. They had pooled their resources and somehow raised enough for us all to be able to celebrate together. Fifteen is a milestone birth-day in the droving calendar. It's when a child steps into adulthood, and it's the same for girls and boys alike." He took a breath and paused for a few moments.

"There were six of us, four boys and two girls, and we were due to meet to celebrate at eight-thirty, ten years ago today," — he checked his watch again, — "three hours from now. We had arranged to gather in the plaza of Nucleo, but Peiite, Miike and me and, er... we were two klix away."

[- "Were there more? I could have sworn I only saw three in the vid Cristi showed me."-] "Did you say...?"

But before her question had even registered he had changed the subject yet again.

"Look, that's the Star-Link where we were this morning, and that's Spher... " But then he turned the picture over. "And that's Dominion, it's the other original sphere. We were in Dominion all afternoon on our boards, my old board," he said. "Pop had a board too, though he was hopeless and Mumma was forever jumping up and cheering and laughing every time he fell off. It was in Dominion on that afternoon that Mumma first met Claude, he bumped into her chair and spilt her drink. He bought her another and they got chatting, and they have been chatting friends ever since."

"And now it turns out he owns this fort too," Lucy added and smiled. "Small worlds, hey?"

"Yes, small."

She waited for him to say more, but nothing came, so she sat back and waited for him to talk. It took a while, but he eventually opened up again. When he did, he spoke openly about their time on the AtomSpheres. Nothing was held back, but he was hard to follow. There were rapid-fire bursts and there were pauses that lapsed into long silences, and all she could do was listen and hope that this was the catharsis his wellbeing needed. She let him speak, nodding where appropriate and letting him go whichever way he wanted to go.

"Only one of us was actually celebrating their birth-day on that holiday. But there's no favouritism in the Rahls, and we were all there to celebrate. We're family and we look after one another, and if we celebrate one, we celebrate all. When we can, we do it in style. We had a booking at an eatery on one of the most prestigious junction crossings in the galaxy, '*Five and Equator*' in the outer skin of Nucleo," he told Lucy and pinpointed the junction on the hologram, "although our restaurant was actually a Burger Bar. But it was still at Five and Equator, and those celebrating would've been able to visit the merchandise outlets at any of the top restaurants. Every birth-day boy and girl would have something to take home. Miike wanted a multi-tool, Peiite had seen a book about the Atom's construction, and Tomii wanted a hoodie..."

[-"*Tomii?*"-] Lucy was puzzled. [-"*He called to Tomii in his sleep. Who's Tomii? Was he having a birth-day too?*"-]

"...But first," he continued, "we had to go back to our apartment to change, and we were keeping the others waiting because we were still two klix away. It turned out that the Beske'rahls had got their timing mixed up too, but we only found that out much later on... "

In his next pause, Lucy decided to prompt him. "Why were you in Spher'rios Jez?" she asked.

"Miike saw a girl, he was fifteen..."

[-"*Ah, so it wasn't Miike, Peiite's or Jez's birth-day then, they were already fifteen. Perhaps it was Tomii's.*"-] She thought she was getting an understanding, piecing things together. But with this new name in the mix, she wasn't so sure.

"... and his hormones were on fire," Jez continued, "so Miike had to keep his board in front of him in public." Jez's face creased as he giggled at the thought of Miike's embarrassment, and Lucy joined in as soon she realised what he meant. "He bragged that she would be on his arm by the end of the week. Peiite and Tomii thought that was hilarious!"

[-"*Tomii again.*"-]

"And they teased him mercilessly every time he mentioned her. So you can imagine how livid he was when she agreed to a selfie with me. I got another shot of her too just before... before..."

[-"*And why does he keep hesitating, or shying away from mentioning the lost sphere?*"-]

"Well anyway, Miike wasn't happy, and he even tried to outrun me on his board, to get there before Tomii could steal his girl, but he just... as usual he just... fell off ..."

Suddenly Jez seemed to run out of words and sat in quiet thought for quite a few minutes.

Lucy was confused, and she was finding this line of conversation hard to follow. [-"*His tenses are all over the place. He says I, but then he says Tomii. He said 'she agreed to a selfie with me'. Then 'Miike wanted to get there before Tomii'. So were there four of them scooting down the conduit? I'm sure I've only seen three. And then there's that comment by RSM Tomsen, 'that he needs to figure out who he is?' This is getting confusing.*"-]

"I saw the girl Miike fancied on the flight up. She was a real babe. I was looking out of the observation window, pushing to see how far I could get my thoughts out into the void," he rambled, "and I was looking back at our lumbering ferry when one of those Ultra Hi-Speed Exec jobbies swept past as if we were standing still, and my thoughts latched on to hers for the briefest of moments, then the cruiser and the girl were gone. But I saw her, saw more of her than she probably wanted to show. I was only fourteen, and she was too old, too posh, too corporate for us. She must've been at least eighteen and looked twenty, too old for any of us," he said, and he chuckled, "but she was gorgeous. Miike always liked to punch above his weight..."

[-"*Seems to run in the family.*"-]

"...He was besotted. But she set my loins on fire too," Jez admitted. "She was just...," and his voice trailed off again.

Lucy corrected herself although she was still a bit puzzled. [-"*So he was still fourteen, but I thought they were tri... no, hold on, that's right, Mumma said they were born in the same year, so his birth-day must be later in the year then. Were there two then from that tri? I'm sure Mumma said that 'My Jez' was the only survivor. But if I'm following his thread correctly, there has to be four!*"-]

Jez reached out and squeezed her hand. "She was a babe, Luce. She had lovely legs, nice ar... you know... and I think about her sometimes when I flick through my pix. I was fourteen and she was lost in the sphere. Miike and Peiite, my brothers, were lost too..."

[-"*Now that's a start, he's not called them his brothers before.*"-]

244

"...and Toh..."

[-"Toh?"-]

"Oh, I miss them so much." Jez got out of his chair and walked through the hologram into the dark corner. "I was there when they went. I saw them go... I nearly went... too."

[-"Toh? Does he mean Tomii?"-]

"Sit down sweetheart," Lucy said, "and I'll brew you up another drink. Come on," she said as she stepped through the picture and took him by the hand, "come on, sit yourself down. I'll get your coat and get mine too. Brrr, it's getting a bit nippy up here. Come on Jez, sit yourself down." Then she asked, "Do you have a picture of her? Was she prettier than me? Can I see?" she prompted, and without a second thought he flicked open his cellfone, tapped an icon and brought up a whole sheaf of teenage faces.

"That's her," he said.

"Oh Jez, she's lovely," Lucy said, then asked, "Who are all the other pictures of? Have you got one of Tomii?"

But Jez's thoughts were elsewhere. "She was always Miike's girl," he said. "I only took the photo to wind him up," he added and smiled. "And it did." Then as his memories overwhelmed him once more, and he muttered, "Was she worth it Miike?" Then he shut his cellfone.

"Which one is Spher'rios?" Lucy asked as she handed him another mug of ziirt and sat down at his side. It was Lucy's turn now to sway the conversation and her sudden request took him by surprise, so he answered without thinking.

"It's the pale yellow one, the one at the end of the Star-Link."

"I thought it was pink?" Lucy was puzzled, but feeling much more confident now to ask him awkward questions. "I'm sure I read that somewhere."

"It turned pink when the power-wave swept over it. It turned orange first, then pink, and the stronger the power got, the more vivid and icy pink the sphere became until the power-wave cut through the conduit, the weakest point. The LSP project that Sam and I are working on is a variant of that power-wave. Andy Hobbins has adapted the technology that caused the disappearance... " Yet again his voice trailed off and there was another long break... long enough for two more cups of ziirt and a chunk of cake.

Lucy was getting worried about his caffeine intake, though. "He won't get any sleep at this rate," she muttered under her breath, "or so you'd think. So why does he keep nodding? His chin is almost resting on his chest, yet he's brim-full of this awful stuff. It's almost liquid caffeine!" [-"He should be buzzing, but he can hardly keep his eyes open!"-]

And whilst they were sitting in that prolonged pause, and he was chewing the arm of his glasses, as he did when he was thinking, she thought back to the second photo Sgt. Reeble had shown her. There were bodies scattered everywhere and Jez was standing there amongst them, defiant, just like he had been a couple of days ago. [-"Is it respect they have for him, or is it fear?"-] she wondered? "But he's always so gentle with me?"

"The other faces, in the pix, they are all the birth-day kids," he suddenly said, catching her off guard.

[-"Pix, I love the way he calls them pix."-]

"There are a few older kids, too, who had come along for the ride to help us celebrate. Jixa was there."

"Oh, I didn't see him, where?"

Jez flicked his cellfone back into life and scrolled through the pictures. "There he is, that's Jix."

"You should print them and put them in an album."

Jez nodded. "Hmm, yeah, I should."

"I could buy you a book... we could do it together... er..." Had she asked too much? "Could I help you? Is there a photo of you and Tomii?"

"I was in that conduit," he said, shifting the conversation again. "We were all on Spher... Peiite, Miike, me and... all of us, minutes before it disappeared," he said as he stooped down to retrieve the pen top. [-"He keeps avoiding it, why? He mustn't."-]

"Hold on, there's something else I can show you," he said as he reassembled his treasured pen. And he picked up his cellfone, and just as he was raising a finger to tap an icon, he hesitated. Lucy waited. "No, no no, I'm knackered, Luce. Would you mind if I had a lie-down?" His face was drawn, his lids so heavy they were almost closed. "I'm worn out Luce," he said as he stood and stumbled to the bed that Cristi had helped make up.

[-"That's so weird,"-] she thought, [-"he's drunk enough ziirt to keep a bull tarsen buzzing, yet he's tired. How does that work?"-] "Of course not sweetheart, you go and lie down. I'm going to call Cris, would that be alright? She said she and Sam wanted to be kept abreast of things."

"Hmm, yeah, of course, no probs," he grunted as he flopped onto the makeshift mattress and pulled up the covers.

49

Was it three or four?

"Hi, it's me," Lucy announced, "have I interrupted anything?" she continued nervously.

"No, not tonight, we're snuggled on the sofa. Sam is snoozing and I'm watching a movie. It didn't feel right making-out and not knowing how you were getting on, as we're worried about you both. It's affected Sam in a big way, and he's been edgy all evening. How's it going?"

"I don't know," Lucy said, honest in her appraisal. She really didn't know how things were going or if she was actually making any difference to his situation. "If anything, Cris, I'm more confused than I was before. How many boarders were there in that vid?" she asked. "Was it three or four?"

"I thought it was three. There were three who went down, two gingerly and one at speed. Then the speedy one — the one registered as T.Devii'rahl — came back up and then was stuck this side of the emergency door. He's the one Andy Hobbins shouted at. And there were the other two who stayed in the sphere. It was just three, I'm sure it was just three. Why?"

"I thought it was three too, but now I'm not so sure. His tenses are all over the place too. I know, I know, semantics, but one second he's saying I did this and I did that, the next he's talking about a Tomii. I know now that Miike and Peiite are definitely his brothers, he talks a lot about them, and their names are on the stone. I saw them etched in gold, but nowhere is this Tomii mentioned. Could he have been lost when the conduit was cut?" she wondered aloud.

"Surely his name would have been on the stone as well? It's a memorial to those that disappeared after all?" Cristi replied.

"Yes, you're right, it is. So, if his name isn't on the stone, but it is in the records, where did he go?" They were both silent for a few minutes, until Lucy said, "Jez showed me a picture of a girl. He said that's why they were on Spher'rios in the first place. Oh yes, and he keeps avoiding saying Spher'rios, avoids it like the plague. Anyway, where was I? Oh yes, Miike fancied this girl and they had followed her. She was a pretty thing, and he told me he caught a glimpse of her on the journey up, latched onto her thoughts, but added that she was much too old for him because she was at least eighteen. Eighteen! Too old? You can imagine how that made me feel," and they both chuckled at the thought.

"And he's actually said Miike and Peiite are his brothers?"

"Yes, he's actually said that"

"Well that's got to be good hasn't it?"

"Yes, that's what I thought, and it's the first time he's admitted a connection," said Lucy. "And they were already fifteen, so it wasn't their birth-day that they would celebrate that evening, but was Tomii his brother too? I don't know. Mae told me that Miike and Peiite were from a triple birth and that the third one didn't survive. She was quite blasé about it, said it was the way of the steppe. And I know that she and Pop are Jez's parents and that he was also from a triple birth, but I'm sure she said '*My Jez*' was the only survivor. But now there's this Tomii! Heaven only knows where he fits in. Jez said something else that I found puzzling too. He said, 'We *were all there, Peiite, Miike, me and... all of us, minutes before it disappeared*'. He paused as if there was someone else. It couldn't have been all the Rahls, we would have seen them in the records. They were all in the Nucleo Plaza waiting. You showed me the vid, so he must've been speaking about the boarders. But I'm certain there were only three. I just don't get it, Cris, and this is getting too big for me. Perhaps I should speak to your dad."

"No Luce, Jez only trusts you. You *can* do this, I know you can. You can't introduce a stranger now, and if we refer it to my dad it will only prolong things. You need to sort this now."

"Yes. Yes, you're right."

The evening was cold, clear and starry and whilst she chatted on her cellfone, Lucy had slowly climbed the winding stairs to the roof. "It's a fantastic clear signal," she said.

"Yes, you could be sitting next to me, which would be nice and better than Sam at this precise moment... he's dribbling. He finally settled. My shoulder is all wet, haha," Cristi said and chuckled.

The two friends chatted for quite some time, discussing this and that, the perhaps' and the maybes. The lines to take, the taboos and things to avoid. But really they were just chatting so that Lucy didn't feel so alone. She felt self-doubts and was terrified of losing Jez to his nightmares.

Then Cristi excused herself. "I'm going to have to say good night my lovely, Sam has just woken up and he has that look in his eye. You know where I am, so call me if it gets too much. You know I will always answer for you, whatever I'm doing. Love you."

50

That's me...

Lucy stayed amongst the ruins, alone in the darkness and staring at the stars, contemplating all that had happened in the last twelve hours. She had been up there for a good while, and it was a cold crisp night, she was cold too and desperately wanted to chat with Cristi again. But she knew her friend; she might have said call anytime, but at this moment she would be dead to the world and wrapped in Sam after their energetic lovemaking. [-*"I'll call her tomorrow at work. Sleep tight, my lovely."-]* she thought as she marvelled at the clarity of the atmosphere and the absence of any light pollution. [-*"Hmm,"-]* she thought, [-*"this really would be a great place to live."-]* Then to the stars, she called, "I've got to ask him outright, haven't I? Waiting for him to let it out isn't going to work. But how do I do it? How, without upsetting him and spoiling everything? Come on stars, how do I ask him?"

"Ask who Luce?" Jez asked. He had just reached the top of the stair as she called out.

"Oh, Jez sweetheart, I... ah..."

"What Luce?"

"What's it all about Jez? Who is Tomii?" [-*"There, I've said it."-]*

"Oh, Tomii, yes, who's Tomii? I thought you would ask sooner or later. You know, you're the first person who has actually asked me outright what it's all about."

Lucy was astonished, and pulled back and looked him square in the face, her eyes wide. "Really? The first person to ask you that? Honest?"

"Honest, the first in ten years. To ask outright, yes. Everyone else just sit and wait for me to volunteer information, or skirt around the subject. You're the first to ask."

"Surely Mumma' n' Pop have?"

"No. No, it's too raw for them as well. It's too raw for me really, so it's easier to shy away and avoid the subject. But I want to tell someone... I've been wanting to tell someone for a long time. Reebs understands, and I wanted to share with him, but he has his own troubles and Sam, well I just want to keep Sam as a neutral friend, someone to ground against. Can I open up to you, Luce, would you listen?"

"Of course I will. Didn't I say that? Whichever way your story takes us, I will listen. But first, who is Tomii?"

"Er..." But instead of opening up like he said he wanted, Jez said, "There's something else you ought to see," and before she had a chance to answer Jez was going back down the stairs. Lucy had no choice but to follow.

[-"That was a simple question, so why didn't he answer? Why is he so evasive, and what's the big secret?"-] She was puzzled and a little taken aback, but at least she could sense a change in him. He seemed to be his old self. [-"That's something, I suppose."-]

Once back in the main chamber, Jez set his cellfone down on his chair and flicked it into life, then he tapped the icon he was going to tap before he had his lie-down and projected another hologram into the corner. It was the video clip that Cristi had shown to Lucy on their girly evening, a few days before the incident on the campus lawn. Once again she saw the three boys scooting down the conduit towards Spher'rios, and the *speedy* one — T.Devii'rahl — scooting back and getting the full force of Andy Hobbins' vented anger as he passed.

Then in a hushed voice, Jez said, "That's me."

"What!?"

"That's me."

"But the records... Cristi and I read them, that's Tomii Devii'rahl," Lucy said, gasping.

"Yes. It is," and there followed another long pause whilst they both marshalled their thoughts. "Tomii went with Miike and Peiite," Jez continued. "The moment Miike and Peiite went, Tomii went too."

Lucy was speechless. Her head was in a spin. That was a bombshell she hadn't expected, and she just stared at him. Once again his shoulders had slumped, so too had his body language. All his re-found confidence seemed to have drained away and it scared her to see him like this. It was her turn now to pause whilst she rolled the facts around in her head. [-*"Tomii and Jez are the same person. Tomii is Jez and Jez, Tomii. One person, two outlooks, so no wonder his head's screwed up. And there's JD, too. Geeze, my poor love. What was it the RSM said, 'He has to figure out who he is'? Oh yes, and how."-*]

"Are you saying you are Tomii?" she asked. She had to confirm what he had just said... she had to be certain she had heard what he said correctly.

He nodded sheepishly. "Yes."

"Tomii is a nice name."

"It is."

"I like the name Tomii, it suits you."

"Hmm, I like it too."

"But I don't understand Jez, what did you mean when you said, 'Tomii went with Miike and Peiite'?"

"I er, me, Tomii, I had two brothers."

"Okay?"

"Pop's pop, Jez'ziah, my grandfather, didn't have any. I thought by taking his name I could handle the loss. Mumma n' Pop went along with it... anything for the one who was left, and if it helped me then it helped them too. I even signed up under that name. But it hasn't worked. I tried living their lives, you see — living their dreams. Peiite wanted to be a Fleet Tech-Officer, so I did that for Peiite. Miike was going to join the Jaegers, so I did that for Miike. Tomii never wanted to leave the steppe. I, me, eh Tomii, I just wanted to be a sheep drover. But then I came here to do the things they wanted to do. I thought I wanted to be a drover, but now I'm not so sure. When I was fourteen, I couldn't think of a better life, but now I just want to be... Oh, I don't know what I want to be. I'm lost, Luce. I did all that for them, put myself through hell to fulfil their dreams, and now here I am. I have done all that for them, but what have I achieved for me?

I just want to be Tomii again. Tomii could do things, Tomii was confident, Tomii was... Tomii was everything Jez isn't. Jez just messes everything up. Everything Jez touches turns to shit."

"I haven't."

"No," he agreed and shook his head. "But I'm a fraud Lucy Hettler, you've fallen for failure and someone who doesn't exist."

Lucy was stunned by the statement. "That's the silliest thing I've heard today!" she exclaimed. "How the mejj can you say such a thing? Of course you exist. Here you are. You are the bravest person I know. You came top of the class in everything academic. You won every race at the Inter-Unit Games. You stood up to and bettered nine, *nine*, fully trained, fully fit Jaeger junior officers. And JB316 put their trust in your hands and followed you – blind - through a forest and across the raging torrent. So how the mejj can you say that you're a failure, or that you don't exist?"

"Yes, but I did those things for Miike and Peiite."

"Did you? Really? Oh, come on. Do you honestly believe that? Do you honestly think JB316 would have followed Miike? Miike and Peiite didn't do those things, you did. They didn't crawl on their bellies across the swampy ground and live in sodden clothes for a month, or do a ten-k run-march every day, or for that matter suffer at the hands of a bullying vindictive instructor. Listen here, you, from what you've told me of Miike, sulking for days on end because he couldn't get his way... He might've been a strapping lad, but he wouldn't have been able to handle the mental torment of Jaeger Basic. He would've thrown his toys in the air in the first few hours and gone home with his tail between his legs. And that's only if he had left home in the first place." Lucy paused for breath, her passion impressive.

"And Peiite? Oh, come on, he couldn't have handled it either. You said yourself how upset he was just losing his cap and badge. Peiite was a reader, not a doer. He might've managed Tech-Basic, he might even have been a better man than Miike, but I doubt it. Do you think either of them could have hacked it?" She looked at him and held his gaze for a few seconds, but before he could excuse his brothers, she said, "No, they would've been on the first craft home. All those things, you did them. Maybe you were thinking of them at the time, but it was you," she said, poking him in the shoulder. "You, Jez Devii'rahl, you did those things."

"But that's just it though Luce. I've done everything as Jez, and Jez Devii'rahl doesn't exist, does he? I courted you as Jez, and you fell in love with Jez. I've been living a lie. I'm not the person you thought I was."

"You courted me?" she said and chuckled. "I thought it was me that courted you?"

"It's not funny Luce."

"No it's not," but she chuckled again. "Sorry sweetheart. No, you're right, it's not funny," she said, but smirked behind her hand. "But it is, really it is. From where I'm standing it is."

He grimaced. "Look, you know everything now," he said, trying to get everything serious again, "so I won't blame you if you call Cristi and tell her it's all been a sham, and ask her to come and pick you up."

"This is just getting funnier and funnier, you silly thing. Do you think me that shallow? They're just names, labels. I chased, courted and made love to you, and it's you that I love. I don't care what you call yourself. You can call yourself anything you like, and put whatever label on yourself you want, I don't care. Because I courted the man behind the label, and I've no intention of leaving you. I'm going nowhere Tech-Officer Devii'rahl. Now come here Tomii, you silly shepherd, and put a stop to all this fretting."

She took him in her arms and held him tightly, and they stayed that way for a few minutes until she said, "Let's go back up and sit amongst the ruins, just as we did in the summer when we watched the sunset."

They sat together, arm in arm for a long while beneath the stars, looking down on the village behind the fort, sharing a bottle of wine that Cristi had thoughtfully packed, and supping out of two military pattern tin mugs. "Is that writing?" Lucy asked as she set her mug down. Then she noticed the mug Jez was using. "Oh, there's writing on that one too."

"They're the signatures of everyone on that Basic Training. This one is from Tech2, yours is from JB316. We all signed each other's, so each one will be unique. The signatures are written in indelible ink, then varnished over. Most people only have one, but I did two Basics. The Jaegers tried to break me and that didn't work. So, I have two, and yeah, you're probably right, Miike couldn't have done a Jaeger Basic."

"Well for someone who doesn't exist you certainly have a lot of friends," she said as she turned her mug to see all the signatures. "And don't forget, you got the Meritorious Award too, and they don't give those out to fraudsters or people who don't exist."

"I s'pose not."

"The boy that brought me up here and got me caught out in the rain wasn't a fraud."

"You waited on the stairs," he protested. Then he saw the twinkle in her eye, and the smile on her lips. "I'm glad you got wet," he said.

"I bet you are," she said, chuckling.

"No, I er... " but he saw she was smiling, teasing.

"Do you feel a bit better now?" she asked. "You certainly sound a lot more relaxed."

"I'm sorry I rushed back down when you asked about Tomii. I've evaded all questions for so long you see, and I didn't know how to respond. I'm only twenty-four and I've lived nearly half my life as Jez. Mumma n' Pop went along with my reasoning because they thought it would help all of us. So, there were never any questions at home, and they never asked me what was going on. It was — *I said didn't I* — too raw for all of us. Meeko and Jix didn't broach the subject either, as they were in shock as well. The Beske'rahls are Meeko's immediate family. He lost an aunt, uncle and a cousin. We never actually got to market that year, just stayed in the same area and grazed. We wandered about the steppe, in circles, for a whole year. I stayed with Mumma n' Pop until I was nineteen, then I left to join the Fleet."

He was slowly opening up, and Lucy just listened, adding or asking here and there when she thought it might help.

"Surely it was difficult remembering who you were, having two names. It must've been difficult when you signed up?"

"At first, I suppose it was, but I'd been Jez for three years, so I signed up as Jez. That's how I was known until I got the JD mantle. I never wanted to leave Mii'een, not even for that holiday. I'm glad I did though. And I never wanted to travel. Travelling up to the AtomSpheres was the first time I had ever been off the steppe and it scared the hell out of me, until I did it. Then I tried to live for them, and I failed. I got found out, and life after that was hell," he said, and he pulled his glasses off the top of his head and started to chew the arm again.

[-"Why does he do that?"-]

"It was all my fault though," he continued. "Peripherals you see, I've never been good with the wider picture. I left myself open to that vindictive bastard. The Memorial Stone incident was the turning point. Up until then, I was a failure... and failing badly."

"You were never a failure, Jez Devii'rahl. Failures don't come out top of their class, do they? Just look at all the good things you've done for others. What about what you did for me the other day? A failure doesn't do something like that. And what about Jon Reeble and Maisie? They'd be most upset if they heard you say that." *[-"He doesn't need glasses? I've never really noticed the arm chewing before!"-]*

"Well I nearly failed with you." Lucy looked at him questioningly. "You made contact and I ignored you, and I don't know why, because that was when I realised there could be someone even better than Peiite and Miike in my life. My life had been empty for eight long and lonely years until you came along. It was exactly two years ago today that you gave me that telling off. I wanted to tell you when you handed in your report to the Prof, but you took so long to come into his lecture room. I was shipping out that day, and I just couldn't be late as I didn't want to be on a charge. It was touch and go, and I didn't think you were going to come in. The Prof was worried too, I could read it in his thoughts."

"Oh dear, I'm so sorry," she said, then asked, "Was it really today I gave you that awful telling off? That was today? Are you sure? Today? I'd have to check my notes."

"How could I forget a telling off like that? You were right, I deserved all you threw at me. Look, you don't have to check your notes, there's no need. That moment... this day... is indelibly etched into my memory. I know it was today. I know because today is my birth-day, and it was my birth-day that we were going to toast on the AtomSpheres ten years ago today. In about," — he looked at his watch — "thirty-two minutes. You're the best birth-day present I could ever have, and I nearly blew it. I slammed the door on you. I heard you the first time you called and I ignored you because I didn't know how to let go of the ghosts of Peiite and Miike, to let go of my brothers. I was just wallowing in self-pity and I didn't have time for some intruding girl doing a college project, so I ignored you."

"Today though? It's *your* birth-day? Oh, Jez, that's wonderful. It's great, and I'm here and we can share... Oh shit... no, it's not, is it?" Suddenly her joy for him quickly turned into sadness when she realised that the most joyful day of his year, [-"*Of his calendar,*"-], and the day that marked his step into adulthood would forever be the anniversary of the day his family was torn apart. "Oh Jez, sweetheart, I'm so sorry, and I gave you that awful telling off too!"

"Shall we go back down," he asked, quickly changing the subject, "and I'll cook us something... a birth-day supper. I'm starving."

"I'm not surprised. Apart from that chunk of cake, the last time we ate anything substantial was on the shuttle on the way up to the Star-Link," Lucy added as they entered the chamber.

"Have we had cake?"

"Yes," she said, laughing, "Golly, you really have been out of it!"

"Oh well, never mind. I'll cook something. What do you fancy?" he asked as he pulled out a selection of freeze-dried pouches. "There's a fruit sponge. We can have that for afters. We also have a Mejjan-Minor curry or a Mii'een Mutton stew. The Mejj's a bit spicy, though the mutton's not bad considering it's in a pouch. But as it's my birth-day I'll mix them, and we'll have a mutton curry."

But Lucy wasn't listening. They had left his cellfone playing the video and it must have been looping all the time they were supping their wine.

258

"I've not seen this clip before." She sounded confused, so he left the packets and trotted across the chamber to see what was troubling her. "Cristi's video clip finishes at the pink flare, and I've not seen this bit before... Is that my coat? This is the missing video, isn't it?" Then she thought she heard voices. "Is someone outside? No, hold on... has this vid got sound?"

"Yes, hold on," Jez said and went to the bag Sam had hastily packed and. "Yes he did, here we are." He took out a remote speaker, held it between them and turned up the volume so they could hear the various conversations going on in the walkway conduit.

The video looped around and played through again. "That's us," Jez said and picked up the narration, "can you hear us? That's Miike shouting, he'd just fallen off his board and it was everyone's fault. He was rubbish on a board, worse even than Pop."

"Is that one Peiite?" Lucy asked as the other brother, staring straight ahead, slid silently past.

"Yep, that's Peiite, and he was good as long as he concentrated, but he fell off a lot. He had fallen at the top of the slope and taken out Miike at the same time, so you can imagine that went down well. Miike was desperate to catch another glimpse of that girl, and he accused Peiite of sabotage. Yes, you're right Luce, neither of them could've hacked it."

Lucy nodded but was fascinated and torn between the hologram and Jez's expressions. She had also noticed a change in the tone of his voice and, not wanting to miss the unfolding action in the conduit, she was only able to steal the odd quick glance with a quick flick of the eyes to her right. When she did she saw that when he spoke about his brothers his whole face lit up.

"Can you see right down at the end of the walkway conduit? Can you see all those people," he asked. "There, do you see them milling about? They're in Spher'rios, and that's the entrance hall, so you can see it wasn't that far." Then another voice cut in, though the speaker was hidden. "That was Andy Hobbins talking to his mate. His mate had been caught by the pink beam the day before. It had literally microwaved him, and he was in a sorry state. I never did find out what happened to him. I must ask Andy."

Jez then paused whilst he watched his former self glide effortlessly past the other two as they continued towards the entrance hall. Then the picture was lost!

"What happened there? Where did the picture go Jez?"

"The picture didn't go anywhere. The cameras were on a different circuit. It was the main power to the systems and the lights that failed, but only briefly. Can you hear the commotion?"

Lucy nodded. "Yes, there's a lot of shouting... Was that when Spher'rios went?"

"No," he said, and chuckled, "no, when the power failed, we were whizzing on our boards into the entrance hall, and when it failed our boards failed too and we ploughed into countless people. The commotion is us, and as soon as the lights came on and they could see the carnage, the stewards were on us in an instant. I managed to drift away because I could find my way in the dark. They caught Miike and Peiite, though and threw them out." [>"They should've stayed out,"<] he thought.

Picking up that thought, Lucy felt sad for him but didn't know what to say.

"And now, can you see? Just to the side of those plants in the entrance, can you see? Can you?" Lucy nodded. "That's Peiite and me. Peiite had lost his cap — this cap," he said and pulled his old baseball cap from his coat pocket. "Peiite wanted to go back for it, but I went instead. Look, that's me scooting up the conduit, and there, do you see? I shot between Andy and the wall. Andy wasn't happy about it..."

"I know," said Lucy, "he shouts something rude at you."

"It wasn't that rude, not workshop rude. I've heard him say a lot worse when a wrench slips! Listen..." Jez wound the video back a couple of minutes. "Here it is ..."

'OY, SLOW DOWN YOU LITTLE BRAT!'

"... and I was a little brat too, as I was showing off and you know what they say, pride comes before the fall. And I fell, big time, on the way back. Look, here I come. Because just as I get level with Andy and his mate, the power fails, and I take a tumble, and he says very loudly..."

'SERVES YOU RIGHT YOU LITTLE SOD'

"... but I was up and riding as soon as the power came on. It failed again almost immediately, and by the time I was back on my feet the iris door had closed and we were on either side of it."

Jez stopped talking for a few minutes and just stared at his younger self standing at the emergency door. Then young Tomii turned and trotted back up to the man, and they heard him ask, *"Excuse me, sir, my brothers wondered if you could tell us how long the doors will be closed?"*

"... and Andy Hobbins replied ..."

"Don't know, nipper. Doubt it'll be long though."

"Somehow, we had managed to engage in mindSpeak, so there must've been a porous membrane somewhere in the skin. I don't think we could have talked through the thickness of that door. We were good, but not that good."

"Was that your voice?" Lucy asked. "Was your voice breaking?"

"Oh, I hoped you hadn't noticed." Jez looked a little bit embarrassed. "But yeah, I was barking like a donkey all week. When we weren't ribbing Miike about that girl, they were ribbing me."

"Do donkeys bark on Mii'een?" Lucy laughed, doing her own bit of ribbing, but quickly realised when she saw his face that this was the wrong moment for levity. "I'm sorry, sweetheart, please go on."

He had stopped the video, and when he started it again the pink flare had come between young Tomii and the doorway. "I heard a hisssss. I didn't know what it was, but Andy did, and I heard him scream, *'Run nipper, run, run, run'*, and that's what I did. Look, you can see me. I'm running back up the hill and all that debris is rushing the other way. The pink beam had cut through the fabric of the conduit and the rushing air was pushing me back. And Andy was shouting, and I *was* slowly getting closer ..."

This part of the video was new to her. "Is this the lost file?" she asked him, and she could see the whole of his face now. "I've not seen this bit before."

Jez nodded. "Yes. There are two copies, I have one and Claude has the other. I watch it from time to time, for the memories. They're probably what fuel my dreams."

Lucy put her arm around his waist, and he put his around her shoulders, and together they watched the young Tomii run towards the camera...

"Come on you little shit, stretch. Come on" they heard Andy shouting.

"*STRETCH BOY, STRETCH,*" screeching against the din of escaping air. "*One more step. Come on, you can do it, stretch boy, stretch. One more.*"

Lucy saw their fingers touch, tip to tip, joint by joint, edging forward.

"*One more, an' y'safe. Come on, come on,*" Andy screamed again and again. "*COME ON, REACH BOY. REACH. STRETTTTTCH.*"

"*Legs don't work. Can't... breathe. Can't breathe. Dragging me... dragging... Aagh, oh nooooo...*" the young Tomii groaned. "*Legs don't work. Can't... breathe. Can't... breathe. Dragging me... back... feet... sliding. No grip... sliding. ... Legs... Can't do it. Can't...*"

Lucy watched on, gaping in horror as the scene unfolded.

"*Iss too much,*" she heard him wheeze, then saw him stumble, then in his final gasps he cried out. "*Legs don't work, no gravity! Can't... breathe. Can't breathe. Dragging me... dragging... aagh oh nooooo...*"

Then silence.

"Oh sweetheart!" she whispered. "I've heard those words in your dreams. You poor, poor thing. What are my demons compared to what you saw when you were just a boy?"

Jez broke the silence. "That's Andy's hand that you can se... he's trying to hook my ankle rope so he can get some oxygen to me. There was no air, nothing to breathe. The conduit had been completely severed and the upper doors hadn't closed yet, so we were being pushed out by the inner pressure into the void. There, do you see? The gravity generator failed and there was nothing for my feet to push against. I was floating, and my ankle rope was the only thing holding me back."

"Oh, Jez, my poor love!"

"I only missed being on Spher'rios by seconds. I saw the iris door close as I sped around the corner. If it wasn't for this cap... if it wasn't for this... " he repeated as the moment got to him, "... this cap saved me, Luce. This cap and the badge that I bought for Peiite in one of those tat markets on that holiday. It's the badge of a Technical Officer. That's what Peiite wanted to be, and I went back for it."

"That's what you are."

"Yeah, that's what I am. I wanted to do it for him. Miike wanted to be a

Jaeger and I've done that too, but it doesn't make me feel any better for doing it. Peiite was beside himself, and he wasn't going to rest until he got the cap and the badge back, so I went back for it. He would've taken ages, so I went. There, look, do you see? Andy's hand has grabbed the rope around my ankle."

"Oh my poor love," Lucy whispered again as the video looped around and she watched the scene unfold once more, and saw Jez's younger self, running in vain against the pull of the rushing air. She saw Andy Hobbins slip the karabiner over the rope and stretch, and pass an oxy mask to the boy, and it dawned on her then that her Jez — her Tomii — was 'The Boy on the Rope!'

"Oh, and to think I went to that club and it's you, you are the boy on the rope." Tears were streaming down her cheeks, and her vision was blurred. "How can my troubles compare to this?" she asked herself again. "Oh sweetheart, I don't know what to say." She hesitated. "Eh, what's that at the end of the conduit, over your shoulder? Is something flickering?"

"That's Peiite and Miike desperately waving their arms, thinking I'd breathed my last. They were trying to attract Andy because I hadn't managed to secure the oxy mask and the air was draining from my lungs."

"It was still there? The sphere was still there? But everything I've read said that it blew up when the pink flare hit it. It was still there? Everyone was still there? Is that what you were reaching for, over the shoulder of *The Boy on The Rope* etching, up at the Memorial? You reached past the boy, is that what you were doing?"

Jez didn't answer her question. Instead, he said, "It hung there for a few seconds, which seemed like an age. Watch." Lucy missed it because she had been looking back at Jez, looking at his reaction. So they watched the whole thing again; the doors closing in his face; his brothers frantically waving, urging him to run; the escaping air turning him; the gravity failing; Andy hooking his rope, and Tomii clutching that rope with both hands, and Spher'rios still there and the faces of the two boys over his shoulder.

"Can I look at that old photo?" she asked. Jez slipped his hand inside his coat and passed her the crumpled paper. "Oh, I see now, it's not the club logo at all, it's you, and it's this scene in the vid. Oh, Jez."

"It's the very last picture of the three of us," he whispered. Then he tapped the icon and they watched the footage play out.

Spher'rios sat there for a few seconds after the flare subsided, and then there was a second flare. It was almost imperceptible, no more than an intense pulse, and Spher'rios was gone and Tomii was once more being pulled towards the void, only Andy's hand grabbing his coat and keeping him in the AtomSpheres as the sudden tug of the departing sphere snatched the rope from around his ankle and out of his hands.

"I saw it go, Lucy. It didn't explode... that's a myth. I saw the white dot disappear into infinity. I heard their voices trailing off across the mindPlain as I stared into the nothingness of the void, held back only by Andy's hand gripping my coat. Your coat, this coat," he said, and he turned and pulled Lucy's coat together across her chest. "This coat. And whilst I hung there, staring out into that nothingness with the air draining from my lungs, I could still hear their voices, thousands of them, getting quieter and quieter, until all there was, was silence. Then it all went black.

"I missed them by seconds, Luce. Just seconds! If the power hadn't failed, if I hadn't tumbled from my board, then that *Club*5 Eight Zero 6 would have been 5 Eight Zero 7, and Mumma would have lost all of her babies, and you and I wouldn't be here watching this."

"Oh Jez... er, Tomii, I don't have the words," she whispered, "don't know what to say."

"There's nothing to say, nothing that needs to be said. I was the last person to touch Spher'rios, and now I've told you everything I know. It's not a pretty story and I've never shared it with anyone else, not even Mumma or Pop, or Meeko. No one. You're the only one I trust with those thoughts. Because I love you, Lucy Hettler. You've filled that hole in my empty life and I jus... I never wanted to leave the steppe. Before that holiday on the AtomSpheres, all I ever wanted to do was follow the flocks."

Jez walked across the chamber and stared out into black night sky.

"I'm going for a walk," he said. "Make yourself a brew. I just want to clear my head. I need to think," he muttered and walked to the stairs. "I won't be long."

51

I needed to think...

Lucy scraped her plate clean and poured herself another coffee, and then stared down at his grubby chewed glasses which he must have put down when he was sorting the food pouches. She wondered why he had them, he certainly didn't need them. She picked them up and held them to the light. "They're almost opaque!" she gasped incredulously, and at that moment Jez sploshed up the stairs.

"What the mejj happened to you? I didn't hear any rain," she said, surprised at how wet he was. "You're soaked through!"

"Do you remember that stream we crossed in the summer, between the fort and the fence?"

"You didn't fall into it, did you? You did, didn't you? I thought you could see in the dark?"

"No, I didn't fall into it. I've been lying in it."

"Lying in it? WTF!?" she yelped. "Why?"

"I needed to think. I needed to clear my head. I needed to tell myself how stupid I've been."

"More stupid than lying in a melt-water stream?" Lucy was stunned. "You never cease to surprise me Jez Devii'rahl. In fact, this whole after-noon/evening... no, the whole day, has been one surprise after another. I can't keep up," she said, shaking her head. And she was just about to ask about his glasses but thought better of it. [-"They'll keep."-] "So, what did you decide?"

He straightened up to attention. "I am Tomii Devii'rahl. Jez to my friends and JD to my colleagues." He hesitated, looked her straight in the eye, then asked, "Lucy Hettler, I want to be your handfast-man. Will you have me?"

Lucy stepped back and stared at him with wide eyes, studying his face. It was serious, determined, with no sign of fear or anxiety. His black-eyed stare was bottomless, and his thoughts were his own. It was her turn now to decide.

"If you would take me as your handfast-lady," — her voice was shaky and excited — "I couldn't imagine anyone else to be my handfast-man.

"Will you marry me then, Lucy Hettler?"

"Yes of course I will Tomii Devii'rahl."

Authors Note & Bio

I believe in the weirdly possible; that in the vast starry soup we call the universe that we are, most assuredly, not alone. And there are such things as faeries and the woodland Green Man, and why shouldn't there be ghosts. I even have my own theory of evolution; not so much a Big Bang as a Big Splash. And one day I hope to share it with you. I read maps as you would read a book, especially the Ordnance Survey, maps have so many stories to tell, and on so many different levels. And I have a keen interest in history (medieval and social), and geography.

I started writing about the AtomSpheres in 1998 when mobile phones were still the size of suitcases and smartphones weren't even a smart idea. I was born in Worcestershire in the English Midlands, moved to the Isle of Wight when I married, I spent a couple of years working in Berlin, and now live with my wife in South Gloucestershire, just across the River Severn from Wales.

My life revolves around motorbikes. I enjoy the music of Vaughan-Williams, Dvořák, Shostakovich, Pink Floyd and Santana. I drink black-coffee or Darjeeling tea and have been known to down the odd pint of real ale. And of course, I absolutely love writing.

It has been a long road to get this book into print. This one has only taken eighteen months, but the book it's developed from - Spher'rios (AtomSpheres) - was started in 1998, and it's not finished yet. I hope to complete Spher'rios, or parts of it, early in 2021, and then you will be able to follow the fortunes of the Devii'rahl family, past and present.

Acknowledgements:

There are a few people who deserve my undying gratitude, my best buddy Chris tops the list by far, she's had to put up with random scenarios being thrown at her when she least expected it; thanks LB. Then there's Jim, you've been a good sounding board mate, thank you. And then there's Emily, Spike, Sue and Val M, I couldn't have finished this without your criticisms, I noted them all, ignored most of them, but they certainly made me think.

Thanks also go to Steve Moore (*www.stevenmooreauthor.com/#condor-publishing*), I wanted to see how a professional and published author proofed, edited and prepared a manuscript. Thanks for your help, Steve.

Brian: You were a good neighbour and you *are* a good friend, your critiques have been invaluable.

And of course, my good mate Steve Lyons, I couldn't have done any of this without your help.

My thanks to you all.

Steve

Reviews and things

Now that you have read '*Club* 5 *EIGHT ZERO 6*' whether you enjoyed it or not, please leave a review on Amazon. Reviews help the author to plot his/her course and tell them if they've got it right or wrong.

And, if you want to follow Tomii and Lucy, and find out more about The AtomSpheres Legacy, and get advance pages of the stories yet to come, please sign up to my email list at *https://www.subscribepage.com/m9f8a9.*

Thank you

Copyright

Club 5eightZero6

First published by **Floating Boy Publishing (Stephen Lyons)** in 2020

Copyright © **Steve Exten**, 2020

Also by Steve Exten

Something I'm working on - due to be released in 2021.

"I'd never heard of the AtomSpheres until last week when Daley wanted that filler piece," Lomax said to Thompson, as she plunged her hands into the sack and took out a random letter. "Golly, according to this one, I hit the nail on the head. Heaven knows how? I just pulled stuff from the archives and chopped it around a bit. Hells teeth it was just archive stuff, it had already been in print, I just rearranged it."

"Maybe it hadn't, maybe you found copy that had been edited out. Just because it was in the archive, it doesn't mean it got into print. You did alright," Thompson smiled and turned to answer the deskfone.

"Geeze, it was huge," Lomax exclaimed. "How come I've never heard of or even seen pictures of this before? It must have been massive."

Arnie Thompson put the deskfone down and leant across to look at the picture spread out on Lomax's desk, "You're right, it was massive. From down here it looked like a small planet. It didn't start that way though. It was supposed to look like an atom, hence the name, it was supposed to be like the diagrams you see stamped on nuclear devices: A nucleus surrounded by encircling protons, and it did for a while.

At its centre was Nucleo, 2km in diameter, a self-contained world – loads of hotels and shops – a paradise for binge shoppers. The proton spheres were the same, 2km in diameter and each had its own theme. Then it all got out of hand. They added on more and more spheres – Spher'rios was the last – the AtomSpheres just got bigger and bigger, until... Until, well until something went wrong. BANG!" and Arnie slammed his hands on the desk.

Printed in Great Britain
by Amazon